2001 05 22

BY A FROZEN RIVER

About the Author

Norman Levine was born in 1923 and grew up in Ottawa.
He served in World War II in the RCAF with a Lancaster Squadron
in Yorkshire. After the war he returned to Canada, and went to
McGill University where he wrote his first novel. On graduation,
he went back to England and spent the next 31 years mainly in St Ives,
Cornwall—where his friends were the leading painters of that time.
His writing has earned him a place as one of Canada's foremost writers.
He has made his home in Canada, England, and France.

Books by Norman Levine

BY A FROZEN RIVER

The Short Stories of Norman Levine

NORMAN LEVINE

Foreword by JOHN METCALF

L &
OD

Canadian Cataloguing in Publication Data

Levine, Norman, 1923–
    By a frozen river : the short stories of Norman Levine

ISBN: 0-88619-403-2

1. Title.
PS8523.E87B9 2000   C813'.54   C00-931633-7
PR9199.3.L468B9 2000

The Canada Council
FOR THE ARTS
SINCE 1957
Le Conseil des Arts
DU CANADA
DEPUIS 1957

The publisher gratefully acknowledges the assistance of the Canada Council and the Ontario Arts Council.

L&OD
is an imprint of
Key Porter Books Limited
70 The Esplanade
Toronto, Ontario
Canada M5E 1R2

Printed and bound in Canada
00 01 02 03 6 5 4 3 2 1

Contents

Foreword

Norman Levine stands at the very centre of achievement in Canadian short story writing. The masterful stories included in this collection are already a familiar part of our mental and emotional furniture. Everyone has their own favourites, but I could not imagine Canadian literature without such stories as "By the Richelieu," "A Small Piece of Blue," "We All Begin in a Little Magazine," and "Champagne Barn."

The stories may be familiar—but they are decidedly not comfortable. In them, Levine conveys various forms of displacement, of discontent, of alienation, of loss. Like Alexander Marsden, the roundabout maker in "A Canadian Upbringing," Levine left Canada "because he [felt] the need to accept a wider view of life." Levine stands aside, observing life's to and fro; he has elected to be a permanent outsider as immigrant, as resident alien, as writer, as Jew.

The Cambridge Guide to Literature in English says of Levine's work: "Written in a tight, economic prose style, his stories evoke places vividly and frequently focus on social outsiders, the problems of the writer's life and his Jewish-Canadian upbringing." *The Oxford Companion to Twentieth Century Literature in English* says: "Levine's spare, understated prose style is seen at its best in his short stories. Predominantly first-person narratives, they exhibit a keen eye for external details, but their prime concern is with the subjective experience of the outsider."

While Levine's writing always *seems* clear and simple, the stories themselves are far more complicated than the simplicity of language suggests. One might say that his work is as simple or as subtle as the people reading it. The stories usually function as an accretion of images—all of which contribute to the story's emotional current, adding tiny detail to what will be the finished shape. Levine refuses to explain or interpret his scenes for us; requiring us, in a sense, to *compose* the story for ourselves. It is that act of composition that turns these stories into such powerful emotional experiences.

Consider "Champagne Barn," for instance. We are treated to a range of scenes and images: the Senior Citizens' Home where one of the residents, Mr. Tessier, has watched 68 corpses carried out over the years; the mindless chatter of the narrator's mother; a restaurant meal with the narrator's spinster cousin who is in her forties and still a virgin; a meeting with a childhood friend who has become a butcher; a tour of the decaying neighbourhood of the narrator's childhood. The story ends with the hack, hack, hack of the butchers' choppers in Reinhardt Foods. The last line: "I would carry that sound with me long after I left."

As we will carry this story with us. Levine creates a world in this marvellous story—a world deftly suggested and then nailed with telling detail. He forces us to compose meaning from the seemingly random encounters and events in five days of the narrator's life. Through the vividness of his detail (steely master that he is) he moves us to brood on the narrator's life, a brooding which overflows the story's bounds and compels us to confront our own direction and mortality.

This way of writing is essentially poetic and it is no surprise that Levine's first two books were collections of poetry: *Myssium* (1948) and *The Tight-Rope Walker* (1950).

> *The beat and the still*
> *And the beat, caught, lift,*
> *Of the rook and the gull*
> *Over sea, roof, hill*
> *Disturb this place from sleep.*

(Norman Levine, *The Beat and the Still*)

Of these lines he wrote: "It was the first line—describing the way the bird flew—that made me realize that the leaner the language the more ambiguous it becomes, and the more suggestive ... The more you tell—the more you are keeping the reader out from bringing his or her experience in. So if you can reduce a thing to a minimum like 'The beat and the still'—then the reader brings his or her associations to that. So contrary to what people think: the more cryptic you are the more resonance there is." (Metcalf, J., and J.R. Tim Struthers, eds. *How Stories Mean.* Erin: The Porcupine's Quill, 1993.)

Levine's work has resonated with readers in England and Europe for many years. Canada has been slower to respond. *The Times* said that Norman Levine's work was marked by "timeless elegance." *Encounter* said: "Norman Levine is one of the most outstanding short-story writers working in English today." *Le Monde*, a paper not given to rhapsody, simply compared him with Chekhov.

By a Frozen River:The Short Stories of Norman Levine is a publishing event of the greatest importance. It gives Canada the opportunity to experience and celebrate the work of one of our finest writers.

John Metcalf
Ottawa

A Father

THERE IS A PICTURE of my father that is still around the house in Ottawa. It shows a youngish, handsome man with a magnificent moustache, waxed ends; a fine head with black wavy hair, and eyes that I know to be brown. That picture was taken in Warsaw. And to it belong the anecdotes: 'Man about Town,' 'Friend of writers and painters' ('Yes, I knew writers. I used to buy them meals'), 'Owner of a shoe concern' ('You can always tell if the leather's good by the way it creases'). And 'Smuggler'—I'd like to think it was of diamonds.

I never knew that man.

The person I got to know in Ottawa was in his early forties, a fruit peddler. Slightly built, bald, with a sardonic face. And very emotional.

He was five-foot-four yet he had the highest wagon of all the Ottawa peddlers. It was painted a bright red. And it had, on its sides, wooden steps and iron rungs to help him get up to the driver's seat and to the wooden boxes where he kept the fruit and vegetables. Over the years the red wagon was pulled by a succession of second-hand horses—discards from the local bakeries and dairies. Yet even these nags could place him in difficulties. The one that was around the longest was called Jim. A heavy white horse with nicotine-coloured tufts, and a delicate slow walk. My father jerked the reins. He said, 'Gid-yup.' He shouted, 'C'mon Jim.' He even used the whip. But the horse ignored them all, until it was time to go home. Then he would gallop—the wagon swayed as it went through red lights, took corners flat out: father pulling back on the reins, standing up, fists against his chest, red in the face—until he turned into Murray Street.

Mother watching on the veranda took this running as a sign that the wagon was empty and father had a good day.

Saturday was a fruit peddler's busiest day. And being twelve, and not having to go to school, I'd go peddling with my father. I'd walk along Murray Street (our lunch in brown paper bags that mother made up), past the houses of sleeping friends. Up King Edward Boulevard. Between the large elms where I skated and skied in winter. Crossed the streetcar tracks at Dalhousie. Hung around the Français, looked at all the stills. By the time I arrived in the Market the clock in the Peace Tower showed after eight. And my father had bought the load and loaded it on the wagon himself. He had left the yard, behind the house, in the dark, before five.

When we came back that night he put the horse in the stable, gave him oats, hay, water. And by the time he had unloaded, washed, eaten, counted his takings, it was nearly eleven. Then he joined the others outside. A whole street sat on the wooden verandas, in rocking-chairs, on the veranda steps, in the shade of the hanging Morning Glory.

In winter, Saturday nights were spent in the kitchen around the linoleum-covered table playing cards. The players came from different parts of Ottawa. How much of these sessions was due to gambling fever, I don't know. But some of it, I'm sure, was just to get together with their own kind. They played from Saturday night right through Sunday and usually Sunday night as well.

The games they played were twenty-one and poker. And for holding the game in our house mother collected ten cents from each pot.

I'd watch. Standing behind the players' chairs, so I could see their hole cards. If they were winning they wanted me to stay behind them. They said I gave them good luck. If they lost, they said I was making them nervous, and I moved on.

Around ten I'd be sent to bed—school tomorrow. Upstairs, in the dark, I listened to the sounds of the game that came through the floor-boards and wondered when we would be raided by the police.

Nearly all the players were born in Europe and had come to Ottawa just before or after the First World War. There was Shalevsky—he used to deliver bread for a Lower Town bakery (he gave me rides on his sleigh) before he went into real estate. There was Joe—the youngest player (he was born in Ottawa)—he drove for the same bakery after Shalevsky left. Then worked as a porter at the Lord Elgin and told me marvellous stories of what went on in the hotel. He was killed delivering a new car from Toronto. There was Harry, our silent roomer, who worked for his cousin in a paper factory—he sorted the rags the rag peddlers brought in. He died of lung cancer. There was Mr Nadolny and Soloway, also fruit peddlers. And Sam Shainbaum, who had a fruit store uptown then went into real estate. And I hear he's made a bit of money too. The only woman among the men was my mother. She won fairly consistently. My father always lost.

He made costly mistakes. He thought the ace of clubs was the ace of spades—in a flush hand. He mistook numbers. He took twice as long as anyone else to decide whether to call, pass, or make a bet. They always had to wait for him. And when he ran out of money he reached over for a couple of dollars from my mother's winnings—a habit she didn't like. After a while of his inept card-playing, Sam Shainbaum said,

'Why don't you give up, Moyshe?'

'You're spoiling the game,' Soloway said.

'Why do you have to think so long when you've got nothing,' my mother said.

'Just one more hand,' he pleaded with her having gone through five dollars of her winnings.

'You'll only lose it.'

'Just Nadolny's deal.'

He tried this time. He had a pair of tens showing, but he didn't raise. When the five cards were dealt my father passed to Soloway who had four hearts showing. Soloway bet a dollar, and my father, who didn't have a dollar to call, folded up his cards.

Soloway began to rake in the money.

'I wasn't bluffing, Moyshe,' he said. 'I've got the flush.'

He turned up his hole card—a seven of hearts.

No one spoke.

'I didn't have to show it to him,' Soloway said angrily to the others.

On the next deal they missed him out. He watched the cards go to either side of him for a couple more deals. Then he got up and stood behind my mother. After that he didn't play any more.

Instead, he went on errands for the players. He went to Dain's on the corner and came back with a brown paper bag of soft drinks. He opened up the bottles, handed them around. In below zero he walked to the Smoke Bar on Rideau Street and came back with corn-beef, smoked meat, rye bread, that he made into untidy sandwiches, gave them to the players, and to me as well. And apart from a quiet game of casino, during the weekdays with his cronies who dropped in for a social call, no one played cards seriously with him any more.

In February 1944, I was on the last day of embarkation leave. I was sitting in the living-room with my parents, in a brand new pilot officer's uniform, waiting for a taxi to come to take me to the Union Station. Mother had cried earlier. She was sure I wouldn't come back. And as we waited she sat in the chesterfield chair staring in my direction. Her anxiety unnerved me as well and I remained in the chair not knowing what to do or say.

'You know this town called Chelm,' Father said. 'A town of halfwits?'

I nodded, wondering what he was getting at.

'They were having trouble with a cat. They decided to get rid of it.' He got up from the chair and stood in front of mother and me. 'They went to the beadle and convinced him that it would be a blessing for him if he put the cat in a sack and went with the sack to the bottom of the river.'

My father paused.

'—the beadle drowned. The cat managed to get out and scrambled ashore.'

My father came over and touched me on the shoulder. 'The wise men had another council. They decided to tell the people to bring pieces of furniture. And the people of Chelm came back with brooms, tables, beds, chairs. Piled the stuff in a heap in the shul. Put the cat inside. Set fire to the wood. Locked the doors.'

My father grinned.

'The shul burned down. The cat feeling the heat leapt through the window ... Then the wise men had another meeting. They decided to approach their hero, Abrasha—he killed twenty Cossacks in one pogrom. They told Abrasha to take the cat up their highest building, the old people's home, and jump.'

My father was speaking with eloquent gestures.

'Abrasha said a weeping goodbye to his wife and children. He took the cat in his arms. All of Chelm came to watch. He climbed to the top of the old people's home. The band played the National Anthem. When they finished, Abrasha jumped. Abrasha was killed. The cat, on the way down, wriggled loose and landed safe.'

My father was laughing. And I laughed because he was. And we both glanced to where mother sat. And though she didn't join us she had visibly relaxed. And suddenly I felt immensely proud of my father— who cared about those cards.

'Two liars met in the street,' my father said with growing confidence. 'And one liar said to the other: *Guess what I saw today——?*'

But the doorbell went. It was the taxi. We embraced and kissed and said goodbye.

I was riding away to war in a taxi. Along the streets I had walked and played as a child. Murray Street looked drab, empty, frozen. Solemn boxes with wooden verandas. Brown double doors and double windows. Not a soul was outside. On King Edward the snow heaped in the centre had a frozen crust. It glittered underneath the street lights. And the houses, on either side, in shadow, appeared even more boarded up, as if you would have to go through several layers before you found something living.

In Quebec City

IN THE WINTER OF 1944 when I was twenty and in the RCAF I was stationed for seven weeks in Quebec City. Fifty newly commissioned pilot officers were billeted in an old building right opposite a cigarette factory. It used to be a children's school. The wooden steps were wide and worn in the middle but they rose only a few inches at a time.

We were sent here to kill time and to learn how to behave like officers. Some of the earlier Canadian Air Force officers who were sent to England lacked the social graces. So they had us play games. We took turns pretending we were orderly officers, putting men on charge; being entertainment officers, providing the escort for a military funeral. We were instructed how to use knives and forks. How to make a toast. How to eat and drink properly. It was like going to a finishing school.

To keep fit we were taken on early morning route marches. We walked and ran through frozen side-streets then across a bridge to Lévis. And came back tired but with rosy cheeks. Evenings and weekends were free. We would get into taxis and drive to the top to the restaurants, have a steak and French fries, see a movie. On Sunday we behaved like tourists. Took pictures of Champlain, Bishop Laval, The Golden Dog, the Château Frontenac, the wall around the city, the steps to Lower Town. There was not much else to do.

On the Monday of the second week Gordie Greenway, who was make-believe orderly officer for the day, came up to me during lunch.

'Someone rang asking for you.'

'Who?' I asked. I didn't know anyone in Quebec.

'They didn't give their name,' he said and continued his tour of inspection.

Next morning I received this letter.

Quebec, 15 January.

Dear Pilot Officer Jimmy Ross,

We would be honoured if you could come to dinner this Friday. It would give me and my wife much pleasure to meet you. If I don't hear from you I'll take it that we'll see you on Friday at 8.

Yours sincerely,
Mendel Rubin.

Out of curiosity I decided to go. The taxi driver drove to the most expensive part, just off Grande Allée, and stopped at the base of a horseshoe drive in front of a square stone building with large windows set in the stone.

I rang the bell.

A maid in black and white uniform opened the door. She said with a French accent, 'Come in, sir.'

I came inside. A short man in a grey suit came quickly up to me, hand outstretched. He wore rimless glasses and had neat waves in his dark hair.

'I'm so glad you could come,' he said smiling. 'My name is Mendel Rubin. Let me have your coat and hat. You didn't have any trouble getting here?'

'No,' I said.

He led me into the living-room. And introduced his wife, Frieda. She was taller than he was, an attractive dark-haired woman. Then to their daughter, Constance. She was around seventeen or eighteen, like her mother, but not as pretty.

'It's nice of you to ask me over,' I said.

'Our pleasure,' Mendel said. 'Now, what will you drink. Gin? Scotch? Sherry?'

'Gin is fine,' I said.

He went to a cupboard at the far end of the room.

'Where are you from?' Frieda asked.

'Ottawa.'

'I've been there a few times,' she said. 'But I don't know it well. Mendel knows it better.'

He came back with drinks on a tray.

'Do you know the Raports?' he asked. 'The Coopers? The Sugarmans?'

'I went to school with some of the kids,' I said.

'Where do you live?'

'On Chapel Street—in Sandy Hill.'

'It's a part of Ottawa I don't know too well,' he said. 'What does your father do?'

'He's a teacher.'

The maid came in to announce that dinner was ready. And we walked towards the dining-room.

'I bet it's a while since you have had a Jewish meal,' he said.

'Yes,' I said, 'it is.'

'Every time a new draft comes in I find out if there are any Jewish officers. Then we have them up. It's nice to be with your own kind—you can take certain things for granted. Come, sit down here.' And he put me in a chair opposite Constance.

While Mendel talked I had a chance to glance around the room. The walls were covered with some kind of creeper. The green leaves, like ivy leaves, clung to the walls on trellis-work and to the frames of oil paintings. The paintings looked amateurish, as if they had been painted by numbers.

'Do you like the pictures?' Mendel asked. 'My wife painted them.'

'They're very good,' I said.

Mendel did most of the talking during the meal. He said they were a tiny community. They had to get their rye bread, their kosher meat, flown in from Montreal.

'We're so few that the butcher is only a butcher in the back of the shop. In the front he sells antiques.'

After the meal we returned to the other room. It was dimly lit. The chandelier looked pretty but did not give much light and there were small lights underneath more of Frieda's pictures on the walls. The far wall was one large slab of glass. It had now become a mirror. And I could see ourselves in this room, in the dark glass, as something remote.

Mendel went to a cupboard and brought back vodka, brandy, whisky, liqueurs. He gave me a large cigar.

'You know what I feel like after a meal like that? How about we all go to the theatre?'

'But it's half past nine,' Constance said.

'How time goes when you're enjoying yourself,' Mendel said. Then he glanced at his wrist. 'I think we'll still catch it.'

He walked to the far cupboard and turned on a radio. A Strauss waltz was being played. It stopped. And a commercial came on. A sepulchral voice boomed *Rubins*. And then *bins ... bins ...* echoed down long corridors. Then another voice spoke rapidly in French. And again *Rubins* and the echoing *bins ...*

He switched the radio off.

'I have a store in Lower Town. We carry quality goods and some cheap lines. Sometime I'll show you around, Jimmy. But what can we do *now*?'

'Mummy can play the piano,' Constance said. 'She plays very well.'

'I don't,' Frieda protested.

'Play us something,' Mendel said.

Frieda went to the piano and played 'Für Elise,' some Chopin, while we drank brandy and coffee and smoked cigars.

At eleven he was driving me back to the children's school.

'Do you know the one about the two Anglican ministers?'

'No,' I said.

'There were these two Anglican ministers,' Mendel said. 'One had seven children. The other had none. The one with the seven children asked the other. "How do you do it?"

'"I use the safe period," the other minister said.

'"What is that?"

'"When *you* go out of the house—*I* come in. It's safe then."' And Mendel laughed.

'Here's another one. There was this Jewish tailor. He had an audience with the Pope. When he got back to Montreal they asked him—How was the Pope? A nice-looking man, the Jewish tailor said. 36 chest, 32 waist, 28 inside leg ...

'Are you taking out Constance tomorrow night?'

'Yes,' I said.

I took her to a movie. We got on fine. On Sunday we went out in the country to ski. We skied for miles. We both seemed to have so much energy. We came to a hill. I went down first. She followed and fell at the bottom. I picked her up and we kissed.

'My father is worried that I'll be an old maid,' she said, laughing.

I didn't think he needed to have any worries about that.

'He only lets me go out with Jewish boys.'

We kissed again.

'Am I going to have a baby?'

'You don't have babies that way,' I said.

'I know. But I have a girlfriend in Montreal. She told me that if you let a boy kiss you like that you can become pregnant.'

Although I was being thrown together with Constance (we went out often for meals; saw movies; had romantic night-rides in a sleigh, wrapped in fur skins, behind the swaying rump of a horse) and Mendel took me to several hockey games, it was Frieda who interested me. But so far I didn't have a chance to be alone with her. If Mendel was there, he didn't let anyone else talk. If Constance was there, I was expected to be with her.

I managed to get away from the children's school early one Wednesday and drove up to the house to find that Mendel and Constance had driven to his branch store in Three Rivers.

'I was just reading,' Frieda said when I came into the living-room.

She got me a drink. We stood by the glass wall looking out. It's a nice time, in winter, just before it gets dark. When the snow on the ground has some blue in it, so has the sky. She told me she came from Saint John, New Brunswick. Her father was a doctor. At seventeen her parents sent her to Montreal. 'Just the way we worry about Constance.' She met Mendel. He was working for his father who founded Rubin's Department Store in Quebec. She was eighteen when they married and Constance came along when she was nineteen.

'After she grew up I found I had nothing to do with my time. And when I tried things—I found that I can't do anything well. That's my trouble.'

'You had Constance,' I said.

'Anybody can do that,' she said contemptuously.

'I tried to paint—I have all these nice pictures in my head—but look how they come out. I tried writing—but it was the same. Sometimes when I'm walking through the streets or in a restaurant I see something. It excites me. But what can I do with it? There's no one I can even tell it to. I hardly go out of the house now. I feel trapped.'

'Can't you leave Quebec City,' I asked, 'for a short———'

'I don't mean by this place,' she interrupted. 'I mean by life.'

This conversation was out of my depth. I didn't know what she wanted. But her presence excited me far more than did Constance.

'I taught myself French,' she said, 'so I could read Colette in the original. And I have my flowers. Do you like flowers?'

'Yes,' I said. 'I like the colours.'

She led me to her conservatory. It was full of orchids: yellows, purples, oranges, pinks, browns. There were other exotic flowers. I didn't know their names. There were several creepers overhead. And a smell of jasmine from the one in a corner. But it was mostly orchids, and in different stages. Some were only beginning to grow. They seemed to be growing out of stuck-together clusters of grotesque gooseberries. While outside the glass of the conservatory the thick snow had a frozen crust. It glittered underneath the street light.

She showed me a striped orchid on the table in the hall. Yellow with delicate brown stripes. It was open and curved in such a way that you could see deep inside the flower.

'Do you know how Colette describes an orchid?'

'No,' I said.

'Like a female genital organ—I have shocked you,' she said with a smile. 'I would be promiscuous if I was a man. I know it. I wouldn't be like my husband. He's so old-fashioned—telling jokes. But I can't do anything like that here. If I step out of line—'

She broke off again. She would talk, follow a thought then, unable to see it through, break into something else.

'Poor Mendel. He desperately gets in touch with every Jewish officer who comes to Quebec. Throws them together with Constance as much as he can. Then they go overseas. They promise to write. But they never do.'

I heard a car drive up. Mendel and Constance came through the door. 'Hello Jimmy,' he said. 'boy, it's a cold night.'

The other officers complained about the deadness of the place. They thought I was lucky. Some met girls through a church dance or YMCA do. A few could speak French. Most tried to pick something up.

Tucker and Fleming got into trouble accused of raping a waitress. But nothing came of the charge, except they were confined for three days to a make-believe cell in the children's school.

I tried to get Frieda alone again. The only time I did she was upset. The boiler for the conservatory had broken down.

'You must get a plumber,' she appealed to me. 'If I can't get a plumber the orchids will die.'

I got a taxi into Lower Town. Half an hour later I came back with a French-Canadian plumber.

Our time was up. To see how we finally passed, the Air Force organized a ball at the Château Frontenac, and all the eligible debutantes from Quebec and district were invited to be escorted by the officers. I took Constance. She looked very nice in a long white gown. We danced, made small talk, ate, passed the carafe of wine around. The dance band played.

> To you he might be just another guy
> To me he means a million other things.
> An ordinary fellow with his heart up in the sky,
> He wears a pair of silver wings.

Air Marshals made speeches calling us 'Knights of the Air', 'Captains of the Clouds'.

At half past two we left the Château Frontenac. In the taxi, driving back, she pressed against my side.

'Don't you love me a bit, Jimmy?' she said softly.

'I'll be gone in a few days,' I said.

She took my hand.

'Would you like to come up to my room? You'll have to be very quiet going up the stairs. I'll set the alarm for six. You'll have to be out by then.'

I wondered how many times this had happened before.

'Is this the first time?' I asked.

'No,' she said. 'There have been other officers passing through.' She squeezed my hand. 'I didn't like them as much as you.'

'How many others?'

'Four. This will be my fifth time.'

She spoke too soon. After we went up the stairs, closed the door of her room, undressed, got into bed, turned out the light. I found I couldn't do a thing. And she didn't know how to help things along.

'Let's have a cigarette,' I said, 'and relax for a while.'

I lit one for her and one for me. We lay on our backs, the cigarette ends glowing in the dark.

I was wondering what to do when I heard a door open. Then footsteps. Someone was walking in the corridor. The footsteps stopped by the door.

'*Con, are you awake?*'

It was Frieda on the other side.

We both stopped breathing. I was aware of Constance's body becoming tense with fear.

'*Con—you awake?*'

She was lying beside me, not moving, breathing deeply and rapidly.

I waited for the steps to go away, the sound of a far door closing. I put out our cigarettes. And took her easily.

'That was the best yet,' she said softly. 'Goodnight darling. Wake me before you go.'

She lay on her side, away from me, asleep. And I lay on my back, wide awake. I listened to the ticking clock, her regular breathing, and thought of Frieda.

Just after five I got out of bed, dressed, disconnected the alarm, straightened the covers on Constance. And went out of the room, down the stairs, and out.

It was snowing. Everything was white and quiet. It felt marvellous walking, flakes slant, very fine. I didn't feel at all tired. I heard a church bell strike and somewhere further the sound of a train whistle, the two notes like the bass part of a mouth organ. The light changed to the dull grey of early morning and the darker shapes of a church, a convent, came in and out of the falling snow.

Next day we were confined to barracks and told to pack. That afternoon we boarded a train for Halifax. And at Halifax we walked from the train onto the waiting troop ship. Two weeks later we docked at Liverpool.

Those first few months in England were exciting. I moved around a lot. A week in Bournemouth in the Majestic Hotel. Ten days leave in London. Then a small station, in Scotland, for advanced flying on Ansons. Then operational training near Leamington on Wellingtons. Before I was posted to a Lancaster Squadron in Yorkshire.

Perhaps it was this moving around? Perhaps it was being twenty, away from Canada for the first time, spring, meeting new people, new situations? The uniform was open sesame to all sorts of places. And there were plenty of girls around. I had forgotten about the Rubins except to send them a postcard from London.

In the middle of May I had an air-letter, redirected twice, from Constance.

> Dear Jimmy,
> I hope this will reach you soon. Probably you are having all kinds of exciting things happen to you … meeting new people … doing things … and you have long forgotten me and the time we had together. I hope not.
> Now my news. We're just getting over winter. It's been a long one, cold and lots of snow. The next lot of officers after you was a complete washout. But the one now has three Jewish officers. Shatsky and Dworkin from Montreal. And Lubell from Winnipeg. None of them are as nice as you … but I like Shatsky best … he's fun.
> Don't forget to write when you can and take care. Mummy and Daddy send their regards. We all miss you.
> Love,
> Constance.

Two months later I received a carton of *Macdonald* cigarettes from Mendel. I bet he sent them to all the boys he had up at the house.

When the war was over I went back to Ottawa and to the job I had in the Government with the construction department. In my absence I was promoted. Now I'm assistant to the Head.

I have not married. Nor have I been to Quebec City, until this winter when I had to go to New Brunswick to see about a proposed dam that the Federal Government was thinking of putting some money in. The plane stopped at Quebec longer than the usual stop to let off and pick up passengers. A blizzard was blowing. Flying was off. A limousine brought us from the snow fields of the airport to the Château Frontenac. We were told the next weather inspection would take place at three.

I took a taxi to Lower Town. Down St Jean. Down the slope. Passed the cheap stores, the narrow pokey side-streets, horses pulled milk sleighs, the bargain clothes hung out, the drab restaurants. An alligator of school-girls went by along the sidewalk with two nuns behind. Even with the snow falling men doffed their hats to priests.

I found Mendel standing in the furniture department. He looked much older and fatter in the face, the skin under the jaw sagged, and the small neat waves of hair were thin and grey.

'Hullo Mendel,' I said.

He didn't recognize me.

'I'm Jimmy Ross,' I said. 'Remember during the war?'

'Of course,' he said becoming animated. 'When did you get in?'

'Just now. The plane couldn't go on to Fredericton because of the snowstorm.'

'Let's go and have some coffee next door,' he said. 'It's been snowing like this all morning.'

We went to the Honey Dew and had coffee. The piped-in music played old tunes. And bundled-up people with faces down went by the plate-glass window.

'I wish Constance were here,' he said. 'I know she would be glad to see you.'

'How is Constance?'

'She's living in Detroit. Married. He came over from Germany after the war. His name is Freddie. He's an accountant. They're doing well. They have four kids. And she's expecting another. How about you?'

I told him briefly what I had done.

'There were some good times during the war—' he said.

'How is Frieda?'

'She died a year and a half ago. I married again. Why don't you come up to the house and meet Dorothy.'

'I'd like to,' I said. 'But I don't want to miss the plane.'

'They won't take off in this weather,' he said. 'But here I am telling *you* about airplanes.'

'That was twenty-two years ago,' I said. 'I couldn't fly the airplanes today.'

We got into his black Cadillac with black leather seats. He drove through all white streets, the windshield wipers going steadily, to the house.

Dorothy was the same size as Mendel, plump, a widow, very cheerful.

'This is Jimmy Ross,' Mendel said. 'He was a young Air Force officer here during the war. He used to be much handsomer.' He went to the far cupboard to get some drinks.

The oil paintings, the creepers, the flowers, were gone. A rubber plant stood by the plate-glass wall. Its bottom leaves shrivelled and brown.

'Would you like some sponge cake?' Dorothy asked.

'She makes an excellent sponge,' Mendel assured me.

'I had lunch on the plane,' I said. 'I can't stay very long.'

It had almost stopped snowing. Only the wind in gusts blew the loose snow up from the ground and down from the roofs.

'Where are you from Mr Ross?' Dorothy asked.

'Ottawa,' I said.

I felt awkward. It was a mistake to have come.

Mendel drove me to the Château Frontenac.

'Don't forget,' he said. 'Next time you're here let me know in advance. We'll have you up for dinner.'

'You used to tell me jokes, Mendel,' I said. 'Where did they come from?'

'From the commercial travellers. They come to see me all the time. All of them have jokes. I had one in this morning. What is at the bottom of the sea and shakes?'

'I don't know,' I said.

'A nervous wreck,' he said and smiled. 'Here is another. Why do cows wear bells around their necks?'

I said nothing.

'Because their horns don't work.'

He stopped the car outside the entrance of the Château Frontenac.

'When I write to Constance I'll tell her I saw you—'

An hour later I was back in the Viscount taking off from a windswept runway.

A Small Piece of Blue

ON THURSDAY MORNING the train arrived at Sault Ste. Marie. Leaving my bag in the left luggage I asked the way to the office of the Algoma Ore Properties. The man in the company's office was tall and wore a loose-fitting summer suit. He had the appearance of an athlete turned salesman. Straight blond hair combed back without a parting, a well-fed face. But there was something deceptive about the way he talked. For his mouth when open seemed unnatural in that position as in those films where animals are made to speak like human beings. I showed him my letter from the Mine Manager. He read it, said I was lucky, for I would be able to get a train out tomorrow.

'There are only two trains that go up a week, Tuesdays and Fridays.'

He walked to a large map on the wall. It hung there framed. The bottom had a large blue area marked Lake Superior. Smaller pieces of blue were scattered all over the map.

'The only other way is by seaplane.' He tapped a spot in the far right-hand corner. 'There won't be a plane till Saturday and if the weather's bad there won't be a plane.'

He enjoyed what he had said for he walked away from the map to his desk and offered me a cigarette.

'It'll cost you twenty more dollars to fly in.'

It was the way he mentioned money that brought back those classes in salesmanship we had at high school where we had to stand in front of the class and pretend we were selling something while the teacher criticized our technique.

'Besides it's a job,' the tall man said, 'finding the right lake. There are thousands like them. And the bush pilots are just as likely to put you down on the wrong one.'

I said I would take the company's train.

Sault Ste. Marie was the kind of place that I had been in before. The quick stay in a small town where I knew that after a few years I would remember very little of it, in this case a zoo. Away from the main street I walked in a residential area. The houses were set back from the sidewalk by lawns; grass, trees, but no flowers. One wooden house with a large veranda had a cardboard sign, *Room To Let*, nailed to a veranda post. Above the bell-button was a metal plate, *L. M. Kalma. Music Teacher. Qualified.* I rang the bell. I could hear the bell ringing inside. But the tall, grey door remained closed. I rang and knocked and waited. A window on the top opened but no one looked out. Then I heard steps.

The woman who opened the door was small. She had a dressing-gown on over a nightdress. Her hair was grey, fuzzy, and held in place by a net. Though it was early afternoon the fact that she had obviously just come out of bed did not seem as startling as her face. The eyes were there. So was the mouth. But where her nose should have been there was a flat surface of scarred flesh with two small holes.

'You caught me undressed.'

I told her I wanted a room for one night. She led me upstairs to a bedroom. A square room with a window and a large four-poster bed. 'It's a feather bed,' she said. 'They are much better than spring or rubber. The feathers they sleep with you like another person.'

My first impulse was to make some excuse, leave, and find another place.

'The clever doctors, to them I ought to be dead.'

She said this without sadness or humour. Then she showed me the bathroom, the light switch, asked me if I liked music, if $1.50 was not too much for the room, and placed on the kitchen table some cold chicken with sliced cucumber that she had taken from the ice-box. She insisted that I sit down and eat. I ate the food and she talked. She talked as if we had known each other for a long time. Like boat-passengers who have been forced into each other's company only for a particular journey and are safe with the knowledge that no matter how much one says or does there is no consequence to be faced. I now found a strong physical attraction to her face.

Later in the evening when I returned with my bag from the station it was difficult to recognize her as the same woman who opened the door. She had on a dark dress instead of a dressing-gown, but her face was different. She wore a false nose attached to a false piece of skin that stretched from one ear to the other and by wearing glasses held it in place. Face powder and rouge generously put on only helped to show the falseness. I preferred the scarred face with the two air holes to this manufactured monstrosity. In her attempt to look normal she looked ugly.

Next morning the train did not begin from the railway station but from a private siding by the Algoma Ore Properties' office. In the coach, besides myself, were four middle-aged Americans dressed in bright lumberjack shirts with fishing gear piled around them. The only other person was the ticket collector who, I discovered later, was also our cook.

The coach was old and of a type I had not seen on either the Canadian National or the Canadian Pacific. The inside was like a worn-out billiard table with large patches eaten out of the green. The seats were hard and uncomfortable. Gas brackets hung from the ceiling. In the centre of the ceiling a light-bulb did not give much light. But we did not go through many tunnels. Travelling into the bush we continually crossed trestle-bridges, curved by small lakes, and moved slowly through miles of pine and soft-wood. By noon the journey had gone on much too long. The total distance was less than a hundred miles north and we had travelled half of it when the ticket collector came and asked me if I wanted some grub. I followed him into his compartment at the head of the coach. One side had deep shelves from the ceiling to the floor and the shelves had tinned goods in them. The ticket collector took a tin from a shelf. He showed me the tin. *Grade A. Specially Selected Ready To Serve Chicken.* 'Want this?' he asked. 'Go to your seat and I'll call you when she's ready. Here. Have a funny. It's on the house.' He went over to the loose papers on top of a bundle. 'What do you want? Annie. Tarzan. The Katzenjammer Kids.'

A dog barked. In the corner opposite to where we were a cocker spaniel was kept in a large wicker cage.

'She's going the same place as you're going,' he said.

I looked out from the small observation window. The train was going through a narrow valley. The earth was banked along the track. We were travelling so slow that it was possible to see the cracks in the soil. The ticket collector put down the chicken tin and filled a bowl with water from a kettle.

'You don't mind if I give her water. Trains give them this thirst.'

He made a clucking noise with his tongue and walked over to the wicker basket and put the bowl down so that the dog could reach it.

'She belongs to an engineer at the Mine. He sends her to the Soo whenever she's on heat.'

He knelt to the dog and fell over as the coach jolted. Instead of getting up he lay sprawled on the floor and talked to the dog.

'Was it good girl? Eh, my beauty. C'mon tell me—'

I left the ticket collector talking to the dog and returned to my seat with The Katzenjammer Kids and looked out of the window. The first excitement of seeing so much green and trees had passed. The trees were monotonous and I wanted the journey to end. I wondered why I was going to the Mine. Part of it was for the money and the experience. But I felt convinced that there was something else. Four years of lectures and campus enthusiasms had given me an overdose of books and words and examinations. I felt as if I was on a see-saw, stuck to the one side that was raised, where my head was the only part involved in 'the goings on.' Not that those four years were unpleasant. They only seem a waste of time, looking back.

I did not see the Mine until sundown. From the train it looked like an old ruin on top of a hill where the hills around were without trees or grass. The station was at the bottom of the hill and we stopped by a long wooden platform. The train picked up water. Parcels and crates were moved from the train to the waiting trucks. Then the spaniel, free from the wicker cage, was given to someone in a car. A cream-coloured bus was also by the side of the platform. Some men were inside. I went to the bus. The driver sat like a sparrow over the wheel, a jockey cap on his head. He wore an orange sweater with a large H in green across the front.

'Your name Tree?'

When I said it was he said, 'Hop in.'

The men by the station were watching the reunion of the spaniel with her owner. There were some guttural jokes made at the spaniel's friskiness, for they knew where she had been. Then the bus backed, turned, and drove off.

We came to a lake with wooden houses on one side. The bus stopped by a General Store. Several men with black lunch-pails climbed in. They called the driver Jack in various accents. He punched small cards that the men held up as they entered the bus. We drove around the lake and up a hill. Above us a steel cable carried large buckets of iron ore from the Mine to the Sinter Plant. We stopped at the top of the hill, beside a wooden building. I asked the driver where the office was. He said to follow him. He carried a mailsack over his shoulder.

'Where you from?'

'Montreal.'

'Play ball?'

'A bit.'

'What position?'

'I pitch.'

He remained silent as we went through a wooden gate and into a frame building partitioned off for several offices. The bus driver dropped the mailsack on the floor and a girl came out of one of the partitions.

'Hi, Glorie. Someone from Montreal.' And he went out.

She came to the counter, unsmiling, and took some paper, spread it flat.

'When did you come?'

A skirt and sweater and on her sweater at the neck she wore a black cross.

She took my name, age, and home address. Her eyes moved nervously. Her other features were coarse. When my card was filled out she told me to go to the cookhouse, a building some twenty yards away, and ask for the cook.

I crossed the bare hard-packed ground and saw a man with glasses, stripped to the waist, holding a white apron. He stood by the cookhouse near several large barrels filled with garbage and looked towards the horizon. I asked him if he could tell me where I could find the cook.

'Where you from?' he said with a Scottish accent.

'Montreal.'

'Montreal,' he said the word slowly, 'it's seven years since I've been there. How are *The Canadiens* doing?' Not waiting for a reply he became excited and talked quickly. 'The last time I was there I did a food crawl. I started at Pauze's with a dozen oysters then I went to the Bucharest for a steak, Ben's for a smoked-meat sandwich, Chicken Charlie's on St Catherine for spare-ribs, and ended with spaghetti and meat balls at FDR's and before I caught the midnight train I took a taxi to a place called *Au Lutin qui Bouffe* where somebody blind played a piano while I had frog's legs and my picture taken giving a baby's bottle of milk to a little pig.' As spontaneously as he started, he stopped. To cover up his embarrassment he became silent, then formal, as he led me to his cookhouse office.

In his office he issued me a new black lunchpail and I signed a slip for it. He told me to scratch my name on the lunchpail with a nail and that supper was at seven-thirty, so that I still had half an hour to get a place to sleep. We walked outside, through the dining-hall. Unpainted large wooden tables. Benches on both sides. The first table near the door had chairs, and a sign, *Staff Only*.

He showed me a building about fifty yards down the hill.

'Go to Room 9, Laddie, and ask for Willie Hare.'

The cable stretched over the cookhouse and I could hear it creak as the buckets kept passing overhead. Where the cable crossed between cookhouse and office a steel net was suspended above the ground.

I found Number 9 in a building smelling of paint. Outside the door a bundle of dirty laundry was tied together by a shirt. Some time passed between my knock and the door being opened. At first I thought he was a boy, then he switched the room light on and I could see that he was old, unshaven, and sleepy. He could not be much more than five feet, a thin frame covered by a dirty white shirt buttoned tight at the neck, collar crumpled, and grey trousers that were too small. He wore no shoes but heavy woollen socks. His fly-buttons were undone.

'My name is Tree. The cook told me that you would let me know where I sleep.'

He hesitated, then turned back to the room leaving the door open. He went to a cupboard and pulled out a large piece of cardboard. Then he sat down on his bed and began to examine the large writing on one side of the board.

I looked around the room. It stank of old age. Shelves covered an entire wall. In these shelves: toothpaste, soap, razor blades, shoe laces, and chocolate bars, were propped up in open boxes. Above his bed, pasted to the wall, was a map similar to the one hanging in the company's office in Sault Ste. Marie. Covering most of the map were pictures of boxers, hockey players, movie stars, old Christmas cards, pin-up girls, and an old calendar advertising Life Insurance.

'Yours will be Number 42.'

He spoke with difficulty for he had no teeth. They were sunk in a glass of water on the floor by his bed. 'You'll have another student in with you later. Tree.' And he laughed. 'That's an easy one to spell.' He licked the end of the pencil and printed my name large on the cardboard. 'You can get most things from me.' He showed me the cupboard built into the wall where he returned the piece of cardboard. Inside sprawled hundreds of paper-backed books. 'Mystery, cowboy, sex stories, no need to pay. It'll come off your cheque.' He gave me the key to my room and returned to his bed entering between the sheets fully dressed.

'By the way Tree, where you from?'

'Montreal.'

I waited. There was no reply.

As I walked out he called back. 'Shut the light.'

Number 42 was a square room freshly painted white, with one window directly opposite the door. Two beds. Two dressers. A naked light hung from the ceiling. I tried to raise the window but was able to move it only a few inches. I could see the side of a hill, the sky, and trees. The outside air tasted cold in my throat.

I unpacked and had put on a sweater and old flannels when I heard a bell tolling. There was nothing urgent about the sound. Silence. Then the sound again. I went out of the room and looked out of the window in the passage. Men were pressed tight to the door of the cook-house. Others were running towards it. Suddenly the door opened and those that were there disappeared inside. By the time I reached the cook-house the tables were crowded with men eating. Late-comers, like myself, were running from one table to the other until we found a place on a bench.

At my table they were speaking German. The only one not speaking was deformed. He sat opposite me. Stubbles for fingers on a wrist which was raw. A large red handkerchief, tied around his head, went under-neath his chin. He used this handkerchief to hold his jaw together. To eat he would loosen the knot above his head and with one stubbled hand he would slide the food from the table to his mouth while the other worked the jaw up and down.

'You a Canadian?'

He had bad teeth.

'Yes,' I said.

'Look at the monkeys eat.'

As a platter of food was placed on the table, often before it reached the table, bodies pushed, hands snatched whatever they could get. In less than ten minutes it was all over.

Outside the tramline continued to creak. The men stood waiting by the side of the cookhouse where, on to the main wall, a wooden booth was built. It stuck out like an ear. Steps without handrails led to a door. Someone shouted. 'Here he comes.' I saw Willie Hare coming from the office towards the cookhouse, his hands full of letters and newspapers. He gave the letters to the first man then went up the ladder to the booth and threw the papers inside. 'Shout them out.' Another man took the envelopes away from the first man and began to call out names. Letters passed from hand to hand. After all the names had been read out several times the DPs went through them again.

I woke next morning to the sound of blasting followed later by the steady tolling bell. Breakfast was a repetition of the supper last night, except that different faces were at the table. After breakfast I walked over to the office. The manager had not yet arrived. Glorie suggested that I go and see the doctor as I had to have a medical before I could begin work.

The doctor's office (a wooden building as were all the buildings on top of the hill) was a few minutes' walk from the cookhouse. His hours according to a sign were 10-12. I arrived after 10.00 and it was now 11.32 and still no one had arrived. A man with a crew-cut, wearing white shorts and an open shirt approached. I asked him if he was the doctor.

'I'm not that lucky,' he said, and walked on.

The doctor arrived at noon. He was the palest person I had so far seen at the Mine. A long head on a tall thin body. His face reminded me of a goat. Straight black hair parted on the side. A thin mouth. It was difficult to guess his age. He could as easily have been in his thirties as in his forties. He opened the door and indicated that I enter.

'They said in the office to come and see you about a medical.'

He remained silent, took off his jacket and flung it on to the leather couch that was near his desk. The room was small and stifling. All the windows were closed. Papers were on the floor. A file, like a broken accordion, lay on the floor with papers sticking out from the bellow pockets. A telephone was on the desk. Beside it, piled high on top of each other, were old telephone directories. On the desk a dish had dried apples, over-ripe pears, and an onion sprouting. A green filing cabinet stood against the wall by the window. On top of it several parcels, tied crudely together, had holes in the brown paper as if the rats had been there. A picture of Mickey Mouse was the only bright spot in the room and it hung as a target on a piece of cardboard underneath the eye-chart. There were three chairs and a leather couch to sit on.

'You another student?'

I said I was.

He began to listen to my chest.

'Where you from?'

'McGill.'

He looked up, surprised.

'And how is the dear place? Are they still after you asking to give money for some building or drive, writing you letters, telling you how important you are to them—'

'I just graduated,' I said.

'You'll get them soon enough.'

He did not bother to examine me further but went over to his filing cabinet, unlocked it, and from the back he brought out two large glasses and a half-full bottle of brandy.

'It's all right, Tree. I was there myself. Good time. Best time I ever had.'

He poured the glasses nearly full and we drank.

'We must have a reunion. You know you are the first McGill man who has hit this God-forsaken hole. The others at the staff table are a bunch of hicks from all the hick colleges across the country.' Then, as if he remembered something, he came and shook my hand.

'My name is Crepeau.'

We continued drinking. I told him who on the faculty had died, who had left, and he appeared to be interested when I said a name he knew. The conversation jumped from the campus, to Montreal, to sport, to the different places we had seen. 'Look at yourself,' he suddenly interrupted, 'You talk. You can talk like I can talk. We both can make talk. Talk on anything. They have seen to that. But what good does it do you, or anybody else? They've sandpapered all your rough edges, your instincts, your intuitions, then turned you out with a fake smartness like a car on the assembly line. You happen to be the 1950 model. I was the 1933. The funny thing is we like it.'

He stood up.

So did I.

'You'd better sit. You're only here for this summer so you'd better listen. I was like yourself twenty years back, perhaps better. I had first-class honours, won prizes, had an offer to continue research in a San Francisco hospital. But I said to hell with them—'

He opened his arms indicating the untidy room.

'—they don't make it easy for you to be a failure.'

Suddenly he seemed to lose interest in what he was saying for he walked to the filing cabinet and from behind it took out an air rifle and a candle. He lit the candle and stood it up on top of the filing cabinet, in front of the crudely wrapped parcels. He broke his rifle and inserted a slug.

'Let's see what kind of shot you are. Go against the far wall and put the flame out.'

The distance was about ten yards. I aimed. I missed. He made me try again. This time I hit the candle, knocking it down, but the wick still burned. He tried. His first shot either went through the flame, or very near it, for it flickered. The next one put it out. He returned the rifle to its place and offered me a cigarette.

'I know I'm tight, but it does not matter. What does any one person matter? They come into your world for a while then leave it just as quickly as they entered.'

He finished what was in his glass, poured more in and drank it down.

'Don't expect the men to like you. When they find out that you've been to university and have come here it's like telling them that what they believe in is rotten. They work hard to save money so that their kids can go to university, get a degree, and not have to come to places like this. Then they see you here—'

The room was stuffy yet all the windows were shut. I was glad that he stopped talking for I found the atmosphere in the room and the brandy had made me sleepy and I wondered how much longer he would go on before I could excuse myself and leave.

'Use your eyes and you can see a lot,' he said. 'Everyone else who is here has not come by choice. The DPs are counting the days, marking them off on their calendars until they can get away to Toronto, Montreal, or Winnipeg. Those who work underground stay as long as the bonus makes it worthwhile, then they drift to some other place. A few scare-crows like Willie Hare and Old Harold hang on because the company ruined them as human beings. For fun the men play crap, smuggle hootch, and pin black lace panties on their walls that they get from the Soo.'

He stopped talking to drink and fill the glasses again.

'I suppose you'll return to Montreal.' He burped and excused himself.

'I don't want any of that kind of civilization. I've contracted out from all of them. I drink, and I write poetry.'

He tried to get more brandy out of the bottle but it was empty.

'Sometimes I go to the Soo. The last time I took a case of Scotch, found myself a hotel room, locked the door, and I didn't get out of bed as long as the Scotch lasted.'

He went over to his desk, unlocked a drawer, and brought out a leather folder. From it he took a piece of paper.

'I wrote this on my last blow.'

All your experiences:
Those bits.
Those pieces you carried away with you.
How long will they last?

At the undertaker she showed me the coffin.
'Oak the best wooden one
Won't last you more than twenty-five years.
It falls away like paper'.

Those bits and pieces you carried away.
How long will they?

He stopped. For some reason he looked embarrassed. He went to his desk and returned the piece of paper to the leather folder.

'I've got a couple of hundred poems. Some day I'll get them put into a nice book and send it to the dear old place with my compliments.'

The effort of reading seemed to sober him up for he threw the empty bottle into a large sack by his desk that had something soft in it for there was no sound of the bottle hitting. He picked up his jacket.

'There's no point staying in here.'

We went out and walked along the slope of the hill. The bell began to toll for lunch. Grass was burnt. And scattered were small patches of blueberry bushes. We walked on a narrow path sunk in the hard ground following the contour of the hill. I could see the tramline going down but we were too far away to hear the buckets creak although the sound of the bell still reached us. The doctor walked in front.

'Fly in?'

'No. I took the train.'

'It only takes an hour to fly in.'

'The manager at the Soo told me pilots can't find this lake easy.'

'There's only one lake in the bush shaped like ours.'

We walked on. The sun was still hot. The bell tolled behind us. And I could now see a gull flying alongside the hill and a small piece of blue locked in the surrounding earth and rock growing larger below. The slope of the land entered the water and split the top quarter in two.

'What does she look like to you,' the doctor said.

I stood on a flat rock looking at the lake that I had come by on the bus yesterday.

'To me it's more like a heart.'

He said this without waiting to hear what I might say.

South of Montreal

I SEE HER NOW. In some kind of outer garment. Tugging at her lapels, as if it was falling off her shoulders. Her hair, a thin yellow-blonde, piled on her head. She was short. A pale white skin. A largish nose. Talking elaborately, closing her eyes, exaggerating her gestures. She could have been an actress in some melodrama. Her name was Madame de Wyssmann. She was French Canadian, a widow, a Huguenot. She wanted her nephew Paul to be taught English so he could go to Loyola in the autumn. That's how I came to Ile Aux Noix. I was to tutor Paul and two of his school friends—Jose and Mario—Guatemalans.

I am writing about the summer of 1947. I had just finished third year at McGill when I went down to the Placement Bureau to get fixed up with a job for the summer months. Madame de Wyssmann's letter giving me detailed instructions on how to get to Ile Aux Noix was written in the largest copperplate I had seen.

On Saturday I left Montreal, by bus, over the light green bridge. And soon we were on a straight highway that led to the United States border. The countryside was uninteresting. Flat fields to the river that went parallel to the highway with a few stilt cottages along the bank. The river had overflowed, in the spring, and the receding water left reeds wrapped around the fence posts and around the trunks of the few trees.

I got off the bus by a telegraph pole that had a sign *Riverside Hotel* pointing down a dirt track to the river. Further along the highway was the white church steeple where the village began. Across the road, this fine row of poplars, a nice lawn, and a large stone house with white trimmings.

'You had no trouble getting here?'

'No Madame. Your instructions were exact.'

'Would you like some coffee? This is *Madame*.'

She introduced me to a gentle old woman in a brown print dress. She had bow legs and a small moustache. She spoke a few sharp words of French to her.

'*Oui, Madame,*' the old woman said and went to the kitchen. It could have been the voice of a young child.

My room was the small room on the first floor. The staircase was wide and wooden and it went up to a large tapestry on the wall showing a battlefield. There were shelves of books, mostly Balzac. And old *National Geographic* magazines. It was a fine house, cool in the middle of the summer, high ceilings, with highly polished wooden floors. Downstairs, the dining-room was filled with Japanese screens and other stage props.

'They were given to me by Tyrone Power, Senior,' Madame de Wyssmann said at lunch. 'He and his wife had a cottage next to us by the river. I taught young Tyrone Power how to drive a car. We had fine times—but the interesting people who were here are gone.'

Her nephew Paul wore glasses and had straight blond hair that he combed back. He was tall but flabby. The two Guatemalans were quite different. Jose had brownish skin, curly dark hair. Until he met me he thought everyone in the world was a Catholic. Mario was smaller, white skin, sharp features. He mispronounced ham and jam at the breakfast table. They both laughed and smiled a lot.

On the second day, after breakfast, when they had gone to the village to collect the mail, Madame de Wyssmann came up to me.

'Sir,' she said. 'Look what I have found in his bed.'

She gave me a rubber doll. It was a miniature nude woman about seven inches long.

'What am I to do?'

'Boys are boys,' I said.

'It's all he thinks about. He's got this little DP in St Johns. A little prostitute.' She closed her eyes and spat out the word. 'He thinks of nothing else.' Then she said something in French that I didn't understand. 'I was married. But we slept in different rooms. He had to knock if he wanted to come in.'

'Were you married long?'

'Six months,' she said. 'He was a lawyer. Much older. I came straight from the convent.'

At the end of the first week I realized why I was here. It wasn't only to get her nephew into Loyola. Madame de Wyssmann believed that English meant refinement. And French Canadian was coarse and provincial. I was expected to help her nephew make the change.

Lessons meant reading from *Vanity Fair* (it was the only English book she had on her shelves) and giving them words from my *Pocket Oxford Dictionary*. We had spelling classes. We had reading classes. We talked in English. Sometimes it was on the grass around the stone house with the poplars overhead. And I would hear Madame de Wyssmann playing Chopin on the piano. More often I would go with the boys down the dirt path to the river. And there, from a garage, take out one of the three boats: the sailboat, the canoe, the dinghy. And we'd go up and down and across the Richelieu River while they read or spoke English.

I liked the river. There were red and black buoys in the middle to mark the channel. But weeds had claimed most of it. And sometimes the boat got so tangled in them that it came to a stop. Towards dusk, swallows would come over the water. And the beeches, the mountain ash, looked very pretty along the shore.

One Saturday afternoon, when there were no lessons, Paul and Jose and Mario came back to the stone house with a large white bird. They said they found it in a field by the river. It couldn't fly. Paul carried it very gently in his arms. Outside the kitchen door he tied its long thin legs to a fence post with a leather strap. Then pulled it by the neck until it stretched fully out, its whole length parallel to the ground, the wings hanging lifelessly by its sides. Jose came out of the kitchen with a knife and gave it to Paul. And Paul began to saw away at the neck. The wings began to beat the air. They were large wings. They made a swooshing sound and sent the dust on the ground moving. All the time he was fiddling away at the neck, the bird was stretched out as in flight, the wings beating powerfully, until he cut through.

At next day's lesson, in the sailboat, I had Paul alone. In the middle of reading Thackeray he said. 'I am French. Why should I try to be like the English?'

'It doesn't hurt to know another language,' I said not very convincingly.

But it was the end of that lesson. After that, Paul went through the motions. He was too polite for any more outbursts. But with his aunt, even when I was there, he spoke French. When she said.

'Paul. *Speak English.*'

He just smiled.

It had been the nicest summer I ever had in Canada. I had gone out fishing by myself, trolling for pike. I had gone out with old Lacosse (he did errands for Madame de Wyssmann). He taught me how to spear carp at night using a light. And I had gone with him in his old Ford when he collected the mail from the tin letter-boxes stuck crookedly to the wooden posts of the farms. And also on Saturday afternoons when he went for frogs. He had a sack and a stick. And he would knock the frogs and put them into the sack then sell them to a Montreal restaurant. One afternoon, late in August, the frogs began to leave the fields by the river and move to the higher ground. But they had to get across the highway. The cars killed most of them. There were thousands of dead frogs lying on the highway for the next few days.

In the first week in September the trees had started to change colours. The swallows flew lower over the river. And splashes of red settled slowly on the reeds by the shore. The nights were cold. One day the radio said snow was expected. Jose and Mario were excited. They had never seen snow. They wanted to stay up all night. So we all did. The moon was large and orange. It was cold. But no snow fell.

Next day it was time to go away. I thanked Madame de Wyssmann. I said I enjoyed the summer. Old Madam brought me some coffee. Paul and Mario and Jose shook my hand. Then we went outside and stood by the spot where Paul had killed the bird waiting for the bus to come.

'What are you going to do?' Madame de Wyssmann asked.

I said I would finish university. Then go somewhere. Where I didn't know.

'You are young,' she said. 'You still have your ambitions.'

PART TWO

A Canadian Upbringing

WHEN PEOPLE ASK ME why did I leave Canada and go over to England, the answer I give depends on the kind of person who is doing the asking.

If it is someone of my own generation, at some party, I tell them it was because of the attractive English girl who sat beside me at college and took the same courses as I did, and who was going back when she graduated. If it is someone like my bank manager, I say it was because of the five-thousand-dollar fellowship I got for postgraduate study. The only condition being that I had to do it at some British university. And if the question comes from an editor, I tell him that at that time I had just written a first novel and my Canadian publisher (to be), having read the manuscript, said that I would have to go to New York or London to get it published, then he would look after the Canadian market.

All of these have something of the truth about them. But what was behind them, and which I could not admit at the time, was the work of Alexander Marsden.

I had never heard of Marsden until I went to McGill. In my second year, Graham Pollack, one of the English professors—poor Graham, he's dead now. No one, apart from the handful of students who took his courses, gave him much credit for the range of his reading, nor understood the kind of humility he brought into the classroom. He lectured, in a weak voice, on Utopias throughout the ages; on Science Fiction; and on Comparative Literature. Wiping away with a large white handkerchief the sweat that broke out on his forehead.

His office, which he shared with an assistant professor, was swamped with his books. Not only were they around the walls, but in piles on the floor. And it was from one of these piles that he pulled out *A Canadian Upbringing* by Alexander Marsden.

'I think you might enjoy this,' he said, blowing off the dust.

I began to read it late that night—in that large basement room on the corner of Guy and Sherbrooke that I rented from the Dean of Christ Church Cathedral. And when I finished the last page I was far too excited and disturbed to go to sleep.

It's a small book, 112 pages. It was published in England in 1939. The first half deals with Marsden's growing up in Montreal. The rest with a trip he made across the country in the early thirties: by riding freight cars, by bus, hitch-hiking, and walking.

What first disturbed me was the shock that one gets when, without warning, you come across a new talent. But I was also disturbed by something else.

Although I was brought up in Ottawa—and Ottawa has, compared to Montreal, a small Jewish community—the kind of upbringing I had wasn't much different from the one Marsden describes in Montreal. He pinned down that warm, lively, ghetto atmosphere; the strong family and religious ties—as well as its prejudices and limitations. And when, at the end of the book, Marsden decides to leave Canada for England, not because he wants to deny his background but because he feels the need to accept a wider view of life, I knew that was the way I would go as well.

From Professor Pollack I found out what I could about Marsden, which was very little. Marsden had gone over to England in the late thirties, and as far as Pollack knew he had never come back.

I graduated that summer and set out for London. With my five-thousand-dollar fellowship; the English girl; the manuscript of my novel; and the well-marked copy of *A Canadian Upbringing*.

In London I soon discovered that I didn't care for the academic. And I dropped it. The attractive English girl went over to Paris and on the cross-Channel boat met an Englishman. And they married.

But I did get my novel accepted by an English publisher. And with this I decided to try and make, like Marsden, some kind of literary career over here.

I also tried to track down Marsden's whereabouts. But the publisher of *A Canadian Upbringing* was out of business. And it was only a chance remark by the librarian at Canada House that put me on his trail. She didn't know who he was, and had never heard of the book. But she remembered his name.

'I send him batches of Canadian papers,' she said. And pulled out a card from a file that had Alexander Marsden on top. And below, a series of crossed-out addresses. The last one she had was: The Little Owls, Mousehole, near Penzance, Cornwall.

I copied it into my address book and there the matter rested.

Until this summer. One of my short stories was bought up for a film. And with the money from that I bought myself a small English car, rented a cottage in Mousehole, and took my wife and kids for our first holiday in Cornwall.

It was very pleasant. The weather was marvellous. The kids played along the rocks at low tide. And found rockpools with sea anemones in them. Towards evening we drove down to Land's End, stopping off at the coves, the small coastal villages, on the way. Or over to Penzance, where my wife did some shopping and the kids played on the lawns of the Morrab Gardens.

On the sixth day I couldn't put it off any longer. I asked the postman where Marsden lived.

The small greystone cottage, without a front garden, was easy to find. Across the unpaved road water flowed in the ditch. A few chickens were wandering about further up the road, from a field. And a black dog was stretched out in the sun.

I knocked.

The man who opened the door was about five foot ten, a little on the plump side. He had a sardonic, very pale, face. And a short pointed blond beard. He reminded me of one of those engravings of Shakespeare.

'Mr Marsden?'

'Yes,' he said gently.

'I'm a Canadian, and since I was in Mousehole I thought I'd come over and tell you how much I've enjoyed *A Canadian Upbringing*.'

The pale face looked very vulnerable.

'Come in,' he said quietly. 'How is Canada?'

'Fine,' I said.

'When were you last there?'

'Eight years ago.'

'What part?'

'Ottawa.'

I then told him my name, that I left for much the same reason as he did. And that since my college days I had carried around his book, like a Bible.

'Would you like some tea?' he said in that gentle detached manner.

'Yes,' I said. 'Thank you.'

'I'm sorry I haven't any spirits,' he said, as he disappeared into the back.

It was a small tidy cottage, very simply furnished. An unvarnished wooden table in the middle. A couple of well-made wooden chairs. A fireplace with some coloured postcards on top.

Marsden returned with a tray that had a small teapot, two earthenware mugs, a loaf of bread, and a sliced lemon. Then he went back again.

'I've got a surprise,' he said.

He came back with a large salami that had 'Blooms' written across it, in white, several times.

'I get this sent to me once a month from a delicatessen in London. I tried to get some rye bread, but they won't send it.'

He cut a thin slice of the salami and, spearing it with the knife, gave it to me.

'Delicious,' I said.

He made me a salami sandwich and one for himself and we had tea and sandwiches sitting by the bare wooden table.

'That's what I miss most, the food,' he said, and for the first time he sounded enthusiastic. 'I tried to make *gefilte* fish. It turned out uneatable.

I tried to make *putcha* and finally persuaded the local butcher to get me some calf's legs. But the thing looked like jellied dishwater, and I threw it away. Where are you staying?'

'In a cottage across from The Coastguards. We rented it for two weeks.'

'Married?'

'Yes,' I said. 'I've got two kids.'

'I never did,' he said, and seemed to go off again on some private thought. But I wasn't going to let this meeting play itself out in small talk about food. I had rehearsed this occasion during too many sleepless nights. I wanted to talk about *A Canadian Upbringing*. And how he had made me aware of my background and why it was necessary to leave it.

'Go home,' he said suddenly. 'Go home while you are still young.'

'But I thought you were critical of Canada?'

'Maybe. But I care less about England.'

He cut some more salami, very carefully, and made another two neat sandwiches.

I decided to change the subject. 'How is your work going?'

'Fine. I do that upstairs. Would you like to see my work-room?'

I said I would and felt somewhat flattered. Writers' work-rooms are usually private things.

I followed him up the stairs—I noticed he wore brown leather slippers—to a largish airy room that had planks of wood on the floor, some packing cases, an electric saw, several planes, several chisels, tins of glue and paint.

He led me to the far side where, in what looked like former bookcases, were standing brightly painted toys.

'I make roundabouts,' he said, picking one up for me.

They were the gayest roundabouts I have seen. Bright blues, crimsons, oranges, yellows, green—with a barber-shop pole in the middle around which farmyard animals went to the tinkle of a small silver bell.

'I make these for various toy shops in London, and they go all over—' Marsden said.

He saw me look at the Canadian newspapers on the floor.

'I get those sent from Canada House. They're handy for packing.'

He had a large mirror on one wall with various postcards stuck along the inside of the frame. They showed Piccadilly with the Guinness clock and several red buses; the midnight sun over a lake at Landego, Norway; a snow scene in Obergurl, Austria; a bull elephant from Kenya; and the Peace Tower and the lawns in Ottawa. On the backs of the cards was written much the same sort of message.

> *I think your roundabouts are*
> *wonderful. They have given my*
> *children much pleasure. Thank you.*

I told Marsden that I thought the roundabouts were splendid.

'Do you make any other kind of toy?'

'No,' he said, 'just this one model.'

Downstairs. The tea was cold. He had put away the salami and we had smoked all my cigarettes. I stood up and shook hands and said I would see him again before we left. He opened the door for me.

'I'm very glad you called,' he said, in that gentle, unemotional way of his.

For the next few days I didn't go and see Marsden but thought of little else. I have not had many heroes lately and as I grow older they get less. But Marsden had meant something personal to me. And I felt I had been cheated. Of what exactly I didn't know. But the man who wrote *A Canadian Upbringing* no longer existed as far as I was concerned. And I was quite prepared to leave Cornwall without seeing him again.

But on the morning we were to leave, and as we were packing things to take back in the car, he turned up, looking very elegant in light cream trousers, brown sandals, yellow socks, and a maroon shirt.

'I hope you don't mind,' he said. 'I thought your children might like these.' And he gave each of the kids a roundabout.

Their reaction was immediate. They kissed him. They jumped around him. They gave little squeals of delight. And Marsden was enjoying it as well.

For my wife he had an enormous bunch of anemones—and my wife is a sitting duck when it comes to flowers.

He played with the children while I and my wife finished bringing the packed things from the cottage into the car. I was trying to close the back when Marsden came up.

'Can I help?'

'Thanks,' I said, shutting it. 'It's all finished.'

'It was good of you to come and see me,' he said. 'You're the first author who has.' He was, I think, going to say something else, but the kids came running around. So we shook hands, and we all got into the car.

'I'll send you some rye bread,' I said starting the engine.

'I don't want to put you to all that trouble, but if you could send me a couple of loaves, just once—'

And he waved.

And we were waving as I drove away. Around the first bend he disappeared from sight. The road went by some large blue rocks and by the briny sea that lay flat to the horizon. It made everything, suddenly, seem awfully silent.

I Like Chekhov

It was a warm afternoon in July. And in the Yorkshire town the sheep were grazing on the grass of the school lawns that sloped to the river. Chester Conn Bell walked along the footpath under the avenue of heavy trees. He was twenty-nine, blond and with a fine profile, he looked more like an actor than a schoolmaster. Beside him the river had little water in it. It was mainly mudbanks with beached rowboats and old bits of wood.

He turned off the footpath, as he had done five days of the week for the past nine months, and went through the small park with its scented gardens of lemon thyme for the blind.

It's over, thought Chester. And then a sudden light feeling of release. How marvellous to be free again.

Tomorrow he would leave this provincial backwater with its bad library and deadness at night. He didn't mind the teaching as much as he disliked being reminded that he was a teacher. When he walked through the streets the schoolboys were always there touching their caps with their hand.

'Good morning, sir.'

'Afternoon, sir.'

'Good evening, sir.'

By the church with the slate spire he left the park and walked along the side street that brought him into a residential area. On both sides were pale yellow brick houses. Halfway down, on the left, lived Miss Fort, who was in her sixties. She taught music. And Chester rented her front room. As he opened the front door he heard the piano and a girl's thin voice singing 'A lover and his lass'.

He took off his navy blue blazer, loosened his dark blue tie, undid his collar button, sat down in the comfortable chair, lit a cigarette. And listened to the singing and the piano. And he began to think that no more would he be coming back to this room. Nor early mornings going out for coffee and toast. Then through the park, by the cemetery, the mist hanging over the river in the winter. Nor going on the stage and singing solemnly the morning hymns. Then the roll-calls, detentions, telling them to stop talking. He had hated it all the time he was doing it. But now that was over.

The singing and the piano stopped. It was five-thirty. He knew he would like to round off his teaching days and his stay in this town with some kind of gesture. And he was looking forward to seeing the Latin Master and the Geography Master later that evening in The Antelope.

It was the Latin Master's idea to go to The Antelope. He had told Chester about Sophie Jewtree, the proprietress, who served behind the bar. And Chester had also heard from the others in the staff room about Sophie and the Latin Master.

Sophie Jewtree was one of the attractive women in the town. When she was behind the bar there were, at various times in the evening, five or six married men who left their wives to be with Sophie. Her husband, a stocky retired RAF officer, did not mind. (The men came regularly, talked quietly, stood together in a small group, like overgrown school-boys.) He called them Sophie's admirers. And the most consistent of all the admirers was the Latin Master.

He was a lean, taut, man with rimless glasses, small neat moustache, and thin lips. He spoke quietly and precisely. But when he became angry with a pupil, his face would flush and leave him speechless.

Every Monday to Friday the Latin Master went to The Antelope to have a few drinks and to see Sophie. They talked quietly, and kept looking at each other. Then the Latin Master went back to his wife. It had gone on like this for three years.

The Geography Master was different. He looked like a corpulent schoolboy whose suits were always in need of a press. And he couldn't shake off the classroom. Away from it he continued, in his conversation, to explain the obvious. He was married with five small children. And while the Latin Master lived with his wife in a neat rented flat, the Geog-raphy Master inherited money and owned one of the finest houses in the town.

What held these two together was that they both went to Cambridge. While the rest were graduates of provincial universities. And Chester, being Canadian and socially unclassifiable, was accepted by both sides. He was invited to the Latin and Geography Masters' homes for dinner—a thing they had never done with the other masters. And when Chester went out to a pub with some of the masters from the provincial universities they told him how stuck-up the two Cambridge men were.

The Antelope was a combination pub and hotel. It had one long copper bar that stretched most of the width of the room and some wooden cubicles against the wall opposite the bay windows.

When Chester came in, the two were already there.

'What are you having?' the Geography Master asked.

'Whisky,' Chester said, '*Teachers.*'

They laughed.

'This is Chester,' the Latin Master said to the woman behind the bar.

'I heard a lot about you,' she said.

She looked handsome but vulnerable. A tallish woman with brown loose hair that she kept pushing back from her eyes. There was something about attractive women that drew Chester to them. Unlike the other masters, Chester felt more comfortable in the presence of women than of men. And women soon realized this.

'You look different,' the Geography Master said to Chester.

'All people look different when they are going away,' Sophie said.

While she was serving at the other end of the bar, the Latin Master asked, somewhat proudly, 'What do you think of Sophie?'

'Wish I'd come here before,' Chester said, noticing how her belly pushed out against the tight stone-tweed skirt.

'—years from now we'll be saying,' the Geography Master said, '*remember the time Chester Conn Bell* ...'

'Couldn't you teach, and write in your spare time?' Sophie said.

'I tried,' Chester said, 'but I didn't do any writing all the time I was here.'

'Have you had things published?' she asked.

This was a sore point with Chester.

'I've had some stories, in a magazine, in Canada.'

Sophie said her husband was born in New Zealand (he was away in London) and told them how they met in London in 1944 when she was a WAAF. And what a gay exciting time she had when she ran her own MG and met new people nearly every day.

'You must miss that—living here,' Chester said.

'When I do I go to see my doctor,' she said. 'He tells me I have good legs.'

'The thing I missed most in this town,' Chester said, 'was not being able to get a decent book. The library here is terrible.'

'I've got books,' said Sophie.

'What kind of books?'

'Chekhov—Tolstoy—'

'You have books like that?'

'Yes,' she said. 'I like the Russians. They're in the back. Would you like to see them?'

The Latin Master didn't like the way the conversation was going.

'You can see them tomorrow.'

But there was no confidence in his voice.

'I'll be gone tomorrow,' Chester said.

'We'll only be a minute,' Sophie said to the Latin Master, and touched his hand as she went by.

She led Chester into an adjoining room. She put on a wall-light that kept most of the room in shadows. Then walked over to the bookcase. There weren't as many books there as Chester expected. He bent over to read the titles. There was a thin olive-green volume of Chekhov's short stories—books of poetry—Browning—some wartime anthologies—Penguin *New Writing*. She was bending over beside him, he could smell her scent. Their hips touched. He turned and they kissed gently on the mouth. Then they straightened out. And they kissed several times, not gently.

'I think we'd better go back,' she said, after a while.

The light in the bar was hard on their eyes as they came in. The Latin Master looked annoyed and puzzled. The Geography Master: as if he had been told a dirty joke and had just got the point.

'She's got some good books,' Chester said to them. Then to Sophie, who was now behind the bar, 'I like Chekhov. He understands people.'

But the atmosphere had changed. And there was something noticeably uneasy among them now. They finished their last drinks in a series of silences and said goodbye to Sophie.

As soon as they were out on the gravel drive the Latin Master came up to Chester.

'What did you do in there?'

'We kissed,' Chester said.

A flush appeared on the Latin Master's face. He looked at Chester but said nothing. Then turned, walked over the gravel to his bicycle, and rode away.

'I'll drive you home,' the Geography Master said quietly.

'Thanks,' Chester said. 'It's my last night. I think I'll walk.'

'Don't forget us,' the Geography Master suddenly called out from the car, as he drove away.

Chester began to walk down the slope. The moon was out and it shone on the water, on the stone bridge, on the small park and the town behind it. A breeze from the river. He turned the collar of his jacket up and put his hands in his trouser pockets and began to whistle. He felt very happy as he walked through the empty provincial streets and heard the echoing sound of his own footsteps. 'It's nice to be on the move,' he said to himself.

English for Foreigners

THE CLASSROOMS WERE above an optician, by a seedy restaurant, overlooking a large bare cathedral. When I started, at the beginning of May, the season had not begun. I had eight pupils, the intermediates. If anyone could carry on a few sentences in broken English he left the beginners—which was crowded—and stayed in the intermediates until there was room for him in the senior class. Each class consisted of a small room with tables pushed together in the shape of a horseshoe. I sat behind a desk, at the open end of the horseshoe, by a portable blackboard. The windows had to be closed because of the traffic noise. On a warm or a rainy day, the room was stifling.

On the first day I wondered whether my Canadian accent would matter. 'Ladies and gentlemen. I'm your new teacher. I'm a Canadian. And the kind of English I speak is not the kind that Englishmen speak. So if you have any trouble understanding what I say—' But I was interrupted by an Italian girl who beamed and said how clear my diction was. And they all said they understood me and complimented me on how clear I spoke. I was getting to feel quite good. But I found out, on the second day, that the Englishman I replaced had a speech impediment. He left without saying goodbye. That was one of the occupational hazards. One was hired without references and left the same way.

Teaching consisted mainly in giving them new words, correcting their pronunciation, dictating to them small pieces of anything I happened to see while looking out of the window. And reading excerpts from Conrad. Or else we played games. I would borrow one of their watches with a sweep second-hand and say:

'Miss Laroque. You are walking in Brighton from the Steyne to the West Pier. Tell me, in one minute, all the words beginning with the letter "M" that you would see. *Now.*'

'Mouse ... Mutton ... Murder ... Mister ... Missus ... Miss ...'

'Sir. That's not fair.'

'Six, Miss Laroque,' I said, 'twenty-five seconds to go.'

'Mimosa … Macaroni … Man …'

They were mainly young girls. Some were there for business reasons: to be a receptionist in their father's hotel; another was going to be an air-hostess; another to work in an export office. But the majority were there for a holiday.

I had been there three weeks when Mrs Siemens came in. The age of the students didn't vary a great deal; they were in their teens or early twenties. But Mrs Siemens, a handsome-looking woman, with grey hair combed neatly back in a bun, and very light-blue eyes, was in her seventies. The immediate reaction to her presence was to subdue everyone. And we got a lot more done. She sat halfway up the left of the horseshoe, listening to what I was saying. Sometimes she took out a handkerchief and wiped her eyes. I took it that she had some allergy. When it was her turn to read she read softly and very slow, and apologized at the end for not doing better.

At eleven we had a ten-minute break. The teachers would go into the office and have coffee. The students would either go to a small café nearby or stay in the room, open the windows, lean out, and smoke. One morning I came back early and a new student, a Mexican, offered me a cigarette.

'Sir. You like Turkish?'

I said I did.

Two weeks later, on a Friday, Mrs Siemens came up to me.

'Thank you very much,' she said graciously. 'This morning was my last lesson. I enjoyed myself very much. I have a small present for you.'

We shook hands. And I went down the stairs holding my books and this package carefully wrapped in white paper with a neat red ribbon.

In the office I unwrapped it. It was a large package of Turkish cigarettes. I was deeply touched. None of the others had bothered to say more than 'goodbye'. Perhaps, I thought, it's just old age that feels it has to pay for even the briefest encounter.

I asked the secretary in the office about Mrs Siemens. She said that Mrs Siemens was a widow. That she was part of *the* Siemens, in Germany. They were extremely wealthy. Her son had died and the doctors advised her to get away and do something to take her mind off things.

And as the secretary was talking I remembered that the words I introduced to the class during her stay—the passages I chose to read or dictate—for some reason kept harping on some aspect of death: on cemeteries, gravestones, funerals, coffins.

But this was Friday and there was little food in the house and I knew that I would have to walk back the three miles. If I had breakfast that morning, I didn't mind the walk. After Preston Circus it was very pleasant. There were the small gardens, each one with the name of an English city and with a single stalk of corn growing incongruously in their middles.

I went into a large tobacconist and told the girl behind the counter that I had bought this package of Turkish cigarettes for a friend as a gift, and I found out that he doesn't smoke. The girl examined the box closely. Finally gave me fourteen shillings.

I went out and bought half a dozen eggs, a tin of luncheon meat, a loaf of bread, some sugar, tea, cheese, a newspaper, and took the bus back.

But that afternoon—though I watched my wife and children eat—I felt I had betrayed something.

Ringa Ringa Rosie

THE BUCHANAN'S fourteenth move in five years was to a semi-detached brick cottage in Bogtown. The front faced the main road. The back had long gardens, then a cricket field which sloped down to brush and a river.

Moving had, by now, become an accepted but reluctant part of their lives. Whenever they moved into a new address no serious attempt was made to change the place or impose on it any sense of possession. All Sheila did was to take down a few of the pictures from the walls and cover with cloths the tin trunks and tea chests until they became part of the set furniture.

Bogtown was a row of labourers' cottages on one side of the main Guildford–Horsham highway. At both ends were filling stations and two pubs. One would have long gone out of business had it not also been a rest point for the coaches plying between London and the south coast. On Sundays the village boys sat on their motorbikes in front of the filling stations and watched the cars go by. At night the place was lit up by a yellow-glass *Shell* sign, above a garage. When the garage closed the village was in darkness except for the sweeps made by passing headlights and the glow from thrown-out cigarettes on the road.

The Buchanans came here, as they did in their previous moves, out of necessity. They were unsatisfactory tenants. They were always behind with the rent. The electricity never received payment until they were threatened with disconnection. And since most of the time they were just trying to make sure that there was enough for the day's food—there was little inclination or time left in seeing that the garden was looked after, or the place kept tidy. In any case the furnished accommodation which they could afford, by the time they had moved into it, had already become run down and seedy.

This time they had moved from a partly furnished semi-detached suburban house in East Finchley. At two pounds ten a week the cottage was exactly half of the rent of the house. But even at that price they were being taken.

The rooms were damp. Patches of grey clotted the ceilings and the walls. The furniture was uncomfortable—a collection of junk that was picked up at various auction sales. And until the cold weather came the place had fleas.

On their second day the Buchanans went on a tour of inspection. In the long back garden dead stalks mixed with new shoots. The grass was over-grown. The rhubarb was wild. There were weeds and two dead apple trees. The middle of the garden was a rubbish dump. And from the rubbish and from every other mound where previous tenants had emp-tied the lavatory bucket, giant nasturtiums with thick fleshy-white tubular stalks twisted magnificently up. The nasturtiums were enor-mous. The white of the stalks swamped the yellow orange brown of the petals. They crawled and twisted over the ground like a series of swollen blood vessels.

In the neighbouring gardens the grass was cut, the dividing hedges trimmed. There were small greenhouses and rose-bushes and apple, plum, and pear trees. There were cultivated blackberries, strawberries, and straight rows of vegetables.

'We always seem to move—'

Sheila said, watching three blue tits on the other side of the hedge—faces like Indians with war paint—picking at a piece of fat dangling from a wooden post.

'—into places where the gardens on either side are always neat and well looked after.'

Whenever the wind dropped there was a smell of decomposition.

He was writing a new book. And she, besides housework and trying to make ends meet, also kept the children out of the cottage by taking them for long walks so he could work in quiet; and on the way filled the second-hand pram with bits of wood which she would hide with the raincover so that the neighbours wouldn't see. And wrote a weekly air-letter to her parents in Ottawa, which was a form of blackmail, for only on that basis did they send her ten dollars every week. Besides this their only other income was the eighteen shillings family allowance.

George and Sheila had never lived in the country before. They had grown up in Kingston and had come over after graduating from Queens for their one trip abroad. But this was extended when Sheila became pregnant. They married. And George refused to return until he had a book published. So far their lives consisted of changing addresses, from one of the outskirts of London to the other, leaving small debts behind. But never had they allowed themselves to be cut off in the way they were now.

In the country when they couldn't pay the monthly newspaper bill—they had to go without newspapers. And likewise when the coal ran out. There was no alternate choice. The coalman lived five cottages away and when George promised that he would pay at the end of the week, and then couldn't, the coalman said, 'I'm a man of principle.' And refused to deliver any. George then took an old sack, went across the snow-covered cricket field, and into the drifts of the brush.

The wind blew the loose snow on to his face and against his eyes. In the fields across the river he could see horses. They swirled in and out of focus, manes blowing. It was, he thought, like a scene in a Russian film. He went to the river, which was frozen, and began to pull the dead branches from the trees. Breaking easily the very green, strong-smelling light wood with his foot and then throwing the pieces into the sack. And carrying the sack on his back, like the coalman, he went back through the gusts. He thought that this should make him hate this kind of life. That it ought to give him some incentive, to do something else. Instead, he looked at the drifting snow, the staring horses, the backs of the cottages, the blurring gardens, and thought it was fine. Someday he would write about it.

It was fine until he brought the sack inside the cottage. The two small children were there with running noses, and they had brought the cot down for the baby as this was the only room they could keep warm in winter. Nappies were around the fireplace, and drying clothes hung on a line from the ceiling across the room. But the wet wood only filled the room with smoke.

They had been living in Bogtown five months. It was a Saturday morning, the middle of February, when she came upstairs and said, 'There's no food for the week-end. You'll have to do something.' He hitch-hiked into Horsham and pawned his typewriter. That lasted them a week.

The following Saturday it was raining when she walked, without her usual knock, into his room. 'The baker is outside. I'm not answering the door. We've no food for the week-end. And the milklady isn't going to deliver anymore unless we pay a pound tomorrow. You'll have to do something.'

So he came down and fumbled with the broken kitchen-door handle. When he finally opened the door he made a joke about the broken handle. But the thin, dark man in white uniform did not find it amusing. He stood there, one hand held the wicker basket, the other his book. George took a plain white loaf. 'We'll pay next week.' The man didn't say anything. He closed his book. But when George put his hand out again to get another loaf, the man said, 'I was told that all you could have was one bread.'

George went back upstairs to his room, sat down in the chair, and looked out of the window. The garden was muddy and drab. The cricket field very green. He saw a large bird at the end of the field, by the river, gently flapping enormous wings. It had a small black body. Then he realized it was a man carrying a long plank of wood on his shoulders. And made a note of this in his notebook.

Downstairs he could hear Sheila becoming irritable with the children. And for his benefit she kept saying out loud, 'It's all right. Daddy will do something.'

He came down again.

'There's nothing I can do,' he said quietly. 'It's raining too hard. I've got nothing to sell.'

'How about the printer?'

'He's away for the weekend. Gone to see his sister at Bognor.'

He went over his list of what he could do. When there was nothing, he could usually borrow ten shillings from the printer down the road. Once, when they were hungry and living in Clapham, he did a song and dance for them, crossing his hands while he moved his knees together and apart. It made them laugh. And laughing they went to bed. But this time she was becoming hysterical.

'You gotta do something.'

'But what can I do.'

The baby fell over a broken plastic flute and began to cry, then ran up to him and buried her head between his legs. The rain came down from the roof, and down the windows, and into the barrel by the drain. It overflowed on to the sogged earth, forming pools in the depressions.

'I don't care what. Long as you do something.'

He went upstairs and looked through his room. Only a few used paper-backs were left on the bookshelves and an old copy of *Gulliver's Travels* that the secondhand bookseller in Horsham had refused to buy. He came down carrying a small green address book and began to telephone. Sheila and the children just stood and watched.

'Hello, Bill. This is George Buchanan. How are you? I bet you are. We're fine. Sheila and the kids. Look, Bill, the reason I rang. I'm hard-pressed at the moment. Could you send me ten pounds. You'll have it back by the end of the month ... I see. Sure, I understand. How's Tangier? No, just raining. I'll tell Sheila. Any time you come to England, drop in. I don't know. Maybe I'll go back home next year. Sure. Bye.'

He hung up. Looked through his address book. Then he was talking again.

'May I speak to Paul de Secker-Remy? Hello, Duke. Guess who this is? No. George Buchanan. Bucky, the genius. Long time no see. I bet you are. Me too. Three, girls. We're living in England. I hear you've got yourself some hotel in the Laurentians. Paul, the reason I called. I'm in a spot at the moment. Could you telegraph a money order for fifty dollars. You'll have it back by the end of the month. Rose Cottage, Bogtown, near—Twenty-five will do. No ... I didn't. I don't worry too much about income tax. Yeh, sure. Sounds like a nice car. I understand. Bye.'

He continued to go through the pages of his address book, calling up people, and he was getting near the end when Kate, the three-year old, said:

'What Daddie doin'?'

'I'm doing something.'

'What Daddie doin'?'

'Talking on the telephone.'

'Don't be silly, Daddie, that's only the top-end of my toy-iron,' Cassie, the eldest, said—a blue-eyed girl of five with blonde, curly hair.

'Daddie funny,' Kate said, 'Daddie pretendin'.'

He had gone through to his last address when Kate ran to him and took his hand. For her that game was over. She began to pull him. 'C'mon, Daddie, play inga-inga-osie.'

Now Cassie took his other hand. And Sheila, standing by the stairs, began to weep. For a short while Cassie didn't know whether she should join her mother and cry as well. But Kate pulled him, then her, and then went over and held out her hand for Sheila. She took hold. And the four of them went around the room in a circle, singing loudly.

Ringa—ringa—rosie.
A pocketful of posie,
A tishoo. A tishoo.
We all fall down.

And they all did, laughing.

I'll Bring You Back Something Nice

I

GORDON RIDEAU'S EYES were closed and he could hear the trucks going by outside the window on the main London to Guildford road. And in-between the trucks, the alarm clock on the floor. At his feet the hot-water bottle was cold. He shoved it to the edge of the bed. Then he opened his eyes and saw the wallpaper: wide yellow bars separated by thin black lines.

His wife, Coral, lay with several blankets over her so that just her dark hair was sticking out. Between them a National Health orange bottle was wrapped in a nappy to keep the milk inside it warm in case the baby woke during the night.

He could hear Kate walking down the stairs. The hall light was on. The brown curtains across the bedroom were drawn. The room was cold. There was a pitcher standing in a large basin; both had a red rose painted on the enamel. And a large bedpan with an old copy of *Vogue* on top. A small triptych of three angels stood on the mantel above the small fireplace which was stuffed with newspapers, cardboard, and bits of coloured crepe paper. All this they had inherited from the owner of the cottage. Their belongings: a steel trunk was open in a corner, in another corner two smaller trunks. Inside were clothes jumbled and spilling out.

Coral sat up quickly, turned back the cover, and looked closely down one leg. Near the ankle she picked off a flea and, carefully, crushed it between her fingers. Then she left the bed.

Gordon watched her. There is nothing graceful about her movements, he thought. She was wearing a grey sweater and put on a blue skirt. She took the nappy with the makeshift milkbottle, the alarm clock, and went downstairs.

Now he lay in bed in a sense of luxury. He was alone, staying in. He drew his knees up to keep warm. He heard the radio downstairs playing dance music. And lay there wondering whether she would bring him a cup of tea.

A door opened below and Kate called out,

'Breakfast is ready Daddy.'

'Coming,' he said.

And remained in bed knowing that in a few minutes she would open the door again and say,

And he would say, 'Breakfast is ready Daddy.'

'I'm just getting my socks on.'

But he had them on all night, and his shirt, and a heavy black sweater.

The child came lightly up the stairs. She had just turned four. A shy attractive child with blonde straight hair and fine small features.

'OK,' Gordon said as she came into the bedroom. 'I'm coming.'

'Post, Daddy.'

She gave him a brown envelope.

He opened it. It was a letter from the electricity company saying that a man had come yesterday to disconnect the electricity but no one was in. He was going to come on Friday at eleven unless they could pay £12. 5s. 2d.

It means a trip to London, Gordon thought. And that was enough to make him get up.

He dressed and went to the window and pulled back the brown curtain. The diagonal crack in the glass was like a scar. The fields, across the road, muddy and drab. The trees on the border of the field—misshapen by the ivy that was slowly killing them—looked very pretty. He watched a motorcycle accelerate as it went by splashing mud on either side and with a muddy wake. Then he closed the light in their bedroom and went down a narrow passage. By the children's open door: the smell of urine, the camp bed, the mug of water, the comics and books on top of an overturned orange case. He turned sharply. Down the narrow stairs. At the bottom he opened a door and immediately felt the warm air. It was the one room that was warm. A coal-fire was going in the fireplace. Beside it, in a corner, was a baby's cot.

Kate stood by the cot dressed in a jumper, a red sweater, which someone had given them when their own children had grown out of the clothes. She was talking to the baby. 'Ah goolie goo Rachel. Ah goolie goo.' The baby stood up in the cot, grasping the wooden struts and gurgled back a couple of vowels. She looked like something caught in a cage.

'Good morning,' Gordon said cheerfully to the children and went into the kitchen.

Coral was at the stove. 'High keeps changing,' she said. 'I don't know if the hot plate is off or on.'

'Use the Master Switch.'

Then he decided it would be better to show her. 'Off,' he said and put the switch up. 'On,' he pulled it down.

'What do you want,' she said. 'There's a bit of cheese—I could make toast.'

'Fine,' he said and went into the other room. Kate was playing with some pieces of paper and a pencil. The baby was crawling on the floor to the coal bucket. She took pieces of coal and tried to put them in her mouth. Her lips were black. Gordon took the bucket away and put it by the side of the fireplace, behind a chair. The child crawled after it.

'What post did you have?' she said bringing in the toast and cheese.

'A reminder from the electricity.'

'When are they coming?'

'Tomorrow.' He tried to appear casual. 'I guess I'll have to go to London.'

'Where Daddy going?' Kate said quickly.

'To London—I'll bring you back something.'

'A dolly,' the child said excitedly.

'What will you do?' Coral said.

'I'll try the bank first—I'll find a way.'

'You know how I hate this place.'

'I know.'

And he prepared himself for her to follow with: you can always get away but I'm stuck here ... my hands are tied ... I'm the one that's always left behind. Instead she said, 'When you're up could you look around.'

'I'll go and see some real estate people.'

'Try somewhere near a park.'

'I'll try darling.'

'This isn't just you saying things to keep me happy? You will do something.'

'Yes,' he said quietly.

'We've got less than two months.'

'You know how I work,' he tried to sound convincing. 'Leave things until the last week. Then I get something.'

She didn't reply. He was nearly there, he thought.

'You won't forget.'

And he was safe now.

'I'll do my best darling,' he said and got up. 'I'd better shave.'

There was some hot water left in the kettle. He emptied it into a tin mould that she used to make cakes in, mixed a bit of cold water from the tap, and shaved in front of the mirror, above the dishes.

He tried to tidy his sideburns and realized that his face looked odd. It was the eyes. The left one set at an angle. He saw it as well in the baby. Around the small mirror was the kitchen window with old spider webs. Cuts in the snow skiers made climbing a hill sideways. And for a moment he was back to the pressure the cold made on his forehead. He was in a sleigh sitting behind the swaying rump of a horse held in its tight harness, with Holly. Past white fields with the telegraph poles just protruding. I could tell, she said, when you held my hand to take my coat off. And Jasmine. It snowed all that day in Montreal. After the lecture we went to the Berkeley and drank Brandy Alexanders until it was time to go. The expensive gloom of her parents' apartment. The thing like a curled bulrush that she took from out her hair. And Lily. How quick it was with her ... she had her own car. Her father owned an entire small town in Northern Ontario. He wondered what would have happened to his life had he made one of them pregnant.

'Don't forget to empty the bucket,' Coral called from the other room.

He took a spade from the shed, walked along the path to the back garden. Halfway down he selected a part of bare earth and began to dig. He emptied the almost full black bucket into the hole he made. Then shovelled the earth back into the hole. It splashed gently. Then the liquid overflowed and stained the earth. He came back into the kitchen. 'I've emptied the bucket,' he said to Coral. He washed his hands. 'Is there anything left?'

She went to the dresser with the few dishes and from a Peter Rabbit saucer took out a halfpenny and a 3d. stamp. He put the halfpenny in his pocket. Then went upstairs, into his room, and put on his one clean white shirt. He took down his trousers hanging from a hook on a hanger in the corner. They were the trousers of his one remaining suit. He saw how frayed the bottoms were. He took the small scissors from his desk and cut some of the hanging threads. He put on the trousers, his tie and jacket. And came down carrying the black winter overcoat that he bought twelve years ago when he was at university. He put it on. Coral brushed him down. The children were crowding around him.

'You look nice Daddy,' Kate said.

'You will look around,' Coral said.

'Yes,' he said, then smiled to the children.

'I'll bring you back something nice.'

'A dolly?' Kate said.

'Something to eat.'

Coral picked up the baby.

He kissed them all goodbye.

They went with him to the front gate. And watched him walk along the road away from them. Kate climbed up the wooden gate and said goodbye several times. And they waved to each other.

From a distance of ten yards, Coral thought, he was still handsome and looked neat and successful. There was the confident manner, the upright walk. He turned and waved back to them. From some thirty yards, she thought, he looked even better. He might have been an executive going off to the office, to work.

He looked for darkness in the windshield. He could tell quickly by the amount of darkness, the outline (like those outlines they had trained him to look at in a tenth, a twentieth, a fiftieth of a second) whether the driver of the coming car was alone or not. He didn't bother to put up his hand if there were two.

II

From Piccadilly Gordon walked down Lower Regent Street and into the bank, across the light marble floor, to the short teller with the Italian-sounding name. They shook hands and asked each other questions as if they knew one another well.

'I've just come up for the day,' Gordon said.

'How is the family?'

'Fine. And yours?'

'They're fine. We went to Connemara for a holiday.' He smiled and took out some photographs. 'It was wonderful—the best holiday we had.'

There were photographs of some children by a pony, by a cottage. And the bank teller in a pair of shorts.

'May I see the manager?'

'I'll see if he is free.'

He left his cage and out of it looked even smaller but long in the arms.

He came back smiling. 'The manager is busy. But our assistant manager Mister Henderson will see you.'

'Come in, Mister Rideau.'

The assistant manager, unlike most North Americans, looked much older than his forty-two years. But his: 'Sit down, Mister Rideau. Cigarette?' had a professional warmth. 'Now, what's the trouble.'

'I have an electricity bill just over twelve pounds that I must meet tomorrow or else they'll cut us off. Could the bank let me overdraw fifteen pounds? It will only be for a short time. I've got money coming in.'

'I'm sorry. It's impossible,' the assistant manager said. 'I can't let you have a pound.' He lowered his voice. '*He* gave me strict instructions.' And his eyes indicated the frosted glass partition of the other room.

'But I've been with the bank for seven years.'

'*He* doesn't consider you a banking proposition.'

They were both silent. The assistant manager looked uncomfortable. 'Are you a veteran?'

'Yes,' Gordon said, 'I was in the army.' And remembered a time in Montreal, after taking a girl home to the Town of Mount Royal he flagged a cab and found he didn't have enough money to get back. He told this to the driver. 'Are you a veteran?' the driver asked.

'I was in the air force,' the assistant manager said. He crushed his cigarette in the green-glass ashtray. Then stood up and walked away from his desk. Gordon also got up. The assistant manager put his hands in his trouser pockets.

'I'm sorry I can't let you have the money. Take this. Pay it back when you can. *Please.*'

'Thanks, I'll pay it back soon as I can.'

'There's no rush.'

He wondered if the assistant manager was now going to give him a lecture. But they shook hands and said goodbye.

Outside, walking up the Haymarket, Gordon took the bill out and saw it was a five-pound note. He was delighted. Imagine getting money from an assistant bank manager I had never met. But a moment later it also registered on him that the probable reason he got the money was because the assistant manager had never laid eyes on him before.

At a small kiosk he bought a pack of tipped Gauloises, a box of matches, an *Evening Standard*. Then walked along Piccadilly to Lyons Corner House. He went into the Wimpy side, found an empty table by the wall, ordered two hamburgers and a black coffee. Around the centre counter North Americans were staring at other North Americans. It might have been the drugstore back home, except they were on good behaviour.

III

The alarm clock woke Mr and Mrs Black at seven even though Mr Black wasn't going to work. He went to shave. And used the foam lather of the company whose assistant accountant he was. Then he sat down in the room with the Van Gogh print on the wall, the souvenir ash-tray from Clovelly, the silver napkin rings, the photograph of himself in the Home Guard, while Mrs Black did his porridge and the two pieces of toast in the kitchen.

'You won't get excited,' Mrs Black said as they were having their second cup of tea.

'No dear.'

'She could have her old room. The children could sleep in the spare room. And there's the camp bed.'

Mr Black put on the jacket of his dark suit, the Homburg hat, the black coat. He was a handsome if stern-looking man with dark straight hair, a lean face, but there was a strain about it, the result of a lifetime of bronchial trouble.

'Do you want to take anything for the train?' Mrs Black said, standing by the glass-enclosed cabinet with her Mary Webb novels and his *Lord Jim*, James Agate, *Quest for Corvo*, the books on accountancy.

'I have the paper.'

'I hope it goes all right,' Mrs Black said at the door.

'I'll be back for tea. Goodbye dear.'

The train went by Eltham, Kidbrooke, Lewisham. Mr Black turned to the *Telegraph*'s crossword '_ _ _ _ _ _ _ _ is mortal's chieftest enemy' (*Shakespeare*). He tried 'dying.' But that wasn't long enough. Neither was 'boredom.' 'Temptation' was too long …

At Charing Cross he changed to a tube that took him to Victoria and here he had to wait another ten minutes for a train to Horsham. At Horsham he took a taxi to the cottage. It was 10.20 when he opened the front gate, but he didn't go to the front door. He went around the side of the cottage, where he surprised Coral hanging up the children's washing.

'Hullo,' he said quietly.

They smiled, then they kissed. And one could see a family resemblance.

She opened the kitchen door and led him into the warm room where he took off his coat.

'How is Mummy?'

'She sends her love.'

He gave the children some toffee candy.

'Gordon is in London,' she said. 'He had to go up on business.'

'Daddy is going to bring me a dolly,' Kate said.

'We haven't had our milk,' Coral said. 'I could make tea without it.'

Mr Black sat in the worn red chair. His breathing was audible. 'You can't go on like this,' he said quietly.

Coral quickly took the children into the next room and closed the door behind them.

'Why don't you leave him,' Mr Black said. 'I'll see that you and the children are looked after. I'll get you a house—'

She didn't reply.

'He's no good,' he said. 'He'll only drag you down.'

'I can't leave him,' she said.

'If he wants to go on like this there's no reason why you and the children—'

'He's got no one except me and the children.'

'I'll get you a house—' he began, but he knew it had not gone right. This wasn't the way he had rehearsed it.

'I think you must hate me,' Coral said.

'I don't hate you,' Mr Black said. But he was at a loss as to what to say next.

Kate came into the room, followed by the crawling baby. Kate had a drawing. 'This is for you Grandpa.' He took the drawing and gave the child a half-crown. He also gave Coral three one-pound notes. She immediately went next door to the grocery and came back with milk, sugar, and some biscuits. They sat in the warm room and had tea while Mr Black told her about a cousin who had gone to Rhodesia to run an Outward Bound School. That an uncle had become manager of a bank in Plymouth. And another cousin had gone to Canada as a physical training instructor. It was time, he said, he was leaving. They walked slowly up the road to the Shell garage, where Mr Black took a taxi. Kate kissed him. So did Coral. 'Goodbye Daddy' she said.

IV

For half an hour Gordon sat in the cubicle by the wall of the Wimpy watching other people. Then he went downstairs to the washroom. He turned the hot tap of the sink and began to wash his hands.

'You can always tell a McGill man. He washes his hands *before*—'

Gordon turned to see a grinning boyish face. I don't know him, he thought. Aloud he said. 'Of course. It's—'

'Not fair surprising you like this. I'm Hugh Finlay,' the man said still grinning.

'Hugh Finlay,' Gordon said. They shook hands. 'What are you doing over here?'

'Passing through. I'm on the way south, to France.'

They were both in their middle thirties, McGill graduates, in London, but there the resemblance stopped abruptly. Hugh Finlay was blond, ruddy, and radiated bodily comfort.

'I heard you were over here,' Finlay said. 'I was going to go to the bank to get your address. You know we're having a reunion?'

'No,' Gordon said. 'No, I didn't.'

'It's our tenth anniversary.'

They returned to the cubicle and ordered two coffees.

'You've worn well, Hugh,' Gordon said.

'The reward for leading a healthy life,' Finlay said. 'You married?'

'Yes. We've got two kids.'

'Do I know her?'

'No. She's an English girl. We live in the country. How about you?'

'I was engaged to Sally Boston. The Boston Biscuits. They give a quarter of a million each year *anonymously*. But she was too good. She's like an angel. If she saw somebody poor, she'd cry.' He took out some coloured snapshots from his jacket pocket. 'This is my yacht at Cannes. Here's a picture of Garbo on it. Here's some of the girls I had on board last summer. She's only sixteen. Hard to believe. Do you know any addresses of girls?'

The pretty West Indian waitress came with the two cups of coffee. Gordon insisted on paying.

'How about coming to the reunion?' Hugh said suddenly. 'Lot of the gang you know will be there.'

'Do you think it will be all right?'

'I know it will. I'll phone Charlie Bishop.'

While he was gone Gordon tried to remember Hugh Finlay at McGill …but he couldn't.

'I talked to Charlie. He said sure, swell. We've a couple of hours. How about if we got some fresh air. I've a rented car outside.'

They were driving through Hyde Park when Hugh Finlay said, 'I saw a friend of yours last week. Mary Savage. Except she's not Mary

Savage any more, she's Mary Troy. Remember Jack? You'll see him at the reunion.'

'How is Mary?'

'Exactly the same. She does some kind of social work.'

'What's Jack doing?'

'Selling beans ... millions of them. They've got a place by the river. Fifteen rooms but no kids. I think they're planning to adopt one.'

V

Because her father left her the money Coral decided to go into London with the children. She washed them and herself, got them dressed, caught a green bus to the station then a train to Victoria.

From Victoria she took a bus to Kensington Gardens. And walked through the Gardens. A man was flying a kite, ducks flew over. The children chased the wood pigeons. She liked London. It was the only place she wanted to live. But what chance had they? She decided to try the Town Hall. The receptionist led her into a separate office where a single yellow rose in a thin glass vase stood on the wooden desk. 'Mrs Troy will be here in a minute.'

A tall angular woman with dark hair and glasses came in. The woman was about the same age as Coral, perhaps a year or two older. 'What's the problem,' she said.

'We have to get out of the place we're living in ... in Sussex ... and I wonder if you can help us find somewhere in London?'

'You have no alternative accommodation?'

'No.'

'Have you funds?'

'No. We haven't.'

'Does your husband live with you?'

'Yes.'

'I'm sorry. I'm afraid I can't help you. We can only help if your husband leaves you.'

Coral came out with the children and walked along Kensington High Street. Everyone it seemed would help her if he left her, or if she left him. Otherwise, what was the future? Moving from one rented place to another, from country village to country village or, with luck, to a provincial town. And she hated living in other people's houses.

She caught a bus to Trafalgar Square and walked among the pigeons. The children clung to her. Then along the Mall. She bought some choc-ices and they had a little picnic of choc-ices on a bench in St James's Park. She wondered where Gordon was, who he was seeing, what he was doing. He always came back with money and food from these trips to London. But she suspected that he never told her the whole truth as to how he got it.

She was walking through the Park—the baby in the push-chair, Kate holding her hand—when a truck, with a camera on the roof, stopped. A man and woman were inside. The man said, 'Do you mind being in a film? Just like you are ... with your children. Can you do that again? Thank you. Thank you very much.' A few minutes later, further into the park, she sat on the grass, underneath a beech, by the water. The sun was out. Kate was feeding the ducks, the baby was on the grass watching. She suddenly felt extraordinarily happy. She hoped the truck would come back and take a picture of them now.

VI

Well-dressed men in their middle to late thirties were standing under the hanging flags or by the windows looking out to Trafalgar Square. They greeted one another enthusiastically. They came up to Gordon Rideau.

'Hi, Gordy old man.'

'Where have you been hiding?'

'Hello Gordon,' Charlie Bishop said and shook hands. 'Nice of you to come. It has been a long time.'

'Ten years.'

'You don't look any different Gordon.'

Mike Gagnon, an energetic head of a publishing firm who was tipped while an undergraduate to be the next Prime Minister, came up. 'Let us in on the secret Gordy. How do you keep so slim? You wearing a corset?' Mike's fine features were slowly being undermined by fat. 'I go to the Y three times a week but I've still got this rubber ring.' And he playfully slapped his middle.

Charlie Bishop hit his glass with a spoon and called Quiet. Quiet. A short stocky man with glasses, almost bald, but hardly a line in his face. He was a director in the London branch of his grandfather's tar company.

'As you know,' he said confidently, 'this is something of an occasion. Our tenth anniversary. And while the main one is being celebrated in Montreal it is fitting that we in London should get together and remember when we all were ...'

'Single,' someone shouted.

'*And* broke,' another replied.

He waited. 'The bond we established at McGill was something special. It's a different kind of loyalty to anything else. It's different from the wife or the kids. And I know that every time we come and get together like this that bond is strengthened.'

'Hear, hear' came from several tables.

'This year I have a surprise. And by now you all must know who the surprise is. He's sitting here beside me ... Somebody has pointed out that our year was a vintage year. And it's true. We've got more people in the Canadian edition of *Time* than any year since. But the only literary man we produced was Gordy. He has lived in England, in the country, since he left us. And he is difficult to get hold of. But when I heard he would be in London today I didn't have to do much persuading to get him to come to this reunion. Fellow classmates, I'm very proud to give you Gordon Rideau.'

There was generous applause. Gordon got up.

'I first would like to say how pleased I am to be back with you.'

'Hey, where did you pick up that Limey accent?' Jack Troy called out. Charlie Bishop detected something else in Gordon's voice and wondered why he was so nervous.

'Although this is the first reunion that I have attended, I've often thought of my college days,' he said hesitantly. 'I really had a good time. And I was just old enough to know it ... I think what made us different from the other years was because we were all returning veterans. And it was difficult to pretend we were college kids straight from high school ...'

He's not a good speaker, thought Charlie Bishop. His voice is too monotonous. But he seems to have the right idea. It looks like a short speech.

'... and that nice secure feeling of walking under the avenue of black trees in winter or in the fall sitting on the grass under the willow ...'

Hugh Finlay seemed, at that moment, to be sitting on the grass under the willow tree watching the grey squirrels, the fallen leaves, on the lawns: and waiting for a two o'clock lecture.

'One is always disappointed by change,' Gordon said coming to the end. 'And these reunions remain a tribute. To one's youth. To gaiety. To optimism. When things seemed continually fresh. And life was a pleasure. And it was all so very easy.'

He sat down quickly to loud applause. Charlie Bishop leaned over and shook Gordon's hand. So did Mike Gagnon from the other side.

Then Charlie Bishop got up, thanked Gordon for his speech. 'Before we leave the formal side,' Charlie said, 'I'd like us all to stand and remember those classmates who are not here with us.'

They got up, some bowed their heads slightly. Charlie waited then nodded to Jack Troy. And Jack began to sing. Holding hands the rest joined in. There were tears in Hugh Finlay's eyes as, with the others, he sang.

For auld lang syne, my dear.
For auld lang syne.
We'll drink a cup of kindness yet
For the days of auld lang syne.

They broke up into small groups around separate tables. And as the afternoon went on, the food, the drink, being guest of honour did something to Gordon Rideau. He went around gaily from one group to another. And he found himself boasting about things that hadn't happened.

'The Russians have brought out my last two novels,' he said, cutting into one group's conversation. 'But I can't spend those roubles unless I go there.'

To another. 'They're making a film in Ireland. It's called *The Millionaire*. I did the script. It's an original.'

A few moments later he tried again. 'I won some prize in Australia. But I don't believe it. How can you believe a telegram that's signed Johnny Soprano?'

But after a while of this he felt their lack of interest. And that he was being left out of their conversation. The others were talking away and they wouldn't let him come in. He had the feeling that he was no longer wanted ...

If anyone was watching this convivial gathering he would have seen, through the smoke of cigarettes and cigars, Mike Gagnon get up from the table shortly after five and make his way across the room to the toilet. Gordon Rideau got up and followed him. They were in there for a few minutes. Then they came out together, not talking. Some ten minutes later, Charlie Bishop made his way to the toilet. And Gordon left his chair soon after Charlie disappeared. They came out together. Charlie somewhat red in the face.

In the next half-hour Gordon followed three more into the toilet, and reappeared with each one.

The talk around the table where Gordon Rideau sat was noticeably subdued. A short while later he got up and said he had to go. 'It's a great reunion,' he said to Charlie Bishop. He wanted to shake Charlie's hand, but Charlie withdrew his. 'See you ...'

After he had gone, Charlie Bishop, Mike Gagnon, Jack Troy, Hugh Finlay, sat around without saying anything. They looked tired.

'Our great author,' Mike Gagnon said finally.

'Maybe he's had a run of hard luck,' Jack Troy said.

'How much did he hit you?'

'Three pounds.'

'He got that from me.'

'That four-flusher—' Hugh said, his voice shaking.

'You guys got off easy,' Charlie Bishop said. 'He hit me for five.'

'*That little four-flusher.*' Suddenly Hugh lashed out at a glass on the table. Then he saw it was on the floor in pieces.

'Don't take it so hard,' Charlie Bishop said. 'There's another one next year. I won't make the same mistake.'

'But why ...?' Hugh said. 'Why did he spoil everything?'

We All Begin in a Little Magazine

WE LIVE IN A SMALL coastal town and in the summer, when the place is looking its best, it becomes overcrowded with people who have come away from the cities for their annual holiday by the sea. It is then that we leave and go up to London for our holiday.

My wife usually finds a house by looking through *The Times*. In this way we had the house of a man who built hotels in the poor parts of Africa so that wealthy American Negroes could go back to see where their grandparents came from. Another summer it was an architect's house where just about everything was done by push-button control. A third time, it was in a house whose owner was in the middle of getting a divorce—for non-consummation—and wanted to be out of the country.

This June she saw an ad saying: DOCTOR'S HOUSE AVAILABLE IN LONDON FOR THREE WEEKS. REASONABLE RENT. She phoned the number. And we agreed to take it.

The advertised house was central, near South Kensington tube station, not far from the Gardens. The taxi took us from Paddington—how pale people looked in London on a hot summer's day—and brought us to a wide street, stopping in front of a detached all-white house with acacia trees in the front garden. A bottle of warm milk was on the doorstep. I opened the door with the key and brought our cases inside.

The phone was ringing.

'Hello,' I said.

'Is this *ABC*?' a youthful voice asked.

'I'm sorry,' I said. 'You have the wrong number.'

'What is your number?'

'Knightsbridge 4231,' I said.

'That *is* the number,' the voice said.

'There must be some mistake,' I said. 'This is a doctor's house.'

'Is the doctor there?'

'No,' I said. 'He's on holiday.'

'Can I leave a message for him?'

'Are you ill?'

'No,' he said. 'Tell him that David White rang. David White of Somerset. He has had my manuscript for over six months now. He said he would let me know over a month ago. I have written him four times.'

'I'll tell him,' I said.

'If he needs more time,' the young man said hesitantly, 'I don't mind—'

'OK,' I said and hung up.

'I don't know what's going on here,' I said to my wife.

But she and the children were busy exploring the rest of the house.

It was a large house and it looked as if it had been lived in. The front room was a children's room with all sorts of games and blackboards and toys and children's books and posters on the walls. There was the sitting-room, the bottom half of the walls were filled with books in shelves. There were more books in the hallway, on the sides of the stairs, and in shelves on every landing. There were three separate baths. A breakfast room where a friendly black cat slept most of the time on top of the oil-fired furnace. And a back garden with a lawn, flowerbeds on the sides, a pond with goldfish, water-lilies, and a copper beech tree at the end.

The phone rang and a shaky voice said.

'May I speak to Doctor Jones?'

'I'm sorry, he's on holiday.'

'When will he come back?'

'In three weeks,' I said.

'I can't wait that long,' the voice said. 'I'm going to New York tomorrow.'

'Would you,' I said, 'like to leave a message?'

'I can't hear what you're saying,' the voice said. 'Can you speak up? I'm a bit deaf and have to wear a hearing aid. The doctors have a cure for this now. If I'd been born two years later I would have been all right.'

'I said would you like to leave the doctor a message?'

'I don't think that will do any good,' he said. 'Could you look in his office and see if he has a poem of mine? It's called "Goodbye." If it is in proof, don't bother. I'll wait. But just find out. I am going over to teach creative writing in night school so I can make some money to come back here. The poem will probably be on the floor.'

'Hold on,' I said.

I went into the office at the top of the house. The floor was cluttered with papers and magazines and manuscripts with letters and envelopes attached. On a wooden table, a large snap file had correspondence. A box had cheques for small amounts. There were also several pound notes, loose change, a sheet of stamps, and two packages of cigarettes. (How trusting, I thought. The doctor doesn't know us—supposing we were crooks?) There was typing paper, large envelopes, a typewriter, a phone, telephone directories, and some galleys hanging on a nail on a wall. A smaller table had an in-and-out tray to do with his medical work, more letters, and copies of *The Lancet*. The neatest part of the room was the area where stacks of unsold copies of *ABC* were on the floor against the far wall.

'I'm sorry,' I said on the phone. 'I can't see it.'

'Oh,' he said. He sounded disappointed.

'Well, tell him that Arnold Mest called. M-E-S-T.'

'I've got that,' I said.

'Goodbye,' he said.

'You won't guess,' I told my wife. 'The doctor edits a little magazine.'

'We can't get away from it,' she said.

Early next morning the doorbell woke us. It was the postman. He gave me several bundles. There were letters from different parts of England and Europe, and air mail ones from Canada, the States, Australia, and South America. There were two review copies of books from publishers. There were other little magazines, and what looked like medical journals, and a few bills.

As I put the envelopes and parcels on the chair in the office and saw the copies of *Horizon* and *New Writing*, the runs of *Encounter*, *London Magazine*, and a fine collection of contemporary books on the shelves right around the room—it brought back a time twenty years ago when I first came over.

There was still the bomb-damage to be seen, the queues, the ration books, the cigarettes under the counter. And a general seediness in people's clothes. Yet I remember it as one of my happiest times. Perhaps because we were young and full of hope and because we were so innocent of what writing involved. A lot of boys and girls had come to London from different parts. And we would meet in certain pubs, in certain restaurants, Joe Lyons, the French pub, Caves de France, the Mandrake. Then go on somewhere else. I remember going over to see another Canadian, from Montreal, who was writing a novel. He had a studio, by the Chelsea football grounds (we could always tell when a goal was scored). I remember best the cold damp winter days with the fog thick—you could just see the traffic lights—and then going inside and having some hot wine by the open fire and talking about writing, what we were writing, and where we had things out. We used to send our stories, optimistically, to the *name* magazines. But that was like taking a ticket in a lottery. It was the little magazines who published us, who gave encouragement and kept us going.

I remember Miss Waters. She was in her late forties, a pale woman with thinning blonde hair and a docile tabby cat. She edited a little magazine founded by her great-grandfather. She had photographs of Tennyson on the wall, of Yeats and Dylan Thomas. And wooden pigeon-holes, like the sorting room at the post office, with some of the recent back issues. She didn't know when I was coming. But she always greeted me with:

'How nice to see you. Do come in.'

She walked ahead, into the dark living-room. Suggested that I take my winter coat off. Then she would bring out a decanter of sherry and fill a glass. Then take out a package of *Passing Clouds*, offer me a cigarette.

I was treated as a writer by this woman when I had very little published. And that did more than anything to keep up morale. And after another sherry, another *Passing Cloud*, and she had asked me what I was working on and seemed very interested in what I said, she told me that her great-grandfather paid Tennyson a thousand pounds for one of his short poems, and two thousand pounds to George Eliot for a short story. (Was she trying to tell me that there was money to be made out of writing?) Then she stood up. And we went into the other room. It was very neat and tidy. Magazines on a table laid out as at a news agent's, books as in a library.

'Is there anything you would like to review?' she asked.

I would pick a novel or two, or a book of short stories.

Then she would say. 'And help yourself to four books from that pile.'

That pile consisted of books that she didn't want reviewed. She had told me, the first time, to take these books to a bookseller in the Strand who would give me half-price for them, and later sell them to the public libraries. But before I could get the money from him I had to sign my name in what looked like a visiting book. And I saw there, above me, the signatures of the leading Sunday and weekly reviewers—they were also selling their review copies for half-price.

And I remember how I would come to her place—with the brown envelopes lying behind the door—broke and depressed. And when I left her, I left feeling buoyed up, cheerful. There would be the few pounds from the review copies. Money enough for a hamburger and a coffee and a small cigar. And there was something to do—the books to review. She always paid in advance.

And before Miss Waters there were others. The press officer at the Norwegian Embassy—he ran a Norwegian little magazine, in English, from London. And another one, from India, also in English. My early stories appeared in both. And when I got a copy of the Indian magazine I saw that my Canadian characters had been turned into Indians. And there was another editor who would ask to borrow your box of matches. Then when you got back to your flat you found he had stuffed a pound note inside the box.

They are all gone—like their magazines.

And something has gone with them.

Those carefree days when you wrote when you felt like it. And slept in when you wanted to. And would be sure of seeing others like yourself at noon in certain places.

Now in the morning, after breakfast, I wait for the mail to come. Then I go upstairs and close the door behind me. And I make myself get on with the novel, the new story, or the article which has been commissioned by a well-paying magazine. I take a break for lunch, then come back up here until four. Once in a while I might take a day off and go on a bus to see what the country is like. I forget that there is so much colour about. Or, for a change, take a train for the day to Plymouth. But otherwise, it is up the stairs to this room. All my energy now goes into work. I light up a small Dutch cigar, and sometimes I talk to myself. I feel reasonably certain now that what I have written will be published. Writing has become my living.

Of course there are still the occasional days when things are going right and the excitement comes back from the work. Not like in those early days when writing and the life we were leading seemed so much to belong together. I had complete faith then in those little magazines. What I didn't know was that what they bred was infectious. They infected a lot of young people with the notion that to be involved with literature was somehow to be involved with the good life. And by the time you learned differently, it was usually too late.

On Friday I had to be up early. In the morning I was to be interviewed, in a rowing-boat on the Serpentine, for a Canadian television program on the "Brain-Drain." And later I was to meet my publisher for lunch.

It was very pleasant on the water early in the morning. The sun made patterns. People going to work stopped to watch. While I rowed the interviewer, the cameraman, the sound-recordist, and their equipment—and was asked why wasn't I living in Canada, and why did I write?

I met my publisher in his club. He is an American, from Boston, bald and short. We had a Martini. Then another. Then we went into the dining-room. Smoked salmon followed by duck with wine, then dessert. And ending with brandy and a large Havana cigar.

He asked me what type would I like for the book, could I send him the blurb for the dust-jacket? He told me the number of copies they would print, that one of the Sunday papers wanted to run a couple of extracts before publication. He told me some gossip about other writers, publishers, and agents. And what was I writing now? And which publishing season would he have it for?

I left him after four and caught a taxi back to the house.

'How did it go?' my wife asked.

'OK,' I said. 'How was the zoo?'

She began to tell me, when we heard a noise. It sounded as if it was coming from the front door. We went to look and surprised a man with a key trying to open the door. He was in his late fifties, short and stocky and wearing a shabby raincoat.

'Is the doc in?' he said timidly.

'No,' I said. 'He's on holiday.'

'Oh,' he said. 'I've come up from Sussex. I always have a bed here when I come up.'

He spoke with an educated accent.

'I'm sorry,' I said. 'But we have the place for three weeks.'

'I always have a bed here when I come up.'

'There isn't room,' I said.

'My name is George Smith,' he said. '*ABC* publish me. I'm a poet.'

'How do you do,' I said. 'We'll be gone in ten days. Come in and have a drink.'

While I poured him a brandy, I asked what was the name of his last book.

He said he had enough work for a book and had sent the manuscript to—and here he named a well-known publisher.

'But I haven't heard,' he said.

'That's a good sign,' I said.

'Perhaps they have lost it,' he said. 'Or they are, like Doc, on holiday.'

He brought out a small tin and took some loose tobacco and began to roll his own cigarette and one for me.

'How long,' I asked, 'have they had it?'

'Nearly five months,' he said.

He finished his brandy. I poured him some more.

'I would ring them up and find out,' I said. 'Or drop them a line.'

'Do you think I should?'

'Yes,' I said.

I went to the door to see him out. And instead walked him to the bus stop.

The street was full of mountain ash and red berries were lying on the lawns, the sidewalk, and on the road.

'I had a letter from T.S. Eliot,' he said. 'I kept it all these years. But I sold it last month to Texas for fifty dollars,' he said proudly. 'My daughter was getting married. And I had to get her a present.'

I asked him where he would stay the night.

'I have one or two other places,' he said. 'I come up about once every six weeks. London is my commercial centre.'

I went and bought him a package of cigarettes.

'Thank you,' he said.

The red bus came and I watched him get on.

When I got back my wife said.

'Well, do you feel better?'

'No,' I said.

It went on like this—right through the time we were there. An assortment of people turned up at the door. There was a young blonde girl— she wanted to lick stamps for literature. There were visiting lecturers and professors from American and Canadian and English universities. There were housewives; one said, over the phone, 'I'll do anything to get into print.' There were long-distance telephone calls. One rang after midnight and woke us up. 'Nothing important,' the voice said. 'I just wanted to have a talk. We usually do now and then. I've had stories in *ABC*.'

There was, it seemed, a whole world that depended on the little magazine.

I tried to be out of the house as much as possible. I went to see my agent. He had a cheque for four hundred dollars, less his commission, waiting for me, for the sale of a story. He took me out for a meal. And we talked about the size of advances, the sort of money paperback publishers were paying these days, the way non-fiction was selling better than fiction. I met other writers in expensive clubs and restaurants. We gossiped about what middle-aged writer was leaving his middle-aged wife to live with a young girl. And what publisher was leaving his firm to form his own house. I was told what magazines were starting—who paid the best.

Then I would come back to the phone ringing, the piles of mail, and people turning up at the door eager to talk about the aesthetics of writing. I didn't mind the young. But it was the men and women who were around my age or older who made me uncomfortable. I didn't like the feeling of superiority I had when I was with them. Or was it guilt? I didn't know.

Meanwhile my wife and kids enjoyed themselves. They went to the Victoria and Albert Museum, the National Gallery, the Tate. And came back with post-card reproductions that they sent to friends. They went to a couple of Proms, to a play, had a day in Richmond Park, Hampton Court, and a boat ride on the Thames.

When the time came to go back—they didn't want to.

But I did.

I had passed through my *ABC* days. And I wanted to get away. Was it because it was a reminder of one's youth? Or of a time which promised more than it turned out to be? I told myself that there was an unreality about it all—that our lives then had no economic base—that it was a time of limbo. But despite knowing these things, I carry it with me. It represents a sort of innocence that has gone.

On the Saturday morning waiting for the taxi to come to take us to Paddington Station, the phone rang. And a young girl's voice wanted to know about her short story.

I said the doctor was away. He would be back later. She ought to ring this evening.

'What time?'

'After nine,' I said.

'Have you read the story?' she asked. 'What do you think of it?'

'We just rented the house,' I said. 'We were here for a holiday.'

'Oh,' she said. 'You're not one of us?'

'No,' I said.

Then the taxi came. And the driver began to load the cases into the back of the car.

PART THREE

I Don't Want to Know Anyone Too Well

I first heard of Al Grocer as a legible signature at the end of this type-written letter.

Dear Mr Bonnar,

I should like to ask you quite well in advance if you would be agreeable to act as my guide while I'm in Cornwall for a week at the beginning of September. I operate an original service for independent radio stations throughout Australia. We offer them tape-recordings of various aspects of European life. For the 1967 season our project is a series of journeys. And after reading your excellent article on Cornwall we have decided to include *A Journey into Cornwall* on our list.

I hope you can come with me, and together we can shape a thirty-minute travel-interpretation of this (your) region. I would be prepared to pay for your services. And I think it would be fun to do. And I hope you can find time to do it with me. By the way, to lug the equipment (and ourselves) around, I'll rent a car because I think of this in terms of my own pleasure and comfort, plus the great benefit of being mobile in our work. At any rate, may I have your initial reaction at this time.

Cordially,

Al Grocer.

I wrote back saying I'd be delighted. It seemed a fine way of seeing the country and having a holiday as well. For though I've lived in Cornwall for five years I haven't been around much. I don't drive.

On Friday I got Sam England to take his taxi and we drove over to St Erth to meet the train. It was a fine blustering kind of morning with white caps in the bay. And I could see the shadows of the low clouds moving over the far shore fields, leaving patches of light green, dark green, and brown. Al Grocer had sent me a brochure of his company. It included a photograph. From the photograph he looked to be an undistinguished crew-cut, in his thirties. But the man I finally approached—the only one left standing on the platform—was clearly in his fifties. Medium height, stocky, bald. He was neatly dressed in a navy blue blazer, grey flannels, a white shirt open at the neck. And on a pale face he had very large black sunglasses.

'Mister Grocer?' I said. 'Good to see you.'

'Ditto,' he said, dragging the word out. And his accent had a trace of central Europe in it.

He smiled. And his mouth showed, contrary to what I expected, one of the finest sets of teeth I have ever seen. We shook hands firmly. Then he put his arm around my shoulder and left it there. Something I do not entirely take with strangers. It was, I discovered, one of his mannerisms. A few days later I introduced him to my bank manager to cash a personal cheque of his as he was running short. In less than five minutes after meeting the manager he was putting his arm around the bank manager's shoulder.

'Call me Al,' he said. And changed his glasses for another pair that he brought out of his blazer pocket. I caught a glimpse of bulging eyes. 'I better make sure the porters don't throw the equipment around, it's sensitive.'

There were no porters. The portable recording machinery was dumped on the platform, and the train moved off to Penzance. I helped him carry the equipment up the steps and across the covered, brown, wooden bridge above the tracks. He was breathing hard and I could smell scent, a kind of bay rum.

'How was the trip?'

'Not bad,' he puffed. 'I really go for these toy English trains.'

'Your first time in England?'

'No. Twenty-five or thirty years ago I lived in Southampton—for three months. Someone got a disease on the boat taking us to Australia. They took us all off the boat and put us in quarantine. Until we all got the disease. Guess who got it last ...?'

On the way back we had to share the taxi with an elderly couple who were staying at the Tregenna Castle. We drove up the long drive of trees, to the plateau, and the taxi stopped. Mister Grocer opened the taxi door and got out, surveying the grounds, the country-house of a hotel, the fine view of St Ives with the harbour, bay, and the Atlantic below.

'I'm going to like this place,' he said, taking off his glasses and inhaling the air.

'This isn't where you're staying,' I said. 'This is the most expensive hotel here. You asked for bed and breakfast. I've got you a place for fifteen shillings a day—it's clean.'

He put his dark glasses back on and returned into the taxi visibly disappointed. I had a feeling this kind of thing had happened to him before. And for some inexplicable reason I wished there and then that Mister Grocer could have stayed at the Tregenna Castle.

My wife took an instant dislike to him. She had gone to some trouble and expense to get a duck and spent most of the day getting it ready.

'What's this?' he said. 'Rabbit?'

'No,' my wife said, 'it's crow.'

He looked so startled that I found myself saying. 'It's duck. It's been done in wine.' And for my wife's benefit. 'It's delicious.' But the damage had been done.

Next morning he came around after breakfast. He had changed and was wearing a fawn gabardine jacket over a dark blue sport shirt, light-blue sport trousers, and the black sunglasses. Apart from his bulging eyes his other features were fine, though age and fat had started to undermine them. 'How do you like the bed and breakfast place?'

'Just fine.'

I fixed him up with a place run by a couple of artists. They had a ter-raced house and took in people, since they couldn't make a living from painting. But I was a bit worried if Mister Grocer would take to their bohemian ways.

'Would you like a walk?' I said.

'You're now about to get one of Bonnar's Conducted Tours,' my wife said sarcastically from the kitchen. I had never known her to take such an instant dislike to anyone.

We were walking towards Carbis Bay—it's a pleasant walk: on the side of a slope, overlooking the bay, alongside flowering gorse, blackberry bushes, and wild garlic—when he said: 'William, you having trouble in your marriage?'

'No.'

'It's no good, William, I can tell. I'm sensitive to people's voices. I can walk into a room and spot immediately by the way a person talks whether he likes me or not. And I could tell from the way your wife spoke that you've just had a row ...'

'But we haven't.'

We walked on, through a stile, in silence.

'You married?'

He shook his head. 'I had a girl once, in Poland. When the war came an uncle in Adelaide said he would bring her out for me. I would come later. He did bring her over. Three years later he helped to bring me. When I came, I found my girl married to his son.' He stopped, plucked a wild garlic. 'I made films in Poland,' and put the green stem in his mouth, 'before the war, historical pictures—I used to be quite well known.'

After about a mile the path leads to the door of the Carbis Bay Hotel. It was a very hot day, the tennis courts were deserted, there wasn't anyone on the close-cropped lawns. We went inside the hotel. No one there either. I suggested that he wait while I try to find out if we could have some tea or coffee or a beer out on the lawn or the balcony. I finally found a student in the kitchen who said he was working here for the summer. He said they didn't provide refreshments for non-residents during the season. I told this to Mister Grocer. But it was obvious that he had his mind on something else.

'Is there anyone about?'

'No.'

He walked behind the reception-desk and calmly helped himself to a considerable number of hotel envelopes and hotel writing paper. Then he sat down by a table in the empty lounge, made himself comfortable, and began to write a letter.

'I like good hotel stationery,' he said.

When we returned to St Ives he fumbled in his fawn jacket pocket. 'I've lost my Biro.'

So I took him to Woolworth's. He tried out several plastic pens at a shilling each, but didn't like them. 'They are much too cheap.'

We came out and walked along the front.

'I think we can get a Biro,' I said, 'in Literature and Art.'

'*But I've got one.*' And he brought out from his fawn jacket pocket one of the plastic pens that were on sale in Woolworth's. 'What's the matter,' he said good-humouredly. 'Haven't you ever taken something without paying for it?'

We rented a car from the North Star Garage. We planned to start next morning. For the first day we would go outward to Land's End along the North Coast, and come back by the South. We decided it would be best to start early and return to St Ives, from wherever we were, to sleep.

We met in the car park by the cemetery. He was there, looking closely through a copy of *The Times*. And he encircled with his pen possible stories that he might record. *The oldest water wheel in England was in the West Country*—that would make an item, he said. *The man who breeds worms for a living.* Then he transferred these into a notebook that was marked *Ideas*. On its front page in his large clear writing was

What is precious is never to forget
The essential delight of the blood.

'I've got the front of this book full of quotations and jokes,' he said, turning the pages. 'Listen to this. What did the young rabbi say to the old rabbi in the French pastry shop as he passed the cakes: *Have another Ghetto.*' And he laughed infectiously.

It was raining when he drove out of St Ives and in a matter of minutes we were on the moors. The sea was beside us on the right. The moor on the left. And the rain kept coming across like folds of a pale white curtain.

'It's wet in England,' he said thoughtfully.

Our first stop was at a filling station. The man who ran it was an old-timer, one of the survivors of a mining disaster. Mister Grocer came in carrying his portable tape-recorder in a green sling over his shoulder. And he began to flatter the man. But the oldtimer stopped him. 'I've been interviewed many times on radio and television. You just tell me what you want …'

Mister Grocer asked him questions. They rehearsed, twice. Mister Grocer checked his equipment. He locked the door. He stuffed paper into the door bell. He put up a 'Closed' sign in the window. And just as everything was set to record, Mister Grocer had an attack of nerves. So he had another rehearsal. The oldtimer was right-on with his replies, while Mister Grocer fluffed his.

'I must take a tranquillizer,' he said and swallowed a pill. He had worked himself up into such a state that I was ready to suggest that I interview the oldtimer.

Then the interview started. And once he began, the voice that spoke into the microphone was authoritative, distinct, and without a trace of anxiety. It was the anonymous 'interview voice' that radio and television have made familiar. As soon as he finished he relaxed. And you could see he was no longer interested in the oldtimer, in mining, in this part of Cornwall. All he wanted to do was to get away from here.

'That's the start,' he said, walking back to the car. He was full of nervous excitement and kept patting me on the shoulder. 'The hard part is always the start.' I said it was the same in writing. As a parting shot he told the oldtimer the only obvious lie I could detect—that he would let him know when it would be broadcast. But driving on to Land's End he said that he came from a wealthy family just outside Warsaw. That his people were in wood. 'My father had forests.' And when he made a bit more cash in Australia he would go back for a visit. 'I would like to see what the place looks like. We had a magnificent white house—I was born there. We had an Alsatian on a long leash attached to an overhead wire— he patrolled the grounds …'

And I didn't believe a word of it.

I could see St Just come out of the mist. And in the town complete silence except for the squawks from the jackdaws and gulls. This is a part of Cornwall not touched by tourists. Instead of *Bed and Breakfast* the signs here said *House for Sale*. Empty square, large Wesleyan chapel, squat church. And right beside them small fields with cows and horses, barns and dung. A gull flew low down a wide empty street and the mist lay on the surrounding hilltops with stooks of corn on the slopes. Around the perimeter: abandoned tin-mine chimneys and the Atlantic.

We went to the Western Hotel—I had once met the owner. Mister Grocer had me rehearse with him before we came to St Just all the facts about St Just that I thought he ought to know, until he had memorized them word-perfect—he might have been an actor learning a part. And, for a few minutes, he did talk intelligently about St Just with the hotel owner. He rehearsed the interview. Then again went into a flap. I was posted outside to keep guard. Doors were locked. And just as soon as the interview was over he wanted to get away from here. It was as if he had done something he knew he shouldn't and was afraid of being found out.

By the end of the second day I was beginning to have doubts whether this little holiday trip would last the week. I was convinced that Mister Grocer was on the verge of a nervous breakdown. He turned up around ten that night at the door of the cottage with his bags and portable equipment, sweat on his face. 'William, I'd like to move.'

'What's wrong?'

'Nothing's wrong. But the place—it's not for me.'

My wife gave me a knowing glance. She was brought up in a London suburb and doesn't approve of the mild bohemian life that flickers here in the summer.

'Why don't you take him to Mrs Richards?' she said.

I walked him over to Mrs Richards, helped carry his stuff. On the way down he suddenly stopped, put his bags on the road. I thought he was tired. 'William, I forgot to pay at the last place. Could you, for me?' And he took out a couple of pounds.

'Sure,' I said.

'Tell them I had to go to London, unexpectedly. And didn't have time to pay or say goodbye.'

I left him at Mrs Richards and went to the other place and saw Leo— one of the owners.

'Leo. Al Grocer had to go to London. Here's what he owes.'

'*Grocer.* That friend of yours is some character.'

'What's up?'

'He came into my room last night, said he had Angst. Said he wanted to tuck me in and kiss me goodnight.'

Next morning when I got to the car park he was putting away *The Times* and his notebook in the dashboard compartment.

'Is Mrs Richards' place OK?'

'Fine, William,' he said cheerfully. 'It's healthy the food here—I've broken out in pimples.'

We drove out. The rain had stopped. And there was a fresh morning smell to the air. He suddenly became concerned about my welfare. 'You must get out of Cornwall—the place is too slow. You have been spoiled living here. You won't be able to survive in a city. I'm not joking. And the longer you live here, the harder it will be. Come to Australia. With your education you could make money over there—like mud.'

He watched me smoke a cigarette, with disapproval. Finally, he said. 'You smoke your cigarettes too much. You must throw more of a cigarette away. You sell yourself cheap …'

We headed for the south coast in sunshine. Over the car radio a crooner was singing.

> *Tear a star from out the sky*
> *And the sky feels blue …*

In Falmouth he interviewed three housewives and got their recipe for making a pasty. In Helston he got the mayor to talk about the Flora dance. Then came cursing out of a public lavatory.

'England's finished—there's no reason for a civilized country to have *such* toilet paper.'

In Bodmin he saw, at a magazine stall, that Daphne du Maurier lived in Cornwall. He bought one of her books. Read about a dozen pages while we were having tea. 'She's a very good writer. I wish I had time to go to a library and get some background reading on Daphne du Maurier. She interests me very much.' And he went to the hotel's phone and rang her up. But she wouldn't see him. As we drove across Bodmin Moor, he tossed her book out of the window.

A couple of miles later the car broke down. The clutch burnt out. We left the car, on the side of the road, on the moor. Hitch-hiked to the nearest phone, and rang up the garage. Then got a lift to St Erth and walked over to the station. Al Grocer wanted to go in a first-class compartment. I told him on these one-track lines they were exactly the same. Anyway, we had bought a second-class ticket. But he wanted first. He had a stubborn streak in him.

And just when it seemed I had enough of him (he pocketed my change when I paid for lunch; he would never buy a round when we stopped off at a pub; and I began to think of the whole thing as a fiasco) I began to like him. I can't explain why. But I found I was looking forward to seeing him again the next day, and being in his company. Perhaps it was no more than knowing he was going away. Or maybe because neither of us belonged here, and we had come a long way to be thrown together. Or maybe the explanation was even simpler: certain things had now happened to both of us—we had a past in common. I told this to my wife. She thought I was crazy. She said she didn't want Al Grocer around any more and wouldn't care if she never saw him again.

He came to the door on his last night. A face made sad by the large bulging eyes. Neatly dressed in a grey suit, and very apologetic. '… you mind William if we have a few drinks?' He held up a bottle of whisky. And for my wife he brought a miniature cherry brandy. She relented.

As he entered he said excitedly. 'I've taken a room for my last night here—bet you won't guess—?'

'The Tregenna Castle?'

'No, not quite. The Porthminster.'

It wasn't a bad evening. He was very good at telling a story, especially against himself. Near the end he began to get introspective. 'I wonder why

I feel insulted after a day interviewing people—I meet people all the time —but I've never got to know anyone—you know what I'm getting at?'

'It's a job,' I said.

'—there's something about the business—it makes you lose something of yourself as a human being—something of your dignity.'

But he had drunk too much and went upstairs and was sick. It was past midnight when I suggested that we'd better call it a day. He said he enjoyed his stay in Cornwall and enjoyed meeting both of us very much.

'Now, could you get me a taxi.'

I told him it was only a three-minute walk to the Porthminster, and I would walk him back. He insisted on a taxi. I didn't think anyone would bother to come at this time for such a short distance—and I was right. But he wouldn't have it. 'I'll get a taxi,' he said defiantly, and walked unsteadily out of the room to the phone. I could hear him putting on his interview voice.

'You know who I am. I'm *Al Grocer*—*Al Grocer*—'

'He says Al Grocer,' my wife said, 'the way other people say Happy Christmas.'

'—*Al Grocer* will put Cornwall on the map—All *Al Grocer* wants is a taxi—to take him to your Porthminster Hotel—where he's staying—' He must have tried a half-dozen places, going through the same routine. Finally a taxi agreed to come. And he came back to the front room. 'I had to throw a bit of that personality stuff around,' he said deprecatingly, 'it comes in useful,' and sank back into one of the chairs. I could see headlights sweeping the dark street. So I went and hailed the taxi. The taxi-man had got out of bed and all he had on was a coat over his pyjamas and slippers. He apologized—with one hand by his mouth—for not having time to put in his false teeth.

But Al decided he didn't want to go. I helped him up and steered him to the door. He kept on about 'dignity.' Then, with great effort, he pulled himself together and said very precisely,

'Come up tomorrow morning, William, and have breakfast with me at the Porthminster.'

I did go up next morning. He was back to the navy blue blazer, grey flannels, and those large black sunglasses.

'You know, William, I've put something of yours in my quotation book.' He turned some pages. 'I got it from your novel. *I don't want to get to know anyone too well*,' he read slowly, '*when I do I don't like them.*'

I was going to explain that it was just a character talking—but he didn't give me a chance.

'It's very true,' he said quietly. 'Sad isn't it.'

Then he asked me if I would carry his bags down to the station while he carried the portable recording equipment. I didn't mind, but as we walked down the slope I couldn't help feeling that the reason I was asked up for breakfast was to carry his bags down for him. And immediately I was annoyed with myself for thinking this. To make up for it, at the station, I went over to the paper-kiosk and bought him a copy of the morning's *Times*.

'Business can wait,' he said with a laugh. And with a grand gesture flung the paper to the corner of the compartment. And shook my hand a long time. Large black sunglasses on a pale face, leaning out of the train, was the last I saw of him.

Ten weeks later I received a glossy picture postcard from Sydney. On the front was a coloured photograph of its most expensive hotel. On the back he had written:

> *I am resting up here after a very rough ocean voyage. I have a few ideas for 1968. How would you like to come over and do a journey through the Outback? Will write again and send address.*
>   Cordially, Al.

A Writer's Story

AT THE BEGINNING OF 1952 we were married. And in the spring we left London (two uncomfortable rooms in a cold house in a northern suburb) for the south of Cornwall. And rented a granite house on the lower slope of a hill. It had a high walled garden with palms, bamboos, copper beech, and hydrangeas. Wild roses were on a frame bent over to form an arch. Blackberries grew on top of the wall. And between two trees was a hammock.

The house was once a schoolhouse. And in the front room, where we would eat and sit in the evenings, there was a long table with fixed benches on either side. And cut in the dark varnished wood were generations of children's names.

I worked in a large building attached to the house. The only furniture was a small stove where I burned wood in winter, a chaise longue where I read the landlord's little magazines (*Blast*, *Tyro*, *Horizon*) and the novels of Henry Green that were in a bookcase against the white wall. And a table where I wrote. The building must have been the gym or the assembly hall for there was a raised platform at one end. And it had a high ceiling and large windows.

From a window overlooking the road I could hear the stream that went by outside and see, in the field opposite, a light pink house surrounded by trees with white blossoms. And further away the small green fields, separated by irregular hedges, sloping gently upwards. And in the distance a farmhouse.

From a window on the other wall I could see—over the garden and over the slate roofs and chimneys of the village—the water in the bay, the long sweep of the far shore. At dusk the land was often coloured purple. And we could hear the curlews as they flew back to the rocks at the sea's edge. And hear them again the first thing in the morning when we were still in bed. That gentle melancholy sound of a curlew flying over the house on the way to the fields above.

Sam, our landlord, looked like a Tolstoyan farmer. He always wore
baggy trousers, worn shirts, a wide leather belt, and large working-men's
shoes. He was tall and broad but he had a small head and a close-cropped
ginger beard. For such a big man he had a gentle voice. And he spoke
well and smiled easily.

He lived with his wife in a cottage on the moors. They believed in the
simple life, in living off the land, in natural foods. They had these handsome blonde children running around in bare feet. And because I had an
MA and because he wanted something better for his kids than the local
school, I signed a form that said I would look after their education. But
it was my wife who taught them how to read and write.

By the time we knew him, he must have been in his middle forties. I
had a feeling that he had lived quite a different kind of life before coming here. It was his voice which told it all. Years later someone told me
that Sam was an Old Etonian. That's part of Sam's story that I don't know.

I only know that he was kind to us. He would arrive, on a bicycle, in
the morning. His lunch in a brown paper bag. He always brought something for my wife: endive, new potatoes, a cabbage, a cauliflower, duck
eggs, or honey that he collected. We would all have coffee in the front
room. Then he would go into the back of the gym, which was partitioned
off and quite separate from where I worked. And here he would do his
paintings. 'My pot boilers,' he said with a smile. But he was still hopeful
that he would make a breakthrough and become known. When he did
show me twenty or thirty canvases—it looked like a class at an art
school—every picture was painted in a different style.

If Sam, dressed like a peasant farmer, was getting away from his past,
so was I. The navy blue blazer with nickel-plated buttons, the grey flannels, the pipe—they belonged to the last four years at university and to
three previous years, in uniform, in the war. But behind them were the
streets of Lower Town, the houses with stables in the back. A working-class
community of French Canadians and immigrant Europeans that I was running away from. I just had a first novel accepted and thought of myself
as a writer. I expected being a writer would be a continuation of the life
I knew at university: where I edited the literary magazine, had poems and
stories on the Montreal radio, and wrote the novel in my final year. Things

appeared to follow one another, and fall naturally into place, without my having to try very hard. The war ... university ... novel accepted ... getting married. And now coming here to write the next book.

But for the first few weeks we took it easy. The early spring days were warm and sunny. Few people were about. The place had an air of nothing happening, of people gently living out their lives. Rooks and gulls flew slowly by. It was so quiet. And full of colour. The sea. The sky. The yellow sand beaches. Things growing in the fields and in the hedgerows.

Around ten in the morning Charlie would come up the granite steps to bring me *The Times*. He thought I was a painter. And if the back pages of *The Times* had a photograph of some disaster (like the Lynmouth flood, an air crash or a fire) he would open the door, grin, and say,

'This make good picture.'

'Yes, Charlie.'

Later I found out that Charlie, though in his thirties, couldn't read.

Or else Sam would come in to tell me some story he heard in the village. 'You can write about that,' he said.

I tried to write.

I spent hours at the wooden table in the large high room. And I didn't know what to write about. That's the trouble with going to university, I thought. I didn't have to try hard enough. The results for a little effort were too immediate and too great. You think you're a writer because those at university say so and make a fuss. But now that I was on my own—?

'You must write,' I told myself. 'It will come if you write.'

But what to write about. I didn't know.

I thought at first that, at twenty-seven, I had run out of material. But as the weeks went by I realized it wasn't that at all. I didn't know what my material was.

I sat at the table, smoked (the pipe kept going out), read the little magazines, went to the windows.

What a pleasant place to be idle in.

I decided to take a notebook and go out. I walked to the sea's edge. And made notes. 'The way the sun appears on the water on a hot summer's day. The blue water sparkles. Then it seems as if it is raining sundrops. They are hitting the water—slanting down—golden moving streaks—just like rain.'

'I walk by the tideline,' I wrote, 'and I can see my footsteps behind me. But a little while later the footsteps disappear in the moist sand leaving no trace.'

Then I sat on the granite pier and tried to describe the colours of the sea, the changing colours of the land as the clouds passed over.

When my wife asked me at lunch, 'How's the writing going?'

'Fine,' I said.

On Sundays we went for walks in the country. She knew all the wild flowers. She would tell me their names. And I would repeat. But when we went out the following Sunday, I had forgotten. So she would name them again.

'What did you do as a child?' she asked.

What did I do, I wondered.

'We had other flowers,' I said.

We passed a field with chickens. Horses in another. It was so still. So quiet.

'See the mole-hills,' my wife said.

I didn't know they were mole-hills.

'That's buddleia,' my wife said; 'butterflies like it.'

She was right. There were butterflies resting on this bush. The sun caught them. Some with their wings spread, others drawn up. I counted twenty. And there were more.

'Those are Red Admirals,' she said. 'That's Tortoiseshell. That's a Peacock—'

But on Monday morning I was back in the large high room by the wooden table. It was much better when I was out looking at things.

That is how I met Mrs Burroughs.

I was out with my notebook. And she was standing by her front gate with a letter in her hand.

'Are you going to the post office?' she said. 'Will you take this for me?'

After three more times taking letters for her she invited me into her house.

We walked along the gravel path with the garden on one side. Mrs Burroughs' ankles were swollen and she had difficulty in walking. She used a cane. She was a large woman, slightly bent, with grey hair combed tight to her head and in a bun at the back. She had a large face, almost like a man's, thin lips, a strong jaw with loose skin under it. But her china-blue eyes were delicate. They slanted upwards.

'I don't go out much,' she said quietly.

It was dark when we came into the house. I thought, at first, it was because we came in from the sunlight. But the walls of the rooms were painted brown. And they had dark Victorian oil paintings on them. Cows by a stream. Trees in a field. In front of the fireplace was a highly polished copper screen. And hammered out in the copper was a sailing ship. On a dark wooden side-table, in a glass case, were three exotic stuffed birds with long tails. Their feathers were blue and green. But the colours had faded. The brightest things in the room were various glass bottles, glass vases, on the window sills. They were all the same ruby colour but with different designs.

'Sit down,' Mrs Burroughs said. 'I heard you are at the old schoolhouse. And you're a writer. What are you writing?'

'I have a novel coming out,' I said.

The phone rang. She didn't appear to hear it.

'The phone is ringing,' I said.

'Oh,' she said. And quickly went out of the room. I could hear her shouting from the next room. When she came back she sat down in her chair and said:

'What are you writing *now*?'

'Nothing.'

'Why not?'

'I don't know.'

She looked puzzled.

'You mean you don't know any stories?'

I didn't know what to say.

'I know lots,' she said. 'I'll tell you.' And she did.

Every time I came up to see her she would show me into the front room, ask me to sit down, and tell me something else from her past.

It began eighty-one years ago. Her father was a farmer. She was a teacher and taught in a country school. Then she married Mr Burroughs, who had a timber business. They moved into Penzance and had two daughters and a son. She packed up the teaching and ran the accounts.

As they made money they put the money into land and houses. They had properties all over Cornwall. When her husband died her son ran the business. Then the youngest daughter, Shirley, died when she was in her thirties. And Mrs Burroughs didn't go out of the house after that. She didn't get on with her older daughter, Brenda.

'I don't go to see her often,' Brenda told me, when I met her a few months later. 'When I do, Mam begins to cry and says: why aren't you Shirley?'

I would sit in the darkened room with the Victorian paintings and watch how the light from the windows caught the ruby glass. While Mrs Burroughs talked.

'Last year,' she said, 'I went to Jean's—my granddaughter's—wedding. One of Jean's girlfriends had a quarrel with her boyfriend. They split up. And she didn't have anyone to take her to the wedding. So she hired a boy from an agency. Someone she had never seen before—to take her. At the wedding I saw this woman. I remembered her when she was a child. Her father and mother—they had their own farm—were devoted to each other. But they didn't have children. Then when she was in her forties she got pregnant. The baby was born. But the mother died in childbirth. The father was out in the fields. When he heard he went and shot himself. And there was this child, now a woman and married, at the wedding. Isn't that a good story for you to write?'

'Yes,' I said.

'I have a cousin,' Mrs Burroughs said. 'She was going out with this boy. He worked as an accountant. Very neat. But the family didn't think he was good enough. So there was opposition to the wedding. But they did get married. Then the war came along. The Second World War. The man was called up. And he cut his throat because he was frightened of being killed in the war.'

I'd go and see Mrs Burroughs on Saturday mornings because her grandson came in from Penzance to play the piano for her. They were old tunes, mostly waltzes.

'It reminds her of the time when she was a girl,' he told me.

I'd be in the front room, looking out over her garden; the sounds from the piano came from the other room, while Mrs Burroughs talked.

'My daughter's husband is called Jack,' she said. 'His grandmother—when she was a girl—fell in love with Mr Doo. Mr Doo was an artist. But he was poor. So she married Mr Wilsher. He was very rich and old. They lived together for seven years. And then Mr Wilsher died. And she then went and married Mr Doo. And they lived happily. Then Mr Doo died. And Mrs Doo lived in that pink house opposite you. She had butlers and gardeners and servants and cooks. All these people to wait on her. And all she could talk about was her darling Mr Doo.

'Her daughter was brought up as a lady. And when she was getting on she fell in love with a young man—he was thirteen years younger. He worked on a farm. They married. And after they married—the daughter began to look more and more like a gypsy. And the young man dressed and behaved like a gentleman.'

'That's a good story,' I said.

'I have lots more,' Mrs Burroughs said.

It was at Mrs Burroughs that I met Mr Oppenheimer. A neat man, about five foot two, bald, and with glasses. He was dressed in a hand-stitched tweed suit, a handmade shirt, and a woollen tie. Mrs Burroughs told him I was a writer.

'I've met a lot of writers here,' Mr Oppenheimer said. 'I used to visit D.H. Lawrence and Frieda on Sundays when they lived at Zennor.'

'How was Lawrence?'

'*D.H.*' Mr Oppenheimer raised his voice. 'He was a gentleman. One time I rode over on a horse. It was a hot day. And the horse gave me a rough ride. When I got there I must have said some swear words. *D.H.* got angry. "No need to say words like that here, Oppenheimer. There is no need."'

'Arthur, my gardener,' Mrs Burroughs said, 'also thought Lawrence a gentleman. Because when he went out there with a pony and trap to deliver a loaf of bread, Lawrence always gave him a shilling tip.'

'After *D.H.*,' Oppenheimer said, 'there was Harris. And after him, another writer, Johnson. He was always talking about money. He stayed only a year. How long are you staying?'

'I don't know,' I said.

I walked back with Mr Oppenheimer to his cottage.

'I've known Mrs Burroughs for over forty years,' he said. 'Very tight with her money. Never gives anything away.'

How could I tell him that she was giving me all these things from her past.

'She can't hear very well,' Oppenheimer said. 'But if you start talking about money. She'll say wait—I'll just get my hearing aid. She had a grand-niece getting married in Canada. She told me she sent her a pound as a wedding present. *A pound*. Come inside and have a drink. I start the day with a small glass of brandy. The doctor told me to take it. It warms the system up.'

His cottage was small and untidy. There was a dog, a terrier, also old, sitting by the electric fire. There were papers, magazines, and books piled everywhere. Often when I would come down to visit Mr Oppenheimer I would look in at the window to see if he was in. The place was in a mess, plates and cups still on the table. And Mr Oppenheimer, sitting in a chair with his feet up, reading a book.

He told me why he came here. His family owned freighters in Wales. He began to work in the Cardiff office. Then he got a spot on one lung. 'The doctor told me to go to a warmer climate. Or else I wouldn't make old bones. I'm seventy-six,' he said proudly. 'I started a restaurant here just after the First World War. But I don't have anything to do with that now. I still have my office there. Come and see me.'

I did go.

His office, above the restaurant, was as untidy as the cottage.

'Augustus John sat where you are sitting and drank a half bottle of whisky. And little Stanley Spencer—he came up to here.' Mr Oppenheimer stood up and put his hand under his chin. 'I don't think he changed his collar once in the three months he was here. Have you heard of Guy Gibson. During the war?'

'Yes,' I said.

'I gave Guy Gibson piggybacks on the sand,' Mr Oppenheimer said. 'He used to come here as a child. Have some more brandy.'

His hand shook as he poured. But it was because of arthritis in his fingers. It was painful for him to shake hands.

'Tell me about D.H. Lawrence,' I said.

'*D.H.* He had a red beard. He worked at night. In the day *D.H.* went for walks on the moors. He was very good with his hands. He fixed things in the cottage. Why don't you come and see my house in the country. I've got a lot of land around it.'

I said I would. But as he had bought the house for his daughter Mary and her husband George—and only went there, reluctantly, on week-ends —I never did go to see the place.

But on Monday afternoons I would go to see him at his cottage. I'd say.

'How are things Mr Oppenheimer?'

And he would say. 'Have some more brandy.'

This time he began to laugh. 'I shouldn't laugh,' he said. 'But George had something else go wrong. George decided to cut some of the old trees—I shouldn't laugh—There are fourteen acres. He got the wood.' And Mr Oppenheimer began to laugh again. 'I shouldn't laugh,' he said, tears in his eyes. 'He got the wood and started to cut it. And *phlewt*— half of his finger flew off. I shouldn't laugh at this. But he couldn't find the piece that flew off.'

'What happened?' I said. I wondered why I was laughing.

'Mary got the ambulance. They rushed him to Penzance hospital. But it was too late. They couldn't sew the two pieces together.'

Next morning, sitting at the wooden table in the high room, I thought how rich Mr Oppenheimer's talk was and Mrs Burroughs' talk. Compared to Sam's and mine. Sam never once talked about his Old Etonian past. Just as I didn't talk or even refer to my past. I was like Sam. We were both trying to cut out our pasts, to cover them up. And it made us boring.

The next time I saw Mr Oppenheimer he said, 'I don't have the dog any more. I took him out for his walk. We went along the harbour. The dog always peed against the railing. This time he went on the wrong side of the railing. There was no rail. He flipped over. Fell into the harbour. The tide was out. He broke his back.'

Besides visiting Mrs Burroughs and Mr Oppenheimer, I also found two places that I would make for on my walks. One was in the country, just off the road. It had a broken-down gate. Then, a slope up, a field of green grass.

And at the top of the slope this house. An ugly house. With two dormer windows downstairs and two upstairs. And a white door that was always half-open. All the paint was peeling. The curtains were grey, half-drawn, and falling to bits. But there was something marvellous about a broken-down place with a sign at the front gate that said *Venton Vision*. No one lived in the house now except the animals: a goose, some cows, chickens.

Then, in December, with a mist closing in, in grey light, I found this field of anemones. The flowers were not very high above the ground. But the colours stood out. There were blues, purples, deep reds, light reds, and whites and pinks. Low colours, rising from the green, moving from side to side in the wind. Some were wide open with their dark centres. Others in bud, others opening. Very delicate colours, in the grey light, the mist closing in. And here and there a tall dead stalk from last summer's thistles. A lovely field. And no one picked them.

And I couldn't get over seeing the anemones, and the surrounding green fields, because it was December. I think of December as snow, ice, double-doors double-windows, and skating on frozen rivers. I would come here just to look at this field. And wish I was back to the snow, the crisp air, the harsh glare on sunny days.

I went to see Mrs Burroughs to tell her about the field of anemones. I found her crying.

'What's the matter Mrs Burroughs?'

'I'm remembering the happy times,' she said.

She was holding a photograph of herself, before she was married, as a teacher with her class.

Meanwhile the problem was getting clear. How was I to earn a living if I couldn't write my next book? I started to make lists. Of the people I grew up with in Ottawa. Of the popular songs I knew when I was at school. Of the streets, the streetcar lines, the market, the library, the parks. But the money was running out. The novel was due in two months. It was time to leave.

I went to see Mr Oppenheimer. The door of his cottage was locked. I looked through the window. Things were just as I last saw them. The newspapers, the magazines, the books.

On Saturday morning the taxi came to take us to Penzance station. We said goodbye to Sam. He still dressed like a Tolstoyan farmer, smiled easily, and talked of his pot-boilers.

We wished each other luck.

I told the taxidriver to go to Mrs Burroughs. As I went along the walk I could hear her grandson playing the piano. And as soon as I came in she said. 'You haven't been up for a couple of weeks. Sit down. I have another story for you.'

'I can't stay, Mrs Burroughs.'

But she interrupted or else she didn't hear what I said.

'You know the farm that you can see from where you are? That farm was run by Mr and Mrs Brill. She died when she was fifty-five. And six months later Mr Brill had a heart attack. And he died. The relatives were saying how sad it was. How he tried and couldn't live without her.

'When the relatives came to divide the valuables they found a camera with a half-used film in it. They had the film developed. And it was full of pictures of Mr Brill and his girlfriend—she was someone else's wife. There were pictures of this woman in his wife's kitchen. In her favourite chair. And Mr Brill had made plans for them to go away to London. *Now* the relatives were saying the heart attack was the best thing that could have happened.'

'What has happened to Mr Oppenheimer,' I said. 'He's not at his cottage.'

'He fell in the street,' Mrs Burroughs said. 'He is gone to live with his daughter in the country. We won't see him again. That's what happens. The family takes over and the friends don't see you any more. When that happens to me, I'll have to go and live with my daughter Brenda. Then no one will see me.'

'Oh, you've got lots of time yet Mrs Burroughs.'

'I don't know,' she said quietly.

'I came to say goodbye,' I said.

'Where are you going?'

'To London.'

'When?'

'Now.'

I could hear her grandson playing *Morgenbläter*. Since living here I had learnt the names of a lot of things.

'Do you like my red glass?' Mrs Burroughs asked.

'Yes.'

'Take the one you like.'

'I couldn't do that.'

'Why not. They will only fight over it when I'm gone. Do you like this one?'

And she gave me a red glass vase with a pair of cockerels etched in it.

I returned to the taxi with the red glass.

'Look what Mrs Burroughs gave me,' I said to my wife.

'It's beautiful,' she said.

But she was looking out of the window as the taxi drove along the coastal road. On one side—the earth with the small green fields, the yellow gorse, a stone church with old gravestones. And on the other— an immense sky against the thin flatness of the sea.

My wife took my hand. 'I'm glad we are leaving,' she said. 'Now things will begin.'

Class of 1949

THE END OF JANUARY is quiet and empty in this seaside town. Martha is away at university in Manchester. A nine-hour train ride from here, on the fastest train. She has just phoned, as she always does on Friday evening. Ella has come back tired from school. She is doing A levels but buys magazines in order to read: 'I was pregnant at 15' ... 'Are my kisses a match for his' ... 'My husband beats me.' She has gone up the stairs to her room and put on a Joni Mitchell record. For I can hear

> *The wind is in from Africa*
> *Last night I couldn't sleep*
> *Oh, you know it sure is hard to leave you, Carey*
> *But it's really not my home*

I am sitting in a comfortable chair, by the side of the open fire, waiting for the news to come on the television. Emily is on the settee, in front of the fireplace, knitting a red sweater for Ella. The black kitten is chasing a shallot as if it was a ball, knocking it from one paw to another.

The phone rings. 'I'll go,' said Emily.

'Who was it?' I said as she came back into the room.

'Someone wanting the old people's home. That's the second time today. If it's not someone wanting matron then it's Linda's the hairdresser.' She took up her knitting. I listened to the clock on the mantel above the fireplace.

> *Maybe I'll go to Amsterdam*
> *Maybe I'll go to Rome*

The phone rang again. Emily went quickly out of the room. I could hear her voice becoming louder. She came back excited.

'It's Victor,' she said.

'Victor. Here?'

'Yes. He's at the Sheaf. I told him you'll go down and bring him back.'

'I guess there is no way I can get out of this,' I said as I put on my coat.

But as I walked down the slope in the light rain—past the terraced houses, a few had lights on in the front rooms; by the closed post office, the closed summer restaurants—I remembered it was Victor who was responsible for my coming here in the first place.

I met Victor in 1946 in Montreal while going to McGill. We were two from the thousands of returning servicemen and women who went to university just after the Second World War. I remember that winter looking out from the top window of an apartment opposite the campus. It was snowing. And bundled-up young men and women in blue and mustard and black overcoats were walking to and from a lecture. Furthest away, through the dark trees—the Arts Building, the Engineering, the Library—bits of light, bits of orange. There was no sound. Just the snow failing. And the moving greatcoats.

Victor would have got to McGill war or no war. But a lot of the others depended on the Veterans Act—fees paid by the government and sixty dollars a month to live on. When Victor came in his car to pick me up for dinner with his parents and saw the basement room I had by the boiler on Dorchester next to the railway tracks, he put it down to some eccentricity on my part. Then he drove through wide streets with trees and lawns and elegant houses. To the paintings on the wall of Emily Carr, the first editions in the bookcase, the butler bringing in the drinks. It was through Victor that I met the rich and powerful English families of Westmount and Outremont. In those days I was attracted by the rich— their houses, their possessions, the way they lived. Perhaps this is what I found interesting in Victor.

But there was something else. We both wanted to be writers. And we were convinced that the first step was to get out of Canada and go over to England. To get over I needed money. That meant putting in for a fellowship. I said I would do a thesis on 'The Decay of Absolute Values in Modern Society.' And got five thousand dollars spread over two years. Victor got his father to give him a chunk of capital in the form of Bell Telephone shares, Canada Packers, Canadian Pacific, and Dominion Tar.

I am trying to be as brief and accurate as I can of those early postwar years. The girls wore their skirts and dresses long, and our jackets had padded shoulders. We had youth and high spirits—but they were held in check. When we graduated the principal made a speech saying what a fine generation we were, how we fought the enemy of civilization and made the world safe for democracy, and now we would take our place as useful citizens. The person they thought most suitable to give the con-vocation address was the Chief of the Boy Scouts—I cannot remember a thing he said.

Next day, Victor flew to England. Two weeks later I took a freighter to Newcastle. We met up in London. Victor had rented a cottage in Cornwall for us both. London, he said, would be too hot in July and August. It was a marvellous summer. The wartime restraint suddenly went. And in its place I felt an exhilarating sense of personal freedom.

In September we went up to London. To a flat in Swiss Cottage. We were both writing first novels in different rooms on typewriters. The house was broken-up into flats. In the others were middle-aged European refugees. And workmen were still repairing the bomb-damage. We went to Soho, to the pubs, the drinking clubs, the small restaurants. We met painters, writers, editors. It was very pleasant.

Now and then Victor would say we were invited for the weekend to some large country house. (They were relations or acquaintances of his family.) And I would rent tails from Moss Bros. and we would go by train into the country. To the lengthy meals with many courses and wines and the mothers complaining that England was dull, that their daughters were not having the time they had. Then the Hunt Ball, champagne, dancing all night to the Harry Lime theme. And back to the seedy flat. To ration books and queues at Sainsbury's for the small egg, the Irish sausage, the cube of butter, the bit of cheese and meat. While the pile of typewritten pages for our novels increased. We both knew we had two years to live like this and finish our books. Then get them published and go on as writers—or else return to Canada.

The Sheaf was ahead. There was one room with a light. From the window I could see an open coal-fire. Two people by a table. The rest of the room was empty.

As I walked in Victor called my name, got up, and smiled. We shook hands. He continued smiling. I saw that his once white teeth were discoloured. That his blond hair was grey. And I wondered what changes he could see in my face.

'This is Abdullah,' Victor said. And introduced a small young Arab, very fine features with a dark moustache, neatly dressed in a brown suit.

'When did you get here?'

'Late this afternoon,' Victor said.

'Will you have the same? Is it draught?'

'Yes.'

I went to the bar and ordered three draught Guinness. Abdullah came up. 'I'll bring them back for you,' he said. I returned to the table and sat down opposite Victor.

'I didn't think you would still be here,' he said. 'I thought you would have gone back to Canada.'

'We've been waiting for the kids to finish school. Martha is at university in Manchester. Ella is in her last year here. So we'll be able to move soon. What made you come down?'

'I thought Abdullah ought to see a bit of Europe. We've been in London the last two weeks. Going to art galleries, plays, movies, walking around—'

'It was very tiring, all that walking,' Abdullah said.

'I decided to take us away from London for the weekend. We took a train to Truro, hired a car, and drove here.'

'Where are you staying?'

'At the first hotel that had a car-park opposite.'

'That would be the Porthminster,' I said. 'Did you remember it?'

'No,' Victor said.

He took out a package of cigars and gave me one. Then brought out a gold lighter and we both lit up. He seemed reluctant to talk. So I said. 'My hair is a bit longer than it was.'

'At least,' he said, 'it's the same colour.'

'Emily and the kids wanted me to have it like this. So I let it grow. I didn't like it at first. In summer some of the places here have signs in their windows, "no undesirables." It means boys and girls with long hair who do not have much money to spend. I began to feel I might be undesirable. Abdullah, have you been to England before?'

'No. This is the first time for me out of Morocco.'

'How long will you stay here?'

'Just the weekend,' Victor said. 'We leave Monday for London then fly to Amsterdam for a few days. Then a couple of weeks in Paris. He learned English himself,' Victor said proudly. 'In three months.'

'You speak very well,' I said. 'What do you do in Morocco?'

'I register births and deaths,' Abdullah said. 'I begin when I get back. It will be my first job. As assistant.'

We finished the draught Guinness.

'Let's go back to the house,' I said. 'Emily is waiting to see you.'

We went out of the pub. The tide was out. The widely separated lights along the front and the pier were reflected in the shallows. Up ahead, in the dark, were clusters of lights from the houses above the harbour. It felt damp and cold.

'I walked around with Abdullah earlier,' Victor said. 'A shame the boats are gone.'

'It's become a tourist town,' I said. 'You're seeing it at the best time of the year. In summer you can hardly walk.'

We went along a dark street. I stopped beside a cottage.

'Pop Short lived here,' I said. 'Remember him?'

Victor was silent.

'He let you read a first edition of *Lady Chatterley*. He used to ask after you. He told me there was a White Russian colony here after the First World War. Like we were after the Second. And I guess there will be others like us later on. Pop showed me a Fabergé egg that he got from the White Russians. He died last year. He was ninety.'

We walked along a bit further on the wet cobblestones. I stopped beside a street light. There was an opening with stone steps going up.

'Do you remember this?'

'No,' Victor said.

'It's where we had our first cottage, halfway up the steps. We were charged two pounds a week for it. At that time we didn't know we were overcharged a pound because we were Canadians. The rooms were damp. The gaslight came from small wire baskets. The toilet was outside in the courtyard.'

'I remember that,' Victor said hesitantly.

We walked a little further along. 'This used to be Maskell's. He would put aside cigarettes for us. The cigarette paper had a thin pin stripe, like on a shirt. He died some years ago. And the Gay Viking? Here. We would go for coffee in the morning. Meet other people and have long talks. The Saint and Elsa ran it. They're both dead.'

'I don't remember,' Victor said.

'Victor's here,' I shouted as soon as I got into the hall. Emily came out of the dining-room, smiling. Victor was also smiling. He opened his arms.

'Emily.'

'Victor.'

They embraced and kissed.

'What a surprise,' Emily said. 'Here we are thinking no one comes to see us. And here you are.'

'You haven't changed,' Victor said.

'You've got taller,' she said.

'It's these new shoes. They have thick heels. It's the latest fashion. This is Abdullah.'

We introduced Ella.

'You remember Victor?'

She stood there smiling.

'How could she,' Emily said. 'She wasn't born.'

I took their winter coats and hung them up. And we went into the kitchen where Emily had laid out the table.

'Someone gave us this pâté for Christmas,' I said. 'We were waiting for an occasion to open it. Do you know what it is?'

'It's pork,' Abdullah said, chewing it slowly. 'In my country I'm not supposed to eat it.'

'It's very good,' Victor said.

I helped myself to a hard-boiled egg.

'Do you remember Tom Slater? We met him in one of the Soho pubs. He wrote short stories—'

'I don't remember him,' Victor said.

'He died nine years ago. He was thirty-six. He used to come down with his wife to see us. He knew I liked sardines. So he would bring a different tin of sardines every time he came down. He said he told a friend of his about my liking sardines. "That used to be the way you could tell a gourmet," the friend said. "Now, it's hard-boiled eggs."'

Abdullah laughed.

'Aren't these plums good. Have some more,' I said to Abdullah.

'As you see, Victor, we are still here,' Emily said. 'We seem to sit here waiting for something to happen.'

'We'll get out soon,' I said quietly.

'I've heard that before,' Emily said.

'We have a chance. Now that the kids have grown up. Ella finishes school this year. Then we'll be able to go.'

'But where will we go *to*—?' Emily asked.

'You two sound like characters in a Beckett play,' Victor said.

No one spoke. Then Emily said sharply,

'How *could* you come back here, Victor?'

He didn't answer. He went on eating, looking not at all at ease.

'Do you remember Keith Haydon,' I said. 'He came over a few years after us and became an authority on nuclear strategy. He used to write articles, appear on television. He died last year in Venice.'

'That's a shame,' Victor said.

'And remember Len Mason? One time the three of us were walking along Sherbrooke Street after a late lecture. It was winter. Lots of snow on the ground. We told him we were going to be writers. And he said he was going to be an actor. So we said we would write plays for him. Len did become an actor. He acted in Canada and over here and in the States. He was killed two years ago while driving a car on a highway.'

'I'm sorry to hear that,' Victor said.

'How do you live in Morocco?' Emily said changing the subject.

'I have a house in the Arab quarter. I designed the inside of the house. Also had my own furniture made up. It's got lots of rooms. Now and then I have some European friends staying with me. But most of the time I only see Moroccans.'

'What do you do in the morning?' I said.

'I go shopping. Buy food.'

'Do you still cook?'

'Yes. But I have a cook and a houseboy.'

'Is it hot there?'

'It can be during the day,' Abdullah said. 'But at night it freezes.'

'What do you wear?' Emily asked.

'He wears a silken—' Abdullah smiled mischievously at Victor.

'It's something I got in Japan,' Victor said nervously. 'A karate suit.'

'It's like the old men wear,' Abdullah said, still smiling.

We went into the other room. I put more coal on the fire. Emily came in with the coffee. I brought in some whisky and brandy and began to pour the drinks. Victor took out the package of small cigars and offered me one. 'I used to smoke one cigarette after another,' he said. 'Now I smoke one cigar after another.'

'What do you work at, Victor?' I said.

'I'm a dilettante,' he said lightly. 'I do several things. But as an amateur.'

'Then you're a professional dilettante, Victor,' Emily said.

'No,' Victor said. 'I'm not professional at anything.'

'But you could cook—very well,' I said.

'He is doing a cook book,' Abdullah said proudly.

'I'm supposed to be doing one,' Victor said. 'But I don't think I will. Just putting down one recipe after another would be boring. I paint most of the time.'

'What kind of paintings do you do?' said Emily.

'Landscapes.'

'Like what painter that we would know?'

'Like Corot.'

'That's a name to conjure with,' Emily said.

'I like being an amateur,' Victor said. 'The good painters and writers I know—they lead such miserable lives. I was going through immigration at London Airport. And the official looked at my passport and asked me. What do you do? I said writer—I still say that sometimes. What have you written? he asked. *Nothing*, I said.'

We all laughed.

'He let me through.'

And for a moment he was like the Victor I knew. The one who used to make me laugh. But just as quickly he went back into his shell of not talking freely and looking uneasy. A few minutes later he stood up. 'I think it's time we went to the hotel.'

'I'll walk you there,' I said.

Back with Emily in bed. She said, 'I was looking out of the window. And I saw three people coming up. And I thought, supposing Victor's married. And he's bringing his wife ... Do you think Abdullah is his boy-friend?'

'I didn't ask. But I guess so.'

'I thought he liked girls?'

'He did,' I said. 'I knew of three at McGill and one over here. Just before I met you he began to see a lot of this girl. I don't remember her name. She was a Canadian in London from the same background as Victor. About your height, only very dark hair, high cheekbones, a nice smile. She looked a bit like Claudette Colbert. *Very* sympathetic. One night he came to the flat I had in Notting Hill Gate (Victor was then living in Chelsea) to tell me that he had just left this girl. And she told him she was pregnant. He didn't know what to do. He said he would marry her. Victor has a great sense of doing the right thing. "The trouble is," he said, "I have enough income from my capital for one person to live. But with two—I'll have to get a job." So he went and signed up as a salesman to sell encyclopedias. He did that for a month. Didn't like it. Then the girl told him it was a false alarm. And that was the end of that.'

We lay in bed for a while not speaking.

'He's not giving much away,' I said.

'Maybe he knows what writers do,' Emily said.

'I don't think so,' I said. 'I remember when he finished the novel and showed me the typescript. The characters were lifeless. I asked him why didn't he write about people he knew. About his family, about Montreal, his private school, McGill. He said he didn't want anything to do with Canada or anything connected with it. I don't know anyone who hates Canada so much. And how can you be a writer if you reject your past? Seeing Victor, I can see the person I was.'

'Yes,' Emily said. 'He can tell little lies. He said we haven't changed. I know we have. It's the kind of small talk you used to make. Why say things you don't mean?'

'It's a form of politeness,' I said ... 'I wonder what would have happened to Victor if that dark-haired girl was pregnant?'

'But he's happy with his life,' Emily said. '"The nice thing about these trips," he told me, "is that at the end I can go back home to Morocco. To my house and my Arab friends." I think he's very lucky to live in a place he likes.'

I didn't reply. I expected her to go on and say: we're about the only ones who live in a place they don't like. Instead she said, 'I think Victor disapproves of me. Every time he looked at me, I felt it.'

'I also think he disapproves of me now,' I said. 'For not living better— for not getting on.'

'Well you have written a few books since you last saw him.'

'But he's not curious about our life at all,' I said. 'He hasn't asked me one question as to what I've been doing these past twenty years. It's as if he looks at the way we live—and doesn't want to know. And he has forgotten a lot. I walked down the street with him, showing where we had the cottage that first summer—where Pop Short lived— Maskell's—The Gay Viking. All he said was: I don't remember. I don't remember.'

'Perhaps that's why he was able to come down here,' Emily said. 'He doesn't have much to lose.'

Next day, Saturday, they didn't arrive until noon.

'I've been walking up and down the street,' Victor said. 'I couldn't find the house. All the houses look so much the same.'

'I've found Morocco in Ella's Atlas book,' Emily said. And showed Abdullah the map. 'Are you anywhere near the coast?'

'We are about three hundred miles from the coast. Beside the mountains.'

From the window I could see the sky was still overcast. 'I hope you'll get a bit of sun while you're here,' I said to Abdullah. 'Then you'll be able to see the colours.'

'I like the way it is,' Abdullah said. 'I have never seen anything like this.'

'Why don't we go for a drive across the moors,' Victor said. 'Stop at a few pubs. Then I'll take you and Emily out to a meal.'

I got in front with Victor. Emily was in the back with Abdullah. And in a matter of minutes we were on the moors. The small green fields with the grey broken-stone hedges. The hedges with gorse and hawthorn on both sides of the road. Last year's bracken a light rust colour. Some deserted tin mine chimneys.

'In Morocco,' Victor said, 'you have these wild flowers. One day they are all yellow. Next day they are pink.'

'I suppose you find this drab.'

'No,' he said. 'I wouldn't mind getting out here and do some painting.'

I can hear Abdullah telling Emily, 'My father has two dozen head of cows, some chickens and sheep.'

'If a Moroccan sheep saw this green grass,' Victor said, 'it would go ga-ga.'

We drive along the turning road. There is a drop to the green fields below us on the right while the moors go up on the left.

I can hear Emily with Abdullah in the back. 'Have you any brothers and sisters?' 'I have thirteen brothers and sisters. My father has fifteen wives. But only four at a time. When my father comes in and tells the women to start cleaning and cooking—I know he is getting a new wife.'

'He has written an autobiography,' Victor told me. 'That's all in it.'

I hear Emily say. 'Why have you written your autobiography?' And Abdullah saying: 'Because I have had a very interesting life. I find life much more interesting than fiction.'

'How old are you?' I asked Abdullah, turning my head.

'Twenty-three.'

'How long have you and Victor known each other?'

'Five years.'

We come to Zennor and Victor stops the car by the Tinner's Arms and we get out and see the old squat church. No clock but a sundial. Inside the Tinner's we stand and drink Guinness and take in the atmosphere. On the wall there is a painting of a stallion.

'It's an Arab,' Abdullah said.

'How can you be so sure?' Emily said.

'See the smooth lines. Your English horses are more heavy in the stomach.'

A group of young people sit at the far end where a fire is going. I recognize one as the son of a painter Emily and Victor and I knew twenty years ago.

'Are you one of the Sparks?' I asked him.

'Yes,' he said, standing up and saying my name. We shake hands. He is the same age as Abdullah and twice as tall.

'Your mother and father,' I said, 'brought you over to see us when we lived in Mousehole.'

'When I was in diapers,' Sparks said laughing.

I introduce him to Abdullah. 'He's from Morocco.'

'I was there last summer,' Sparks said. 'I was thrown in jail. My friend the chief of police got me out and then I was in even worse trouble.'

There is an immediate rapport between the small Arab and the tall country-faced young man.

While Abdullah is talking to Emily, Sparks tells me: 'Abdullah—it's like Fred over there. You see all these mothers come running out of their houses calling: "Come here Abdullah you naughty boy."'

'He's just like his father,' I said when we were getting back in the car, 'outgoing—giving of himself.'

'He tried to say goodbye to me in Arabic,' Abdullah said.

We drive over to Mousehole. (We are covering old ground that Victor knew.) We came here just after Emily and I married. Lived for a year in a large granite house on the side of a hill. It had a nice garden with bamboos, copper beech and palm trees. In the morning, when we were still in bed, we could hear the melancholy sound of curlews flying over to the fields above. And again at dusk when they flew back to the rocks at the sea's edge. Victor was living in St Ives and he would come on Friday night for meals that Emily made. Our novels were finished and were making the rounds of the publishers ...

Now, we look through the bare hedge at the granite house in silence. Emily wants to get away. 'Some things are best left undisturbed,' she tells me. Victor shows no interest at all.

'Let's go,' he said, 'and have a meal.'

The little village is very clean, the colours as fresh as paint, the streets deserted. But we are too late for lunch.

We drive into Penzance. The restaurants are shut. Finally we find one open in Market Jew Street. It is packed. Every seat taken. People are standing up. I see stairs. I suggest we go up the stairs. Here it is all empty. The tables nicely set with white table-cloths and facing a wall-window overlooking Market Jew Street.

'I see the advantage of a university education,' Emily said.

'Now,' Victor said, 'we'll have a feast.'

The menu was brought to us by a stocky middle-aged waitress. She had white shoes on. And gave the impression that there was still lots of life in her yet. We all agree to have soup and scampi.

The waitress came carrying the bowls of soup close to her breasts. And she was singing, '*Isn't It Romantic*—'

The soup was terrible. The scampi wasn't very good either. But we were hungry.

The waitress came back with a bottle of standard fish sauce. Her hips swaying.

'Let's try some of this exotic sauce,' Victor said, putting his knife into the bottle.

'I'll have some too,' I said.

'*Isn't It Romantic*—' she sang.

Abdullah didn't like the scampi. The waitress went back and sat down by another table. I guess she had her eye on Abdullah. But Abdullah was looking out into Market Jew Street.

'In Morocco,' he said to Emily, 'the people would be on the road and the cars on the pavement.'

An old man came up and sat down at a table.

'Hullo, my handsome,' the waitress said loudly. And went over carrying a cup of tea.

That night in bed Emily said. 'Yesterday, early Friday, it was raining. And you know how it is here sometimes. You think it's all coming down on you. I just wanted to talk to someone. And there was Mr Care outside his nice pink house with a broom. And I said, You're not going to change the colour? No, he said, I've been away for a few days. I'm just tidying up. Where did you go? To Brighton. My son is a vicar there. He is the vicar for the crematorium. And I remembered our neighbour with her obsession about the dead. It was all getting me down. Then Victor phones to say he's here. And the next day I am out driving in a car across the moors and there were the green fields and this very English landscape. And sitting beside me is a dark little Arab. Suddenly life seems to have all sorts of possibilities. If this can happen—there's hope. I was so excited I was almost jumping up in the back seat. Thank God for Abdullah. Victor is too glum for me. And his talk is so superficial. I don't suppose you would have anything to do with him now if you met him.'

'I don't suppose either of us would,' I said. 'He didn't expect to find us here when he came. I don't think we'll even exchange postcards when he gets back.'

'That happens all the time,' Emily said. 'People who know each other when they are young drift apart. Are they coming tomorrow for lunch?'

'Yes,' I said.

'I'll do a roast chicken and make a nice dessert.'

'Fine,' I said. 'And I'll get some wine.'

Soon after they arrived at noon I brought them upstairs to this room. It seemed necessary, for me, that Victor should see what I had done with all those years. I showed him the books. For twenty years they seemed so few. But I tried to make it look better by showing him the various editions. Knowing his predilection for the exotic I showed him an article on some of the books in *The Bangkok Post* of 2 August 1970.

'This is nice,' Victor said as he read it.

'Do many people come to see you?' Abdullah asked.

'A few.'

'What do they want?'

'I think they want something to happen to them. Then they go home.'

'Do you write about them?'

'Sometimes,' I said. 'People are very generous. They let you into their lives. So you don't want to hurt them by what you write. In any case I write about people I like or have liked. And only about people I know. Their visit is only the tip of an iceberg.'

The meal went all right. Victor kept touching his chin when he talked. Abdullah was much more at ease. He told us that he was circumcised when he was six, that the Jews and Arabs were cousins, and what was all this stupid fighting for.

After lunch I took them both for a walk. 'That's Emily's garden,' I said. 'There used to be a greenhouse but the storm blew it down. Underneath the pear tree there is a little cemetery of children's animals—part of Martha's and Ella's childhood—two cats, one kitten, two hamsters, a goldfish.'

I walked them through the twisting back streets and around the harbour. 'You have seen the small stone cottages,' I said to Abdullah, 'and the kind of terrace houses we live in. Now I'll show you how other people live here.'

We got in the car and I told Victor to drive out of the place. Then down a road with trees. And through a wide gate. And there were the fine lawns with the large house at the end. The sides with trees. And a sheer slope down to the sand and the water of the bay. Abdullah could not contain his excitement. 'Shall I take some pictures?' he asked Victor.

'I don't think the light is good enough,' Victor said woodenly.

And I wondered why Victor hadn't taken any pictures of where we lived or of Emily, Ella, or myself.

'You might remember Henry Nicolle,' I said to Victor as we walked towards the house. 'He was a painter. We went to his first show in London in 1949. His widow still lives here.'

But Victor didn't remember.

The front door was shut. I looked inside the front room with the paintings on the wall, the antique furniture. 'I guess no one's in,' I said.

But Victor had already gone back to the car. He looked impatient to get away. Did it remind him of the house in Westmount, of summers in Murray Bay, St Andrew's Ball, Sherbrooke Street, McGill? I didn't know. When we got in the car he said. 'I'll drive back to say goodbye to Emily.'

For a while Victor and Emily looked at each other in the hallway. Neither knew what to say. Then they embraced and kissed. 'If you are ever in Morocco,' Victor said. And Emily laughed. 'Yes, Victor—'

I went out to walk them back to the car-park. It was dusk. Most of the houses were in darkness.

'You'll be able to get back to work,' Victor said.

'The importance of work is highly exaggerated,' I said. 'Sometimes I think it is just another con trick.' I didn't know if I believed this or not. Or was I trying to tell him that I understood his life. 'It's probably just another way of passing the time.'

He didn't reply.

When we got to the car, Victor turned and said, 'It's been fun.'

He said this with something of the gaiety that I remembered. I shook hands with both of them. And walked quickly away.

For the next three days I came up here and tried to get on with some work but couldn't. Victor's visit had made me dissatisfied with the sort of life I was living. Why am I chained to this desk? I asked myself. What's so important about writing? Victor was living a much freer life. He had travelled and continues to travel all over the world. But when I make a trip it is back to Canada—to keep in touch with the past. Another chain. I deliberately remain uninvolved with things here because I don't want to lose the past—to put too many layers between. While Victor—? I suddenly envied his life. I don't mean living in Morocco or his house or Abdullah—I envied him his freedom. Chains and freedom, I thought. Chains and freedom.

But on the fourth day the visit began to fade. Things here were getting back to the way they were before. Emily came up at ten-thirty in the morning with a cup of coffee and a biscuit. And I began to go on with the writing where I left off.

A week later I had a letter from Montreal, from the Graduates Society of McGill, letting me know that this year was our silver anniversary. 'Dear Classmate,' it began. 'Yes indeed it is hard to believe that a group as young as we are graduated from the old Alma Mater 25 years ago! But that's the way it is!'

By a Frozen River

IN THE WINTER OF 1965 I decided to go for a few months to a small town in northern Ontario. It didn't have a railway station—just one of those brown railway sidings, on the outskirts, with a small wooden building to send telegrams, buy tickets, and to get on and get off. A taxi was there meeting the train. I asked the driver to take me to a hotel. There was only one he would recommend, The Adanac. I must have looked puzzled. For he said,

'It's Canada spelled backwards.'

He drove slowly through snow-covered streets. The snowbanks by the sidewalk were so high that you couldn't see anyone walking. Just the trees. He drove alongside a frozen river with a green bridge across it. Then we were out for a while in the country. The snow here had drifted so that the tops of the telegraph poles were protruding like fence posts. Then we came to the town—a wide main street with other streets going off it.

The Adanac was a three-storey wooden hotel on the corner of King and Queen. It had seen better times. Its grey-painted wooden verandah, with icicles on the edges, looked old and fragile. But the woodwork had hand-carved designs, and the white windows had rounded tops. Beside it was a new beer parlour.

Fifty years ago it was the height of fashion to stay at the hotel. It was then called the George. The resident manager told me this, in his office, after I paid a month's rent in advance. His name was Savage. A short, overweight man in his sixties, with a slow speaking voice, as if he was thinking what he was going to say. He sat, neatly dressed, behind a desk, his grey hair crew-cut, and looked out of the large window at the snow-covered street. The sun was shining.

'Well,' he said slowly. 'It's an elegant day.'

His wife was a thin, tall woman with delicate features. She also hardly spoke. But would come into the office and sit, very upright, in a rocking chair near Mr Savage and look out of the window. The office connected with their three-room flat. It was filled with their possessions. A small, bronze crucifix was on the wall. Over the piano a large picture of the Pope. There were a few coloured photographs: a boy in uniform, children, and a sunset over a lake.

I rented the flat above. I had a room to sleep in, a room to write and read, and a kitchen with an electric stove and fridge. To get to them I would go up worn steps, along a wide, badly lit corridor—large tin pipes carried heat along the ceiling. But inside the rooms it was warm. They had radiators and double windows.

I unpacked. Then went to the supermarket, by the frozen river, and came back with various tins, fruit, and cheap cigars that said they were dipped in wine. I made myself some coffee, lit one of the thin cigars, and relaxed.

I saw a wooden radio on the side-table in the sitting-room. A battered thing. I had to put twenty-five cents in the back. That, according to a metal sign, gave me two hours' playing time. But that was only a formality. For the back was all exposed, and the twenty-five cents kept falling out for me to put through again.

Listening to the radio—I could only get the local station—the town sounded a noisy, busy place, full of people buying and selling and with things going on. But when I walked out, the first thing I noticed was the silence. The frozen, shabby side streets. Hardly anything moving. It wasn't like what the radio made out at all. There was a feeling of apathy. The place seemed stunned by the snow piled everywhere.

I quickly established a routine. After breakfast I went out and walked. And came back, made some coffee, and wrote down whatever things I happened to notice.

This morning it was the way trees creak in the cold. I had walked by a large elm when I heard it. I thought it was the crunching sound my shoes made on the hard-packed snow. So I stopped. There was no wind, the branches were not moving, yet the tree was creaking.

In the late afternoon, I made another expedition outside. Just before it got dark, I found a small square. It began to snow. The few trees on the perimeter were black. The few bundled-up people walking slowly through the snow were black. And from behind curtained windows a bit of light, a bit of orange. There was no sound. Just the snow falling. I expected horses and sleighs to appear, and felt the isolation.

That evening I had company. A mouse. I saw it just before it saw me. I tried to hit it with a newspaper, but I missed. And as it ran it slipped and slithered on the linoleum. I was laughing. It ran behind the radiator. I looked and saw it between the radiator grooves, where the dust had gathered. It had made a nest out of bits of fluff. I left food out for it. And in the evenings it would come out and run around the perimeter of the sitting-room, then go back behind the radiator.

Birds woke me in the morning. It seemed odd to see so much snow and ice and hear birds singing. I opened the wooden slot in the outside window and threw out some bread. Though I could hear the birds, I couldn't see them. Then they came—sparrows. They seemed to fly into their shadows as they landed on the snow. Then three pigeons. I went and got some more bread.

On the fourth day I met my neighbour across the hall. He rented the two rooms opposite. He wore a red lumberjack shirt and black lumberjack boots with the laces going high up. He was medium height, in his forties, with pleasant features. And he had short, red hair.

'Hi,' he said. And asked me what I was doing.

'Writing a book,' I said.

'Are you really writing a book?'

'Yes.'

'That must be very nice,' he said.

And invited me into his flat. It was the same as mine, except he didn't have a sitting-room. The same second-hand furniture, the used electric stove, the large fridge, the wooden radio.

I asked him what he did.

'I work in a small factory. Just my brother and me. We make canoes. Do you like cheese?'

'Yes,' I said.

He opened his fridge. It was filled with large hunks of an orange cheese.

'I get it sent from Toronto. Here, have some.'

I met the new occupants of the three rooms behind me next morning. I was going to the toilet. (There was one toilet, with bath, for all of us on the first floor. It was in the hall at the top of the stairs.) I opened the door and saw a woman sitting on the toilet, smoking a cigarette. She wasn't young. Her legs were close together. She said, 'Oh.' I said sorry and closed the door quickly. 'I'm sorry,' I said again, this time louder, as I walked away.

A couple of days later she knocked on my door and said she was Mrs Labelle and she was Jewish. She heard from Savage that I had a Jewish name. Was I Jewish? I said I was. She invited me back to meet her husband.

The people who rented these rooms usually didn't stay very long. So there was no pride in trying to do anything to change them. But Mrs Labelle had her room spotless. She had put up bright yellow curtains to hide the shabby window blinds. She had plastic flowers in a bowl on the table. And everything looked neat, and washed, even though the furniture was the same as I had.

Her husband, Hubert, was much younger. He looked very dapper. Tall, dark hair brushed back, neatly dressed in a dark suit and tie and a clean white shirt. He had a tripod in his hand and said he was going out to work.

'Savage told us you were a writer. I have started to write my life story—What the photographer saw—I tell all. You wouldn't believe the things that have happened to me.'

His wife said that the mayor was trying to get them out of town. 'He told the police that we need a licence. It's because he owns the only photograph store here. He's afraid of the competition. We're not doing anything illegal. I knock on people's doors and ask them if they want their picture taken at home. He's very good,' she said, 'especially with children.'

After that Mrs Labelle came to the door every day. She knew all the other occupants. And would tell me little things about them. 'He's a very hard worker,' she said about the man who made canoes. 'He doesn't drink at all.' Then she told me about the cleaning woman, Mabel. 'She only gets fifteen dollars a week. Her husband's an alcoholic. She's got a sixteen-year-old daughter—she's pregnant. I'm going to see her this afternoon and see if I can help. Be careful of Savage. He looks quiet, but

I saw him using a blackjack on a drunk from the beer parlour who tried to get into the hotel at night. He threw him out in the snow. Dragged him by the feet. And Mrs Savage helped.' She complained of the noise at night. 'There's three young waitresses. Just above me. They have boys at all hours. I don't blame them. But I can't sleep. I can't wash my face. It's nerves,' she said.

Then I began to hear Mr Labelle shouting at her. 'God damn you. Leave me alone. Just leave me alone.' It went on past midnight.

Next day, at noon, she knocked on the door. She was smiling.

'I found a place where you can get Jewish food.'

'Where?'

'Morris Bischofswerder. He's a furrier. Up on the main street.'

I went to the furrier. He had some skins hanging on the walls. And others were piled in a heap on the floor.

'Do you sell food?' I said.

'What kind of food?'

'Jewish food.'

He looked me over.

He was below middle height, stocky, with a protruding belly. A dark moustache, almost bald, but dark hair on the sides. He was neatly dressed in a brown suit with a gold watch chain in his vest pocket. He was quite a handsome man, full lips and dark eyes. And from those eyes I had a feeling that he had a sense of fun.

'Where are you from?' he asked. 'The West?'

'No, from England.'

'All right, come.'

He led me through a doorway into the back and from there into his kitchen. And immediately there was a familiar food smell, something that belonged to my childhood. A lot of dried mushrooms, on a string, like a necklace, hung on several nails. He showed me two whole salamis and some loose hot dogs.

'I can let you have a couple pounds of salami and some hot dogs until the next delivery. I have it flown in once a month from Montreal.' He smiled. 'I also like this food. Where are you staying?'

'At the Adanac.'

His wife came in. She was the same size as Mr Bischofswerder but thinner, with grey hair, a longish thin nose, deep-set very dark eyes, the hollows were in permanent shadow, and prominent top teeth.

'He's from England,' he told her.

'I come from Canada,' I said quickly. 'But I live in England. The place I live in England doesn't have snow in winter. So I've come back for a while.'

'You came all the way from England for the snow?'

'Yes.'

They both looked puzzled.

'I like winters with snow,' I said.

'What have you got in England?'

'Where I live—rain.'

'Have you got a family?' Mr Bischofswerder said, changing the subject. 'Is your mother and father alive?'

'My mother and father lived in Ottawa, but they moved to California eight years ago.'

'I bet they don't miss Canadian winters,' Mrs Bischofswerder said.

'We have a married daughter in Montreal and five grandchildren,' he said proudly, 'four boys and one girl.'

'Sit down,' Mrs Bischofswerder said. 'I was just going to make some tea.'

And she brought in a chocolate cake, some pastry that had poppy seeds on top, and some light egg cookies.

'It's very good, isn't it?' she said.

'I haven't had food like this since I was a boy,' I said.

'Why are you so thin?' she said. '*Eat. Eat.*' And pushed more cookies in my direction.

'I wonder if you would come to *shul* next Friday,' Mr Bischofswerder said.

My immediate reaction was to say no. For I haven't been in a synagogue for over twenty years. But sitting in this warm kitchen with the snow outside. Eating the food. Mrs Bischofswerder making a fuss. It brought back memories of my childhood. And people I once knew.

'I'll come,' I said.

'Fine,' he said. 'If you come here around four o'clock, we'll go together. It gets dark quickly.'

That night the Labelles quarrelled until after two. Next day, at noon, Mrs Labelle knocked on the door. 'He didn't turn up. This woman was holding her children all dressed up. I told her to send them to school.'

'Is this the first time?'

'No. It's only got bad now. He's an alcoholic.'

She began to weep. I asked her inside. She was neatly dressed in dark slacks and a small fur jacket. 'My sisters won't have me. They say I've sown my wild oats.'

'Would you like some coffee?'

'Thanks. We had a house in Toronto. I have in storage lots of furniture—a fur coat—real shoes—not shoes like this. And where would you see a woman of my age going around knocking on doors? I'm sure I'm going to be killed. He calls me a witch. I found a piece of paper with a phone number. And a name—Hattie. I called up and said to leave my husband alone. I found another piece of paper. It said Shirley. They're all over him. He's a good-looking guy. And when he's working—these women are alone with him. You know—'

That afternoon, while I was writing, the phone went. It was Mrs Labelle.

'I'm in someone's house waiting for him to come and take the picture. Can you see if he's in? He hasn't turned up.'

I knocked on their door. Mr Labelle was sitting on the settee with a middle-aged man in a tartan shirt, and they were both drinking beer out of small bottles.

I said she was on the phone.

'Say you haven't seen me,' he said.

'Yes,' the other man said. 'Say you haven't seen him.'

But Labelle came after me and stood by the open door. 'Why don't you just say hello?' I said.

He went in and I could hear him saying, 'I'm not drunk. I'm coming over.' He hung up and closed the door.

'I'll tell you,' he said. 'Man to man. I'll be forty-one next month. And she's fifty-eight. We've been married fifteen years. I didn't know how

139

old she was when we married. Then she was seven months in a mental home. I used to see her every day. At two. I had to get my job all changed around. But I'll tell you what. I knocked up a woman two years ago. And she heard about it. The child died. She can't have children. She won't give me some rein. I've had her for fifteen years. Don't worry,' he said. 'I won't leave her. You may hear us at night. I shout. I'm French Canadian. But I'll look after her.'

He went back and got his camera and tripod. And he and the other man went down the stairs.

Ten minutes later she rang up again.

'Is he gone?'

'Yes,' I said.

That evening around nine, there was a gentle knock at the door. It was Mrs Labelle, in a red dressing-gown. 'He's asleep,' she said. 'Thank you very much. He hasn't eaten anything. I make special things. But he won't eat.'

It was quiet until eleven that night. I could hear them talking. Then he began to raise his voice. 'Shut up. God damn it. Leave me alone. You should have married a Jewish businessman. You would have been happy.'

On Friday afternoon I put on a clean white shirt and tie and a suit. And went to call on Mr Bischofswerder. He was dressed, neatly, in a dark winter coat and a fur hat. We walked about four blocks. Then he led me into what I thought was a private house but turned out to be the synagogue. It was very small. Around twenty-four feet square and twenty feet high. But though it was small, it was exact in the way the synagogues were that I remembered. There was a wooden ark between a pair of tall windows in the east wall. A few steps, with wooden rails, led to the ark. The Ten Commandments, in Hebrew, were above it. A low gallery extended around the two sides. In the centre of the ceiling hung a candelabra with lights over the reading desk. There were wooden bench seats. Mr Bischofswerder raised one, took out a prayer book, and gave the prayer book to me.

'Shall we start?' he said.

'Aren't we going to wait for the others?'

'There are no others,' he said.

And he began to say the prayers to himself. Now and then he would run the words out aloud so I could hear, in a kind of sing-song that I remembered my father doing. I followed with my eyes the words. And now and then I would say something so he would hear.

I had long forgotten the service, the order of the service. So I followed him. I got up when he did. I took the three steps backwards when he did. But most of the time we were both silent. Just reading the prayers.

Then it was over. And he said.

'Good Shabbus.'

'Good Shabbus,' I said.

On the way back, through the snow-covered streets, it was freezing. Mr Bischofswerder was full of enthusiasm.

'Do you realize,' he said 'this is the first time I've had someone in the *shul* with me at Friday night for over three years?'

For the next seven Friday nights and Saturday mornings I went with Mr Bischofswerder to the synagogue. We said our prayers in silence.

Then I went back with him to his warm house. And to the enormous Sabbath meal that Mrs Bischofswerder had cooked. Of gefilte fish with chrane, chicken soup with mandlen, chicken with tzimmes, compote, tea with cookies. And we talked. They wanted to know about England. I told them about the English climate, about English money, English society, about London, Fleet Street, the parks, the pubs. How I lived by the sea and a beautiful bay but hardly any trees.

And he told me how the trappers brought him skins that he sent on to Montreal. That he was getting a bit old for it now. 'Thank God I can still make a living.' He told me of the small Jewish community that was once here. 'In 1920 when we came there were ten families. By the end of the last war it was down to three. No new recruits came to take the place of those who died or moved away. When we go,' said Mr Bischofswerder, 'all that will be left will be a small cemetery.'

'Have some more cookies,' his wife said, pushing a plateful towards me. 'You have hardly touched them. You won't get fat. They're light. They're called nothings.'

Mrs Labelle knocked on my door. She looked excited. 'I'm selling tick-ets,' she said. 'The town's running a sweepstake—when will the frozen river start to move? Everyone's talking about it. I've already sold three books. Will you have one? You can win five hundred dollars.'

'How much are they?'

'Fifty cents.'

'I'll have one,' I said.

'Next time you go to the supermarket,' she said, 'you'll see a clock in the window. There's a wire from the clock to the ice in the river. As soon as the ice starts to move—the clock stops. And the nearest ticket wins.'

She gave me my ticket.

'Good luck,' she said. And kissed me lightly on a cheek.

She looked, I thought, the happiest I had seen her. My ticket said: March 26th, 08:16:03.

That night I noticed the mouse had gone. No sign of it anywhere. It was raining. The streets were slushy and slippery. But later that night the water froze. And next morning when the sun came out it was slush again. The snow had started to shrink on the roofs; underneath the edges I could see water moving. I walked down to the river. It was still frozen, but I saw patches of blue where before it was all white. Crows were flap-ping over the ice with bits of straw in their beaks. The top crust of the river had buckled in places. And large pieces creaked as they rubbed against each other. Things were beginning to break up. It did feel like something was coming to an end here.

Next day, just before noon, Mrs Labelle came to the door. She looked worried. 'Savage told us we have to leave. I went to see him with our week's rent in advance. But he said he didn't want it. He said we were making too much noise at night. The waitresses make noise, but he doesn't mind them. I don't know where we'll go. We've been in Sudbury, in Timmins, in North Bay—'

'It's OK,' Mr Labelle said, coming to the door. 'We'll be all right,' he said to her gently. And started to walk her back towards their door. Then he called out to me. 'If we don't see you, fellah, good luck.'

'Same to you,' I said.

'But where will we go Hubert?' Mrs Labelle said, looking up to his face.

'There's lot of places,' he answered. 'Now we got some packing to do.'

After the Labelles had gone, it was very quiet. I had got the reminders I wanted of a Canadian winter. I had filled up three notebooks. It was time that I left. I went down to the office and told this to Mr Savage. He suggested that I stay until the ice started to move.

But I left before it did.

I took a light plane, from the snow-covered field with a short runway. From the air, for a while, I could see the small town. But soon it was lost in a wilderness of snow, trees, and frozen lakes.

The Girl Next Door

In October 1976 I came back to Ottawa and rented three rooms in an old house on Cobourg Street just below Rideau. It wasn't anything—plain bare rooms with brightly coloured wallpaper—but the windows looked out over a small park. And that made all the difference.

For the first two days—apart from going out to buy some small cigars and groceries—I stayed in and looked at the park.

It's a lovely little park ... made for the human scale ... people look right when they are in it. The two Lombardy poplars. One, at the edge of the park, by the sidewalk, in front of the window. The other, towards the middle of the park but off centre, raised, where the earth formed a mound. And on top of the mound, on a small plateau, a gazebo. And beside the gazebo—with its open arches, its sloping brick-coloured roof—this other, very tall, Lombardy poplar.

I could tell a wind's direction not only by the arrow on top of the gazebo but, from the near poplar's leaves showing their light green underside, I could also tell its strength. Elsewhere there were maple trees—young and old—their leaves, in autumn colours, some lying thick, underneath, on the grass.

I was quite happy to stay by a window. There was always something moving. A leaf from a maple, people walking, grey and black squirrels, boys throwing passes or kicking a rugby ball, others rolling from the gazebo down the slope. Pigeons, sparrows, and the occasional gull flying slowly over.

I watched until the park lights came on. Then it was too dark to see. That's when I switched on a small radio and listened to the news (the local, national, international), the sports, the time, the temperature, the weather forecast, and the commercials in between.

On the third day I woke up, drew back the curtain, and there was snow. It was the first snow I had seen in years. I made some coffee, lit up an Old Port cigarillo, and watched a man dressed in black with a black umbrella above his head walk through the all-white park. The wind picked up some loose leaves and moved them swiftly on top of the snow. Fascinating to see fallen leaves lifted then carried by the wind across the snow. They look like small birds. They are small birds.

I decided to go out. I had no destination. I walked along Rideau to the Château Laurier. In the lobby I took off my coat and sat down in a leather chair, as if I was waiting for someone. There were others also sitting down and watching.

I left the lobby as the bell in the Peace Tower was ringing ten and walked across Confederation Square, down Elgin, to the National Gallery. And found this Monet.

There was a Renoir to the left, of a mother and child. And a Braque to the right of the Port of Antwerp. And elsewhere in the room: a red landscape of Vlaminck; a red nude of Duchamp; a Derain, a Leger, an Epstein; some Cezannes, Pisarros, Sisleys, and Gauguins; several Degas; and a Van Gogh of some irises.

But it was this Monet, *Waterloo Bridge—The Sun in a Fog, 1903*, that I kept coming back to see.

When I was close to it it was just paint. But when I went back, about ten feet, the sun was round at the top coming faintly through the fog. The sun was orange on the water in the front and, further away, on the water through an arch of the bridge. While the darker shapes, of the bridge, the barges, came visibly through.

At the end of the second week Lynn moved into the apartment next door. I had pulled back the curtain and saw that the little park was almost hidden by fog. Only the gazebo—the arches filled with fog—and the near poplar and the near maples were visible. The rest was fog and the sun trying to come through. When a taxi drove up, a slim girl with long hair that almost hid her face came out. She was about five foot six or seven, dressed in jeans, a black sweater, and a black duffle coat. The taxi driver helped bring in her few things.

Next evening I knocked on her door.

'I saw you move in yesterday. I live in the next apartment.'

'Come in,' she said quietly.

The room was like mine. But she had put up art posters of Chagall and Picasso. And a Snoopy poster that said:

> *No problem is*
> *So big that you*
> *Can't run away*
> *From it.*

There were picture postcards and a row of paperbacks by the wall. There was a small wooden table and two wooden chairs.

'I haven't had time to do this right. Would you like coffee? It won't take long.'

She filled an electric kettle and plugged it in. I noticed that she was left-handed.

'How long have you been here?'

'Two weeks.'

'Will you stay?'

'I don't know. How about you?'

'I've got to sort myself out,' she said.

I saw Jung's *Modern Man in Search of a Soul*, Sylvia Plath's *The Bell Jar*, books on psychology, poetry, philosophy. And art books on Klee, Magritte, Kandinsky, Munch.

'I go to the National Gallery,' I said. 'They have a lovely Monet.'

'I like Monet,' she said.

'Where are you from?'

'From New Brunswick,' she said, 'near Fredericton, in the country.'

'I've been to Fredericton,' I said, 'about ten or eleven years ago. I deliberately go to places—some I know, some I don't—and isolate myself because I want to work. Why don't we go to my apartment? I have a bottle of wine and some records.'

I put on Bix Beiderbecke and Sydney Bechet. And she took off her shoes and began to dance in heavy white woollen socks. She danced, for a while, by herself. Then she came over and stretched out her hands.

'Dance.'

I got up and we danced. She was very firm, no fat at all.

After that we would see each other every day.

She had dark straight hair that she parted in the middle that almost hid her face. Now and then I caught a glimpse of her blue eyes, the longish straight nose, a small mouth and, occasionally, a shy smile. When she smiled she also seemed to look amused. I liked her from the start.

After I told her I was a writer she would turn up at the door with a piece of paper and say, 'Do you know this?'

When Spring comes round
If I should be dead,
Flowers will bloom just the same,
And trees will be no less green than they were last Spring,
Reality doesn't need me.

She wouldn't read it aloud. But give me the paper that she had written it on. It was through Lynn that I got to know the poetry of Pessoa and Osip Mandelstam. She also gave me several paperbacks of Herman Hesse. I think he was her favourite. But I didn't get very far with Hesse. I didn't try. I don't read much when I'm writing. And I was working on a long story, a novella, and I was often thinking of that even when I wasn't writing.

She would come to see me in the morning, in bare feet, a Hudson's Bay blanket draped around her shoulders.

'Walking in bare feet,' I said, 'that's the quickest way to get a cold.'

'It's the way I grew up,' she said.

She would light a cigarette and we would have coffee together and talk about writers, books, painters, movies, music, the weather …

After the coffee she would go out shopping. She always asked me if I wanted anything. About twice a week I would ask her to get some apples, grapes, tins of soup, salmon, coffee, rye bread (if she was passing Rideau Bakery), or nuts, if she was going near the mall. She always came back with a small white paper bag full of warm nuts from the Nut House. That's another thing we had in common. We both liked nuts.

She also went out every day for walks. And she would come back and tell me what she saw. She didn't tell me right away. There was this reserve—the silences—the shy smile—then she would say:

'I saw some gulls. Against the snow they looked dirty.'

Or else I would have to guess what took place when she said,

'I went to the cafeteria at the National Gallery to have a cup of coffee and listened to the conversations around me. People talk a lot of nonsense—don't they?'

'Do you know anyone in Ottawa?'

'Only you,' she said.

'Why did you come here, Lynn?'

'I had a quarrel with my boy-friend. He's white. But he works for a black revolutionary organization in Africa. We were together nearly a year. I let my heart rule my head. Because I was in love with him I became interested in politics. Then we had a quarrel. And he left.'

'What did you do before?'

'I went to college for a while. Then to Art School. I was trying the wrong things. I left Art School after two years. They were all on an ego trip.'

'Can't you go home?'

'There's only my father. We don't get on. He wanted boys. But he got three girls. I'm the eldest.'

'How old are you?'

'Twenty-three.'

'You're young,' I said. 'You still have your life ahead of you.'

'I don't know,' she said. 'There are times when I don't see any point—'

I thought, if I was twenty years younger it would be different.

'I'm the wrong person for you,' I said.

She didn't say anything. But she appeared at the door more often. And now I found that she began to stay too long. Her visits became more like interruptions. I would say.

'Yes, come in, Lynn. But you can't stay long. I have to do some work.'

Finally I said. 'I'm sorry, Lynn—I'm busy.'

She went away. But the next time I became annoyed.

'Lynn—I can't see you. I'm working.'

'Work. Work. That's all you do. What's so important about work?'

'Without my work,' I said, 'I'm nothing.'

She walked away, slamming the door.

I didn't see her next morning. But in the afternoon the phone rang.

'Hello.'

Silence.

'Hello,' I said. 'Hello—'

I thought I heard a voice but far away.

'—is that you Lynn?'

Silence.

Then quietly she said, 'I'm going to kill myself.'

'Where are you?'

'In a phone box—by the Château Laurier.'

'Stay there. I'll be right over.'

I got a taxi on Rideau and saw Lynn inside the phone booth, leaning in a corner with her head down. Her hair hiding her face. I put my arm around her and brought her to the taxi.

'I'm sorry,' she said when we were inside her apartment. 'I'm all right now. I feel tired. I'll lie down. You can go now.'

Next morning she came around for coffee—in her bare feet, the Hudson's Bay blanket around her—and we talked as if nothing happened. She asked me if she could do any shopping. Was there anything I wanted mailed.

'No thanks,' I said.

When she came back that afternoon from her walk she came back with a small present, a jar of honey, that she wrapped up very neatly in Snoopy wrapping paper.

She left me alone, but not for long. The following day she came around and wanted to talk. We did for a while. Then I had to say,

'You'll have to go now. I must get back to work.'

She went out. A few minutes later a piece of paper was pushed underneath the door. On it she had written. 'I'm going—and I won't come back.'

That afternoon I found myself going to the window, looking out to see if I could see her.

She did come back as the light in the park was fading.

'Where did you go?'

'To the Château Laurier,' she said. 'I sat in the lobby and watched people. I did that for an hour. Then I went to the National Gallery and looked at the Monet. Then I walked. I walked until I got cold. So I went into department stores to keep warm. What's wrong with me?'

'Nothing,' I said. 'Just wait. Time has to go by. Things have to happen.'

'You're lucky,' she said. 'You are doing what you want to do. I don't know what I want to do. I like going out for walks. I like looking at things—paintings, reading books.' Tears appeared in her eyes. 'Isn't there a place for someone like me?'

I went over and kissed her.

'Yes,' she said quietly. 'There's always that.'

For the next three days it went more or less all right. She still went out for her walks. But instead of telling me about them when she came back, she showed me sketches that she did. Of the market, and people in the market, of people crossing near the cenotaph, of the mall, the frozen Rideau river with the snow, the trees, and the white Minto bridges.

On Friday she came in, around noon, with her sketch-book and a pencil. She wrote something on the paper, tore the piece off, and gave it to me. It said,

'I can't talk.'

'Of course you can,' I replied.

'No,' she wrote. 'I woke this morning and I wanted to speak but I couldn't.'

'It will come back,' I said.

Silence.

'Has this ever happened before?'

'No,' she wrote.

Silence.

'I had a letter from my boy-friend,' she wrote. 'He wants me to come to Toronto.'

'Why don't you go?'

'Do you think I should?' she wrote.

'Yes,' I said.

She must have packed before she came to see me for when I saw her again, a half-hour later, she was ready to leave.

'Thanks for talking to me,' she said. 'You don't know how much all those talks we had meant to me.'

And I felt bad. All I could think of was how abrupt I was with her. How little I did give of myself.

I watched her go with her few belongings into a taxi.

A month later I walked to the National Gallery to see the Monet again. And as it was a particularly cold day I decided to go to the Lord Elgin, into Murray's, to have a cup of coffee. The large room was crowded with civil servants having their morning break. I found a seat by a table in a corner. It was pleasantly warm. The coffee was hot. I sat and smoked a small cigar and looked at the lights near the ceiling. They were set in round wooden circles, like wooden crowns. When I noticed a lively group of boys and girls come in. They were talking and joking together. They all looked excited, handsome. Lynn was one of them. Her hair was short. She wore a bright yellow sweater. A tall young man was beside her. And like the others she smiled and laughed a lot.

To Blisland

SUNDAY MORNING ON a hot warm August day. And we were in a train that was going to London. Two hours later, at Bodmin Road, we got off in the country. A long outside platform with upward-sloping green fields, trees, and hedges. The sun shining on them.

We crossed the tracks, to the other side, by the covered wooden bridge. And to a waiting small green bus.

Marie carried a carrier bag. I another. Hers had a carton of six eggs that she had boiled with onion skins to make the shells dark brown, a jar of gooseberries that she had cooked the night before, some panties, socks, soap, and writing paper with envelopes and stamps. I had several comics, grapes, apples, bars of chocolate, a paperback, and a kite.

It was warm in the bus. We were the only passengers. After twenty minutes it drove along a country road, then a small bridge, over a narrow river, and onto the main road.

Fifteen minutes later we came to the town. It was deserted. The bus went, slowly, up the rising main street. (The houses, the buildings, looked as if they had resisted change.) At the top, at crossroads, we got out and began to walk along a straight wide road.

On the side we were walking were small houses with small front gardens and, at the back, farmers' fields.

On the other side was a continuous brick wall. Behind the brick wall, cut grass lawns and, further away, Victorian brick buildings. The brick buildings had many windows and fire escapes—an institution, looking stark against all the greenery around it.

About a quarter of a mile down the road the brick wall had a gap. A drive went from this gap, down a short slope, to a small new bungalow-like building.

Carol was sitting outside on a wooden bench.

She saw us.

We both began to walk quickly towards one another.

'Hullo love. Happy birthday.'

Tears appeared in her eyes.

'You both look so handsome,' she said quietly.

Marie wore a light blue summer dress with short sleeves. I had a light grey summer suit with a dark blue sport shirt open at the neck. Carol was all in black—black trousers and a long black sweater. Her black hair almost hid her face.

'We got some things for you—'

I took the kite. It was made and painted to look like a red butterfly.

'I don't think we can fly it today. There's not enough wind,' I said.

'We brought a picnic,' Marie said. 'Shall we leave the other things in your room and tell Mister Patrick. Is he on today?'

'Yes,' said Carol.

We went into the bungalow-like building, into the corridor. It was dark. A door was open, the office, and an outgoing young man in a white coat was sitting behind a desk. He was medium sized, stocky, with dark hair.

Marie went with Carol further along the corridor to her room.

I went into the office.

'We thought of taking Carol out for a picnic.'

'It's a good day for it.'

'Can you suggest anywhere?'

'Have you been to Lanhydrock?'

'We were there a few weeks ago.'

'Altarnun—?'

'We have been there as well.'

'There's a nice spot—just down the road—you can walk it from here. Down a hill. Go to the railway tracks. Then walk along the tracks. No trains run there on Sunday. And you will get to a river. It will be cool by the river.'

'How is she?'

'Some weeks there is a step forward. Others not. At least she hasn't gone back.'

Marie appeared with Carol.

'What time do you want her back?'

'Not later than five,' Mr Patrick said.

'Could you order us a taxi for five?'

'I'll do that,' he said. 'Have a nice time.'

Carol didn't say a word.

We walked along the short drive, to the opening, then along the main road. On the horizon, the white grey hills of China clay.

'Have you been down this way?'

'No,' Carol said.

'They've made a poster for Carol,' Marie said. 'They put it on the inside of her door. It says Happy Birthday. Everyone signed it. I remember my eighteenth birthday. My mother made a large party, invited all my relatives, and I didn't like it at all.'

'Have you still the room to yourself?'

'No,' Carol said. 'They put someone in with me on Tuesday.'

'How old is she?'

'Seventeen.'

We walked along the side of the road, down the slope, in silence.

'Someone else came in on Tuesday—' Carol said. 'His name is George. He sits beside me at the table when we eat. He did the poster.'

'Mrs Smith asked after you,' Marie said. 'So did Flossie. And the woman in the paper place always asks how you are getting on.'

Where the road levelled out we came to the railway tracks. We left the main road and walked between the tracks. There were trees on either side and overgrown grass. After a while the trees became thicker and the earth sloped more steeply down. There was a path near the top of the slope. We walked on the path, between the trees. It began to get dark. And we could see water.

It was a strange light. The sun (not able to come through the trees except for a shaft here and another some way along) left the top parts of the trees a bright yellow-green. Halfway between the tops of the trees and the river the light changed from bright to dark. The river was dark—dark green, dark blue, with large rocks in it. Sounds carried. We could hear boys and girls talking and splashing somewhere ahead. A dog barking. It was very still. We were walking in the dark light while above was this bright light-yellow and light-green. And all the colours seemed softened.

We sat on the trunk of a fallen tree, on the slope, where we could see the river. And had a picnic from the hard-boiled eggs, apples, grapes, and bars of chocolate.

'You look better,' I said.

'I don't take the pills.'

And she brought out, from her trouser pocket, some small red pills.

'They give them to me. I put them in my mouth, but I don't swallow. If they find out I will be in trouble.'

'I'll take them,' I said. 'And get rid of them. If they get to know about this they may not let you go out.'

'What's the girl like that is in the room with you?' Marie asked.

'She lies on her bed most of the time,' Carol said. 'They brought her in because she took an overdose.'

'What's wrong with George?' I asked.

'He broke all the clocks in his house. Then the mirrors. Then the windows … How's Min?'

'She had kittens,' Marie said. 'In the cupboard under the stairs. Five this time. Four ginger and one black and white.'

'I miss Min,' Carol said quietly.

'We painted your room,' I said changing the subject.

'I don't know,' she said. 'Sometimes I think home is my room here.'

We got up and walked by the river stepping over rocks and fallen branches and smelling the mud. The river turned. And as we came around the turn the sun had come through a gap in the trees ahead and we could see, in the shaft of light, a boy, two girls, and a dog. The boy was splashing in the water with the dog. While the others sat on the rock. They were in bright sunlight. The water, near them, a light bright blue. While all around it was dark.

We clambered up the slope to the railway tracks and into the sunlight. And walked farther along the tracks until we came to a road. The fields, on either side, were lush with grass and wheat. We came to an avenue of trees. They led to wide lawns and banks of flowers. And behind them, slightly raised, a large stone house with farm buildings. We walked on the lawns, picked some flowers. There was a small bridge over a stream. When we crossed the bridge we dropped the white and light pink flowers in the water.

Then we walked towards the farm buildings. They looked very old and used. A large pile of cut wood was neatly stacked by a barn. Others had machinery. In a stable a white horse with blue eyes had his head out of the stable door. He stood there not moving.

There was no one about.

We walked to the house. From the front it had a magnificent view over the lawns, over the trees, and onto a valley with the higher fields and trees on either side. The house was dark. It looked tatty, as if it had been lived in a long time.

'It looks so feudal,' Marie said.

We crossed the lawn to go out on the far side. And crossing the stream we saw the flowers that we had dropped at the start, passing by, carried on the slow moving water.

Some way down the road were two neat cottages.

'My grandma worked on an estate like this,' Marie said. 'She was a teacher on the Royal Estate at Windsor. But that was nearly a hundred years ago.'

'I would like a small cottage in the country, near here,' Carol said. 'I'd have a goat and a cat or a dog. I would grow my own vegetables. And I'd get better, if I can be left alone for a while. If no one bothers me. If there is no noise ... I looked in an estate office window in Bodmin. There are cottages at two thousand pounds. When I'm twenty-one, I'll be getting five hundred pounds from the policy—maybe they will take that as a deposit—'

'Yes,' I said. 'That's a good idea.'

We came to crossroads. One sign said to Bodmin, the other said to Blisland.

'Let's go to Blisland,' Carol said.

'It's too late,' I said looking at my watch. 'We have to get you back by five.'

'I don't want to go back.'

'We'll go to Blisland another time,' Marie said.

By the time we came back to the town we were all tired.

I tried to find a restaurant or a café. But all of them were closed. I saw a filling station open. Part of it had a small room with several tables with plastic tops.

We went in. We all had coffee in silence.

Then two motorbikes drove up. And four young people in white crash helmets and black leather jackets and jeans came in. When they took their helmets off I could see they were two young boys and two young girls. They talked loudly and laughed a lot. They had soft drinks standing at the counter. One of the girls went to the juke box and put some money in. The music came out loud and clear.

Nothing's gonna change my world
Nothing's gonna change my world

We remained sitting not saying a word. Marie and I finishing our coffee. Carol hunched over looking down at the table.

'What's wrong love,' I asked Carol.

'It's the noise,' she said. 'I can't stand it.'

Nothing's gonna change my world
Nothing's gonna change my world

I got up and awkwardly we left.

Outside it was warm. I started to walk briskly. I was first, then Marie, then Carol. And Carol became further and further away. I stopped to wait for her.

'I don't want to go back there,' she said.

'You can't come home yet.'

'I'll never come home,' she said.

We were approaching the hospital when I saw Carol leave the side of the road and start to walk towards the middle.

A car, coming from the opposite direction, blew its horn.

'Carol,' Marie shouted.

I ran over to Carol to try to make her come to the side of the road. But she shrugged me off.

More cars were coming at speed. They blew their horns. They took evasive action. One angry driver leaned out and shouted.

'Do you want to get killed?'

We were near the opening in the wall that led to the short drive and the bungalow-like building. The taxi was there. We waited for Carol. She came, slowly, away from the centre of the road and walked through the opening.

'I'm sorry,' she said quietly.

'Thanks for all the nice things. I had a lovely time. Will you come next week?'

'Yes,' we both said.

'You better go in, love,' I said.

We kissed outside the door.

She stood there with a plastic bag that had the remains of the hard-boiled eggs and the apples.

We went into the taxi that would take us to the railway station. As it drove away we waved.

And she went inside.

Why Do You Live So Far?

'WHY DON'T YOU go out?' Emily said. 'Do you know it's over a week that you haven't been out of the house?'

'I went out on Tuesday to the post office.'

'I meet people in the street. They all ask, And how is Joseph? What can I say? He's working. He's up in his room. He's busy. Why don't you go out and see people?'

'It costs money to see people,' I said. 'If I meet anyone they say let's go in for a drink. I'm too old to go bumming.'

'So what do we do? Play cards, read newspapers, and watch television. I'm tired watching television.'

'You're tired when we go to bed.'

'You expect me to be excited just because we're going to bed? Why don't you go out for a walk now? You'll feel better. Walk around the harbour, or through the town, go to the library.'

'I hate this place,' I said. 'All I can think of is how to get us out. I've got a sign up on the wall of my room, *You've got to get out of here*, facing me all the time. I don't want to end my life in this cut-off seaside joint.'

The phone rang.

'You answer it.'

'Now you don't even want to answer the phone,' she said and went out of the room to the kitchen.

I went up to this room, looked at the collection of picture postcards stuck on the large mirror. (When I look in the mirror, to see myself, the postcards give a 3-D effect.) They were from people scattered over North America, Africa, and Europe. I've stuck them on with sellotape with spaces of glass in between. I even have a postcard of Carnbray in with the others. A summer's day ... palm trees ... the sea a shade darker blue than the sky ... a large green-and-white yacht in the harbour ... people on a sand beach ...

As a postcard, I thought, I could like this place.

I went to my desk and looked at the pieces of paper listing what payments I expected to come in. They added up to £325. But I had learned not to count too much on other people paying when they said they would.

Next morning Emily had a letter from her mother in London, and with it came a money order for ten pounds for Christmas.

I got a small tree and put it up in the front room. I went and got some ivy and Emily put it around the room, on the walls near the ceiling. Cards began to come in. And I went out and had a drink in a pub with people I hadn't seen for several months.

On the evening of December 23rd we were waiting in the front room, which looked very nice and warm. We had the fire going in the fireplace. There were some coloured balls hanging from the lights. There was this nice-fitting red carpet. It's a splendid room with a large bay window and we only use it when people come, or perhaps in summer, for it's too cold. Emily had made some sandwiches and I got a bottle of sherry and wrapped it in coloured paper, and bought some extra glasses. We were waiting for the people Emily had been evacuated to during the war. They lived near Truro. Since our marriage they've sent a chicken for Christmas and I've given them a bottle of sherry. We sat in the large second-hand chairs with the scratched sides where the cat sharpened its claws, waiting for them to come. It was past seven. I thought they were late.

'They have to put the cows away,' Emily said, 'and do a lot of things before they can leave.'

A few minutes later we heard sounds outside the front door.

'That's them.'

'No,' I said, without knowing why. And it wasn't.

It was a wizened, hunched-up little woman, determined, thrusting her face forward. It was not a pretty face, although it had new blondish curls.

'Does Joseph Grand live here?'

It wasn't so much a question as an assertion. And it was said by my sister Mona from Meridian. I hadn't seen her for ten years.

Afterwards, she said I just stood there not saying anything but shaking my head.

I went outside and saw Oscar. He looked like a gentle wrestler. A squat little man with sleepy eyes, a hat on, a camera around his neck, a brand-new black coat and black gloves.

I shook Oscar's hand.

'Why didn't you write or phone or send a telegram?'

'I wanted to,' Oscar said, 'but your sister didn't let me.'

I looked into the taxi, half-expected to see my father and mother inside.

'I bet you're surprised,' Mona said excitedly when we were inside with the bags and hung up their coats. Oscar kept his hat on.

'Why didn't you let me know when you got to London?'

'We didn't want you to go to any trouble,' Mona said.

Oscar said: 'I've got a movie camera—I wanted to record the expression on your face when you saw your sister.'

I steered them into the front room. Mona lit a cigarette.

'You don't look like your pictures, Emily,' Mona said. 'You've lost weight,' she said to me. 'It suits you. The last time I saw you, you were fat. I thought you had heart trouble.'

Then the kids were introduced.

'This is Martha—this is Ella—this is Rebecca—.'

'They're like dolls,' Mona said.

'—this is your Uncle Oscar and your Auntie Mona. They've come all the way from Meridian in Canada. How was the trip?'

'Terrible,' Oscar said. 'We had to change twice on the train. You know it took longer to come down here from London than to fly from Montreal over to England. Why do you live so far?'

'If you sent a telegram or phoned,' I said, 'I would have told you what train to get. You wouldn't have had to change—'

'I told her,' Oscar said.

'I didn't want to put you to any trouble—shall we give them the presents?'

They brought their new bags into the front room and brought out gay bunny pyjamas for the kids. They gave Emily a Norwegian ski sweater.

'He always wears black,' Mona said. 'Why, I don't know. So I thought I'd get him a white sweater.'

It was a splendid sweater with a turtle-neck.

'You smoke?' Oscar said. And gave me several red-and-white flat tins of duty-free cigarettes.

'Thanks. Why didn't you write from Canada?'

'We didn't know if we were coming or not. You know your sister. She was terrified of flying.'

'Everyone told us to go to Miami,' Mona said. 'At this time of the year England, they said, would be full of smog, fog, accidents.'

'It was a toss-up,' Oscar said, 'whether to go to Disneyland or to come here.'

'Didn't you know *some*thing was in the air when I didn't write?' Mona said.

I didn't say anything to that. I couldn't remember when she last wrote.

'Here,' Oscar said to the children, taking out his wallet from his back buttoned-down pocket. 'From your Grannie and Grandpa in Canada—your Chanukah gelt.' And he gave them two pounds each. Our kids never had so much money.

My sister looked at the Christmas tree, the decorations, the cards.

'Do they know about Chanukah?'

The kids were silent.

'Your Daddy will tell you.' Then back to me in the same low disapproving voice:

'You celebrate Christmas?'

'We sort of have a tree—and I give out the presents on Christmas Day.'

'I always say, how you want to live your life that is your business,' Mona said.

The kids went upstairs to their rooms to try on their pyjamas.

'What would you like to drink?' I said confidently. It was the first time that year I had so much drink in the house. 'Scotch, gin, sherry, beer—'

'You have no rye?' Mona asked.

'No.'

'I won't bother.'

'Oscar. What'll you have?'

'I don't care for the stuff.'

'Won't anyone join me in a drink?'

'I'll have some sherry,' Emily said.

'Let me taste,' my sister said. 'It's not bad. I'll have a drop.'

'How's Maw and Paw?' I said.

'The same,' she said. 'Maw still works at the hospital.' Then suddenly brightening up. 'If they could only see the kids—Paw's got to go in for a check-up when we get back. You should see how nervous he was when we told him we were flying.'

I remembered the last time I saw him. We were waiting for the taxi to take me to the station. He was in his shirt. A towel around his head. He was in the middle of shaving. 'I hope I'll still be here next time you come,' he said and began to weep. 'Sure, Pop,' I said. How pathetic and kind he looked. Then we saw each other in the hall mirror. He pointed to his weeping face in the glass. 'I look like a Chinaman.'

I suggested to Emily that Mona and Oscar might like to have some coffee.

Mona hunted in one of their bags and came out with a jar of instant coffee and gave it to Emily.

'We drink a lot of coffee, and I heard you can't get good coffee over here.'

'We've got instant coffee,' Emily said.

'Oh, you have,' Mona said, puzzled. 'Well, we like it strong.'

As soon as Emily was out of the room, my sister said:

'I thought you said she was *half* Jewish.'

'I said that long ago, because of Maw. She asked me where did I get married? Who was the rabbi? Now she knows. I know she knows. She said if this happened in her time the family would be sitting Shiva.'

'I always say, the way you live your life that's your business,' Mona said.

Emily came back with the coffee, and she also had some hamburgers in buns that she made earlier and heated up.

'Gee, these taste good,' Oscar said.

'They're like we make them,' Mona said, somewhat surprised.

I was surprised how she had aged. I knew she was two years younger. But she looked in her forties. Except for her body, which was very slim. She sat hunched, her back curved, jaw thrust forward, smoking one cigarette after another.

I heard a car go up. We live on the side of a hill. Mona stopped eating. 'What was that?'

I told her.

She heard a rail outside the house rattle. People hold onto it for support as they walk up the hill. But it was loose.

'And what was *that*?'

We were all quiet.

'I heard something—it's upstairs,' she said.

I went upstairs.

'Nothing,' I said.

'Are you sure?'

'I've got to do this every night,' Oscar said. 'You should see the locks on our doors. And the bolts. And the chains. When I go away after breakfast she locks the double doors with double locks—they're special locks. Then the chains. And then the bolts. She even has a gun and a dog.'

'But what for?' I said.

'I don't know,' Mona said quietly.

'You weren't like that,' I said.

'Let me tell you,' Oscar said, with a sleepy grin. 'You've got some sister.'

Just before nine the farmer and his wife came. And it became a small party. They drank several gins too quickly. They gave us a chicken and pressed tongue. I gave them the bottle of sherry. They left presents for the kids under the tree. They thought it was marvellous to come and find people who had only twenty hours before been in Canada. The farmer's wife—bright faced, plump—and Mona found something to talk about.

'—I also had my gallstones out.'

'Mine burst,' Mona said, 'as the surgeon was putting it on the tray.'

But they couldn't stay as they had to get back to the farm.

Though the room had become much warmer, Oscar had not taken his hat off all evening. He had removed his suit-jacket, sweater and tie. With his hat on his head he went to sleep in the chair by the fireplace.

As soon as Mona saw that Oscar was asleep she said:

'What do you do about teaching the children religion?'

'We don't,' I said.

164

'Our kids celebrate Chanukah. They all wear Mogen Dovids around their necks—*This* is the Star of David, Emily,' Mona said, showing her the thin gold chain around her neck. 'In my home I have two sets of dishes. I light the candles on Shabbus. We eat bacon—but outside, in someone else's house. You might think that was hypocritical. Do you light the candles on Friday night?'

'If I did that, Mona, I'd feel hypocritical.'

'Who did you name Rebecca after?' Mona quickly changed the subject.

'After Aunt Rocheh,' I said. 'You may not remember her. She's the one that never married. I think she died when we were kids. How did you get Francine?'

'After Fruma—Oscar's grandmother.'

'Fruma is Frieda or Fanny,' I said.

'No,' she said. 'You can take anything from the Fs ...'

'But why just the Fs ...?' I said.

'Well, it's got to be *like* Fruma—you can have Faith, Felicity, Fawn.'

'They don't sound like Fruma to me.'

'They don't have to sound, long as the first letter's the same. For instance, your Rebecca is after Auntie Rocheh. Then you could have had Roxana, Roxy ...'

'That's the name of a cinema,' I said. 'Who's Lance after?'

'He is after Oscar's grandfather Laybel—he could have been Lawrence, Lorne ...'

'What about Lou or Lionel?'

'They're old-fashioned.'

Mona stubbed out her cigarette and immediately lit up another. I had noticed earlier the area of nicotine on her finger, but it was while I gave her a light that I noticed her hand was shaking.

'We don't let Francine go out with any English boys in Meridian. We send her away to Montreal during the holidays. She also learns Hebrew.'

'Girls in Canada,' I said, 'learn Hebrew?'

'Why not?' Mona said aggressively. 'I believe in God. Don't you?'

'No.'

'Don't *say* that,' Mona said. 'You must *never* say that.'

'Don't believe him,' Emily said, trying to calm her down.

'I believe in fate,' Mona said, 'that between Rosh Hoshannah and Yom Kippur your fate for the year is decided.'

'I don't go along with that,' I said.

No one spoke.

Then Mona chuckled. 'It's a good thing Oscar's asleep, otherwise he'd never forgive me for talking like this.'

We gave them our bedroom. We slept on a mattress in my office with coats over us. This arrangement was all right for tonight. But tomorrow we'd have to try and get some sheets and blankets from the woman next door.

Emily and I were trying to get to sleep. Our eyes seemed level with the gap at the bottom of the door that showed the light from the hall.

'She must have been saving that up for a long time,' Emily said. 'I wanted to like her.'

'I know,' I said. 'I've never felt terribly close to my sister.'

Fifteen years ago, in Montreal, I was asked to leave the middle of an English 10 class.

'Someone to see you,' the Dean's secretary said.

And there in the dark cool hall, under the Arts building clock, was my mother. A bit frightened but dressed nicely in a small blue hat, a new black coat, and dark gloves. She had come up, on her own, from Ottawa to try and make me change my mind about coming to Mona's wedding. I don't know what excuses I gave for not going. And I don't know why I chose my sister's wedding to make a stand.

My mother took me out for a meal, in a small restaurant on St Lawrence Main, which I enjoyed. It wasn't as good as her cooking, but it seemed ages since I had Jewish food. And the signed photographs on the wall of Max Baer, Al Jolson; her, all dressed up, across the table— the food—brought back my childhood on Murray Street; the stillness of the house on the Sabbath, with my mother, a handsome woman, sitting out the afternoons by the window. She wept—she may even have given me a few dollars—and I said I would come.

At the wedding I remember my father coming down the aisle with Mona. He was about the same size as Mona, but looked smaller. In a double-breasted blue serge suit which was cut down to fit him from one of my uncle's discarded suits. His lips pressed tight, near to tears, a little frightened. Away from the house he always looked lost.

Then the reception downstairs in the vestry rooms. There was something like three hundred guests. Most of them I didn't know. Perhaps I had, even then, gone further away from home than I thought. (The way the waiters were openly helping themselves to the booze—the way the people were stuffing themselves.) It seemed to me—at university because of the Veteran's Act, sixty dollars a month, which meant eating peanuts in the last week—that my mother, who had cleaned out her bank account for this wedding, was feeding a lot of strangers.

I remember the young rabbi sitting in front of me, eyes moving continuously. He was new, 'from outa town.' And ate very quickly. Then he got up to make his speech. He talked of Mona, whom he had never seen before.

'Mona, today you are a Princess. Oscar, you are a Prince.'

Earlier that week Princess Elizabeth and the Duke of Edinburgh had got married.

Then he sat down, mumbled quickly and indistinctly his after-eating prayers, gave a few little shakes of his body, and vanished.

Next morning Emily and I and the kids were up early. The kids were very excited. Oscar and Mona came down after ten. Said they slept well. Didn't eat very much but drank endless cups of coffee that Emily kept making and smoked cigarettes.

It was the coldest winter England had for over a century. And though there have been Christmases in this resort where I have been able to walk about without a coat, this time we had fires going in every room. Fortunately our lavatories didn't freeze, though the neighbours' did.

Oscar became a great favourite with the kids. He had a way with children. He sat two of them on one of his knees. He told them stories about Canada and their summer cottage by a lake.

'... we've also got a speedboat and we go through the lakes. You could come up and stay at the cottage with us and have some of Mona's blueberry pie and see the animals. You've never seen a skunk. They come right up to the cottage ...'

He spoke in a sleepy, genial way. The kids loved him.

'Why don't you go back?' he said.

'We'll see—maybe next year.'

'You owe it to the kids,' he said.

Mona began to speak in Yiddish. 'Was it a question of money?' Emily and the kids just looked on, puzzled.

'It's a bit more complicated,' I said in English.

'How about if we take the kids back with us?' Oscar said. 'We'll take Martha and Ella. We'll look after them and they can go and stay with us in the summer at the cottage.'

Martha and Ella were hugging Oscar.

I didn't think for a minute he was serious.

'Look,' Oscar said. 'We can take them back for nothing on our tickets. We'll feed them, look after them. It's not a question of adopting them. They're yours.'

'We'll see,' I said to the two excited kids. It hurt the way they were so willing to go away from us.

Whenever Mona didn't want the kids to understand something she began to talk in Yiddish. Until I finally decided to send the kids into the other room. Only to have Rebecca come back upset.

'They're whispering,' she said. 'They've got secrets.'

It was nearly noon and we hadn't left the kitchen table. I suggested I might take them out, show them the place, and get some fresh air, so as to give Emily a chance to clear up and do some shopping.

It was freezing outside. There was no one out. The puddles in the narrow streets were frozen. The long fine sand beaches were empty. The water in the bay was grey. No boats in the harbour, only a few gulls were huddled together at the harbour's entrance, facing the wind.

'You should see it in the summer,' I said.

'I can imagine,' Mona said, huddled up in her Persian lamb coat. 'It sure is a nice-looking place.'

Oscar took coloured moving pictures of Mona and myself and the kids. And of the empty streets, the empty restaurants, the empty beaches, and boarded-up shops. Then we came back with rosy cheeks and sat around the fire in the dining-room.

'It's healthy the fire here,' Mona said, lighting up a cigarette. 'Not like our place—so stuffy.'

I went outside in the courtyard with the coal-bucket and came back with it full to the top.

'You know what you remind me,' Mona said, 'you coming in like that—with the pail of coal?'

'I know,' I said. 'Paw.'

There were times when I went out to get the coal from the shed in the courtyard that I remembered my father coming up from the cellar in the house on Murray Street, with a bucketful of coal for the Quebec stove in the hall. Just as there were times, upstairs in my room, when I was making out a list of payments to come, and remembered him and his black book with his list of people owing him money.

'Do you remember you telling me: Don't let boys touch you between *here*,' she drew a line across her neck, 'and *there*.' Another line at the knees. 'And you remember when you were at university and I saw you in Montreal. You had written that song. When you met me you gave me twenty dollars. I said no. What, you said, it's not enough. And gave me another twenty.'

I didn't remember either of these.

Instead, I remembered when she was about eight or nine. When she was hit with a stone from a slingshot. It cut her head. They had to shave her head. And she wore a beret. She wore it in school. And the kids made fun of her.

'And you remember my wedding?' Mona said. 'You remember Betty's fiancé, Sam? He was supposed to take a movie of the reception. But all he took was pictures of Betty ...'

I didn't remember that either. I remembered Mona being sick. The doctor came to examine her. He gave her a large bar of chocolate for being a good girl. She gave me some. And we went upstairs and ate it in her room. Later, I watched the long, thin, white-yellow worms come out of her mouth and lie slowly twisting on the floor.

Mona and Oscar had never seen Christmas before except in the movies. So I briefed them.

'This is the way it's going to be tomorrow. We wake up in the morning. We say Happy Christmas to each other. Then the kids come down. We have breakfast. Then go into the front room. And I read out the names and give out the presents.'

When they heard this they went out and came back loaded with presents that they wrapped up in their room and put under the tree.

'I arranged for a taxi to come on Boxing Day,' I said. 'We'll drive around and see some of the country around here.'

'I thought you told Maw you had a jalopy.'

'I might have said that,' I said, 'for Maw's sake.'

In the evening we sat around and watched television.

'They've got the same programs here,' Mona said, 'as we've got in Meridian.'

'They're American shows,' I said.

We watched a quiz show for children. 'Your TV is so much better than ours,' Mona said. 'It's so educational.'

But they were mainly interested in the commercials.

After the news I switched off and we sat around the fire, drank coffee, and smoked cigarettes.

'Why don't you go back to Canada?' Oscar said.

'It takes money to get out of here,' I said. 'And maybe, now, I've lived too long away.'

'With your education you could have been a doctor,' Mona said.

'Its true,' she said to Emily.

'But I'm a writer,' I said. 'How many doctors has Canada got—thousands. How many writers? A handful. It's easier to be a doctor than a writer.'

'Yeh, I know,' Mona said sadly. 'But it's hard.'

I went and got some whisky—no one joined me.

'In a year's time I figure I'll make enough money to retire,' Oscar said.

'Talk, talk,' Mona said. 'That's easy.'

'You'll see if I don't,' Oscar said. 'I'd be half way there if it wasn't for her operations. You know, she's had half a dozen already.'

'It's true,' Mona said.

Oscar I knew was in the scrap-metal business. But he bought anything that he could sell at a profit. He would fill up his warehouse and then load up a truck and drive the stuff to Montreal or Toronto and sell it.

'I've got to ring her up *every* night,' Oscar said, 'when I'm away from Meridian.'

'We've got a system where we don't have to pay,' Mona said. 'If we don't want to talk but just let the other one know that he arrived in Montreal or Toronto—Oscar asks person-to-person and makes up some name like Johnson. 'May I speak to Mr Johnson,' he says. And I say, 'I'm sorry Mr Johnson is not in.' And I know he got there all right.'

'You think *that's* something,' Oscar said. 'We know a woman who rings up Montreal long distance to get her kosher meat. She'd call up the butcher and say. 'Is Chuck in?' And of course the man would say that Chuck wasn't in. But he knew that meant she wanted chuck that week.'

'We've got three properties in Meridian,' Mona said. 'So you could come and stay there. I know it's a small out-of-the-way place. But until you find your feet.'

'Thanks,' I said.

But I didn't see much point in exchanging one small town for another. I desperately wanted to get out of this seaside town and live in London again. It's a cosmopolitan city that I miss. I try to go to London as often as I can, but it's expensive. Even so, a few days in London and I come back as if I had a shot in the arm. I feel sharper in London. I go through the streets and feel like singing. I do sing. I go to bed in London feeling slim and not the way I feel here, as if I'm carrying a large body with lots of weight and deadness.

'I've got to get us out,' I told them. 'There are times I've just got to take myself away from here. So I take a train to Plymouth. And just to walk down straight streets again. Until about noon it's fine. After that, I know I've got to come back to this place.'

'Do you miss London, Emily?' Mona said.

'It's my home town. There are days here when I feel life is going by—day after day the same—and you're waiting for something to happen.'

'Like us coming,' Oscar said.

And we all laughed.

On Christmas morning the kids were up early. Emily had filled up their stockings by their beds when they were asleep. And by the time we all came down for breakfast the kids were excited and some of that excitement went over to us. We all said Happy Christmas. And after some coffee we went in the front room. It looked cold outside, no snow but the puddles were frozen. Emily had the large open fire blazing away in each room.

I began to call out the presents. The children's first.

'This is for Rebecca from Uncle Oscar and Auntie Mona—I wonder what it is?' And the excited child undid the parcel and showered Mona and Oscar with kisses. 'Who's this for——?'

Martha, just over nine, got a toilet set from them. There were things for cleaning her nails, plucking her eyebrows, putting on nail polish, and some perfume. The others got the most expensive dolls in the place. I know, I saw them in the store window. It embarrassed Emily more than it did me. There were boxes of candies from Emily's relations, reading-books, and colouring-books for the children, toys, bits of jewellery, and soap, and lots of handkerchiefs.

Around two we sat around the table in the dining-room, all seven of us, for dinner. Emily brought in the turkey. 'It's nearly twelve pounds,' I said. And all the kids said Ah and looked excited.

'You think that's big,' Oscar said to the kids. 'If you come to Canada you'll have turkeys twice that size. You remember,' he said to Mona, 'the turkeys we had that time?'

'Canadian turkeys are a little bigger,' Mona said politely.

On the last night we were sitting around the fire, watching some play on television. I decided to switch off. I went out to get some more coal in the bucket. When I came back Oscar was saying:

'... one thing we got for sure. A place in the ground. It's six feet long, three feet wide.' He moved his hand as if he was measuring. 'And six feet deep.'

I noticed Emily getting flushed. She turned her head away from Oscar. 'Stop it. Stop it,' she said quietly.

'It's all the same,' Oscar went on taking no notice. 'We'll all have it in the end.'

Emily turned her head away from us all. 'I'm sorry,' she said. And, weeping, got up and went out of the room.

Mona and Oscar looked astonished.

'Is she upset?' Mona said.

'No,' I said, sarcastically.

'She's got to accept this, you know,' Oscar said. 'It's no use running away.'

'She doesn't accept it,' I said.

'But we all got to die,' my sister said.

'I think,' I said, 'you brought back her father.'

'So?' Oscar said. 'I buried my mother.'

'Maybe you better go and speak to her,' Mona said.

I went. Emily had stopped crying, although her face looked as if she hadn't. I put my arms around her and kissed her.

'I'm sorry,' she said. And I kissed her again.

'It was a lot of things. It was suddenly as if I realized that she, they, being a Jew. As if I was an outsider and we weren't close, man and woman, like we are when she goes on talking Jewish. This is my house she's in and I suddenly felt we'll die and they are able to believe in something—that you are part of, and I'm not. And there isn't anything I could do about it.'

I kissed her again. 'Let's go back in.'

We did.

'I'm sorry,' Emily said.

'He's going to put us all in a story,' Mona said, 'just watch.'

'I don't care,' Oscar said. Then turning to me. 'If you can make a buck out of it—that's okay with me.'

I phoned up London and fixed them up with a room in the Strand Palace. 'It's so much with a bath and so much without,' I said.

'We'll have without,' Mona said.

They were going to London because Oscar wanted to do a round-up of some of the places he knew when he was a soldier over here in the war.

'I'll cry when I say goodbye,' Mona said. 'I don't know why. I'm not like him. I'm like Paw. I cry.'

We had to wait for the train at the station. Mona looked at Oscar. And Oscar put out his hand to shake mine.

I felt a piece of paper in my palm. I looked and saw it was a five-pound note.

'Thanks,' I said, and gave it back to him. Since two of the kids were with us there was no scene.

'My pocket is deeper than yours,' Oscar said, still holding the note out for me.

I put my hand in my coat pocket. Then put my hand in his pocket.

'It *is* deeper,' I said.

Then the train came. I went in with their luggage and got them an empty compartment and kissed my sister. She wept, without a sound, her face screwed up. And I thought how like my father she looked. I shook hands and embraced Oscar.

They rang up that night to say they got in OK and the room was fine, the hotel was fine and a blizzard was on. I told them to go to Blooms in Whitechapel for a meal.

Next night Mona spoke to Emily. They decided to go back tomorrow morning. London they found was expensive. ('There are no bargains.') The weather was miserable. And they missed their kids.

On the morning they were to take off, we returned the bedding to our neighbour, cleared the rooms. Nothing had really changed. And again that feeling of being cut off, and the need to get out of here. Luckily one of the payments came through. So I took myself off to Plymouth. Went to see the new books and the new magazines at W.H. Smith's. Had some coffee and doughnuts at Joe Lyon's. Saw a bad movie. Had a meal. And came back. On the following Monday we got a letter from Mona. On page two she said:

> ... Dad was operated on this morning and it's a good job they did as both doctors said he wouldn't have lasted four months. I never saw such a big stone that he had in his bladder. The doctor said he got through better than average. We saw and spoke to him but he was in pain and got his hypo so thought we had better leave so he could rest. Poor Mom she looks terrible and it's taking a lot out of her. As soon as I hear anymore will let you know.

On January 22nd came another letter.

It has been sometime since we heard from you and hope all is well. Saw Dad yesterday afternoon and he got his stitches out and is looking better. I saw the doctor and asked him how he is getting along and he said as well as can be expected. Dad seems confused at times though. We brought the children yesterday and he was happy to see them. He's well looked after.

February 2nd, Meridian.

Hope all is well with you. Haven't been down to see Dad the last while and everytime I spoke to Mom she seemed upset so yesterday afternoon I got the cleaning woman to watch the children and went down to see him. I also saw the doctor. He says Dad is coming along but is confused and that he doesn't know if he'll get better. He wants to put him in a rest home if he can get him in. The other day he went out in his pyjamas and it was below zero. I don't think he realizes he's in hospital. He recognizes us all but talks as if we were still living on Murray Street and gets confused.

February 25th, Meridian.

Dad was moved to the nursing home on Friday and went down yesterday to see him. He seems much happier and I don't know if he realizes where he is or not. At night they put a restrainer on him so he won't get out. Thursday morning at the hospital they found him outside at the Parking Lot. It was his fourth time out.

March 10th, Meridian.

Hope all is well and what's the matter I haven't heard from you? Saw Dad on Thursday and he was so happy to see me. Apparently he got out again so when I was there the Director of the Nursing Home spoke to me and asked me to tell him not to go out and he got angry with me and said how can I get out as you see I'm lying here.

April 6th, Meridian.

Last week he got out with just his clothes and slippers and the Nursing Home is past the exhibition grounds and he walked to Bank Street and went in a restaurant (he had no money) they gave him a cup of coffee and phoned the Nursing Home and an orderly came with a taxi and got him.

'For some reason he wants to get out,' I said to Emily. 'But once out he doesn't know what to do. It's at the opposite end of town from where we live. He doesn't know how to get home from there. I don't know why, but I'm proud of him running away like this ...' Tears were coming to my eyes. And with Mona's letter I went upstairs to my room. There was the sign. *You've got to get out of here*, facing me on the wall. The mirror with the postcards.

I went to the window. It overlooked a small valley of cottages. There was a funeral taking place in the street immediately below. The hearse with the glass sides had driven up outside a small stone cottage. Men in black brought out the light wood coffin. And heaped it with bright yellow flowers in the hearse. The mourners walked behind it. They seemed to walk like mechanical toys.

I stood at the window, over to the side, so they couldn't see me and watched them go by.

From this window I have now watched several funerals. They were all of people I didn't know.

A Visit

THE PHONE WOKE US.

We let it ring. And looked anxiously at one another.

'Answer it,' Emily said urgently.

I got out of bed and ran up the stairs to the office in the attic. At this time of night it could mean only one thing, someone was calling from Canada.

'I have a call for you,' the operator said. 'Go ahead.'

'Gordon,' an excited woman's voice said. 'It's Mona.'

'Hullo Mona.'

'Did I get you out of bed?'

'Yes. It's after three in the morning.'

'I'm sorry,' she said. 'Nothing's wrong. But I thought I'd ring to let you know that I'm coming over with Ma on Wednesday. We're flying from Montreal.'

'I thought Ma was to come on her own?'

'It's the first time for her in an airplane. She asked me if I could go with her. Is that OK?'

'We can put Ma up,' I said. 'But there's no more room.'

'I don't mind where you find me a place,' she said. 'I thought I'd bring Chuck as well. It will probably be the only chance he'll have.'

'July is the height of the season,' I said. 'It will be difficult to find a place.'

Suddenly I felt cold in the almost dark attic room. The only bit of light, moonlight, came from the uncurtained windows. And I could see the slate of the roofs glistening, the stars.

'I don't mind where you put us up,' she said. 'Any hotel will do, Gordon. As long as it's near you. Is that OK?'

'Yeh,' I said. 'That's great.'

'Are you sure?'

'Yes,' I said. 'That's fine. What time have you got?'

'After ten—I'm sorry I got you out of bed. You're sure it's OK?'

'It's fine,' I said.

Back in bed I said to Emily. 'You heard the conversation. My mother is coming over with my sister on Wednesday. I told her to spend the first day in London and come down the next so they won't be too tired. Mona is bringing her boy.'

'I could hear you say fine, fine,' Emily said. 'And I knew you didn't think it was fine at all.'

We lay on our backs unable to sleep. I didn't know what Emily was thinking. But I guessed she was as anxious about this visit as I was. For neither she nor the kids had met my mother. All these years, I thought, I managed to keep the two sides of the family apart.

'Where do you think we'll get them in?' Emily asked.

'We can try Miss Benson down the road. It's only for a couple of weeks.'

'Remember when your sister came with her husband? They walked in from Canada unannounced.'

'I remember.'

'You don't think they will do something like that again?'

'No,' I said. 'I told Mona to stay Wednesday in London. They won't be here until late Thursday afternoon.'

But I was wrong.

They arrived on Wednesday. No one to meet them. They opened the door and stood in the hall, looking tired and nervous. Mona grey in the face, Chuck vacant, mother neat and self-contained in her navy blue suit. As I came further down the stairs, I called out to Emily, who was in the kitchen. There was some kissing and tears from mother, Emily, Mona, and the children. I paid the taxi-driver. We moved into the front room. And they sat down exhausted.

'Why didn't you stay the day in London?' I asked Mona.

'We couldn't get into a hotel.'

'How many did you try?'

'One,' she said. 'Then they told us at the air terminal that if we rushed we might get the train for down here. You should have seen how fast that taxi went. We got to the station. No time to get tickets. We ran to get on the train. It's been like that since we left Montreal.'

Mona lit another cigarette.

'I was told back home not to go Air Canada. That BOAC was better. *She* got the tickets. She said we're going first class. I told her, no. Our tickets were economy. She insisted they were first. At Dorval the British plane had engine trouble. Another scramble. I was going around getting nervous, while she goes on as if she has all the time in the world. When they said we *had* to go Air Canada—I just stood there and laughed.'

'It was a very good flight,' mother said. 'I enjoyed it. She looks like a Raport,' she said about our eldest girl, Martha. 'Except the Raports are dark and she is blonde. Kate must look like your side of the family, Emily. Judith looks like one of us.'

They brought out their presents. Emily made tea. And, on the quiet, sent out Martha to get some fish for supper. Mother said she wouldn't eat meat, it wasn't kosher, only fish. I got Chuck and Mona into Miss Benson's. And they went there after supper. Mother had our bedroom. Emily and I would sleep on the mattress in the attic-office. I thought I'd better see if mother had settled in.

I saw her, sitting up in bed, giving candies to the kids. She looked refreshed and excited. She was patting the bed around her and saying:

'Come, sit down. And I'll tell you—'

Next morning when I went to open the front door to get the milk there was Mona and Chuck.

'Hi,' Mona said. 'We've been up early. I couldn't sleep. Neither could he. He came and sat outside my door until I got up.'

Mother came down. She said she slept well. And while Emily was making breakfast she and Mona opened their purses, gave the kids five pounds each and ten pounds to Emily and me.

'Where is the nearest bank,' Mona said. 'I need to cash some traveller's cheques.'

'Me too,' mother said.

When they came back they had bags filled with grapes, peaches, apples, oranges, cherries, bananas, pears. I don't remember having so much fruit in the house—not since I lived in Canada.

'People live differently over here,' mother said. 'It's more slow. I like it.'

She was curious about British money. And in no time she was doing sums in her head faster than any of us. They had bought postcards—showing the harbour, the beaches, the bay—to send to people in Canada. Mother insisted that Mona write hers for her since she wrote English phonetically. (I remember her criticism of my last book: 'Why do you always write about bed people.' Or the time after father died she wrote: 'He was not used to go out with the hearse'—meaning horse.) And they soon got into an argument. Mona wanted to write the same message on each card. Mother wanted each one to be different. You would think they disliked each other the way they were talking.

'That's a lot of cards,' I said in an attempt to break up the squabble.

'I've sent twenty-five,' mother said. 'And I'm not finished. Everybody likes me. All my friends are millionaires.'

'That must be comforting,' I said.

'It's true,' mother said.

'I stayed at the Queen Elizabeth,' Mona said. '$31.75 a night. Hamburgers and chips cost $3.75.'

'The way you do your washing,' mother said to Emily who had come in from the courtyard, 'and hang it on the line and pull it up. It's just like the old country.' And when she saw the enamel casserole with the purple-blue cover. 'I haven't seen one like that since I left Poland.' We looked at the bottom. It said *Made in Poland*.

But I remember in Canada when I asked her why did she leave Poland. She wouldn't say except something about taxes being high. When I said I'd like to go to Poland and see where she and Pa lived, she said, 'It would be better if you didn't go. If you could do without.'

And here she was excited because of seeing washing on a line, an enamel casserole, and narrow cobblestone streets.

The kids took them to the beach. They stayed there until late afternoon. Mona swam and lay on the sand. Mother walked by the tideline and picked small delicate pink shells that she brought back to her room. In a few days they looked much better, especially Mona, more relaxed. And they had caught the sun.

'We met this couple on the beach,' Mona said. 'They're on holiday from Scotland. They pay forty pounds a week rent for a house here. He earns fifty pounds a week—he must save up. They have a car—it cost them twelve hundred pounds—is that a lot?'

'Guess how much this tan is costing me?' mother interrupted.

'I don't know,' I said.

'Take a guess.'

'Five hundred dollars?'

'Seven hundred and fifty,' she said with pride.

Chuck was left with us. He didn't like to go outside. He was frightened of steps, of a hill, and the beach. The first time he saw the sand he couldn't understand why we didn't fall through it. And when he was left on his own he would talk in these two voices. One was high, the other low. He would talk rapidly, in a sing-song. High. Low. I couldn't make out what he was saying. The first time I heard him I asked.

'What are you doing?'

'Talking to myself,' he said quietly.

He liked to watch television. The Americans were sending two men to land on the moon. And Chuck knew all the astronauts' names and what they had to do. He knew every stage of the journey into space. He rushed in.

'Halfway—moon gravity—'

He would stand in front of the television, only a few feet away. When he became excited he would bring his hands up by the side of his face, fingers wide apart, and they would quiver.

On days that it rained we sat around the breakfast table listening to the noise on the roof while Mona told the kids' fortunes in their tea leaves. She had complete faith in doctors and tea leaves. And mother asked Emily for the recipes of some of the things she had baked—cakes and desserts— so that she could make them for her Golden Age club when she got back. She showed us photographs. They were of elderly ladies sitting, all dressed up, by long tables with white table-cloths.

On the fourth morning it was drizzling. I was coming down the stairs. There was a nice smell of cooking from the kitchen. I saw Chuck at the bottom.

'You're *fame-us*,' he said to me as I came down. 'Me see you on TV. *Fame-us*.' Then he looked at his face in the hall-mirror and said to himself 'Fame-us. Fame-us.'

Inside the front room Mona continued to chain-smoke. Mother was in a chair by the window, looking out. She looked at the valley of granite cottages, the houses on the other side of the hill.

'I like this,' she said.

It was a summer light rain. It gave the slate roofs of the cottages a blue colour.

'Could you live here?' I asked her.

'It's nice. But not for me. I'm used to a different life.'

She looked around the room, at the shabby furniture, the damp walls, the shelves of books, the worn red carpet.

'Did you ever think of changing your job?'

'And do what?'

'You could work yourself up and become a journalist.'

'Journalists come down to interview me.'

'But what have you got?' she said. 'No home of your own. No new furniture. Children need nice clothes. Appearance *is* important.'

I didn't think it mattered much. But perhaps it mattered more than I ever admitted. Else why did I always meet people who came from Canada, to see me, in a pub. Then take them for a conducted tour of this seaside town, ending with a call on a rich acquaintance who had a large granite house with a drive, wide lawns and gardens, above the bay. So they could go back with that. Was that so different from what she was saying?

'You remember Lionel?' mother said.

I said nothing.

'I betcha he makes thirty thousand dollars a year. Maybe more. And his brother, Jackie, the one you played ball with. He makes forty thousand dollars, at least.'

And Mona said. 'Cousin Lily's daughter got married. You should see what they got. They have black leather Mediterranean chairs and settee. They have a new sports car. They pay two hundred dollars a month and they have a swimming pool. And it's so nice. Music comes in all the rooms—all the day.'

'It's wonderful,' mother said. 'I'm telling you—it's wonderful.'

Emily had come in to join us. I wanted to change the subject. Mona had put out a cigarette and lit up yet another.

'Why don't you ease up on the smoking,' I said to her.

'I tried. But I can't. It's my nerves. I need a cigarette. I tried candies but they don't work. What can I do?'

'Many men smoke,' I said. 'But Fu Manchu.'

Only Emily laughed.

'You should go and see Israel,' mother said. 'It's wonderful. For three hundred and fifty dollars you stay at the David Hotel. You have a table full of fish. You take what fish you want. You pay no more. No tips. Nothing. It's wonderful.'

'But you haven't been there,' I said.

'People who have tell me,' she said quietly.

I went out of the room and when I came back mother was saying: 'I have had two proposals so I went and asked the doctor. He said what do you need another man to get sick on you and you have to look after him. I'm sixty-seven but I look sixty-one or sixty-two.'

I didn't expect to be but I was taken back by this.

A few moments later tears appeared in her eyes. 'Next year will be the fiftieth anniversary of my getting married.' She rubbed the back of her hand against her eyes.

'How old is Chuck?' I quickly asked Mona.

'Twenty,' she said.

'What are you going to do when he gets older?' mother said.

'What do you mean?' Mona came back.

'You should get out of Meridian,' mother said. 'Go to Toronto—you might meet someone there. You ought to marry again.'

Chuck came in very excited.

'Landed on moon. Landed.'

Then he went back, to the other room, to watch television.

'What do you and Gordon do, Emily, on Saturday nights?' Mona asked. 'Do you go out?'

'We stay in and watch television.'

'That's just like Chuck and me. That's what we do, every Saturday night.'

Next morning it was bright and sunny. We were sitting around the kitchen table having breakfast. Mother was talking. She was telling the children: '—your grandfather was an architect. He came over to Montreal in 1904. He stayed a couple of years. But he didn't like the life. So he went back to Poland.'

When the phone went.

Emily answered. She spoke quietly, didn't say much, and hung up.

'That was my mother to say Florrie died,' she said and went into the back kitchen.

'I knew someone was going to die,' Mona said. 'Because of the birds. They were so loud this morning. They woke me up.'

'Those are gulls,' I said. 'They are with us all the time.'

'I thought it would be one of us,' she said.

I went to see Emily. She was standing in the sunny courtyard against the whitewashed wall crying.

Mother, Mona, and Chuck went with the kids to the beach.

I remember Florrie. We spent our honeymoon at their farm, about forty miles from here. Emily was evacuated from London during the war. She came to Cornwall with her name on a luggage label around her neck. Florrie picked her out, at the station, from all the other kids because she said she was dressed in a nice fawn coat. She lived the war years with Florrie and her husband, Morley. Helped to bring the cows in, helped with the milking. Bicycled and walked around the country roads, the fields with the derelict mine shafts. 'I used to write letters to my parents,' Emily said, 'saying I hate it here, take me away, they make me work. Now I look upon it as one of the happiest times of my life. I was lucky— it's like having a bonus. Now Florrie is dead and something has ended.'

And I remembered Florrie coming every Christmas with our Christmas goose or turkey. 'A dear little family,' she called us. And the last time, when we told her we were all going up to London for a holiday and would be on the Cornish Riviera Express, Florrie said she would come out and wave a white table-cloth. We all stood in the corridor of the train looking out as we came near the place where Emily grew up. And there, in the distance, the white table-cloth moved slowly in the breeze—as we waved our handkerchiefs back.

The funeral on Sunday was in a Methodist Chapel. Very plain except for the organ. The chapel was packed. The singing was loud and excellent. And I sang as loud as I could because Florrie was the only one who said I could sing. Everyone else says I can't keep a tune.

Then we went to the cemetery. There was this tall church on top of a hill with the cemetery on the steep grass slope. There were fields with hedges and trees on both sides. As we stood by the open grave, a cow was going across the field opposite us. Emily saw faces of people she knew twenty-five years ago. And she showed me the gravestones of Florrie's father, of Morley's mother and cousin. Trees, grass, fields. It somehow felt right, here, in the cemetery. And I envied people who knew where they were going to be buried.

When we came back and opened the front door we could hear singing. Mother and Mona were in the courtyard clapping their hands and singing with the kids.

Oh, how we danced
On the night we were wed ...

We didn't want to see them. So we went upstairs to the attic room. Emily went to the window and looked out at the deep blue water in the bay, the stone cottages, the far shore fields.

'I hate the sea,' she said and began to cry. 'I wish I belonged to some-thing. I don't belong to anything. There's your mother, your sister, and yourself—you all belong to something. Even if you have run away from it. And there's Florrie and Morley—they belong to something.'

I thought, where do I belong? Where does Emily? Mother? Mona?

Although it was after six in the evening the light was still bright. The sky had high summer clouds. And they were lit up by greens, light pinks, and orange. A gull was making its honking noise close by. And further away it was answered by another.

I could hear the children, inside, around the piano. They were playing a duet and singing loudly, 'Things aint what they used to be.'

There was still another week to go but I was marking off the days. I found myself coming up to the attic to get away from the constant talk they kept up. Even the kids no longer listened to what they were told and had stopped being on their best behaviour. Judith had one of her little bursts of temperament and answered Emily back. When Mona heard this she said,

'Judith, you remind me of me. What's the matter honey? You don't look pleased.'

Emily was also becoming edgy. When she asked me to do something. And I said I would do it later.

'You're like your mother,' she came back sharply. 'You both live as if life goes on forever. But I don't think that way. I know there isn't much time. When a week goes by and I haven't done something, I feel I've squandered a bit of my life. But both of you think you have all the time in the world.'

They could have stayed another week with us. But I told them they ought to see London while they were over here. They didn't want to very much. I said I would phone and get them a room in a hotel. It had to be central as Chuck couldn't get on a bus.

'How about twenty-five dollars a night?' I called from the phone. Mona agreed.

Mother was against it. 'Twenty-five dollars just to sleep in a bed?' In the end I got them something cheaper.

'Type me out a list of what to see,' Mona said. 'Put, first, *Fiddler on the Roof*. And I want to travel on the train first class.'

The last morning came.

'How time flies,' mother said at breakfast. 'It went so quickly.'

Mona came in without Chuck. She seemed to shrink physically in size and become anxious. Except for the tan, she looked like she did when she arrived. 'I can't get Chuck out of bed,' she said. 'He's hiding under the bed-clothes. He doesn't want to get up today. He thinks if he doesn't get up we won't have to go.'

'I'll go and get him,' mother said.

And she did. She came walking back with him, holding his arm in a tight grip so that she took most of his weight.

'Look at us,' she called out. 'We are going steady.'

When the taxi came Mona and mother wept as they kissed the kids. We went with them to the mainline station.

'It's like Europe,' mother said as the taxi drove through the country. 'It looks so nice here, the fields, the trees.'

Mona and Chuck looked lost. I had a feeling, even then, that they were waiting for me to say: why don't you stay the last week here.

But I didn't say it.

At the mainline station we had to wait for the train. I walked up and down the platform. Mother came over.

'You wear your heels down the same way as your father.'

And when I went to kiss her goodbye she offered me her face sideways —just like Kate, I thought.

Coming back in the taxi Emily and I were silent for several miles. Then Emily said:

'She came too late.'

'Yes,' I said.

The hedges, the small green fields, were by us on both sides. Then the first glimpse of the sea and the hovering gulls.

When I opened the front door one of the kids was playing Happy Birthday on the piano. I had forgotten it was Emily's birthday. The kids had set the kitchen table. In the middle there was a chocolate cake with small candies. And birthday cards were on the dresser.

We sat in our places around the table. Emily lit the candles on the cake. Judith pulled the curtain across the window. It was nice by candlelight.

We joined hands and sang Happy Birthday.

Then Emily stood up and took a deep breath.

'Make a wish,' Kate said excitedly.

Emily hesitated. Then blew out the candles.

We all applauded.

Judith moved the curtain and let the daylight back into the room.

Then we began to eat.

Thin Ice

IN THE SPRING OF 1965 a book of mine was published. And it got more notice and sold more copies than all my previous books combined. It was translated into several languages. The CBC and the BBC made half-hour films because of it. It went into paperback. Money began to come in from various places. Someone in Madrid wanted to use extracts in an English for foreigners textbook. Someone in Halifax wanted to make a recording of it for the blind. I was interviewed for British newspapers and magazines. Articles were written. I received a number of invitations: to open a new primary school in Cornwall, to give talks, to give readings. And one invitation came from the head of the English department of a university in the Maritimes offering three months as resident writer beginning in January. As I didn't know the Atlantic provinces and as I wanted to be back in Canada, I decided to go.

I arrived by plane on January 6th. I was met at the airport which consisted almost entirely of fields of snow piled high and long drifts. 'I can't remember when we've had so much snow and such cold weather,' the head of the English department said. 'We're blaming the Russians.'

His face reminded me of an Indian Chief but he smiled easily and was smartly dressed in a black winter coat, a white scarf, and a black Astrakhan hat that he wore tilted to the side. He drove, in a large low car with chains on the tires, to the best hotel in the city and led me to the top floor, to two comfortable rooms.

'Will this be all right?'

'Yes,' I said.

Suddenly the life of a near-recluse that I had lived before changed. I was interviewed for the student newspaper, the town's daily paper, the local radio and TV. I was invited to contribute a regular article to the local monthly magazine. The commercial radio station would phone up and ask what did I think of a particular current topic? And what I said on the phone was taped and then broadcast. There was a display of my books and manuscripts (in glass cases) in the university library. The main bookshop in the place filled a window with my books. I gave talks and readings to a variety of women's and men's clubs. The leading Jewish businessman, Pettigorsky (he owned the largest department store), gave a dinner in my honour at the Jewish community centre. After a filling meal (that included soup and mandlen, chicken, blintzes, and lockshen kugel) and I had made my speech and everyone was standing up and drinking and smoking, Mr Pettigorsky came over.

'It will take you a while to get used to living here,' he said apologetically. 'The first year you'll hate it. The second won't be so bad. After you have lived here three years you won't want to leave.'

But I liked it from the start.

I enjoyed going to the various teas, luncheons and dinners. I liked being asked to meet visiting VIP's who were passing through. Besides professors and undergraduates, I was also meeting judges, politicians, engineers, surgeons, scientists, army officers, restaurateurs, businessmen.

And I had this warm office in the Arts building that overlooked the snow-covered campus and the city. I would go to the office, twice a week, and there would be people outside the door waiting to see me. I was like a doctor. Undergraduates would come—possibly with their ailments, but they would express it differently. Girls would say: 'My boy-friend's too shy to come, but I've come,' and say that he was trying to write a novel.

I was the first resident writer the university of this town had. And, after the early hectic weeks, it was mainly people not to do with the university who came to see me.

The first were two Army Officers' wives from the large Army camp some miles outside the city. They told me that they were from Toronto and Vancouver and were only temporarily at the camp. They were going to put on a musical and wanted my approval. They intended to use the tunes of familiar songs—'Somewhere Over the Rainbow,' 'You Made Me Love You,' 'It's All Right with Me'—but they would put their own words to the tunes. And these words were to be witty comments on local events, especially Army camp gossip.

'We thought of beginning,' said the lady from Toronto, 'by having a voice come over the loudspeaker. It would be a pilot on Air Canada speaking to his passengers: "You are now approaching the Maritimes—please put your clocks back fifty years."'

Most of the others wanted to tell me things.

When I was having a haircut the barber thought I should know the best ways to hunt duck and moose. A scientist, in charge of a unit to help the surrounding farmers improve their productivity, came over after a reading and said,

'This is a true story. I thought I would tell it to you. Perhaps you can use it. There was this priest. He lived in the country near here. He was middle-aged. And he liked women, especially girls. Whenever he went to visit people who were sick in hospital or at home—if they were girls—he put his hand underneath the covers. Things got so bad that the local mothers got together and wrote to the Bishop. Finally the priest was moved. And he was replaced by a much younger man. This young man didn't have the other's habits. But he began to ask for things. He said he needed a new car. The old one was too old. He wanted the house redecorated. Some special food he liked had to be flown in from Montreal. He wanted the best cigars. After a while the people again wrote to the Bishop this time complaining at the money this young priest was costing them.

'Being chaste is expensive, the Bishop wrote back.'

And Peter, the young owner of a Chinese restaurant where I sometimes went to eat, told me that before coming here he attended university in Red China. He thought I should know the best way to steal chickens off a chicken farm.

'You get this candle,' Peter said. 'It only comes from China. When you light it it gives off smoke. And you let the wind blow this smoke over to where the chickens are. You do it at night. One whiff and the dogs go to sleep for twenty minutes. So do all the chickens. They just lie down and go to sleep. You get a handkerchief and put it around your mouth and pick up these sleeping chickens and put them in your truck. Twenty minutes later, when they wake up, you are miles away—'

I listened to the strangest confessions, humiliations, suffering. And, as if to balance them, an amazing endurance.

By the beginning of February I was so well known in the town that strangers in the street would smile and say hello. A tall blonde woman with glasses came up to me: 'I saw your picture in the paper—it looks like you.' Kids stopped throwing snowballs to call out: 'I know you Mister —you write books.' When I went into a restaurant heads would turn.

Meanwhile the invitations kept coming in.

One of the early ones was from the Professor of English at St Vincent's —a teachers' college which was affiliated to the university. But as it was a hundred and sixty miles away, I kept putting it off. Until the head of the English department told me that St Vincent's was after him to get me to come.

'It will be the usual thing,' he said. 'A small dinner before. Then you give your reading at the college hall. And there will be a party afterwards.'

I agreed to go next Friday.

Four days later, in the faculty club he came over. 'I've just got back from St Vincent's. They're very excited about you coming. They've got posters stuck all over the place. There is a piece about you in their local paper. And they have put you up at the best hotel.'

He ordered coffee and doughnuts for both of us.

'The Board of Governors asked me to tell you that you can be resident writer with us for as long as you like.'

'That's very nice,' I said.

I was to fly to St Vincent's at noon. But fog came on Friday morning. The planes were grounded. The train no longer ran although the tracks were still there.

I took a small green bus from the bus station. Four other passengers were on the bus at the start, but they got off at the small towns on the way. For the first hour the roads were clear. Then it began to snow. The wind increased. It turned into a blizzard. Fewer cars and trucks were coming from the opposite direction and more were abandoned by the sides of the road. The driver kept stopping to wipe the windshield. The snow was coming down so fast and thick that the wipers were not clearing it. Then he stopped at a filling station to get a tow-truck.

'We'll never get to St Vincent's today,' he told me.

'But I'm supposed to give a reading—'

'It's impossible. I can't get through.'

I rang St Vincent's, told the Professor of English the position. He said he understood, that the weather was bad there as well, and it would be best to postpone it.

I went back to the bus and sat inside.

'How about going back?'

'Nothing is getting through *either* way,' the driver said.

The tow-truck towed us for about an hour and a half—where I don't know—as I couldn't see for the falling snow. Finally we arrived in a small town. The street lights were on but there was hardly anyone in the street—snow covered everything.

I asked the driver when he would go back.

'Soon as the roads are open. There will be an inspection tomorrow morning at nine.'

I said I would be there.

I went to look for a hotel but as soon as I stepped off the main road I sunk to my knees in snow. I walked that way until I came to cross streets—the road was covered with freshly fallen snow but it was hard-packed underneath. I finally found a sign on a drab-looking wooden building that said it was a hotel.

'Can I have a room for the night?' I asked the man.

'It's eight dollars a night,' he said.

'OK,' I replied. And waited for him to give me the room key.

'Is that all your luggage?'

'Yes,' I said holding on to my attaché case.

'If that is all your luggage you will have to pay in advance.'

'I'm the resident writer at the university and I was on my way to St Vincent's to give a reading when the blizzard came—'

'Is your car outside?'

'No. I came by bus.'

'And that is all your luggage?'

'Yes.'

'You will have to pay in advance—eight dollars.'

I paid him the eight dollars. It seemed a long time since I was treated this way. I took the key and went up the creaky stairs to Room 2 on the first floor.

It was a small gloomy room—the kind I used to have in my early days when I was poor. A bare light hung from the ceiling. And I needed it on all the time. There was an iron bed, a rickety wooden dresser. No chair. A cracked enamel sink with only one tap working. And every time I turned on the tap it made a wailing noise. The wallpaper was stained. I felt cold. I went over to the thin green-painted radiator. No heat. There were two grey blankets at the foot of the bed and a disinfectant smell when I pulled back the covers.

I felt hungry and tired. I looked in my attaché case and took out the toothbrush, the toothpaste, the shaving lather and razor, and the copy of my book that I brought for the reading. But in my rush, or absent-mindness, I had forgotten to take my cheque book. Not that I would have had any luck cashing a cheque here.

I took out all the money I had and counted. It came to nineteen dollars and some change. If I'm stuck here another night that's another eight dollars. The ticket back is ten dollars. That left me a dollar and the change. I counted the change—thirty-seven cents. No need to worry, I said, I might be able to get away tomorrow. What I need now is food (I had been five hours on that bus) and a good night's sleep.

I went out to find a restaurant. It was still snowing. I went to the main street. The stores were on one side. The other side consisted of open fields covered in snow and some trees that were almost hidden. I went into a small supermarket and bought a loaf of bread, a tin of sardines, and two apples. That left me forty cents to spare.

I came back to the room. I ate the bread and the sardines sitting on the bed with my coat on. Then I dipped pieces of bread in the sardine oil. And washed it down with an apple.

I lay on the bed with the coat and the grey blankets over me. I thought that now that I was earning my living from writing and giving readings I was past things like this.

I went to sleep. And when I woke I was hungry. I ate the rest of the bread with the last apple. I remembered from my hard-up days that it was important to have something to keep up morale. I went out, found a small restaurant, had a cup of hot coffee and asked the woman if she sold any cigars singly.

'These,' she said, 'are twenty-five cents each.'

I looked at it wondering if I had enough.

'This one is fifteen cents.'

I took the fifteen-cents cigar, smoked it slowly. The tobacco was kind of green. I took a long time over the coffee. Then went back to the room in the hotel to lie down. Instead I went to sleep.

Next morning when I woke up I was cold. I brushed my teeth and shaved in cold water and went out. The snow was still falling but it wasn't so thick. I walked to the bus station. The bus was in the garage. I found the driver—a different driver—in a stand-up eating place next to the bus depot. He was finishing his breakfast.

'No—no buses today,' he said. 'Next inspection tomorrow.'

'What time?'

'Around nine in the morning.'

'I know the ticket back cost ten dollars,' I said. 'Could you give me a ticket. And I'll pay when we get back?'

'We don't run the company on those lines,' he said.

I felt hungry and light-headed.

'I'll buy you a cup of coffee.'

'Thanks.'

He paid for his breakfast and handed me the saucer with the cup of coffee.

'I'll see you tomorrow,' I said.

When he had gone—in my nervousness—I spilled half of the coffee before I had my first sip.

I went back to the hotel.

'I'll stay another night,' I told the man.

'That will be eight dollars.'

I paid him.

All I had left was the ten dollar bill. I put it in my back buttoned-down pocket.

'How cold is it?' I asked the man.

'Thirteen below. But near here it's been thirty-five below.'

Saturday morning, I thought I'll go to *shul*. It will be warm. There might be a Bar-Mitzvah or some kind of Kiddish afterwards.

'Is there a synagogue here?'

'No,' he said, looking suspiciously at me.

'Where's the nearest church?'

He gave me directions.

It was a wooden church painted grey in a snow-covered field. There was a narrow path freshly cleared to the door. A few cars and a few trucks were sunk in the snow by it.

As I opened the door a man in an ill-fitting blue suit said:

'Bride or groom?'

I must have looked puzzled. For he said:

'What side are you? Bride or groom?'

'Bride,' I said.

'—to your left.'

I went to the left side and sat down on the wooden bench at the back beside the Quebec stove that had large tin pipes going up and across near the ceiling. I don't know what kind of church it was but it was very plain, very austere. There weren't any religious figures or stained-glass windows. About thirty people were separated by a wide aisle. Those on one side looked at those on the other. We all had our coats on. Up ahead, slightly raised, were the bride and groom. And the preacher in a plain grey suit. There was a small wooden organ to the right where a woman was playing.

The wedding ceremony didn't last long.

Afterwards the guests walked in ones and twos along the snow-covered street, icicles hung from the boarded-up houses, down a turning to the main street and to a better hotel. And at the top of the stairs, in the centre of a large room, the bride and groom were sitting, side by side, on chairs against a wall. The guests came up to them, in ones and twos, with their presents.

I stayed near the door. There was food. A buffet. I guess that friends and relations of the bride thought I belonged to the other side. Just as the other side thought I belonged to the groom.

'Where are you from?' a man asked me.

'Out of town,' I said.

I didn't stay long. Long enough to have three ham sandwiches and two cups of coffee.

Then I went back into the street.

For some reason I couldn't find the hotel where I was staying. The town wasn't that large. If you walked five minutes in one direction on the main street that was it. There were several side-streets to the one main—but I kept getting into places that ended in dead ends.

I managed to get back to the main street. The place was now packed with people walking, people shopping. Outside a music store, over a loudspeaker, someone was singing, 'Everyone's Gone to the Moon.'

I felt like a vagrant.

I saw a bit of ice on the road and with a run I went down it. I was hungry and cold. But when I came back to the room my cheeks were rosy.

I lay down on the bed. Because of these last few years I had forgotten how it was to be poor. Now that I was back in it, I was hungry. All that had happened to me since the last book was published seemed some kind of fraud. I was a writer. In my world nothing is certain. I needed this reminder, I told myself.

Now, I must get myself out of it. I tried to remember what I used to do. I went though the pockets—of my suit, my overcoat. Not a cent. In my hard-up days I always left a coin or two in the pockets. What could I sell? There was the copy of my book from which I was going to read at St Vincent's.

I went out again. I couldn't find a bookstore. But I did find a second-hand place that had a lot of junk (mostly furniture) lying inside in heaps all over the place. There were some battered paperbacks on the floor.

A woman finally came.

'Yes.'

'I'd like to sell you this book,' I said.

She picked it up, turned a few pages. I hoped she wouldn't come across the parts I had marked with a pen that I usually read.

She closed the book. 'Fifty cents.'

'It sells for $5.95. And it is almost new.'

'Take it or leave it.'

I took it.

If I had to stay another night I could try and sell her my watch. But she would never give me eight dollars for it—of that I was certain.

With the fifty cents I went out and got myself a hot dog and a cup of coffee. And wondered what I would do tomorrow if I couldn't go back.

Outside it had stopped snowing. I went to the hotel room. I felt hungry and cold and went to sleep.

Sunday morning I slept in. I looked at my watch—ten to nine. I didn't have time to wash or shave. I walked as quickly as I could to the small bus depot. The bus was outside, its engine running. The door was closed. The driver was not inside.

Two men, also unshaven and unwashed, were standing by the door.

'Is it going?'

'Yes,' they said.

I went into the office and gave the driver the ten-dollar bill. He gave me a ticket.

When I came out the two men asked me if I could buy them a cup of coffee as they hadn't had any breakfast and they were broke.

'Sorry,' I said.

I got back to the University town at noon. That evening I was a guest at a dinner party given in the Army Camp, in the Officer's Mess of The Black Watch. There were fourteen of us, some with wives in evening dress. The young officers wore their dress uniforms. We sat in tall straight-backed chairs around the table. The lighting was by candles. We were waited on by two waiters. There was fish and white wine. Roast beef and Yorkshire pudding with red wine. Then champagne with some exotic dessert.

I looked at the others. They were young, attractive, well-fed, well-dressed. How secure they all appeared. And how certain their world.

But outside I could see the snow, the cold, the acres of emptiness that lay frozen all around.

Grace & Faigel

In October I was on my way to Ottawa to give a reading at Ottawa U. But when the taxi brought me to Montreal's Central Station I realized something had gone wrong with my watch during the Atlantic flight for I arrived forty minutes early. There was nothing to do but wait. I didn't mind that. There were these small purple-blue lights, and soft music being played, and plenty of room. In the soft light the men and women walking by were well dressed. They wore bright clothes. They looked carefree. It was very pleasant just to sit, to look and listen. Or to walk along the marble floor. The signs, by the newsstand and cafeteria, were in French and English. The public telephones were of the kind that you touched the numbers, no dialling. And when you touched a number, it gave off a delicate plaintive note. It was so different from the run-down English stations I had left behind.

Then on the train, sitting in a soft seat, by the window, looking at the trees. With the sun on them they looked like coloured smoke. How smooth the train moved. How comfortable, I thought. How clean. What luxury.

I am forty-nine. And since I was twenty-five I have been living away from Canada in England. It was in England that I met my wife, had our children, watched them grow up. But every so often I leave wife and children and make these visits to Canada.

In England we live an isolated life. The apathy of a seaside town in Cornwall, out of season, is hard to believe unless you have ever lived in it. So these trips to Canada. They shake up the system. I always come back to England wanting to do things. And for the first two weeks I do phone London, send cables, write letters. But then the life that we live in Cornwall takes over. I begin to feel cut-off. And soon it is as if I have never been away.

I looked at the young woman on the seat across the aisle. She was reading a paperback with a large *L* on the cover. She had a small boy, of about eight, opposite her. He was half-sitting on the seat and standing up. He began to recite, in a rush: 'A Cub Scout always does his best thinks of

198

others before himself and does a good turn every day I promise that I will do my best—'

He stopped. His eyes looked upward. Then he repeated the words just as fast. And stopped in the same place. The woman said something to him. The boy said quickly, 'To do my duty to God to the Queen help other people and keep the Cub Scout law.'

He laughed. And pushed himself back onto the seat, his feet dangling.

She stood up and, from a small travelling bag in the rack above her, took out a book, a pencil, and some pieces of paper. And gave them to the boy.

She was tall, on the thin side. She had blonde short hair close to her face and two wisps curled upwards beneath her ears. She wore a tight green sweater and a Scotch plaid skirt with a large safety pin on its side. She sat down and went back to her book. As she read her mouth twisted into a frown.

I saw that the paperback was Doris Lessing's *The Story of a Non-Marrying Man*.

She caught me staring. She smiled. And her face changed. She looked beautiful.

'Do you like the book?'

'Yes,' she said.

'I met Doris Lessing,' I said. 'She wanted us to have her house one Christmas and New Year because she was going to be away in Scotland. Who else do you like?'

'Graham Greene,' she said.

'Have you read Henry Green?'

'No. What has he written?'

'*Living. Loving. Caught. Back. Concluding.* I hadn't heard of him either until I went to England.'

'Do you live there?'

'Yes,' I said. 'I was in London yesterday.'

'How was London?' And she smiled again. Her face looked radiant.

'It was raining when I left,' I said. 'What's his name?'

'Justin,' she said.

The next thing I knew I left my seat and came over and sat beside her. Justin's large brown eyes stared at me.

'Do you want to see a trick?'

I took his pencil and held it in the middle by my thumb and first finger, and slowly began to move my hand up and down. The pencil appeared to be bending.

'It's in here,' Justin said. And opened his book, turned a few pages, and there it was illustrated.

'He's advanced for his age,' she said.

'You know any other tricks?' Justin asked.

I stared into space. Then I put my two hands together, fingers apart. I slid the middle finger between the opposite fingers, turned one hand right over, and wiggled the two middle fingers, that stuck out, on opposite sides.

She was laughing.

Justin said. 'What do you call *that?*'

'Milking the cow,' I said. 'Why don't you go over to my seat and see if you can see any animals from the window. I'll give you a cent for every cow that you see, two cents for every horse, twenty-five cents for every goat. And a dollar if you see an elephant or a lion.'

'Boy,' he said. And took his pencil and papers and went eagerly to the window on the other side.

I looked at the large safety pin on her tartan skirt.

'I think,' she said, 'it's the weight of the pin that keeps it down. I don't usually talk to people on a train. Not for long. But you have an interesting face. What do you do?'

I said I was a writer.

'Can you tell me your name?'

I told her.

'I'm sorry,' she said. 'I have not heard of you.'

'No reason why you should,' I said. 'What's your name?'

'Grace.'

'What do you do?'

'That's my trouble,' she said. 'I don't do anything well.'

This time I smiled. 'The only other woman who said that to me turned out to have a very strong character.'

'Oh, I'm a bitch,' she said. 'I know it. I'm selfish. I'm difficult to live with. I lived for a year in England. I used to knock around with the jet set in Knightsbridge. They were a bunch of layabouts just preening themselves. I worked in Selfridge's.'

'How old are you?'

'Twenty-nine,' she said. 'I'll soon be thirty. Are you married?'

I said I was.

'Is your wife in England?'

'Yes.'

'I'm getting a divorce,' she said.

We were coming towards Ottawa. I called to Justin: 'How many animals did you see?'

He came over, adding up pencil marks. 'Ten cows,' he said slowly. '*And* six horses.'

I gave him a dollar.

'Wow,' he said to his mother. 'I've now got a dollar and a quarter.'

He carefully folded the dollar and put it into the back pocket of his jeans. Then went back to the window on the opposite side.

'Besides England,' she said, 'I've been to South and Central America.'

'I've only been to England and Canada,' I said. 'Wasn't it a lucky accident for us to meet?'

'I don't think these things are *accidents*,' she said. 'I think we were intended to meet. We have good vibrations,' she said quietly.

'I'm coming here to give a reading—on Tuesday night,' I said. 'I'll be staying with my mother while in Ottawa. Let's meet tomorrow.'

'All right.'

'How about in the morning? In the lobby of the Château Laurier. Ten o'clock. Is that too early?'

'I'll be there,' she said. 'I'm here for the weekend to see my parents. It's a kind of duty. They live just out of Ottawa. The last time I saw them was in August.'

She took a piece of Justin's paper and, in pencil, wrote her parents' phone number then her address and phone number in Toronto.

We were coming towards the new Union Station. I took her case. We got out of the train and walked into the clean, all-glass station. It was quite empty.

'Anyone meeting you?'

'No,' she said. 'I'll have to phone my father at the office. He'll come and get me.'

'I'll take a taxi outside. Will you be all right?'

'Yes,' she said and smiled. 'I'll see you tomorrow.'

The taxi went down Rideau to Cobourg and stopped by the small park with the gazebo, the poplars, the maples, and the yellow dead leaves on the grass.

When my mother opened the apartment door I kissed her on the cheek.

'I expected you yesterday,' she said. 'You look tired. Why didn't you phone when you got to Montreal?'

'The plane was late,' I said. 'There were no trains. I had to spend the night in a hotel.'

'Which one?'

'You wouldn't have heard of it,' I said. 'The big ones were full. The room I was in had no heating. I was so cold I couldn't sleep. I put on a heavy sweater, socks, and my coat on the bed, and I was still cold.'

'I have something that will warm you up,' she said.

And brought out a third-full bottle of brandy from her fridge. She keeps everything she can in the fridge. And what she can't she pushes in the cupboards. There were so many tins, jars, bottles, and plastic bags filled with food—it was like a siege.

She poured herself a bit of brandy.

'To life,' she said.

The brandy was cold.

'It will soon warm you up,' she said. '*Watch.*'

'I'm not cold now.'

'How is everyone?' she asked.

'I'll tell you later. How are you?'

'I've got high blood pressure, I've got to take pills every day. But why do we have to talk about unpleasant things?'

Above her head, on the wall, was a photograph of how I looked when I was twenty.

I brought out presents from my bags—English honey, English marmalade, packs of tea—and gave them to her.

'You shouldn't have bothered,' she said. 'Come and sit down and have something to eat.'

'How is Esther?'

'Fine. She rings me every morning at eight to see if I'm still alive. There was an old lady here. She was dead four days before they found her. Since then Esther rings in the morning, after lunch, and at night. Anyway, I've got good neighbours. Mr and Mrs Budnoff—they are on one side. And someone from the Gatineau—on the other. I don't know him. In front there's Mrs Nadolny—We all wear the same suits.'

It was only then I realized that she was talking about the cemetery on Metcalfe Road.

She returned from the kitchen with a large banana. 'I've bought some bananas for you,' she said. 'If you have two or three a week—it's good for the heart and protects you from high blood pressure.'

That night I couldn't sleep—and my mother's apartment was warm. Perhaps it was jet lag. But I kept looking in the dark, at the electric digits telling the time in the bedside radio … watching the minutes, the hours, change … and thinking of Grace.

Next morning I was in the lobby of the Château Laurier ten minutes early. She didn't come through the doors until twenty past ten.

'What an early hour.' She was out of breath. 'My mother drove in.'

'I nearly gave you up.'

'I left word at home in case you telephoned.'

She had on the same clothes as yesterday but wore, on top, a hand-knitted woollen jacket. She looked cold.

'Let's go,' I said, 'and have some good hot coffee.'

We crossed the War Memorial (I saw them putting this up, I told her) and walked down to the Lord Elgin and into Murray's. We sat at a table by a window and had coffee. Outside it looked cold, blustery, deserted.

'When I was seventeen,' I said, 'I saw the Lord Elgin being built. I worked in a government building across the road. The Department of National Defence. It's not there anymore.'

'I didn't come to Ottawa until I was five,' she said. 'I don't like the place. It depresses me. I went around with the cocktail crowd at Rockcliffe.

They liked me because I was pretty. I became a revolutionary at university. I met my husband there. He was a Che Guevara character. He wore a black beret and a black leather jacket. I was gun-running in South America. Some of my friends who were caught were tortured.'

'What do you do now?'

'I work in a lawyer's office and go to school at night to learn Greek.' She smiled. 'I'm learning Greek because of my Greek workman. But it's so difficult. I'm seriously thinking of marrying him.'

She must have seen an expression in my face for she quickly said, 'He's not a workman. He's an architect.'

As if that made any difference.

I lit an Old Port cigarillo, drank some coffee, and remained silent.

'Will you come back to live in Canada?'

'I hope to—in the Spring,' I said. 'I have to go back to England and sort things out.'

'You don't talk about your wife.'

What could I say. 'She's pretty,' I said.

'Is she English?'

'Yes.'

'You're the first Canadian I have liked,' she said. 'All the others have been Europeans. You must meet my friends in Toronto. George and Isabel. They've been very good to me. George was my lover for a while.'

'While he was still with Isabel?'

'Yes.'

'Lucky George,' I said.

'Yes,' she said. 'Lucky George.'

'Do you like sex?'

'I like the power it gives me over a man,' she said.

We came out of Murray's, arm in arm, and went across to the National Gallery. It was enclosed in scaffolding. All the rooms were closed except for a small Matisse exhibition of drawings by the stairs. The best paintings were the picture postcards on sale downstairs. I got her a Francis Bacon *Pope*. She didn't like it. She preferred Lawren Harris's *Side Street* of old houses in winter.

From there we walked up to the mail.

She was shivering.

'I didn't bring enough warm clothes. I don't like the cold. I have bad circulation.'

She saw Fisher's. She wanted a Scout cap for Justin and she was told she could get it there.

I remembered Fisher's. When I started university I bought a black winter coat from them. But they were on the other side of the street. I'm sure they were—

After she paid I asked the young man who served her. 'Wasn't Fisher's on the other side?'

'That's the old store,' he said, 'before my time.'

We came out.

'Hungry?'

'Yes.'

'Where shall we go?'

'You choose.'

'Let's go to Albert Street,' I said. 'There used to be a couple of Chinese restaurants.'

We went into the first one. We were the only customers. We had soup to warm us up. Then sweet and sour.

'You're under-nourished,' I told her.

'I don't like eating by myself,' she said. 'I've been living an isolated life these last few years in Toronto.'

Halfway through the tea and cookies I leaned over the table and kissed her.

'That's the second time I've been kissed this visit,' she said. 'My father had some people in last night for a drink. And this friend of my father's said. "Are you Grace? How you've grown." And kissed me.'

'Can you come to Montreal next weekend?'

'I'll see if I can. I have a friend in Montreal. I could come and stay with her. But I've got to think of the money.'

By the time we came out of the Chinese restaurant it was twenty past four. The light was fading and it was colder. We walked along the empty street towards a bus stop. The wind lifted loose papers about.

'Do you like Stephane Grappelli,' she said, 'and Django Reinhardt?'

'Yes. I have their record,' I said. I didn't say it was a present from our eldest daughter for our twentieth wedding anniversary. 'Le Jazz Hot—'

'They've made a lot of records,' she said. 'Do you like Alan Stivell?'

'The Celtic Harp. Yes, I have the record.' Again I didn't say it belonged to our youngest daughter.

We walked about twenty yards along Queen Street.

'I can take a bus from here,' she said.

I put my hand in my raincoat pocket and saw that my mother had put in a bus ticket.

'Here,' I said.

'You are prepared for anything.'

'When will I see you again?'

'Tomorrow, I have to be with the family. And I'm going away early on Monday morning—'

'I'll ring you sometime tomorrow,' I said.

She was shivering. I put both arms inside her woollen jacket and drew her closer. We kissed.

'What would people in Ottawa say if they saw you behaving this way in the street?'

'I couldn't care less. Are you still cold?'

'Not now,' she said. 'I'll see if I can arrange things for Montreal.'

Then the bus came. We kissed, awkwardly, goodbye. But I was singing as I walked back to my mother's place.

Next morning, just after breakfast, I phoned her.

'I was going to ring you tonight,' she said quietly.

'Can you come to Montreal?'

'I can't talk freely,' she said, 'the telephone is where my parents can hear every word.'

'I'm the same way,' I said. 'I have taken the phone into the bedroom —but I have to sit on the floor to talk.'

'I won't be coming to Montreal,' she said.

'In that case I can fly to England from Toronto,' I said. 'I'll come to Toronto—'

'But I'm working during the day and going to school at night. I don't think you're thinking clearly. You are living a very isolated life while you are over here. I told you that I'm considering getting married again—'

I didn't say anything.

'Ring me before you fly,' she said. 'And I'll write to you in England. And when you come back I'll see you.'

Later, I thought how silly. But for two days I felt excited and happy. As though I was experiencing something I thought I had lost.

My mother finished another long telephone conversation. 'That was Mr Laroque,' she said. 'He does memorial stones. He phones me every few months and asks: anyone sick—anyone dying? Everybody here is trying to make a living. Have something to warm you up. The lecture isn't until tonight and you're already nervous.'

She brought a bottle of Bristol Cream from the fridge and gave me a glass full.

The reading went all right. Though at the start I was blinded by the lights and my mouth and lips became dry.

When it was over around twenty people—mostly students—came down from their seats and asked me to sign copies of my books.

As I was getting near the end I noticed a plump middle-aged woman, in a brown cloth coat, with glasses and grey hair, standing about ten feet away, and staring. A grey-haired man was beside her. The woman's lips were pressed tight. She didn't move, just stared. Then she said:

'Don't you remember me?'

I thought—I have never seen this woman before.

She said a name. It didn't bring back anything.

I felt awkward. 'I'm sorry,' I said.

Behind her was a small thin woman. The first thing I noticed was her eyes—large dark eyes set in a white face. Then how smart she dressed. She had on a new camel-haired coat with black leather boots. And there was a nervous vitality about her. Although her shape belonged to that of a young girl—she was clearly in her late twenties or early thirties. She had high cheekbones, a wide mouth, very good teeth. And dark red hair cut close to her head.

As soon as the grey-haired woman and her husband walked away, the small woman with the large eyes came up and said.

'I'm Faigel Shore. I enjoyed this evening very much.'

She spoke with an accent which I couldn't place.

'It's nice of you to say that,' I said.

'I've heard other writers come here and talk,' she said. 'They say how wonderful their work is. But you sounded different. Honest.'

'Aren't you?'

'No,' she said. 'I tell lies.'

'But why?'

'It makes life much more interesting.'

The engineer was turning off the lights. Everyone else had gone.

'Why don't we go and have some coffee,' Faigel said.

'All right. But I can't stay long. I'm expected at a party a professor is giving for me.'

As we were walking through the leafy streets of Sandy Hill, I told Faigel that I knew these streets, that they were part of my childhood.

'But your parents come from Poland?'

'Yes,' I said.

'Then we have a lot in common,' she said. 'I was three when I left Poland after the war. My mother and father fought with the Polish resistance. We all went to Australia then to England before coming to Canada. I went to school in England. We lived there six years—in London—just off the Fulham Road.'

'I know where it is,' I said.

'You know what I miss—from England?'

'No,' I said.

'Kippers. I liked eating them raw—with juice squeezed from a lemon and pepper on top. And with brown bread. It tastes like smoked salmon.'

'I thought I was the only one who did that,' I said.

She put her arm through mine.

'We have a lot in common,' she said.

I expected that we would have coffee in a restaurant on Rideau Street. But she crossed Rideau and began to walk into Lower Town. She stopped in front of a run-down wooden house which was divided into two apartments.

'This is where I live.'

It looked shabby on the outside. The grey wooden steps and grey verandah, with wet fallen leaves, needed repairing and painting. Inside was worse. The wallpaper was peeling, the curtains were old and torn. There were books, magazines, paperbacks, all over the place. Things were in cardboard boxes.

'It's a mess, isn't it?' she said. 'But I can't throw anything away.'

She pushed aside unwashed dishes in the kitchen and put some coffee on a small electric stove. The light was a bare bulb hanging from a wire from the ceiling.

'Come, sit down here,' she said.

It was her bed—a mattress, on the floor, with a patchwork cover full of colour, made-up of small snowflake shapes. Beside it were boxes of matches, burnt-out matches, saucers for ashtrays, candles, and loose change scattered on the bare floor. How it brought back those early years in England after the war. And people I once knew with little money.

Faigel took off her camel-haired coat—she had on a smart black suit— then her leather black boots. And went around in her stocking feet.

When she goes out, I thought, she takes such care to look nice and neat but she lives in such disorder.

'Clothes are very important,' she said as if guessing my thoughts. 'They tell a lot about a person. When I'm depressed—I go and buy something new to wear.'

'Where's your husband?'

'He works all week at a mining camp north of here. I work in a library. We live quite separate lives during the week. He has his women friends. I have my men friends. But he comes home for weekends. We spend our weekends together. I like my husband very much. I can't find any milk or sugar—'

'I have coffee black.'

'Good. So do I.'

She brought the coffee in two cups without handles and lit a cigarette and one for me. She sat, opposite, on the bed, her legs crossed underneath her.

'You write so beautifully,' she said. 'But if I may make one criticism—you never tell enough. Especially with sex. You say people go to bed. Then it's done. I want to know details.'

That would be telling about my wife, I thought. 'I don't know why I don't describe details,' I said.

'You belong to the nineteenth century,' she said. 'What films do you like?'

'Antonioni,' I said, 'and Ray.'

'Have you not seen *Jules et Jim*?'

'No.'

'You must. What about books. What do you re-read?'

'Turgenev,' I said. 'And you.'

'Proust,' she said. 'I also shop-lift, about once a month. I've taken cocaine. I've slept with my husband and with another woman in the same bed. I'm just going to change into something more comfortable.'

What is she telling me this for, I wondered. Is this the way the younger generation get to know one another? Instant intimacy.

She came back wearing a silk blue blouse with black buttons in front—the top three she left undone. And I could see a lace see-through bra.

'I'm not on the pill,' she said. 'I tried it. But I put on weight.'

'Then what do you do?'

'I'm very cautious,' she said.

Cautious, I thought. Shop-lifting, cocaine, three in a bed.

We kissed.

'Do you like large breasts?'

'Yes,' I said. 'But most of the women I have known had small. What are you, 36?'

'No, 34.'

I moistened a finger and ran it lightly over her lips—it was part of my wife's pre-love making.

But Faigel said. 'Are my lips dry? I don't wear lipstick.'

'They are not dry,' I said ...

'Stop it,' she said. 'You are working me up. We have gone too far already.'

She sat up on the bed and lit another cigarette. 'You haven't told me about your wife.'

I now knew what she meant when she said she had 'men friends.' I had a feeling that when this point was reached—the others told Faigel about their wives. But what was I going to tell her?

'She's attractive,' I said. 'Intelligent.'

'I expected her to be that,' Faigel said. 'What else?'

'She's not well,' I said. 'She had a lump in a breast removed—about nine months ago. But why should this interest you?'

'I'm *very* interested,' she said. 'My mother died from cancer. I go for check-ups every six months. Does it affect sex?'

I hesitated. 'Yes.'

And to change the subject I said. 'Do you like Stephane Grappelli and Django Reinhardt?'

'I don't like jazz,' Faigel said. She looked at her wrist-watch. 'I think you had better go. I have to get up early.'

She left the bed and walked across the room to a cluttered table. It wasn't only the neatness in her dress, the care she took with her appearance, that stood out. But also the style with which she moved in these shabby rooms.

She came back carrying a small diary-like book. 'I can't see you tomorrow,' she said looking in the book, 'I have an appointment tomorrow. It was made a long time ago … And my husband flies in on Friday night … How about next week on Tuesday? I can see you on Tuesday. Let's have an appointment for Tuesday.'

'I don't like appointments,' I said quietly.

She took no notice. She wrote in the book and said. 'We'll come together on Tuesday. I look forward to that.'

And I left her.

When I came out, to my surprise, I saw that the clock in the Peace Tower said it was almost half-past one in the morning. In any case I had forgotten the address of the professor's house.

For the next three days I enjoyed myself. After living cut off from people—I felt as if I was suddenly thrown into life again. I didn't think anything of going a hundred and twenty-five miles to Montreal for dinner with a film director who was interested in one of my stories and coming back later to Ottawa that night. And I like the Fall—the colours, the trees, the fallen leaves, and the thin veneer of comfort that modern machinery and money give.

My publisher arranged for me to give another reading next week. But on Saturday morning I received a cable from England—sent by our neighbour—to say that my wife was not well, could I come back. The earliest flight I could get on was Sunday.

I didn't phone Grace. But I did try to phone Faigel. I tried several times, even from the airport. But I guess she didn't answer the phone when her husband was home. Or perhaps they had gone away for the weekend.

My wife was in bed when I returned. After three days she was able to get up. But Canada had a mail strike. The mail strike went on for six weeks. And by the time it was over there didn't seem to be any point in writing to either Grace or Faigel. What was there to say.

I remember the Merchant Navy man who joined the train at Truro. He was going to Glasgow. He had just left his ship at Falmouth. His wife didn't know he was coming back today. He hadn't seen her for three months.

'I have her picture on my cabin wall,' he said. 'For the first few days of the voyage she's nice and big. But as the weeks go by—she gets smaller and smaller …'

Perhaps, I thought, even when we are with people it's a kind of pretence. Nothing really matters.

Champagne Barn

I DIDN'T NOTICE THE birds until I saw them flying. Red-winged blackbirds. A flutter of black. Then a flash of red on the black. Lovely to see. I'd follow a bird as it came level with the window, then watch it go quickly back and disappear from sight. Then I'd look ahead to pick up the next flutter of black, then the flash of red on the black. And follow that for as long as I could.

I was on a train from Montreal to Ottawa. It was early June.

On the second day in Ottawa the local CBC people came to interview me in the small park opposite to where my mother lives. I was sitting on a park bench talking to the camera.

'That new building. Across the road. It's for Senior Citizens. But when I was a kid it was the terminus of an Ottawa streetcar line called Champagne Barn—'

When a thin old woman came up. She walked right into the film and said to me. 'Aren't you Mrs Snipper's boy?'

'Yes,' I said.

'You look like your mother. I'm a near neighbour of hers in the Senior Citizen building.'

Then she noticed the camera on the tripod, the cameraman behind it, the sound recordist.

'Who are these people?'

'From television.'

'Have they come to take a picture of our building?'

'No.'

'What are they doing?'

'Interviewing me.'

'*You*. What for?'

'I'm a writer.'

She didn't say anything after that. Just had a good look and walked away.

When the interview was over I went across the road, through the glass doors of the Senior Citizen building, to the elevator. Mr Tessier was also waiting. As we were going up he said, 'I've seen a lot of people die here since I first come five years ago.'

'How many?'

'Sixty-eight,' he said.

I got off at the second floor, where my mother had her apartment, and Mr Tessier went up to his on the third.

'How did it go?' my mother said soon as I came in.

'All right. Except a thin, tall lady came up in the middle of the interview and began talking to me. She said she was a neighbour of yours.'

'That's Mrs Sobcuff. She has to know what's going on. Come, sit down and eat.'

I went to wash my hands in the bathroom.

'I can't eat all that fish.'

'It's delicious,' my mother said.

'But I can't eat two pieces.'

'Try.'

I began to eat a piece of fish with a sliced tomato and sliced cucumber.

'Eat with bread,' she said.

'I'm trying to watch my weight.'

'You're not fat.'

I finished one piece. And began the other.

'Why don't you eat?'

'I had something earlier,' she said. 'I eat a little bit but every two hours.'

And to prove her point she came back with a piece of hot chicken on a plate.

She ate quickly.

'Slow down,' I said.

The phone rang.

She had it beside her on the table.

'We're in the middle of eating,' I said. 'Let it ring.'

'No,' she said. 'Hullo. Yes. Hullo, how are you?'

She walked with the phone into the next room, her bedroom. And I could hear her say: 'Did you go to Rideau Bakery? Did you get bread? What did you get? Rye. Was it sliced?'

She talked like that for twenty minutes while everything got cold.

When she came back she said, 'Without the telephone I don't know how I would go through the day. It takes up three or four hours. That was Esther. She would like to take you out for a meal. She'll pick you up at six.'

'How is Esther?'

'Her health isn't very good. But she phones me every day.'

It had been hot and sticky. A few minutes before six I went down to the entrance of the Senior Citizen building to wait for Esther. And a sudden summer storm. The wind increased. The poplars began to sway and rustle. The sky got darker. And the rain came slanting across the park.

When Esther drove up I ran to get in beside her.

'We need this rain,' she said. 'I know a good place in Eastview. The food is excellent. It's French.'

Esther's my spinster cousin. In her late forties. Around five foot eight and a hundred and fifty pounds. Large, dark eyes, black hair, heavy bones. Her nicest feature is her eyes. She was made a fuss of as a child, as she was the youngest. Then, when she was twelve, her brother Hank was born. And the fuss was all about Hank. Esther worked in the office of my uncle's wholesale fruit and vegetable business in the market. She did the accounts, saw that the drivers had the right load to deliver, checked the money when they cashed in at night.

I liked going to the market and to Uncle's store. It was always a bit dark when I walked in. But there was the immediate smell of rotten fruit and crates lying all over the wooden floor. Hank would throw me apples and oranges until my pockets were full. Esther would give me a hand of large bananas to take back. And, when no one was looking, Uncle would slip me a dollar and say: 'Go and see a movie.'

Uncle died while I was away in England in the war. And two years ago Hank died from cancer. Then Esther sold the business.

'How are things?' I asked her.

215

'I wish I could have a rain check,' she said. 'I sure would live it differently. I had to go to a doctor for an examination. He said it was the first time he had seen an intact hymen in someone of my age.'

This was the first time Esther had talked to me like this. I guess I was too young before.

'Things have changed,' she said, 'since the business was sold. I don't get up early any more. I go to the library. I take out books. But I can't remember what I read. In the evenings I stay up. I've got some Bristol Cream. I drink that and watch television. I get so involved with what's on. I talk back to it. Throw things at it—'

The rain stopped as we drove into Eastview. The sky got lighter. The grass, the trees, the painted wooden houses, looked full of colour. She parked the car by a small wooden hotel.

The restaurant was on the ground floor. There were round tables with white tablecloths. The two waiters wore some kind of theatrical soldier's uniform. We both ordered steak and mashed potatoes and vegetables.

It arrived covered in gravy.

She tasted hers.

'It's cold,' she said. '*Waiter.*'

I tried mine. It wasn't cold.

A waiter finally came to the table. 'The meat is cold,' Esther said. 'The potatoes are cold. I would like it changed.'

He took our plates away without saying a word.

'Why shouldn't I tell them to take it back?' she said angrily. 'We used to sit like dummies before. Not any more. If you keep quiet and don't make a fuss—you go under.'

After what seemed a while the waiter returned with both plates.

She tasted her steak.

'It's better now,' she said quietly.

I tasted mine. It was just the same.

'Yes,' I said. 'Much better.'

Esther drove me back to the Senior Citizen building. When I came in mother was reading *The Journal*.

'How did it go?'

'Fine,' I said.

'Did you have a good time?'

'Yes.'

'What did you have?'

'Steak, potatoes, and vegetables.'

'Esther will be home now,' she said. 'Why don't you give her a ring and tell her you had a good time.'

'But I just saw her.'

'It won't hurt to ring her up and talk to her.'

'But I only left her fifteen minutes ago. And I was with her a couple of hours before that.'

My mother picked up the receiver and dialled.

'Hullo, Esther. Yes, he said he enjoyed himself very much. Thank you. It's very good of you. All right. We'll talk again tomorrow.'

She hung up.

'The important thing,' she said, 'is for people to think well of you. So they will have good memories of you.'

'They don't remember for very long,' I said.

And to change the subject I asked her. 'Where are my things? Where's the officer's uniform?'

'I gave them away when I moved into here,' she said. 'What's the use of carrying all those things along.'

'I wish you hadn't given away the uniform.'

'But you weren't here,' she said.

The phone went.

'Hullo, Sonia. Yes, he looks fine—'

This time she was on the phone for over half an hour. When she came back she said, 'That was Sonia. I'll be going with her to Toronto for a wedding. Then we'll come back through Montreal. I'll be away about five days. Why don't you move in here instead of staying at the hotel? Why spend all that money just to sleep? You have everything you want. And it's quiet. Here are the keys.'

That's how I came to be living in a Senior Citizen place in Ottawa. I was thirty-eight. Everyone else was over sixty-five. Most were in their seventies and eighties.

Next morning I rang up Harvey Reinhardt.

'Have you had breakfast?'

'No,' I said.

'Let's have breakfast. I'll pick you up in half an hour. OK?'

'That'll be eleven-thirty.'

'Yeh. I'll pick you up and we'll go to Nate's and have breakfast. OK?'

'OK,' I said.

Harvey Reinhardt is the only one left in Ottawa from the old Lower Town gang. Just before eleven-thirty I went down to wait outside the front glass doors. Mr Tessier was also standing there. His shirt sleeves rolled up.

'It's going to be a hot day,' Mr Tessier said. 'It's almost eighty now.'

We looked at the small park opposite, at the still trees, the grass. It was very quiet.

'I played in this park when I was a kid,' I said.

'When I was a kid,' Mr Tessier said, 'it was a cemetery. When they widened the road they dug up skeletons.'

Harvey Reinhardt drove up in a large olive-green car sending a wake of dust behind him.

'When did you get in?'

'A few days ago.'

'You look the same,' he said.

So did he. His straight black hair had thinned. But the stockiness, the grin, were the same.

'How long is it since you were here?'

'Five years,' I said.

'Before we go to Nate's,' he said, 'I want to stop for a minute in Murray Street.'

He drove by Anglesea Square—where Harvey and I used to play touch rugby—by the Bishop's Palace, Brébeuf School, and into Murray Street. One side of the street had all the houses knocked down. The other side still had the houses I knew when we both lived here. But the doors and windows were boarded up. Sparrows flew in and out from the roofs. Harvey's old house had become a store with a plate-glass window and REINHARDT FOODS painted on it.

'Are you still in the butcher business?'

'No,' he said. 'I let my brother Albie have it. I set it up for him. He pays me two hundred dollars a week. I realized early on that there was more money to be made out of the by-products than in meat. For a while I made smoked meat, salami, hot dogs—then I got bored with it. I'm in hides. I'll take you out there later.'

And he grinned.

'I'm the biggest hide man in eastern Canada.'

I followed Harvey into Reinhardt Foods. The room was arranged as a supermarket selling only meat and poultry. The brother was not around so Harvey took me into the back. There was a room with carcasses hanging on hooks. Another room had meat in large vats soaking in brine. Sawdust on the floor. But the only activity was coming from another room. Beside thick wooden tables five men were energetically hacking away at hunks of meat. Separating the meat from the bone. They didn't look at us all the time we were there. They just went on attacking the meat.

Back in the supermarket Harvey's brother appeared.

'When did you get back?'

'A few days ago.'

'Staying at the Château?'

'No, in a Senior Citizen place.'

He looked puzzled.

'It's where my mother lives. But she's gone for a few days to Toronto.'

He gave Harvey a cheque. As we were going out he said, very proudly, to me, 'We supply the Prime Minister with food. We've got two smoked turkeys in the back. You know the address on Sussex Drive? Go and take a look.'

'I believe you,' I said.

From there we went into Nate's on Rideau Street. It was much cooler inside than in the street. Harvey ordered large plates full of smoked meat, chips, pickles, and rye bread.

'Not bad, uh?' Harvey said eating a forkful of smoked meat.

'Delicious,' I said.

'They get it from us,' he said. 'I never thought you would be a writer. Christ, I thought Gunner would be a writer—not you.'

'How is Gunner?'

'He's a professor at some university. He comes back every winter and we go skiing. We still go to Camp Fortune, Fairy Lake, Ironsides—'

And I remembered the last time I went with them. But that was more than twenty years ago.

'I want my son Henry to go to university,' Harvey said. 'I told him he could learn about literature, art, science, philosophy, economics. But he wants to be a butcher. He likes it all. The blood, the killing, the whole lot. It must be in the blood.'

He brought out two thick cigars, gave me one. And we had second cups of coffee smoking the cigars in the air-conditioned room. A large blown-up photograph of Trudeau was on the wall opposite.

'I'm still a socialist,' Harvey said. 'But you can't be a socialist in a capitalist economy.'

He carefully took out a large wad of bills from his back pocket, paid for our breakfast, then put the money in the back pocket and buttoned it down.

I felt the sticky summer heat as soon as we went out.

'How long are you here for this time?' Harvey asked.

'Just a couple more days.'

'Next time you're here,' he said, 'I'll take you out to see my plant. It's in the country. I built it all myself—the machinery—the conveyor belts—the whole process.'

We got back into his car.

'The government health inspector is after me,' he said mischievously. And grinned. 'I'm a polluter.'

I like Harvey. I like his style.

He drove slowly through the streets of Lower Town. 'Before,' he said, 'the small park, the playground, the streets and houses—all fitted together. Now, they knocked down a lot of the wooden houses—left gaps—and put up these high-rises. Suddenly the park is too small. The playground is dwarfed. Nothing seems to fit.'

From Lower Town he drove over the Minto bridges to Rockcliffe and stopped at the lookout. We got out. It was warm and silent. The trees. The grass slopes. A heat haze over the river. Everything here looked so right and in its place.

'I've got a problem,' Harvey said. 'My daughter Clare won't eat. She's a sweet affectionate girl. But if you ask her to eat something—she refuses. If you insist, she gets angry, loses her temper. I don't know how she keeps going. To get her to eat a cracker or a small piece of cheese we have to go through a whole performance—talking and coaxing. And when she finally does have a spoonful of something, I have to behave as if I've just won first prize in a sweepstake … We've been butchers for three generations. I love food. And what she's doing is like a personal insult. She told me that she thinks life is pointless. I can understand someone in their thirties or forties or fifties saying that. But a sixteen-year-old girl.'

'When my sister Mona was growing up,' I said, 'she didn't feel like eating either. She kept to her room. She would go and close the door and stay there. Then we tried to get her to come outside. We had this dog kennel in our backyard. And she used to go in that. My mother would leave out some food for her. In front of the kennel. But she didn't touch it. This went on for weeks. Until my mother put a toy blackbird in the grass by the food. Mona began to show some interest in this bird. And from that day she got better. It took a little while, but she began to eat … I miss red-winged blackbirds. I don't see them in England.'

'Don't they have blackbirds there?' Harvey asked.

'They have lots,' I said, 'but I haven't seen any with red on their wings.'

We drove for a while in silence. Then Harvey said, 'We ought to spend a few days together. I'll tell you the story of my life. And you can write it. It will be a best seller. We can go fifty-fifty on it. I'll show this society up for what it really is. I can tell you things. Christ, did you know we were the poorest family in the street? We burned the furniture one winter to keep warm. When the electricity was cut my grandfather got some tallow and made candles, big candles, and we did our homework by this light. Did you know about that?'

'No,' I said.

'And when I started going to high school they gave three things free at the cafeteria: Heinz ketchup, hot water, soda crackers. This combined together made a delicious soup. This was my daily lunch. I'll tell you things that go on in business that you won't believe. Everyone bullshits.'

This is the best. That is the best. It's all bullshit. If you want to get on you either have to screw somebody or charm somebody ... When the kids were small I advertised for a nanny in England. She gave me the baloney about being an Oxford grad. She came over. She had beautiful manners. She had character. But no money. What's the good of having good manners, talking nicely, if you've got nothing to eat? Christ,' Harvey said, 'why live now in England? That country is on the skids. The last good time they had there was during the war.'

'I'm thinking of coming back here,' I said.

We were now back outside the Senior Citizen building. The heat haze had gone with the afternoon and it felt cooler. Small, pink clouds were in a clear blue sky.

'My mother believed,' Harvey said, 'that there had to be rich people so the poor could live off them. Let me know when you're next in town. Give me a ring. I'll come and get you, show you the plant, and tell you about my life.'

'OK,' I said.

I left Harvey and went into Champagne Barn. It was like going into a quiet residential hotel. I decided to walk up the two flights of stairs to my mother's flat. The carpets in the hall. The copies of *The Citizen*, *The Journal*, *Le Droit*, outside the numbered doors. Between the buildings there was a connecting passage with the walls all glass and where some men sat in their shirt-sleeves and played cards. Above their heads, on the wall, were large posters of Betty Grable in a tight sweater and red lips, and another poster of Ann Sheridan.

A woman went by and said, 'Is that all you've got to do, play games?'

Next morning I was sitting by the window, looking at the park and thinking (This is what I miss in England—trees. Living, as we do, by the sea and all that stone. It's as if something is missing in the diet. The lack of trees. When I'm with trees I feel better.) when a police car with its flashing light drove up, followed by an ambulance. Men went into the building and came out carrying a woman on a stretcher, an oxygen mask over her face. She looked very grey. She still had her hair in curlers.

Then they drove away.

I went downstairs. I went over to Mr Tessier.

'I was just talking to her,' he said. 'About an hour ago. We were watching them pull down that house. And I said—it sure don't take them long to pull down a house.'

'Have they taken her to hospital?'

'She's dead,' he said.

I went to my mother's flat and made myself a cup of coffee. There were the reminders of the past on the walls and on top of the dresser. I looked through a drawer. And found my logbook from the Air Force. And a pile of unused cards. There were Get Well cards, Deepest Sympathy cards, Happy Birthday cards, Happy Anniversary cards, Speedy Recovery, several said Congratulations on your Success.

Next morning my mother appeared just after six.

'Look what I brought you,' she said.

And excitedly took out pieces of wedding cake and assorted pastry from the reception, as well as salami, smoked meat, smoked salmon, hot dogs, bagel.

'I know you like these things,' she said. 'And what you get in Montreal tastes better than here. *Now* what would you like me to make you for breakfast. Some salami with a couple of eggs?'

'Just coffee,' I said.

'What's wrong. Don't you like this food any more?'

'I do,' I said. 'But I don't want it now.'

After the coffee I thought I would go out. It was my last day here. And mother had started to make cookies for me to take back to England. She's happiest when she's cooking. Sometimes I think the only way she can reach you is through food.

I put on my light summer trousers, a sport shirt, and my favourite light shoes so well worn that the leather was split on top in several places.

'You can't go out like that,' my mother said. 'You've been on television. You've had your picture in the paper. Suppose someone sees you?'

Outside it was like walking in a hothouse. It had just gone seven. I walked by Anglesea Square. The row of poplars was still. But now and then their leaves caught a passing breeze. York and Clarence had all the houses bulldozed to the ground. And all that remained standing were the trees. And a signpost saying *Clarence Street*. Another said *York*.

On St Patrick—Percy the Barber was closed. The door boarded up. But from a window I could see the layers of the years on the walls. Haircuts 10 cents ... minnows for sale ... Ken Maynard at the Français ... pictures of King Clancy ... Albert Battleship Leduc ... Howie Morenz ...

By the river it was quiet. The water hardly moving. The sun was coming through a haze. Trees. White bridges. A silver church steeple on the opposite shore. It was like an Impressionist painting.

Then in Murray Street. The wooden houses, with the wooden verandahs, only on one side. As I came near Reinhardt Foods I began to hear the hacking. Then I saw the men. Their window was open. They were the same five men I saw before. By the thick wooden tables ... with the knives ... the choppers ... attacking the meat from the bone. Hack, hack, hack. While the birds sang. The black squirrels moved quickly and stopped on the grass. And now and again a breeze set the small leaves of the poplars moving. Hack, hack, hack ... Hack, hack, hack ...

I would carry that sound with me long after I left.

PART FOUR

Because of the War

I LEFT CANADA IN 1949 and went to England because of the eighteen months I lived there during the war. I met my wife because of the war. She was evacuated to Cornwall from London. She also had a weakness for displaced Europeans who had left their country. And I am European—one generation removed. For almost twenty-seven years we were happily married, raised a family, then she became ill and died.

Soon after that the writing stopped. I'd go out in the morning to get *The Times*, do shopping, cook something to eat. Then go for long walks. Or I would sit in the front room, look out of the window, and listen to the wind, the clock, the gulls. The evenings were the most difficult.

After seven months I realized I couldn't go on like this. So I came back to Canada, to Toronto. A city I had never lived in before. I came mid-February (two months before a new book was to be published ... it was the last thing I read to her in manuscript). I like Canadian winters. But after two weeks in Toronto I didn't want to go out.

I would only leave this room to walk to the corner store and buy two packs of cigarillos. And mail my letters. Then I would go to Ziggy's supermarket. The neat piles of fruit and vegetables. Such lovely colours. And in sizes I wasn't used to. The cheeses from all over. The different bread, bagel, salami, hot dogs—what abundance. Equipped with this I stayed inside, cooked, listened to the radio, made cups of coffee, smoked the cigarillos, and wrote letters to England, Holland, and Switzerland. I like a foreign city. But there was something here that made me uneasy every time I went out.

My publisher had got me this apartment. A large bare room on the seventh floor in the centre of Toronto. It looked shabby from the outside. But one wall was all glass. I watched passenger jets, high-rise office buildings, clusters of bare trees, and some magnificent sunsets. It was even more impressive at night. The lights inside the glass buildings were left on. They made the city look wealthy, full of glitter, like tall passenger liners anchored close together in the dark.

On my first day I went to a bank on Bloor Street to open an account. A small grey-haired woman with glasses came to the counter. 'What is your job?'

I told her.

She lowered her head and mumbled.

'Unemployed?'

'No.'

As she wrote my name, address, and other particulars, I could see she didn't believe I was in work. I wondered why. I had on a new winter coat. I was wearing a tie, a clean shirt, a dark suit. I had good shoes.

I walked to the Eaton Centre. From the outside it reminded me of Kew Gardens—one greenhouse above another. And seeing people moving sideways on the escalators—like something from 'Things to Come.'

I had come to get a telephone. And when I came out, with the telephone, I was on a frozen side-street. I didn't know where north was. So I asked a woman in a fur coat.

'Don't talk to me,' she shouted angrily, waving her hand. 'Go away, go away—just walk along—'

I did walk along. The panhandlers kept asking, 'Can you spare a quarter?' 'Any change, sir?' Then told me to have a good day or else to take care. The cold wind blew loose newspapers down Yonge Street. It looked shabby and raw.

But inside it was different.

I'd come in from the cold to this well-heated building. Though the room was warm the air was dry. The toothbrush I left wet at night was

like chalk next morning And when I left out a piece of sliced bread
In the morning I woke to a high-pitched sound. It was the dry bread
drying even more.

In those first weeks I went for walks. And discovered a large Chinese
section, a Portuguese, Italian, Polish, Jewish, Greek … with their restaurants, bakeries, butchers, bookstores, and banks.

On a cold morning I walked into a district of large houses, wide lawns,
a small park. Icicles were hanging from the roofs. And on the lawns the
snow had a frozen crust. It was garbage day. The garbage cans, and the
tied black-green plastic bags, were on the snow at the edge of the lawns.
In the road steam was rising from the manholes.

Because of the ice I was walking slowly through the park when I saw
a red bird fly to a young tree. This small red bird in this frozen landscape
looked exotic. I was watching this bird when three large dogs appeared.
They attacked the garbage cans, ripped the plastic bags, and foraged. They
did this, from lawn to frozen lawn, without making a sound. Then went
away leaving garbage scattered and exposed.

Some days I gave myself destinations.

One afternoon I decided to walk to the Art Gallery of Ontario. At
a busy intersection I had to wait for the lights to change. I looked up
and saw a black squirrel on a telephone wire slowly crossing above the
crowded street. No one else seemed to take any notice.

Because I saw the squirrel get across and because the sun was shining,
I said to the man waiting beside me,

'Isn't this a lovely day?'

'You too,' he replied.

Late on a Saturday, I went and bought a paperback of *Heart of Darkness*.
Then walked back through fresh snow to the apartment. As the elevator
started it began to vibrate. At the top it stopped. The door remained
shut. I pressed the number seven button again. It went to the bottom.
And stopped. The elevator door still wouldn't open. I tried all the buttons, the switches. Nothing happened except the lights went out. It was
then that I realized I was trapped.

I began to call out.

I don't know how long I was there. The air had become stale. I thought: how awkward it will be if I die here. Finally someone did hear me. 'OK fellah,' I could hear him on the other side. 'Don't worry. I'll get the fire department. They will have you out in a matter of minutes.' And they did. They forced the door open. I was at the bottom of the shaft. And climbed out into the light and the cold air.

That's how I met Nick, the superintendent of the apartment. He was standing with the firemen. He looked distressed. 'Not my fault. I start work yesterday. I no work weekend. Not my fault.'

'Of course it's not your fault,' I said.

After that Nick and I talked whenever we saw each other. His wife had left him. He had custody of their son. When he left for school in the morning, I watched them wave and smile until the boy finally turned the corner. Nick told me he was Yugoslavian. That he grew up with the Germans in his country. 'I see people die. I see people hang. These things I cannot forget.'

'I work for the two sisters. They need to fix here plenty. But they no like to spend money.'

The two sisters came from France after the war and spoke English with a French accent. They owned the apartment and ran it from an office on the second floor. Every morning—Monday to Friday at ten—I'd go down to see if I had any mail. And be greeted by smiles and good mornings from one of the sisters. 'Please sit down. A cup of coffee?'

Edith, the older one, despite her straight grey hair, looked the younger. She was tall, slim, with dark eyes deeply set. She had a long intelligent face. But there was something awkward about her presence. Both sisters were generous, sociable. And both were elegantly dressed.

'These shoes,' Edith said, stepping out of one and going easily back into it. 'I went to Paris to get them.'

'I too go to Paris for my clothes,' said Miriam.

She was stocky: blue eyes, black hair, a round face. She smiled a lot and liked to talk. But often when she started to tell a story she would forget the ending and stop in mid-sentence with a startled look.

Edith was separated with two children. Miriam was divorced with two children. They thought I was too much on my own.

228

'You won't meet people staying in,' Miriam said, 'or going for walks by yourself. Go to dances. Go to political meetings. Join something—' She forgot what she was going to say. Then in a flat voice said. 'In this business you can tell a lot about a person from their luggage.'

At the end of March I met Mrs Kronick. She lived on the floor below. A small Jewish woman, seventy-eight, a widow. She came with her husband from Poland after the First World War. He died ten years ago. She had a son, a doctor, in Vancouver. But he rarely came to see her. Mrs Kronick was still a striking woman, very independent. And she looked after herself. Every time I saw her she wore a different hat. But she couldn't tolerate the cold. I was in the lobby, waiting for the elevator, when she walked in from the outside. Her face was pale, her eyes watering.

'It's a Garden of Eden,' she said, trying to catch her breath. 'A Garden of Eden.'

'What have you been doing, Mrs Kronick?'

She was silent. Then quietly said. 'Sewing shrouds.'

'It's an honour,' she added quickly. 'Not everyone gets asked.'

Next morning Edith knocked on the door of my apartment.

'Did you see what they did in the elevator?'

'No.'

'Come, I'll show you.'

On the inside of the elevator I saw, scratched on the metal, a badly drawn swastika. And on the inside of the elevator door: *Kill Jews*.

'They don't like us,' she said.

Edith's student-daughter told me, 'My mother wears dresses from Dior. She has a woman to help her in the house. But she can't throw away a small piece of cheese. She will wrap it up and save it. She also saves brown paper bags that she gets from shopping—to use again. It's because of what happened to her in the war.'

Both sisters were delighted with Nick.

'He is so much better than the last one,' Miriam said. 'He never stops working.'

'The last one was too old,' said Edith. 'He came from the Ukraine. After forty years here—he was still in the Ukraine.'

'You must come and meet our friend Henry,' Miriam said. 'He is very intelligent. Come for brunch next Sunday.' And wrote an address and drew a simple map. 'Do you think you will be able to find your way?'

'In the war,' I said, 'I found my way to Leipzig.'

On Sunday I took the subway north and travelled as far as it could go. Then began to walk. I had not seen a Canadian spring in thirty years and I had forgotten how colourful the trees were. The flowering crab-apple's pink and crimson; the horse chestnut with its miniature white Christmas trees. And all kinds of maples.

I was walking through a suburb, several cars were beside each house, but no sidewalks.

I walked on the road.

A car drove up, on the opposite side, and stopped. A man got out. He stared at me. Perhaps because I was walking. As I came opposite I called out, 'Why didn't they build sidewalks?'

'I'll only be a minute,' he said nervously. And ran inside the nearest house.

'This is Hannah,' Miriam said.

And I was introduced to a handsome woman in her late fifties: thinning red hair, brown eyes, high cheek-bones, a pleasant face, but there was a certain arrogance.

The man opposite was Henry, a professor of Russian at the university. He was wearing jeans and a blue sports shirt. I felt over-dressed in a grey suit. Miriam had on an expensive-looking sack dress in pastel colours. Edith had gone to New York for the weekend. In the other room the table was set.

We were sitting in the adjoining room. A blue Chagall of flowers was on the wall. And faded photographs of young women with attractive faces in old-fashioned clothes.

Henry was around my age. He spoke English with an accent. I told him that he looked very fit.

'I go jogging every morning. I play tennis. I swim. You realize you are the only Canadian here. Hannah comes from Poland. She came just after the war. I came a few years later. What Russian writers do you like?'

'Chekhov and Turgenev.'

He smiled. 'And what modern ones.'

'Babel, Mandelstam, Akhmatova.'

'Yes,' he said and kept smiling.

I felt my credentials were being examined.

'I have not long come back from Moscow,' he said. 'The status of a writer in Russia today is determined if he is allowed to visit the West. It is the highest accolade. It is higher than getting your book published.'

And I remembered a Russian writer who came to see me in England. He was hitch-hiking. And it was pouring with rain.

'What are you doing?' I asked him.

'Right now, I'm doing an article on suicide in Dostoevsky. Then I will lecture on it.'

We went to the other room and sat around the table. In front of each plate there were wine glasses and tall thin glasses with a yellow rose in them.

Miriam came in with a platter of bagel and croissants.

'Don't let them get cold,' she called out, 'they are delicious.'

I sat next to Hannah. She told me she was leaving tomorrow for Israel. 'I know a lot of people but I don't like staying with friends or relatives. I will stay in a hotel. My mother told me: Guests and fish stink after three days.'

Miriam poured wine into the glasses.

'Why,' Hannah asked, 'is it so difficult at our age to find another person?'

'Once you have been married,' Henry said, 'when you meet someone who has also been married, you are both carrying trailers with you. It is this that makes it difficult.'

'But people do marry again,' Miriam said.

Then Hannah told us how someone she knew got out from Eastern Europe. 'He was running across the border when he heard a whistle. He didn't turn around. He kept running. Then he heard the whistle again.

He kept running. He expected shots. When he got to the other side he heard the whistle again. And saw it was a bird.'

Hannah took a croissant.

'I don't know why,' she said, 'but people from Europe that I meet in Canada seem to be smaller. I don't mean in size.'

'Because in Europe,' Henry said, 'things are small and intimate, therefore the importance of a person is exaggerated. And over there people talk better.'

Miriam brought in ice cream with a hot chocolate sauce. Then waited until she had everyone's attention. 'Today,' she said with a smile, 'I would like us to talk about happiness.'

'You cannot generalize about happiness,' Henry said. 'What is true for one person is not true for another.'

'With the truth you can go around the world,' Hannah said. 'My mother told me that.'

'What is happiness for you?' Miriam asked.

'Moments,' I said. 'You're lucky when they come.'

'For me,' said Miriam, 'it is getting to know another person.'

'But Miriam, don't you agree,' I said, 'that it is impossible, really, to know anyone else at all. At the most it is just speculation.'

'It's living with another person,' Hannah said. 'That's what people can't do without. Once you've had that you want it again.'

'On a visit to a mental hospital,' I said, 'I met a patient. She was in there a long time. She was in there because she was always happy. If someone she liked died, she laughed.'

Miriam suddenly stood up. 'Such a nice day,' she smiled. 'Why don't we go for a walk.'

So we did, the four of us. We walked on the road in the sunshine. Then Hannah said she had to leave as she had to pack. And Henry became restless. He said to me: 'Can I drive you to where you live?'

When he had gone to get the car Miriam said, 'Henry must be lonely. He is always the last one to leave a party.'

The book came out and the publisher arranged a promotion tour. Everywhere I was taken to be interviewed there was a young rabbi ahead of me. He was being interviewed because he claimed to be 'an authority on Death.' There was also a singer making the same tour. In Vancouver she said, 'I love Vancouver. In Calgary, I love Calgary, I love Ottawa, I love Montreal ... it's beautiful, beautiful.' A man from the States said: 'I fell in love with Canada. I changed my nationality. I'm going to die here.' People were going around saying 'I ... I ... I ...' At the end of the week I felt I had given enough radio and TV interviews to satisfy a minor Head of State. But when an article appeared in the *Globe* I had a phone call.

'Do you remember Archie Carter from McGill?'

'Of course,' I said, recognizing his voice and seeing a tall man with dark straight hair, thin lips, a sharp nose, a sharp jaw. He used to be an athlete, then something happened, for he had a limp. In our last year at McGill, Archie Carter started a small recording business. He got me to interview visitors as if they were visiting celebrities. Then they would buy the record to take home. In return Archie let me make recordings of the poems of Thomas Hardy.

'Can you come and see me. Or are you busy?'

'Of course I'll come.'

'Today?'

'Yes.'

He gave me his address.

It brought me to an expensive high-rise opposite a grove of young birches. A doorman, his war medals on a pale blue uniform, saluted me.

I pressed the button outside Archie's door. He called out: 'Prepare yourself for a shock.' 'I'm not the same either,' I shouted back. When he opened the door I didn't recognize him. He was bald. He had put on weight. All those sharp features were gone. Only his voice was the same. And I wondered what he was seeing in my face.

We shook hands. He led me into a room with a glass wall overlooking the birches. He limped more than I remembered.

'What would you like to drink? I only have Italian wine. But it's a good one.'

He came back from the kitchen with two glasses of red wine. We drank in silence.

'I have three daughters,' I said. 'When they were small a friend from London, a painter, would come to see us once a year. When he arrived he would give the three of them five pounds in separate envelopes. The last time he came he only had two envelopes. He had forgotten the youngest. So he quickly asked me for an envelope and a piece of paper. As I went to get them the youngest ran into another room. I could hear her crying. I thought she was crying because he had forgotten her. So I went in to tell her that people often forget. ... But the tears were trickling down her face. And she was sobbing. *He's got old. He's got old.'*

'I'm not a failure,' Archie said.

'In the end, Archie, we're all failures.'

'Oh, I don't know about that. Do you like the wine?'

'Yes.'

'I'm in love with Italy,' he said. 'The food, the climate. Everything. I go there every two years ... I got this foot in Italy. I was leading my company. A mortar bomb hit me. They had to remove the ankle.'

'What happened after McGill?'

'I taught English for a while. Then I began to paint. I'll show you the paintings later.' He paused. 'Of course I'm mad.' And paused again to see what I would say. I said nothing. 'When it's bad it's just boring. It was the pain from the wound that brought it on. The first time was in the hospital ship going back from Italy to England. The next time was fifteen years ago.'

'What happened—?'

He hesitated. 'It's because I have an economic theory that I believe will cure the world's economic problems.' He hesitated again and smiled. He had a pleasant smile. 'I believe we wouldn't have inflation or unemployment or high prices—things would be more abundant and we would be a lot happier—if people didn't *gyp* one another.'

'Did they put you into a mental hospital for that?'

'I went to Lakefield,' he said, 'before McGill. Some of my friends are ambassadors—people like that—scattered all over. I called up Cairo, Amsterdam, London—and told them about this theory.'

'That still doesn't seem bad enough to be put away.'

'But I called them at two in the morning. Some of them became concerned and called the police. It was the police who brought me in ... I thought at this point I was a genius. The hospital I was in was full of people who thought they were geniuses.'

He filled the glasses with more wine.

'A nurse in the hospital tried to make me pee. She got a jug full of water and emptied it into an empty jug. So I could see and hear it. She kept repeating this. I still couldn't go. But the other patients, who had been watching, all wet their beds.

'I have invented a word game that I intend to put on the market. I still think I'm not a failure, you know. But I must not forget. I must call this number.' And he took out an envelope. And dialled very determinedly. 'There is a studio going. And I must get this woman before she lets it to someone else.'

He let the phone ring a long time before he hung up.

'What was I saying?'

'What happened after you came out of the hospital?'

'I began to paint. My shrink quite likes them.' He brought several small canvases from his bedroom. They were gentle landscapes of fields and trees by a river. 'What do you think?'

'I like the colours.'

'I better phone that woman or else that studio will go. And I need a studio.'

He dialled. No response.

'Remind me to try again.'

'Yes,' I said.

'It's good you are in Toronto. We have lots to talk about.'

'I'm going to England,' I said.

He looked disappointed.

'But I'm coming back.'

I got up. 'I'll ring when I get back.'

'Fine. I better call that woman again.'

He took out the envelope. We shook hands. And I left him dialling the number.

On the way back I saw Mrs Kronick.

'What have you been doing?' I asked.

'I was walking down Yonge Street,' she said, 'and I thought of the people I knew who are dead. What have I done with my life?'

I didn't know what to answer.

'You have a son,' I said.

'Yes,' she said gently. 'That's what I have done with my life.'

The two sisters continued to ask me to small parties that they arranged for people separated or divorced. But I met Helen in the supermarket. I could not find the roasted peanuts in their shells. She was standing near by. I asked her. And she walked over to show me where they were.

She was tall. Light blue eyes, a small fine nose, a small mouth, colour in her cheeks, short blonde hair with a fringe. She smiled easily and had a pleasant voice. Because I detected a trace of an English accent in it I said,

'Where in England are you from?'

'Devon—from Exeter.'

'How long have you been here?'

'Thirty-four years.'

'I've not long come from England.'

The next time I saw her was in a small cemetery. I was coming from my publisher. She was arranging flowers by a stone. 'I don't come here often,' she said. 'It's my husband's birthday.'

'Shall we go and have some coffee?'

'My car is here,' she said. 'Why don't we go home?'

There were oil paintings on the wall, books, and black and white photographs of a handsome-looking man.

'He was a very private person,' she said. 'It's almost four years. He had come back from a business trip when he had a heart attack.'

She made me a cheese and tomato sandwich.

'I met Jimmy during the war. He was with the RCAF. We got married when the war was over and he brought me to Toronto. Then Jimmy's father died. And he had to run the family business. We had a very good marriage for almost thirty years.'

Then she told me about her early life in England. How she was brought up by two grandmothers. The one in the city ran a theatre. The other, in the country, was a farmer's wife.

'Why don't you write it down,' I said. 'It would make a good book.'

'I wouldn't know how to go about it.'

'Talk into a tape recorder.'

'I can talk to you,' she said. 'Leave me a photograph. That will help.'

'No, I'll come up.'

That's how it started. Twice a week I would leave the apartment and go there in the late afternoon. She would give me a drink. And talk into the tape. And I would ask her questions and she would answer. Then she would give me dinner. And do another hour of talking into the tape.

One evening there was a thunderstorm.

'Why not stay the night,' she said. 'There's a bed in the spare room or you can sleep with me.'

As I got into bed she said,

'I bruise easily.'

Later she said, 'I wanted you to know that you had a choice.'

Did I have a choice, I wondered.

It was very pleasant having breakfast together. Then walking, in the early morning, down Yonge Street.

After two weeks Helen said, 'Why don't you move in here? One room could be your study and where you work.'

'I'll have to go to England first and settle things. Then I'll come back.'

'The sooner the better,' she said.

The two sisters decided to buy a small coffee and cake store for their children. But the children were hardly there. Only Edith and Miriam. And they seemed to be enjoying themselves. As I came in Edith said. 'You must have a croissant. They are the best in Toronto ...'

'Did you know Nick will be leaving us?'

'No,' I said. 'But why—'

'He takes too many days off. He doesn't do his work.'

Miriam came in. 'You're just the person I want to see. We are having a small party on Saturday night. There will be some interesting people.

Henry will be there—'

'I have come to say goodbye.'

'I don't like goodbyes,' said Edith.

'Ella Fitzgerald used to sing,' I said:

Every time we say goodbye
I die, a little.
Every time we say goodbye
I wonder why, a little.

'That's Lamartine,' Edith said. '*Chaque fois qu'on se dit, au revoir, Je meurs un peu*—Imagine being in a store like this in Toronto and quoting Lamartine.'

'I'm sure that in small stores in Toronto—Czechs are quoting from Czech writers, Italians, Hungarians, are doing the same. The Portuguese here are quoting from Portuguese poets—' when I noticed grey airplanes in the sky. I could see them from the store window. They were coming in all directions. I counted a Dakota, six Mustangs with their clipped wings, two Bostons, a Lightning, a Tiger Moth, another Dakota.

'They're airplanes from the Second World War,' I said.

'It must be from a museum,' Miriam said in her flat voice.

I watched the low-flying planes. They looked so slow. Then they began to circle as if they were going to land.

I went outside to watch the airplanes and saw Nick coming across the car park. He was carrying a loaded shopping bag from the supermarket. I wanted to tell him about the airplanes. But he had his face down. As he came closer I could see tears in his eyes. I thought it was because he had lost his job.

'Tito is dead,' he said. And walked by.

The airplanes had disappeared. There was not a trace of their presence. Only a seagull flew low between two high-rises.

I was walking by the store that showed the time in the capitals of Europe when I saw Mrs Kronick on her way back to the apartment. She had on a smart black and white suit and a large black hat.

'I'm leaving, Mrs Kronick.'

She looked at me for a while. Then said,

'When I leave a person, I don't care if I never see them again.'

'But what about those you love?'

'Of course,' she said, 'with those you love there's always regret.'

Something Happened Here

I FELT AT HOME SOON as I got out of the Paris train and waited for a taxi outside the railway station. I could hear the gulls but I couldn't see them because of the mist. But I could smell the sea. The driver brought me to a hotel along the front. It was a residential hotel beside other residential hotels with the menu in a glass case by the sidewalk. It had four storeys. Its front tall windows, with wooden shutters and small iron balconies, faced the sea. On the ground level was the hotel's dining-room. The front wall was all glass. And there was a man sitting alone by a table.

It looked a comfortable family hotel. The large wooden staircase belonged to an earlier time when it had been a family house. The woman who now owned and ran it liked porcelain. She had cups and saucers on large sideboards, on every landing, as well as grandfather clocks and old clocks without hands. They struck the hour at different times. There were fresh and not so fresh flowers in porcelain vases. There were large mirrors, in wooden frames, tilted against the wall, like paintings. There were china plates, china cups, and china teapots on top of anything that could hold them.

My room on the third floor didn't face the sea but a courtyard. I watched a short man in a chef's hat cutting vegetables into a pot. The room was spacious enough but it seemed over-furnished. It had a large double bed with a carving of two birds on the headboard. A tall wooden closet, a heavy wooden sideboard, a solid table, several chairs, a colour television, and a small fridge fully stocked with wine, brandy, champagne, mineral water, and fruit juices. On the fridge was a pad and pencil to mark what one drank.

After I partly unpacked and washed I went down to the dining-room and was shown to a table by the glass wall next to the man sitting alone. He was smoking a cigarette and drinking coffee. He had on a fawn shirt with an open collar and a carefully tied black and white cravat at

240

the neck. He also had fawn-coloured trousers. He looked like Erich von Stroheim.

The proprietress came to take my order. She wobbled, coquettishly, on high heels. Medium height, a little plump, in her late forties or early fifties perhaps. She had a sense of style. She wore a different tailored dress every day I was there. A striking person. She had a white complexion and black hair. And looked in fine health. Her teeth were very good. There was a liveliness in her dark eyes. Every time I walked by the desk and the lounge she never seemed far away: doing accounts, dealing with the staff, talking to guests.

I gave her my order in English. I ordered a salad, an omelette, and a glass of *vin rosé*.

When she had gone the man at the next table said in a loud voice, 'Are you English or American?'

'Canadian.'

He began to talk in French.

Although I understood some of what he said I replied, 'I can't speak French well. I'm English Canadian.'

'I speak English,' he said. 'I had lessons in Paris at the Berlitz school. My English teacher, she was a pretty woman, said I was very good because I could use the word barbed-wire in a sentence. My name is Georges.'

I told him mine. But for some reason he called me Roman.

'Roman, what do you do?'

'I am a writer.'

'Come, join me,' he said. 'I like very much the work of Somerset Muffin and Heavelin Woof. Are you staying in this hotel?'

'Yes. I arrived a half-hour ago.'

'I live in the country. Since my wife is dead I come here once a week to eat. What do you write?'

'Short stories,' I said, 'novels.'

'I read many books—but not novels. I read books of ideas. The conclusion I have come is that you can divide the people of the world. There are the sedentary. There are the nomads. The sedentary—they are registered. We know about them. The nomads—they leave no record.'

A young waiter, in a white double-breasted jacket, poured more coffee.
'Do you know Dieppe?'

'No, this is my first time here.'

'I will show you.'

And he did. When I finished eating he took me along the promenade.
A brisk breeze was blowing but the sea remained hidden by mist. He
brought me to narrow side-streets, main streets, and squares. He walked
with a sense of urgency. A short, stocky man, very compact and dapper,
with lively brown eyes and a determined looking head. He had a bit of
a belly and his trousers were hitched high-up. He carried his valuables
in a brown shoulder bag.

In a street for pedestrians only we were caught up in a crowd. It was
market day. There were shops on both sides and stalls in the middle.

'Look, Roman, at the *wonderful* colours,' Georges said loudly of the
gladioli, the asters, lilies, roses, geraniums. Then he admired the peaches,
apricots, butter, tomatoes, carrots, the heaped strands of garlic and
onions. He led me to a stand that had assorted cheese and large brown
eggs, melons, leeks, and plums. And to another that had different sausages
and salamis. On one side he showed me live brown and white rabbits in
hutches. And laughed when, directly opposite, brown and white rabbit
skins were for sale. The street fascinated him. He stopped often and talked
loudly to anyone whose face happened to interest him.

We had a Pernod at a table outside a café that had a mustard and orange
façade. He lit a French cigarette. I, a Canadian cigarillo. The pleasure of
the first puffs made us both silent. Nearly all the tables were occupied,
shoppers were passing, and music came loudly from a record store.

I asked Georges, 'What do you think of Madame who runs the hotel?'

'*Très intelligente,*' he said and moved his hands slowly to indicate a large
bosom. '*Et distinguée.*' He moved his hands to his backside to indicate
large buttocks. And smiled.

He had a way of talking English which was a lot better, and more
amusing, than my French.

He brought me inside an old church. He was relaxed until he faced
the altar. He stiffened to attention, slid his left leg forward, as if he was
a fencer, and solemnly made the sign of the cross. He remained in that

position for several seconds, looking like the figurehead at the prow of a ship. When he moved away he relaxed again. And pointed to a small statue of the Virgin with her arms open.

'Roman, the Virgin has opened her legs in welcome.'

I was feeling tired when we came out of the church. The train journey, the sightseeing, the conversation ... but Georges walked on. He was heading for the docks. I said I would go back to the hotel as I had some letters to write.

'Of course,' he said, 'forgive me. You must be exhausted. Tomorrow, would you like to see where I live in the country? I will come for you after breakfast.'

And he was there, as I came out of the hotel, at eight-thirty, sitting in a light blue Citröen, dressed in the same clothes.

'Did you sleep, Roman?'

'For eight hours.'

I could not see the sun because of the mist. But the surf, breaking on the pebbles, glistened. As he drove inland it began to brighten up. He drove fast and well. And he talked continually. Perhaps because he needed someone he could talk English to.

He said he had been an officer in the French navy. That in the last war he had been a naval architect in charge of submarines at their trials.

'I was at Brest, Cherbourg, Toulon, Marseille. My daughter was born when I was stuck in submarine in the mud. My wife told me the nurse came to say, "The baby she is lovely. But the father—it is dead."' And he laughed.

On a low hill, ahead, a large institution-like building with many windows and fire escapes.

'Lunatic asylum,' Georges said, 'full of patriots.'

The government, he said, had a publicity campaign for the French to drink more of their wine and appealed to their patriotism. After this whenever he mentioned anyone who liked to drink, Georges called him 'a patriot.' And if anyone looked more than that, '*Very* patriotic.'

The asylum was beside us. A cross on top. And all the top windows barred.

'When I was a boy … this place made big impression. Before a storm … the wind is blowing … and the people in lunatic asylum scream. I will never forget.'

He drove through empty villages, small towns. He stopped, walked me around, and did some shopping. I noticed that the elaborate war memorials, by the churches, were for the 1914–18 war. The only acknowledgement of the Second World War was the occasional stone, suddenly appearing in the countryside, at the side of the road, that said three or four members of the Resistance had been shot at this spot.

'I have been to America,' Georges said. 'I like the Americans. But sometimes they are infantile. Nixon—dustbin. Carter—dustbin.'

He drove up a turning road by a small, broken, stone bridge that had rocks and uprooted trees on either side. 'There is a plateau,' he said, 'high up. It has many meadows. The water gathers there for many rivers. Once in a hundred years the water very quickly goes down from the plateau to the valley and turns over houses, bridges, trees. Last September a priest on the plateau telephone the Mayor and say the water looks dangerous. But the Mayor, a young man, say it is only an old man talking. Half-hour later the water come down and drown thirty people and took many houses. It was Sunday so many people were away from the houses otherwise more drown. All happen last September. In a half-hour. But it will not happen for another hundred years. And no one will be here who knows it. The young won't listen. They will, after some years, build houses in the same place. And it will happen all over again.'

In one of the large towns he stopped and showed me the cemetery where his family is buried. It was a vault, all stone, no grass around. Nor did any of the others have grass anywhere. On the stone was a vertical tablet with two rows of de Rostaings. The first was born in 1799. 'He was town architect.' A few names down. 'He had lace factory … He build roads … See how the names become larger as we come nearer today.'

'Will you be buried here?'

'No. My wife is Parisian. She is buried in Paris. I will lie with her.'

He continued on the main road, then turned off and drove on a dirt road. Then went slowly up a rough slope until he stopped, on the level, by the side of a converted farmhouse.

'We are here,' he said.

We were on a height. Below were trees and small fields—different shades of green, yellow, and brown. Instead of fences or hedgerows, the fields had their borders in trees. And from this height the trees gave the landscape a 3-D look.

Georges introduced me to Marie-Jo, a fifteen-year-old schoolgirl from the next farm who did the cooking and cleaning during the summer. Short blonde hair, blue eyes, an easy smile. She was shy and tall for her age and walked with a slightly rounded back. While Marie-Jo barbecued salmon steaks at the far end of the porch, under an overhanging chimney, Georges walked me around. In front of the house, under a large elm, was a white table and white chairs. It was quiet. A light wind on the small leaves of the two near poplars. 'They say it will rain,' he said. And beside them a border of roses, geraniums, and lobelia.

We ate outside on a white tablecloth. I could hear people talking from the farm below. Further away someone was burning wood. The white smoke rose and thinned as it drifted slowly up. On top of the house was a small stone cross. A larger metal cross was embedded in the concrete of the front fence.

'I am Catholic,' Georges said. 'There are Protestants here too. My sister married a Jew. A Pole. From Bialystok.'

Marie-Jo brought a round wooden board with cow and goat cheeses on it. And Georges filled my glass with more red wine.

'When I was young boy of seven we had great distilleries in my country. We hear the Russians are coming. We wait in the street. It is beginning to snow. But I do not want to go home. Many people wait for the Russians.

'Then they come. They look giants with fur hats and big boots and long overcoats. *Very* impressive.

'After a while—what happens? First the women. They say to Russian soldiers—you want drink? They give them drink. A little later, in the street, you see the women wearing the Russian furs for—'

Georges indicated with his hands.

'Muffs,' I said.

'Yes, muffs, muffs. The women all have muffs.

'Then the French men give drink. Later, the French men you see in the street—they are wearing the Russian boots.

'The peasants—they *drowned* the Russians.'

Marie-Jo brought ripe peaches, large peaches, lovely colours, dark and light, red to crimson. They were juicy and delicious.

'How did your sister meet her husband?'

'At the Sorbonne. My sister always joking. He serious. I did not think they would stay together. When she go to Poland to meet his family we are worried. We Catholic. They Jew. They have two children. Then the war. The Nazis. He is taken away. My mother, a tough woman, get priest and doctor to make fake certificate—say the two boys baptized. But my mother did not think that was enough. She tell me to take the boys to a farmer she know in the Auvergne. I take them. When I meet the farmer I begin to tell story. But the farmer just shake my hand. Say nothing. The children stay with him for the war.'

'What happened to the Polish Jew?'

'He died.'

We went to have coffee in the barn. The main room of the house. High ceiling with large windows and the original beams. To get to it from the inside you would go up some stairs. But you could walk to it from the garden by going up a grass slope. 'All farmers have this for the cattle to go up and down,' Georges said.

It was also his studio. On the walls were oil paintings by his uncle who was dead. Impressionist paintings of the landscape around here. 'They sell for 40,000 francs,' Georges said. 'I have about thirty good ones. Some in the flat in Paris, some in the flat in Cannes. A few here.' He also had his own paintings—on the wall, and one on an easel—like his uncle's but not as good.

Marie-Jo appeared with a jug full of coffee.

'I am working on book,' he said. 'I have contract with Paris publisher. Eleven years—I am not finished. It will be traveller's dictionary of every place in world that someone has written.'

We had coffee. He lit a cigarette and went over to his record player.

'Roman—have you heard the Japanese Noh?'

I answered no with a movement of my face.

'Very strange. Sounds like a cat ... and a chain with bucket ... and a man flogging his wife. I was twenty, a midshipman on cruiser. We visit Japan. Suddenly I was put there, for six hours, listening to this.'

He put a record on. 'This is the cat ...' a single note vibrated ... 'looking for another cat ...' Georges was standing, talking with gestures. 'Now, the long chain with a bucket going down well ... it needs oil. ... This is a man flogging his wife ...'

He stopped the record.

'The Japanese they are different from the French. They believe the dead are with us all the time.'

He showed me a photograph of his wife, Colette.

She looked a determined woman, in her late forties. A strong jaw, thin lips, blonde hair pulled back on her head, light eyes.

'She had beautiful voice,' Georges said. 'One of the things I like in people is the voice. If they have bad voice it is difficult for me to stay long with them.'

'How long is it since she died?'

'Three years.'

He must have thought of something else for he said abruptly, 'If you do not come into the world—then you cannot go.'

He took me for a walk through the countryside. There were all kinds of wild flowers I didn't know and butterflies, and some, like the small black and white, I had not seen before either. But it was the trees that dominated. And I like trees. Probably because I have lived so long in Cornwall facing stone streets and stone terraces.

I wondered why Georges was not curious about my past. He appeared not interested in my personal life. Though I did give him bits of information.

'How long will you be in Dieppe?'

'Two, maybe three days more,' I said. 'I want to go to England, to a flat I have in Cornwall, and do some work.'

It was after nine, but still light, when we got back to Dieppe. 'I know a small place but good,' Georges said. And brought me to a restaurant opposite the docks called L'Espérance.

We were both tired and for a while didn't talk. I ordered marinated mackerel, a salad, and some chicken. And Georges ordered a half-melon, veal, and cheese. Also coffee and a bottle of red wine.

Two tables away a man and a woman, both plump, in their late fifties or early sixties, were eating with relish. The woman had a large whole tongue on her plate to start with, the man a tureen of soup. He tucked his napkin into his open-neck shirt. Then they both had fish, then meat with potatoes, then cheese, then a large dessert with whipped cream on top ... And all the time they were eating they didn't speak.

Beside them, going away towards the centre of the restaurant, were two young men. They were deaf and dumb. They were talking with their hands. They also mimed. When they saw us looking they included us in their conversation. One of the men looked Moroccan, with a black moustache on the top lip and down the side of his face. He was lean. And he mimed very quickly and well. He pointed at Georges' cigarette and at my cigarillo. And shook his head. He touched his chest and pretended he was coughing. And shook his head. He then showed himself swimming, the breast stroke. He was smiling. He showed us that he was also a long-distance walker, getting up and staying in one place, he moved heel and toe, heel and toe, and that curious rotation of the hips.

'Roman,' Georges said loudly. 'The woman you see is fat. Her husband is fat. Look how they eat. Beside them two men, slim, young. They have to talk with their hands. They look happy—all the time the food comes— they are talking. But the two beside them—they do not talk at all—they concentrate on next bite. If I had movie camera—that is all you need. No words. No explanation. If I was young man, Roman, I would make films.'

As he drove me to the hotel, Georges could not forget the scene in the restaurant. On the hotel's front door there was a sign saying it was full.

'Tomorrow,' Georges said, 'I no see you.'

As tomorrow was Sunday I asked him if he was going to church.

'No, I do not like the clergy. The elm tree need spray. They get disease. I know a young man. He will do it. But I have to get him. And I go to see an old friend. He was officer with me. He now alone in Rouen. We eat lunch on Sunday when I am here. Two old men. I see you the day after.'

And we shook hands.

Next morning, I opened the large window of the room. The sun was out. It was warm. A blue sky. After breakfast I decided to go for a walk. I crossed the harbour by an iron bridge. And went up a steep narrow street of close-packed terraced houses. It looked working class. The houses were small, drab, unpainted. And the sidewalks were narrow and in need of repair. They had red and pink geranium petals that had fallen from the window boxes on the small balconies.

I passed an upright concrete church with a rounded top. It stood by itself, stark, against the skyline. I went through tall undergrowth and, when clear of it, I saw I was on top of cliffs. They were an impressive sight: white-grey, sheer, and at the bottom pebbles with the sea coming in.

I walked along for about an hour, on top of the cliffs, when I noticed the path becoming wider as it started to slope down. The cliffs here went back from the sea and left a small pebbled beach. People were on it.

I was looking at the dirt path, as I walked down, because it was uneven and steep when I saw a shrew, about two inches long, over another shrew lying on its side. The one on its side was flattened as if a roller had gone over it. I watched the head of the live shrew over the belly of the dead one—there didn't seem to be any movement. Then, for no reason, I whistled. The live shrew darted into the grass. And I saw the open half-eaten belly of the one on its side, a brilliant crimson. The colour was brighter than any meat I had seen at the butcher's.

The small beach wasn't crowded. The surf gentle ... the water sparkled ... a family was playing boules. Someone was wind surfing across the length of the beach ... going one way then turning the sail to go the other, and often falling in. A man in a T-shirt brought a dog, a terrier, on a leash. Then he let him go into the shallows. Under an umbrella a young woman was breast-feeding a baby. Nearer to the water a tall woman with white skin and red hair was lying on her back, topless. People were changing using large coloured towels ... while the continual sound of the low surf as it came in breaking over the pebbles and sliding back.

I had brought a picnic: bread, a hard-boiled egg, cheese, tomatoes, a pear. And a can of cider to wash it down. After I had eaten I took off my shirt, shoes, socks, and lay down on the stones.

A loud noise woke me. It was two boys running over the stones between my head and the cliffs. I sat up. I didn't know how long I had been asleep. The surface of the water sparkled. The click of the boules was still going. From somewhere a dog was barking. The cliffs, a few yards behind me and on both sides, had light green streaks in the massive white grey. And high up, on the very top, a thin layer of grass.

The tide was coming in. I put on shirt, socks, and shoes, and walked over the pebbles to a paved slope that led from the beach to the road. I could now see a narrow opening between the cliffs. And as I walked up the slope the opening fanned out to show a suburb of houses with gardens, green lawns, and trees. As I came to the top of the paved slope I saw, across the road, on a stone, in French and English.

On this beach
Officers and Men of the
Royal Regiment of Canada
Died at Dawn 19 August 1942
Striving to Reach the Heights Beyond

You who are alive on this beach
remember that these men died far from home
that others here and everywhere might freely
enjoy life in God's mercy.

When I got back to the hotel the 'full' sign had been taken down. Madame greeted me with a smile.

'You have caught the sun. I have surprise for you.'

She soon reappeared with a thin blonde girl of about twelve or thirteen.

'This is Jean. She is from Canada,' Madame said proudly. 'From Alberta.'

'Where from in Alberta?' I asked.

'Edmonton,' the girl replied in a quiet voice.

'How long will you be in Dieppe?'

'I live here. I go to school.'

'When were you in Edmonton?'

'Three weeks ago.'

'Is your father there?'

'No, he is somewhere else. He travels. I'm with my mother.'

'Can you speak French as well as you can English?'

'I can speak it better,' she said.

And she was glad to go off with Madame's only daughter, who was older and not as pretty, to roller-skate on the promenade.

'She is charming,' Madame said as we watched both girls run to get out.

'I went for a walk today, Madame,' I said, 'and came to the beach where in the war the Canadians—'

'*Ah.*' She interrupted and shook her head, then raised an arm, in distress or disbelief. She tried to find words—but couldn't.

'I have read many books about it,' she said quickly. 'Do you want to see the cemetery?'

'No,' I said.

That evening, while in the dining-room, I decided to leave tomorrow. For over three weeks I had been travelling in France. All inland, until Dieppe. It had been a fine holiday. I had not been to France before. But now I wanted to get back to the familiar. I was also impatient to get back to work. I had brought with me a large notebook but I had written nothing in it.

I said to Madame at the desk, 'I will be leaving tomorrow. Could you have my bill ready?'

'Of course,' she said, 'you will have it when you come down for breakfast.'

'It is a very comfortable hotel. Are you open all year?'

'In December we close.'

'Has it been a good season?'

'I think I go bankrupt,' she said loudly. 'Oil—up three times in two months. It is impossible to go on—' She held up a sheaf of bills.

'I will tell my friends,' I said.

'Is kind of you,' she said quietly. And gave me several brochures that said the hotel would be running a weekly cookery course in January and February of next year.

Late next morning, with my two cases in the lounge, I was having a coffee and smoking a cigarillo, when Georges appeared. He saw the cases.

'Yes,' I said. 'I'm going today.'

'What time is your boat?'

'It goes in an hour.'

'I'll take you.'

He insisted on carrying the cases to his car. Madame came hurrying away from people at the desk to shake my hand vigorously and hoped she would see me again.

While Georges was driving he gave me a card with his address in the country, in Cannes, and in Paris. And the dates he would be there. Then he gave me a large brown envelope. I took out what was in it— a small watercolour of Dieppe that he had painted. It showed the mustard and orange café with people sitting at the outside tables and others walking by. On the back he had written, 'For Roman, my new friend, Georges.'

'When I get to England,' I said, 'I will send you one of my books.'

'Thank you. I should like to improve my English. Perhaps I find in it something for my traveller's dictionary.'

At the ferry I persuaded Georges not to wait.

'Roman, I do not kiss the men.'

We shook hands.

I sat in a seat on deck, at the stern, facing Dieppe. The ferry turned slowly and I saw Dieppe turn as well. The vertical church with the rounded top, the cathedral, the square, the houses with the tall windows and wooden shutters and small iron balconies.

Then the ferry straightened out and we were in the open sea. After a while it altered course. And there were the cliffs where I had walked yesterday and the narrow opening. I kept watching the cliffs and the opening. And thought how scared they must have been coming in from the sea and seeing this.

The sun was warm, the sea calm. And when I next looked at the cliffs the opening had disappeared. All that was there was the white-grey stone sticking up. I thought of gravestones ... close together on a slope ... You could see nothing else. Just gravestones. And they were gravestones with nothing on them ... they were all blank.

On the loudspeaker the captain's voice said that coming up on the left was one of the world's largest tankers. People hurried to the rails with their cameras.

I went down to a lower deck and stood in the queue for the duty free.

Django, Karfunkelstein & Roses

IN LATE OCTOBER, on the morning of my fiftieth birthday, we had breakfast early—my wife and three daughters. On the plain wooden table: a black comb, a half-bottle of brandy, a red box of matches from Belgium, a felt pen, a couple of Dutch cigars, a card of Pissarro's *Lower Norwood under Snow*, and a record. They wished me Happy Birthday. And we kissed.

After breakfast the children went to school. We continued to talk, without having to finish sentences, over another cup of coffee. Then my wife went to make the beds, water the plants, do the washing. And I went to the front room, lit the coal fire, smoked a Dutch cigar, drank some of the brandy, put the record on, listened to Django Reinhardt and Stephane Grappelli—The Hot Club of France. And looked out for the postman.

The mimosa tree was still in bloom in the small front garden as were some roses. To the left, a road of terraced houses curved as it sloped down to the church steeple and the small shops. And at the end of the road—above houses, steeple, shops—was the white-blue of the bay.

Directly opposite, past the garden and across the road, was Wesley Street. A short narrow street of stone cottages. I watched the milkman leave bottles on the granite by the front doors. Mr Veal—a tall man with glasses, a retired carpenter, a Plymouth brethren ('I have my place up there when I die,' he told me pointing to the sky)—came out of his cottage holding a white tablecloth. He shook the tablecloth in the street. From the slate roofs, the red chimney pots, came jackdaws, sparrows, and a few gulls. They were waiting for him. Mr Veal swirled the tablecloth—as if it was a cape—and over his shoulder it folded neatly on his back. He stood in the centre of the street with the white tablecloth on his back, the birds near his feet. ('I need to get wax out of my ears,' he said when we were walking. 'I don't hear people—but I hear the birds.') Then he went inside.

The postman appeared and walked past the house. This morning it didn't matter. My wife hung the washing in the courtyard and pulled up the line. Then left the house to buy the food for the day. The sun came through the coloured glass of the inside front door and onto the floor in shafts of soft yellow, blue, and red. I went upstairs to the large attic room. And got on with the new story ...

Within a few years this life changed. And for my wife it ended. The children left home. I would get up early—the gulls woke me—wondering what to do. (I wasn't writing anything.) Living by oneself like this, I thought, how long the day is. How slow it goes by. I went from one empty room to another ... looked outside ... such a nice-looking place ... and wondered how to go on. And there were times when I wondered why go on?

Then a letter came from Zurich. It came from the people who worked in a literary agency. They told me that my literary agent was going to be seventy. They were planning a surprise party. Could I come?

At the airport a young man with curly brown hair and glasses, just over medium height, was holding a sheet of paper with my name on it. He was shy. (No, he hadn't been waiting long.) He smiled easily. He said he did the accounts.

'You have not met Ruth?'

'No,' I said.

'How long is she your agent?'

'Fourteen years.'

Zurich was busy. In sunny end-of-May weather he drove to the heights above ... to a cul-de-sac of large houses. They had signs, *Achtung Hund* ... except in front of the large house where he stopped.

As he opened the door there were red roses, in the hallway, lots of them. And more red roses at the bottom of the wide stairs. The wall opposite the front door was mostly books. But in a space, waist high, a small sink with the head of a brass lion. Water came out of its mouth. There were more roses, as well as books, in the large carpeted rooms that he led me through. Then outside, down a few steps, to a grass lawn. People were standing in clusters talking and eating. A tall attractive woman with straight blonde hair was cooking over a barbecue. She talked loudly in Italian. A man in his thirties—regular clean-cut face, black curly hair—was moving around slowly with a hand-held camera, stopping, then moving again.

The person at the airport came towards me with a lively short woman. She looked very alert, intelligent, and with a sense of fun.

'What a surprise,' she said. We embraced quickly and kissed. Then we moved apart and looked at one another.

'This is very moving,' she said quietly.

I could hear the whirr of the film camera.

'You must be hungry.'

She linked arms, led me to the barbecue, and introduced me to Giuli—the tall blonde Italian who was her housekeeper. (She would die, unexpectedly, in two years.) There were frankfurters, hamburgers, salad, grapes. I had a couple of frankfurters and walked to the lawn's edge and to an immediate drop. The churches, the buildings, the houses of Zurich spread out below and in front. Across some water I could see wooded hills. And further away, hardly visible against the skyline, mountains.

More people kept arriving. I could now hear French and German. It was pleasantly warm. Sparrows flitted around us. Giuli, and others, threw them bits of bread.

That night cars brought the guests into Zurich. The birthday party was in a Guildhall near the centre. A narrow river was outside. The water looked black. I could see several white swans on it. The guests came from different parts of Western Europe. They were mostly publishers. But I did meet Alfred Andersch. A gentle man with a pleasant face, a nice smile ('Why write novels if you can write short stories'). He would die within a year. And Elias Canetti. A short stocky man with a large face, high forehead, thick black hair brushed back. (He would be awarded the Nobel Prize.)

There were speeches, toasts, in English. Then the guests went in line to another room where—on a long table with white tablecloths—there were lit candles and all sorts of food. Platters of shrimps ... asparagus ... a large cooked salmon ... roast beef ... the salads were colourful. I looked ahead to the far end where the cakes were. And saw, on the table, what I thought was one of the white swans from the river. As I came closer I realized it was made of butter.

Later that night, in the house, seven of us who were staying as guests sat with Ruth in the kitchen. We talked and drank. I was the only male. The women's ages spread from the late thirties into the seventies. The youngest was the girl from upstairs who rented a room and worked in Zurich. She was waiting for her gentleman friend to phone to let her know when he would be in Zurich. After she spoke to him she came down and joined us. She started to sing, *It's All Right With Me*. She had a fine voice. We joined in. There were more Cole Porter songs. And Jerome Kern. Then the older ladies sang, very enthusiastically, European Socialist songs. And went on to folk songs, mostly German. (Ruth was born in Hamburg.) The one that made an impression was a slow sad tune about the Black Death.

Giuli, sitting beside me, said in broken English how her husband, a pilot in the Italian air force, was killed while flying. And how lucky she was to find Ruth. Then, with more wine, she began to talk Italian to everyone and stood up wanting us all to dance. We formed a chorus line, Ruth in the middle. We kicked our legs and sang as we moved around the kitchen. Then, tired, we sat down. This time Ruth was beside me, a little out of breath. While our glasses were being filled again I asked her— what was she thinking when she saw those large bunches of roses all over the house?

And she said that during the last war she worked as a courier for the Resistance. They sent her to Holland. The Nazis tracked her down. 'Things became difficult. I was on a wanted list. I had to stay inside my small room. I couldn't go out.

'In the next room there was a man called Karfunkelstein. He told me he was going to commit suicide. I asked him why.

'"One can't live with a name like Karfunkelstein in these times."

'I managed to talk him out of it.

'"Wait," he said. And left me.

'When he came back he had his arms full of roses and other flowers.

'"For you," he said.

'And gave them to me.

'My small room was full of flowers. And I couldn't go out to sell a rose for food.'

Four and a half years later, early this December, I saw Ruth again. I had been invited to Strasbourg to give a lecture at the university. After the lecture I took a train to Zurich. Outside the station I went into a waiting taxi. I gave the driver the name of the street.

He replied with the number I wanted.

'How did you know?'

'Many people go there.'

This time no guests or flowers. But the same warm welcome. The young man who met me at the airport was still doing the accounts, still looked shy, and smiled easily. His hair was grey. I met the new house-keeper, Juliette. She came from France. About the same age as Ruth.

It was cold and foggy. At dusk I could see the lights of Zurich below. Juliette brought in some coffee and for over an hour Ruth and I talked business. She phoned up the Canadian embassy in Bonn and spoke to the cultural attaché about an East German translation. She phoned a radio station in Cologne about a short story that had been broadcast. We went over a contract line by line. Then Ruth said,

'I must go and lie down for twenty minutes.'

She went upstairs. I went into the kitchen. And talked to Juliette while she was preparing the food. Juliette told me she used to be a pho-tographer in Paris before the war. Then worked in London. She had a studio in Knightsbridge. And talked nostalgically of the time she lived there. A small radio was on. Someone was playing a guitar. I said I liked Django Reinhardt.

'I knew him,' Juliette said. 'My husband, André, was his best friend for some years.'

Ruth appeared looking less tired.

'You didn't stay twenty minutes,' Juliette said in mock anger.

Ruth and I finished the rest of our business over a drink. Then it was time for supper. The three of us sat around a small table in the kitchen, in a corner, by the stove. We had red wine. We clinked glasses and drank to our next meeting.

Juliette passed the salad bowl.

I asked her about Django Reinhardt.

'He couldn't read or write. He was a gypsy,' she said. 'Very black hair but good white teeth. You know how he got those two fingers? His wife was in a caravan making artificial flowers when there was a fire. Django ran in and saved her. His hand was burned ... Oh, he was a bad driver. He had so many accidents ... the car looked a wreck. One time he came to see us with a new shirt, a tie, and a new suit. He asked my husband what was the proper way to wear it. André showed him. Django stood in front of the mirror, wearing the new clothes, looking at himself, very pleased at the way he looked.' (Juliette acted this out with little movements of her face and hands as she spoke.) 'We listened to him play ... he would play for hours ... if I could have recorded it. ... He only began to make records so he could give them to his friends. But he could be difficult. To get him to the recording studio on time my husband would say: "Django, you are late ... the machinery is all set up ...there are people waiting ... they have their jobs." And Django would not go. André tried again. And Django got angry.

'"I need my freedom. If I can't have my freedom ... it's not my life."

'Later he bought a château near Paris. That life didn't suit him. He was ruined ... by money ... by women ... fame. He couldn't handle it.'

Juliette stood up and from the stove, brought a small casserole and served the meat and the vegetables.

'What happened to Karfunkelstein?' I asked Ruth.

'He probably committed suicide,' she said in a flat voice. 'In those days people like him did ...

'On May 10th 1940,' she went on, 'the Germans came into Holland. Next day there was an epidemic of suicides. There weren't enough coffins. They put them in sacks.

'I knew this young family. They had two small boys. The man was a teacher. His wife was in love with him. She would go along with whatever he wanted. And he wanted to commit suicide. He kept saying: "Life as it is going to be ... will not be worth living."

'I knew someone in the American embassy. I arranged for them to see him next morning so they could get out of Holland. But I wanted to make sure they would be there.

'I went to their house. The man was still saying that life without freedom to live the way he had lived would be impossible ... when the youngest boy swallowed a small bulb from a flashlight. (At least his mother said that he did.) She was very worried. She asked me: What should she do? How could she get a doctor? After a while the child got better. Because I saw how worried she had been I thought it was all right to leave them for the night. I said I would be back in the morning.

'When I arrived, the two boys were dead. The man and the wife had sealed all the doors and windows. Turned on the gas. And they had cut their wrists.'

When we had finished, Juliette began to clear and wash up while Ruth went into the other room to dictate letters into a machine for the secretary next morning. I went up to the room where I would sleep the night—a large bare room in the attic with a low double bed, books all over, and a wide window with a view of Zurich. I looked at the lights and thought of the people who had come to Zurich, from other countries, for different reasons. And how few of them stayed.

Juliette came to the door and said, 'There is a Canadian film on television. Have you heard of it? It is called *Mon Oncle Antoine*.'

'It's the best Canadian film I have seen,' I said.

'Then we shall all see it,' she said.

I went down with her.

Juliette drew the curtains. Ruth put in a hearing aid. 'I only do this for television,' she said.

I looked forward to seeing the film again. I had seen it, about twenty years ago, in St Ives on television and remembered how moved I had been by it.

'There is a marvellous shot,' I said while the news was on. 'It is winter. On the extreme left of the picture there is a horse and a sleigh with a young boy and his uncle. The horse has stopped. And on the extreme right of the picture is a coffin that has fallen off the sleigh. In between there is this empty field of snow. It is night. The wind is blowing ... no words are spoken. But that image I have remembered all these years.'

Mon Oncle Antoine came on. The first surprise—it was in colour. I remembered it in black and white. Then I realized ... it was because in St Ives we had then a black and white TV set. There were other disappointments. It might have been because of the German sub-titles, or my memory.

I told them the scene was about to come on.

When it did—it wasn't memorable at all.

Was it because it was in colour? Or had it been cut? I remembered it as lasting much longer. And it was the length of the shot, in black and white, that made it so poignant.

When the film was over I could see they were disappointed.

'I remember it differently,' I said. And told them how I had seen it on a black and white TV set.

'It would have been better in black and white,' Ruth said.

'There may have been cuts.'

'It seemed very jumpy,' Juliette said. 'You could see it had the possibility of a good movie.'

That night in the attic, in bed, I heard midnight by the different clocks in Zurich. I didn't count how many. But there were several. Each one starting a few seconds after another ... and thought about *Mon Oncle Antoine*. How it differed from what I remembered. I saw how I had changed that shot. Just as I had switched the candles from around the man in the coffin at the start. And had them around the boy in the coffin at the end. I had, over the years, changed these things in order to remember them. Is this what time does? Perhaps it was a good film because it could suggest these things.

And was this what Juliette had done when she told about Django Reinhardt? And Ruth with Karfunkelstein?

But some things don't change.

I remembered my wife having to go into Penzance hospital to drain off some fluid. It was in the last two weeks of her life. She hadn't been outside for over a year but in that front room where I brought down a bed. And from there she looked out at the granite of Wesley Street and Mr Veal feeding the birds. Two men carried her out on a canvas and put her in the back of the ambulance.

When she returned she said, 'It's so beautiful. The sky … the clouds … the trees … the fields … the hedges. I was lying on my back and I could see through the windows …'.

Early next morning Ruth drove me to the railway station. The streets were quite empty. The sun was not high above the horizon. And here it was snowing. The sun caught the glass of the buildings, the houses, and lit them up. And the snow was falling … thick flakes.

'My aunt in Israel is ninety,' Ruth said. 'And drives her car. Isn't that marvellous?'

We were going down a turning road, down a slope, then it straightened out. I asked her,

'Will you go on living in Zurich?'

'I don't know. The only other country would be Holland. I like Holland.'

After she left I went inside the station and gave all the Swiss change I had to a plump young girl who was selling things from a portable kiosk. In return I had a bar of chocolate, a large green apple, and a yellow pack of five small cigars.

Gwen John

EARLY IN JANUARY 1984 I flew from Toronto to London. Then a train to Sheffield. My son-in-law, Kevin, met me at the railway station. And from there he drove out of the city onto moorland that led to a valley and to a stone house in Hathersage. Ellen, my eldest daughter, was having their first child. And as her mother was not alive I wanted to be there. The baby was a boy, Hugh. I stayed with them a week. Did the shopping. Helped to prepare the evening meal. (Kevin was in Chesterfield, during the day, teaching science.) Took the dog, a whippet named Gemma, out for long walks in the surrounding countryside.

It was a pleasant village, in a valley, hills all around. A few churches. A school. A short busy road. Above it, on the sloping fields, sheep. There was a butcher shop, a bakery, several fruit and vegetable stores, an Italian restaurant, some old pubs with early photographs of local cricket teams, and a good inn. It looked like a village in a children's book. The postman on his bicycle ... the farm off the main street with working horses in the stables ... ducks by a stream that went by a playing field ... a small library (a room in a house) open some afternoons.

An Air Force jet appeared low overhead. Then climbed and banked quietly above the hills. I saw coaches and cars arrive with hikers and climbers. And walked in a section, up from the lowest part, where the large houses were, with magnificent views of the hills. And, closer, the neatly cut bowling green with the delicate bandstand. Ellen told me that Eyam, a nearby village, was isolated in the Middle Ages because of the Black Death. People would not go in but leave food. And on a postcard (in a small newsagent post office) I read that Charlotte Brontë stayed in Hathersage, then used parts of it in *Jane Eyre*.

When it was time to leave, Kevin drove me to Chesterfield railway station. Across the moor ... before the sun was up ... frost was on the stubble. He went on to his school. I got on the train that arrived from the North and was going to Penzance. I couldn't see an empty seat. Everyone looked asleep. When I heard a voice say,

'You can sit beside me.'

Bright, alert. She could be in her late twenties. Her black hair all over the place—probably I had woken her up. Her face was pale with dark eyes. And she wore an elegant, dark-purple, woollen suit.

'You can have the window-seat,' she said. 'I'm going to get some breakfast.'

She came back with two fried eggs, toast, and coffee. I saw a small black case by her luggage. Perhaps a flute. After she had eaten, tidied up, we started to talk.

She had been visiting her parents in the Lake District. I told her I had just flown from Canada and was going to Cornwall.

The train was moving along. Past small fields. And, in the depressions, water. I remember the American student in the airport bus from Heathrow. In England for the first time. And excited by what he saw. 'This is watercolour country,' he said.

'Have you been to East Germany?'

'Yes,' she said.

'How long were you there?'

'A year.'

'I was there two weeks. Where were you?'

'Halle.'

'I was in Halle ... a few hours ... between trains. What were you doing?'

'Teaching English.'

'Did you go to Leipzig?'

'Yes.'

'When I was in Leipzig I was taken to the Thomaskirche and shown where Bach played the organ. In the aisle, on the floor, there's an area of aluminum where he is buried. And in the middle of the aluminum, in large clear letters, it had B A C H. Someone had placed a red rose in a corner. The organ was at the far end of the church. It's small. The pipes look like children's crayons standing on end.'

'My boyfriend is an organist,' she said. 'A good one. He came to see me. We went to Leipzig. In the Thomaskirche he was given permission to play Bach's organ.'

Outside. A grey sky … low clouds … small fields … hedges …

'Where are you going?'

'Oxford.'

'What are you doing in Oxford?'

'A Ph.D.'

'In what?'

'English.'

'On what?'

'Decadence.'

I thought, how marvellous. On a train in England just after eight in the morning. And we are talking about decadence.

Neither of us was certain what it was. But she was interested what form it took in art. She thought it might be when something—a way of painting, of writing, a style—goes on after the life of the original is over.

Oxford came too soon. She got off. I was on my own until St Erth, where I got off, walked across the covered wooden bridge, took the branch line that went by Lelant estuary, then the coast, to St Ives.

I keep coming back. To this place. To this house. Although now it is only the top floor and the attic that I rent. I keep coming back to these shabby damp rooms, with the paintings on the walls given to me by people no longer here. The old black gas stove, the small (rust-on-the bottom) fridge, the plain wooden table. I can't leave go of this place. The life that was lived here is no longer here. The ceiling is cracked and peeling and when it rains patches are wet. The wood of some of the windows is worn and splintered. It all looks used and worn-out and not repainted or repaired. Yet I feel comfortable here even though the life wasn't comfortable. Nor is it now.

I live opposite stone—stone cottages—stone terraced houses—street after street of stone—no trees.

But there are the windows. In the rooms on the top floor. And when I go up the turning stairs to the attic. And see the colours of the far shore fields, the sun over the bay, the lighthouse, the gulls, the low clouds moving from the land to the sea.

And, from the windows, on the other side. The back and front gardens of the larger houses farther up on the slope with the neat rows of vegetables, the poppies growing wild in the tall grass, the shrubs, the flowers.

And I like being here because I'm on my own. I do what I want to do when I want to do it. I get up—the gulls wake me—before the sun is above the horizon. Make breakfast (a grilled Manx kipper), have cups of coffee, read the morning paper. Listen to the radio. For the first few days that is all I do. Except for walks by the coast, the estuary, in the country (the foxgloves), on the moor (the changing colours of the bracken), or through the town. I get fresh mackerel from the fishmonger, hot bread and saffron from the bakery. There is a familiarity ... as if I have never been away.

But after a week, sometimes less, I am ready to leave. I've had enough. This slow pace, these uneventful days and nights, these spartan and used rooms. When I now walk through the town I see it for what it is—a backwater. A few more days ... I feel strangely exhausted doing nothing. I go to bed, while it is still light, draw the curtains. And it's as if I'm in a small cabin, on a large passenger ship, on an ocean. The ship has its engines stopped. And it's drifting.

Gradually the pace that is here takes over. The tiredness goes. I go upstairs to the attic, to this familiar desk, and start to write.

I remain here, living like this, until I finish something, or a first draft of it. Then I fly back to Toronto, where I live a different life with Mrs Garrens, a widow of forty-six. She has a large secluded house in three acres of grounds (lawns, gardens, trees), a gardener, a housekeeper. In winter we travel.

So these two lives. The one with Mrs Garrens began four years ago— eighteen months after her husband, an industrialist, died. The one in St Ives, in 1949, when I was twenty-four and living in London for the first time.

There was still food rationing, bomb damage, cigarettes under the counter, *The Third Man*, cheap Algerian wine, large Irish sausage at Sainsbury's. And a lot of displaced people.

I had come over to do postgraduate work at the University of London and rented two rooms above the Institute of Child Psychology in Notting Hill Gate. Opposite was a garage. The door beside the garage had *Theosophy* painted above it.

In my third week, I returned late from a party and couldn't get the key to open the outside door. I saw a light in the garage. And walked across the street. A bare bulb hung from the ceiling and a thin man in a white shirt, in his sixties, was reading a newspaper and smoking a cigarette.

I told him I lived above the Institute and couldn't get in.

He remained silent. Then said,

'Come with me.'

I followed him in the dark to the back of the garage where cars were parked.

'You want a Rolls or a Bentley?'

'Bentley,' I said.

He opened the boot of a car, brought out a blanket, unlocked a back door, put the light on, gave me the blanket, and said goodnight.

It was all white inside. A shiny white, like satin. I stretched out across the back seat. It was like being in an expensive coffin.

When I woke it was raining. And almost nine next morning.

That evening I went to Chelsea to see Nicholas Kempster, who was with me at university and lived in a bed-sit on Oakley Street. He left a note on the door saying he'd be back in a few hours.

I went to wait in the nearest pub. It was dark and gloomy (the walls were painted brown) and empty except for an old man sitting by the side of the fireplace. He seemed to be staring into space. A pint of beer was on a small table in front of him. He didn't touch it all the time I was there. He had on an officer's fawn greatcoat, unbuttoned. His hair was grey and uncombed. I recognized him as Augustus John.

The next time I saw Augustus John was two years later, in a black and white photograph on the wall of a pub, The Globe, in Penzance. The others in the photograph were Maurice Mayfield (a war artist) and his attractive wife, Nancy, dressed like a gypsy. Maurice Mayfield tried to look and live like Augustus John. I knew this because, in those two years, I met Elizabeth. We married. And decided to come down to Cornwall. We rented a large granite house with a walled garden from Maurice Mayfield. When he heard what I was doing he let me have it cheaply.

So we lived in this fine large house (it was the finest house we ever lived in) while the owner and his wife and four young children lived in a small primitive cottage on the moors. Maurice would come in every morning on an old bicycle to his studio—a small partitioned section of the building, near the house, where I worked. He always wanted me to see his new paintings. They were of peasant or gypsy women. Stylized figures, often in black, like the one above our bed called *The Angel of Sleep*. Though I didn't care for his work, I liked Maurice. Years later, I was told he came from a working-class family by the London docks. You wouldn't have known from the way he spoke. The soft voice, the careful diction, the good manners. A large man with a small head, short red hair, blue eyes, a face that looked as if he had just caught the sun. He went around dressed like a peasant farmer. And he smiled easily.

He told me he was trying a new technique (bees' wax) and wanted me to see what he had done. I didn't like any of them. Then I saw on the wall a small unframed oil of a woman's head and shoulders. She wasn't smiling. The hair was close to her head, parted in the middle and pulled back, to form a bun. She didn't have much of a chin. It was mostly in browns. But there was an immediacy, a human quality, that none of the others had.

'I like that,' I said. Glad that here was something I could be enthusiastic.

'It's not by me.' Maurice smiled. 'It's by Gwen John.'

It was the first time I had heard her name.

At Mousehole we lived on the slope of a hill in this cut-granite house, with the high granite wall around it, and the copper beech, bamboos, roses, inside. At night, in bed, we could see the roofs of the cottages sloping to the harbour. The boats, in the bay, fishing between the chimneys. We had little money. I went out with the fishermen from Newlyn. And bicycled back after midnight ... the moon on the water ... heard a fox

... an owl from Paul. Then going up the outside granite steps, wondering if we still had electricity. Two days later an elderly man, from the electricity company, came to disconnect our supply. I held the ladder so he could climb and do it.

That night we ate our meal by candlelight.

The fishermen left pilchards and mackerel outside the front door. The farmer, from the fields above, left broccoli, new potatoes, and lettuce. Ellen was born. The butcher, Mr Brewer, left five shillings on her pram when she was asleep. Then the money ran out and there was little I could do here to earn any. So we moved: to London, Devon, Brighton. When things improved we went back to Cornwall and to this house.

A few years later I read that Augustus John had died. And on the television news caught a glimpse of Maurice Mayfield at the funeral. Then Maurice Mayfield died. Our children left home. Elizabeth died. I went back to Canada, to Toronto, where I met Mrs Garrens.

It started as a business arrangement. Mr Garrens had left instructions that he didn't want a memorial stone. But Mrs Garrens wanted to do something. She told me he liked books and thought of having a book prize, in his name, to be given every two years to a promising writer. And she wanted me to select the writer. We continued to meet in her house to discuss this. Soon we talked about other things. The prize was never mentioned. We were both still young enough to miss the physical side of marriage. And we didn't like living on our own.

But I have this illness. What other men do with other women I can only do with my wife. And when she died I thought, now I have to learn to be promiscuous.

When I moved in with her it was Mrs Garrens's life that I began to live. Not only the house with the spacious grounds. But the large rooms with floor-to-wall white carpets, the walls painted a delicate green. The paintings on the walls. The one I liked was a drawing, a nude, by Matisse. The meals cooked by the housekeeper. The dinner parties. I also began to travel.

She took me first to France. (Mrs Garrens grew up in the South of France and talked about the fields of blue cornflowers in the long grass that were part of her childhood.) I had never been to France. It was the country Elizabeth always wanted to see.

In Paris we stayed in a hotel by the Luxembourg Gardens. We often went into the Gardens. Then to a restaurant, then back to the hotel. We went to Marseille and did the same. We both seemed to have a lot of energy, especially early in the morning, as if we had to catch up on lost time. She would make a sound from her throat as she reached her climax. Then give me these quick little kisses all over my face.

At breakfast, she said,

'Your eyes go up when you're happy.'

Next morning at breakfast she said,

'Your eyes tilt when you come.'

On our last day in Marseille she asked,

'Is there any place you would like to see?'

I said Dieppe.

So we went to Dieppe. Went for walks by the coast. Had picnics in the countryside. And to a different restaurant every night. And sometimes we ate in the hotel where we stayed along the front. The bed was wide and high. And there were long mirrors on the doors of the wardrobe.

'I'm your last fuck,' Mrs Garrens said.

That's the way our life has gone. And I like the life we have together. But after seven or eight months, I become restless. Another month or two and I need to leave. I am pulled back (why I don't know) to this pretty backwater, these seedy rooms, to being alone. And to work here.

This January I told Mrs Garrens.

'I need to go to St Ives.'

Mrs Garrens doesn't like this. When I tell her I need to go she becomes anxious. We have little quarrels. And when I'm packed, the bags downstairs, waiting for the limousine to come up the drive to take me to the airport, I feel sad about leaving her.

We sit in the front room, having a drink and talking quietly.

She never uses my name but calls me you.

And I always call her Mrs Garrens.

⌒

I arrived back here on January 10th. There had been continual rain in England for weeks. Drizzle. The sky was overcast. It was raining now. And in the passing small fields there was flooding.

When I arrived in St Ives it was grey and wet. The open railway station above the beach was deserted. I began to walk with my bags. The streets were empty. Just the sound of the gulls. The rooms, the attic, were cold. They were damp. There was no heat except from the gas rings of the black kitchen stove. I put the three on that were working. There was also a strike. The water was cut off. When it came on I was told to fill the bath. I would take saucepans of water from the bath to the kitchen, to make coffee, to wash the dishes, to shave.

I had caught a cold and had a temperature. I decided to go to bed. But I wanted something to read. I went to the small library. Saw a biography by Susan Chitty of Gwen John. I returned to the cold damp and dusty rooms, put on two sweaters, thick woollen socks, and several extra blankets. I went to bed, in the narrow front bedroom, with the bottle of duty-free brandy that I had bought.

And began to read.

How Gwen John led a middle-class upbringing in Wales. Went to Paris to be a painter. Became a model to earn some money. Met Rodin. They became lovers. She was, for a while, happy. Then he discarded her. She wrote him letters every day. And waited in Luxembourg Gardens hoping to get a glimpse of him.

After that she withdrew ... she continued to paint ... but didn't look after herself ... hardly eating ... little money ... she ended up in a shed at the bottom of a garden ... the rain coming in from the roof.

The Second World War. The Germans invaded France. Augustus John was in the south of France with some of his women friends and several children. He was to drive and pick up Gwen John in Paris. Then head to one of the ports. But he avoided Paris. And got on the last ship for England.

With the Germans invading, Gwen John left Paris. Got as far as Dieppe. Collapsed in the street. People thought she was a vagrant. Took her to a hospice. Where she died. No one knows where she is buried. Augustus John was supposed to do a memorial stone. But he never got around to it ...

Soap Opera

I PHONED MY MOTHER in Ottawa just after 6:00 p.m. No reply. A few minutes later I tried again. Then I took Fred, mostly beagle, out for his walk ... through the small park ... (at twelve he still has this rapid acceleration and expects me to throw a tennis ball for him to chase) ... around the reservoir and the wall of green trees that hide the ravine. In front, by the path, were the four saplings planted a few years ago with the name-plates: *In Memory of My Beloved Papa, Joseph Podobitko*. I wondered who Joseph Podobitko was. I had asked the Portuguese gardener, who looked after the grounds, if Joseph Podobitko had worked here. He told me that Joseph Podobitko didn't work here. He didn't know who he was, and it cost three hundred dollars to put up one of those saplings.

I came back to the house with Fred and phoned again. I tried the Civic Hospital. I asked if she was a patient. Silence. Then her voice (slow and shaky) said,

'Hello.'

'When did you go in?'

'This morning at ten.' It was an effort for her to talk. 'I'm just played out.'

'I'll see you tomorrow,' I said. 'I'll take the early train.'

That evening I phoned my sister Sarah in Carleton Place. She had come to Ottawa and had been staying with Mother for a week.

'I couldn't take it any more,' Sarah said. 'She doesn't want to live. She has given up.'

'A person who calls an ambulance and gets herself admitted as an emergency case hasn't given up.'

'But you don't know what she talks about.'

'I'll take the early train,' I said. 'It gets in around noon.'

'I'll be with her in the morning and you will be with her in the afternoon.'

'Yes,' I said. 'We'll get together later.'

My mother was on the fifth floor of the surgical ward in a room by herself. When I walked in she was asleep, propped up by pillows. I was dismayed at how she had changed. I brought one of the grey leather chairs to the side, sat, and waited.

It was a large air-conditioned room with two windows. The blinds were half-way down, the curtains half-way across. On a small table, by the bed, a telephone. On a chest of drawers some flowers wished her a speedy recovery. On the wall a painting, a reproduction, of two rowing boats by a blue pier with the moon out. The room had another room within it. A private bathroom. All the walls were orange and cream. And the doors light blue. The large front door was opened as far as it could go. And on it a name-plate: *Donated by Mr Thomas Sachs*.

She opened her eyes.

'Hello, Mother.'

'Have you been here long?'

'No. It's a nice large room.'

'I paid into Blue Cross,' she said weakly, 'for semi-private. But they put me in here. Do you think they made a mistake?'

'I wouldn't think so.'

She looked up at the two standing metal forms beside her. One had a bag that was giving her blood. It was almost empty. The other, water. And that was full. She watched closely, as I did, as the drops appeared.

'What did the doctor say?'

'That I have jaundice. That I'm bleeding inside. But they say they can stop that. He's a very nice man.'

'Was Sarah here in the morning?'

'Yes.'

'How is Sarah?'

'Hysterical. She looks at me and laughs. Then she cries.'

We were silent. 'Help me up.'

I put my hand behind her back and eased her forward. I was surprised at the thickness of the spine, how much it protruded, and how light she was. She sat, with her head down, as if waiting for strength to return.

'I can't eat,' she said in despair.

Soap Opera

There were small cardboard containers on the table by her bed. 'Would you like this?' It was prune juice. 'This one?' Orange juice. 'This?' A white-purple thing labelled *Ensure*. She answered by an almost imperceptible movement of her head. I put in a stubby straw, bent it near the top, and held the *Ensure* while she sipped it all. Then she reached, slowly, for the box of Kleenex on her bed and, carefully, dried the corners of her mouth.

Again we were silent.

'You will stay in the apartment?'

'Yes.'

With a finger she pointed to the dresser by the wall. I opened the top drawer and saw a large beige purse.

'Take the keys ... Have you got the keys?'

I showed them to her.

'In the fridge ... help yourself. There is coffee. Eat whatever you like. You have my permission.'

'I'll water the plants.'

'It would be better if I didn't have them.'

'How much water do you give?'

'Not too much. Every two or three days.'

'Anything you want me to bring?'

'The small key is for the mail-box ... See if any mail. In the dining-room ... in the drawer ... are two cheques. Six hundred dollars and something. Take the bank-book ... pay in my account.'

I said I would.

She wanted to be eased back to the way she had been.

'Mrs Tessier, across the hall, takes in *The Citizen*. Tell her you are in the apartment and you will have the paper. I have paid three months in advance ... I don't think I'll go back there. I'll go to some other place for a rest.'

The large blue eyes. The grey hair, usually neatly combed up, was loose on the sides. She did not have her teeth in and her mouth looked small. I thought of her independent nature, the quick intelligence, and how she coped with things.

'I'm all played out,' she said. 'But I'm not tired of living.'

She watched the blood and the water drip.

'It's working,' I assured her.

But she continued to watch.

'Another doctor came,' she said. 'A young doctor. He asked me questions about my operations. He said I had some kind of anaemia that only Jews from East Europe have. Did you know about that?'

'No.'

'He said the mother passes it to her siblings. Does that mean daughters?'

'Sons and daughters.'

We were silent.

'Do you want to see anyone?'

She said no with her head.

'If anyone phones. If anyone in the building asks. Say I have gone in the hospital for tests. Don't say anything more. Just tests.'

'Yes.'

Again we were silent.

'I'm going to close my eyes now,' she said.

The closed eyes made the socket bones more visible. Faint sunlight was on her face and on the far wall. I knew nothing of her life in Poland except what she told me. 'I liked a young man, a red-head. He was a scholar. My mother and father didn't think he could make a living ... At my wedding they threw money in pails ... We had a large house and a servant. When I was coming to Canada she begged me to take her.' Then the difficult early years in Ottawa that she doesn't want to be reminded of. And for the last twenty-one years on her own, in a senior citizens' building, opposite a small park. I thought again of her generous nature, how independent she was, and how she came out with unexpected things.

Her eyes opened.

'I need a bed-pan,' she said in a low voice.

A white flex, with a white button on it, was held to one of the pillows by a safety pin. I picked up the flex and pressed the button. A snapping sound and a slight electric shock.

'When the nurse comes I'll go,' I said. 'And I'll come tomorrow. Sarah said she would be here as well.'

I went over and kissed her on the forehead. 'With jaundice I don't think you should kiss.'

I opened the door of her apartment. In the half-light I could see the three small rooms. Brought the suitcase in, quickly drew the curtains, and opened the windows. All the clocks had stopped.

The place looked as if it was left in a hurry. In the kitchen, dishes on the draining-board were upside down. In the bedroom the large bed was not made. A dress was on the back of the rocking-chair. Two-tone, beige and brown shoes were under the bed. The calendar, by the window, had not been changed in two months.

She had kept everything neat and clean. Now a thin layer of dust was on the furniture and on the wooden floor. And on the leaves of the plants in the front room. The earth was dry. I watered the plants. Looked in the fridge. A few potatoes were sprouting. The pears were bruised and had started to go rotten. I couldn't understand why Sarah hadn't tidied up. There was some half-used cottage cheese, a bottle of apple juice, a tin of *Ensure*. The cupboard, by the sink, was packed with tins as if for a siege. I made a cup of coffee, brought it into the front room, sat by the table, and started to relax.

I had not been here on my own before. How small and still. And full of light. The chesterfield set, from the house, was too large. She brightened the settee with crocheted covers—bands of red, yellow, green—that kept slipping down. And cushions with embroidered leaves of all kinds. The same was on the chair, by the side of the window, overlooking the street and the small park. (The Lombardy poplars are gone. But the gazebo is there. And kids throwing a ball around.) On the other side of the window, against the wall, a large black and white television was on the floor. No longer working. Its use, to support the plants on its top. Beside it: the glass-enclosed wooden cabinet with her best dishes, best cups, saucers, the Chinese plate that goes back to my childhood, the Bernard Leach mugs and bowl that I brought back on visits from St Ives. On top of the cabinet a family tree. Small, round, black and white photographs in metal frames hung from metal branches. Father and mother, in the park by the river, some fifty years ago. Sarah and I … when we were around ten and eight … the people we married … our children … with their husbands their children …

The room's centre-piece was the nickel-plated samovar. On the long wooden dresser, against the far wall, with the mirror above it. Two silver candlesticks were on either side. A brass pestle and mortar. A silver tray. And more plants, lots of them, just leaves in various shapes and sizes.

Above the settee, two small paintings of people at the Wailing Wall. Beside it a framed diploma-looking paper with a red seal at the bottom.

First Distinguished Service Award
Presented to
The Dedicated Men and Women
Past and Present Of
The Ottawa Burial Society

'What do you do?'

'Sew shrouds.'

I said nothing.

'It's an honour,' she said indignantly. 'Not everyone gets asked.'

On the wall, a watercolour of St Ives (signed Holland). It was done from the Malakoff, overlooking the harbour, before TV aerials were on the cottages. I grew up, in Ottawa, with this watercolour. And in all those years we didn't know what it was. In 1949 I left for England. Five years later I made my first visit back. Paid the taxi, walked into the house, kissed them, and saw the watercolour.

'That is where I live in England.'

No reaction from either of them.

The phone rang.

'Hello.'

'Annie?'

'No, it's her son.'

'Where's your mother?'

'In hospital.'

'Not again. What is it this time?'

'They don't know. She has gone in for tests.'

The telephone was loud. I had to hold it away.

'Who shall I say phoned?'

'Tell her that Phyllis Steinhoff called. We belong to the Golden Age Club. We go and play bingo together.'

'I'll tell her.'

Silence.

'Your mother is a lovely woman. She is intelligent. And she is nice.'

I went to the door, directly opposite in the hall, and knocked. Mrs Tessier, small, gentle, dumpy, with brown eyes and glasses, opened the door. She always looked cheerful.

'Hello, Mrs Tessier. I came because my mother is in hospital.'

'How is your mother?'

'Not well.'

'What is wrong?'

'They don't know. She is in for tests.'

'You want the paper?'

'Yes.'

She disappeared.

'You want the others?'

'No, just today's.'

'How long you here?'

'Two or three days.'

'I hope your mother comes home soon.'

I decided to change the bed linen. The linen cupboard was packed tight with neatly folded sheets, pillow-cases, and towels. I was taking out a couple of pillow-cases when I saw a used brown envelope. It was unsealed. Inside were dollar bills. Twenties, tens, fives, twos and ones. I counted. It came to a hundred and eighty dollars. When I took out the sheets I saw more used brown envelopes, unsealed, also with money. I counted all the money. It came to $2,883.00. I put my hand between other sheets, pillow-cases, towels. No more envelopes but a small battered cardboard box held together by red elastic bands. Inside, large silver coins that I remembered as a child. A double eagle on one side, two heads on the other. She had brought them over with the samovar, the candlesticks, the pestle and mortar, the silver tray.

It was humid and hot. I had a bath. Then phoned Sarah. She was staying with her daughter Selina and her family on the outskirts. I asked Sarah if she knew about the money.

'Yes.'

'Do you know how much there is?'

'No.'

'Two thousand eight hundred and eighty-three dollars.'

'It's for her funeral. She told me what to do when she dies. I have to call Pettigorsky from the burial society right away. She wants no autopsy. The coffin must be the Jewish way. No nails. Shiva she wants private. At her place. Only the family. And she wants me to get someone to say Kaddish for her. I'll pay him from that money.'

'She hasn't mentioned any of this to me.'

'When I'm with her that's all she talks about.'

Next day I walked to the bank on Rideau near the market and paid the government cheques into her account. Then to the Rideau Centre, got on a bus to the hospital. Sarah was sitting in a leather chair by the bed. Mother was asleep. She was having another blood transfusion. The water was dripping as well. Sarah saw me. 'Hi,' she said and smiled. We both walked quietly over and kissed.

'How is she?'

'Most of the time she sleeps.'

'Has the doctor been?'

'Yes.'

'What did he say?'

'He said, "We are not going to let your mother die."'

We were silent.

'She doesn't have cancer,' Sarah said.

Another silence.

'Why didn't she keep the money in the bank?'

Mother opened her eyes.

'I couldn't put the money in the bank,' she said slowly. 'If I did I would have to pay more rent.'

I sat her up. Got some juice and a straw. She didn't have the strength to hold it. When she finished and wiped her lips she said, 'It is not necessary to put this in a story.'

'I only write about people I like.'

She wasn't convinced.

'Phyllis Steinhoff phoned,' I said.

'You didn't tell her anything.'

'That you were having tests.'

Silence.

'And Dinka called,' I said.

'Is she in Ottawa?'

'Yes, for the weekend. Do you want to see her?'

'No,' she said quietly.

We were silent again.

'How old is Dinka?'

'She is four years older than me and she runs around like a girl.'

'Did she marry again?'

'She did. But she asked him to leave.'

Another silence.

'In your letter-box,' I said, 'you had a notice saying that men are coming next week to clean your windows.'

'No,' she said. 'I don't want anyone to go in there. It's dirty. Write on a piece of paper Mrs Miller doesn't want her windows washed. Then stick the paper, with tape, on the outside of the door. You get the tape in the dresser of the living-room.'

Another silence.

She wanted to be eased back, propped up by the pillows. I suggested to Sarah that as I'm here she might like a break and have coffee in the cafeteria.

When Sarah left I told mother what was in the news. 'Waldheim was elected President of Austria.' She looked surprised. 'The Blue Jays are not doing so good. It's their pitching.' I showed her photographs of St

Ives that I took on my last visit. 'Do you remember that summer … the two weeks you were there?'

'It was the best holiday I had.'

'You used to walk along the beach and pick the small pink shells at the tideline.'

'I still have them.'

We were silent.

'I'm going to close my eyes now,' she said.

When Sarah came we went out in the corridor.

'What else did the doctor say?'

'That she still has jaundice. Why, they don't know. He said they were thinking of doing an operation to find out. She is all for it. "I don't want to go on like this," she said, "if they can do anything—let them do it." But they think she is a poor risk and wouldn't survive. She's not eating.'

A nurse came and woke her to take a sample of blood. I told Sarah I would go to the waiting-room at the end of the corridor.

On the way I saw a young doctor.

'They took a piece of her liver,' I said.

'When was that?'

'On Friday. How long will it take?'

'The pathologists are in a class by themselves. They take their time.'

'I guess we'll just have to wait.'

'I don't think whatever they find will make much difference.'

In a room with the door open I saw a nurse by the bed of a patient. A tube was being shoved down her throat.

'Let me die.'

'Swallow it, dear, as if it is a piece of bread.'

'Let me die.'

'I'm not allowed to. Now swallow it for me, dear, as if it is a piece of bread.'

I returned to my mother's room.

'Selina is coming in a half-hour,' Sarah said, 'to pick me up for supper. She's invited you as well.'

'You'll go,' Mother said.

She knew I didn't want to.

Whenever I arrived from Toronto to see her, and after we had eaten and had a talk, she would say, 'Call up Sarah. Call up Selina.'

I said nothing.

'Do it for me.'

Selina had been in Toronto for two days at a real-estate conference. (She is high up in the company.) And was coming from the airport to the hospital. We were walking, from the hospital, to Selina's car when Selina stopped.

'She's going to die.'

'Yes,' I said.

Selina was Sarah's only child. A tall pale woman with blonde hair, a small face, a nice smile, blue eyes. She looked pretty but anaemic. And there was a toughness about her. The few times I did go to their house she inevitably forced a confrontation.

She had tried teaching, advertising. But she hadn't found what she was good at until she went into real-estate. She was married to George (he was fourteen years older), who smoked a pipe, worked in the Civil Service, and spoke in a slow, deep voice. They lived in a large new house, in a windswept field, on a housing estate near a lake. The nearest place, Rockliffe, was some ten miles away. Their son, Scott, had his mother's eyes and complexion. But looked oddly serious. 'He's very clever,' my mother told me. Then, lowering her voice as if she was going to tell me something she shouldn't, 'He's a genius.' Scott's favourite reading was stocks and shares. But at twelve he wasn't allowed to play the market. I once asked him if he played sports. 'Football,' he said. 'What position?' 'Centre forward—I'm very good.'

I don't remember the meal. It was afterwards—when we went into the large sitting-room with the Eskimo carvings, the Indian paintings—that Selina started.

'This is the first time for you. All the other years you weren't here. We had to take her to the hospital. See her through the operations. While you were away in England.'

'You're lucky,' I said. 'You know her in a way that I don't.'

An awkward silence.

'Why did you go away?' Selina said.

'I had to.'

'You didn't have to. You could have stayed and got a job in the government.'

'I had to leave,' I said. 'The family doctor told me to get away.'

'Why would he say a thing like that?'

'Because of her,' I said. 'He told me to get as far away from home as possible. She was too strong. She dominated the rest of the family. Because she could do things well she wouldn't let anyone else do anything. I saw what she did to father. And he was devoted to her. She was trying to do the same to me.' I stopped from saying—and look what she did to Sarah.

Then George said, 'When you come on a visit she doesn't want us to know you are in Ottawa.'

Another silence.

'Selina thinks we should sit Shiva here,' Sarah said.

'What's wrong with her apartment?'

'It's too small,' Selina said. 'Three people in there and there's no room to move.'

'But here—it's miles from anywhere.'

'All the people who would come,' George said, 'have cars.'

I thought I knew what was not being said. My mother's apartment was not only small it was in a senior citizen's place. And I could see it was no longer going to be private, a small family thing, but a social occasion.

'I'll be here for the funeral,' I said. 'But I won't sit Shiva.'

'Why not?' Sarah shouted. 'It's therapy.'

'I don't believe in it.'

'But for Ma.'

'To remember someone,' George quietly said to Sarah, 'you don't have to sit Shiva.'

He had, on marrying Selina, converted to being a Jew.

'You don't have any feeling for this family.' Selina was angry. 'You just don't have it.'

In my mother's apartment I couldn't go to sleep. I finished reading *The Citizen*. There were no books. Only those I gave her that she kept hidden, in the bedroom, in drawers. They were in mint condition signed to my father and to her. Then only to her. She is the only one in the family who reads my things.

I was looking for a photograph of my father—a studio photograph, of how he looked before he came to Canada—and couldn't find it. But I did find a glass jar with the small pink shells that she collected on the beach in St Ives. And faded cuttings—from *The Journal* and *The Citizen*, of my early books—that I had forgotten. Some large boxes of chocolates unopened. Horoscopes that she cut from the paper. (Sarah was also an Aries.) A flyer that said, 'Your psychic portrait rendered by the combined skills of an astrologist and of an artist. Strategically placed in your home, it allows for meditation on self, and to work out one's destiny.' And it gave two telephone numbers.

In her clothes closet, at the bottom, large leather purses. Brown, beige, black. And none looked used. Inside they had loose change and a wrapped toffee or two. There were small yoghurt containers filled with pennies. One had American pennies. The others Canadian. Some were bright as if newly minted. I saw a small hand-mirror. The glass was cracked. I remember it because of the black and white drawing on the back—a woman's face and neck and dense black hair. I last saw it as a child on her dresser in the bedroom. Now, the drawing didn't look right. I turned the hand-mirror upside down. The drawing became another drawing. A woman had her hand in her pubic hair. I felt an intruder. I didn't want to look anymore.

Next morning I walked to Rideau Street and to the Rideau Bakery. On visits I always drop in to buy some bread. I bought a rye, to take back to Toronto, when one of the owners came in from the back. (We both went to York Street School.) He was talking to a well-dressed woman when he saw me.

'Going to see your mother?'

'Yes.'

'This is Mrs Miller's son,' he introduced me to Mrs Slover, a furrier's wife.

'Your mother,' said Mrs Slover, 'is a very nice person.' Then looking directly at me. 'Are you a nice person?'

'No,' I said.

'Give her my regards when you see her. She is a lovely lady.' And walked quickly away.

The owner of the Rideau Bakery looked confused.

'And remember me to your mother,' he said quickly.

'She is in hospital,' I said.

She was asleep when I entered her room. There was only the drip. I went out, in the corridor, towards the reception desk, when I met the surgeon. A stocky man, with glasses, from Newfoundland. He was in-between operations. They were, he said, still trying to find out why she wasn't eating. I told him I had someone coming from England. Would it be all right if I went back to Toronto? How long would I be away? About five days. He hesitated. 'That should be all right.'

I returned to the room. When she opened her eyes I gave her some *Ensure*. And said I would be going to Toronto as Henry, a friend from St Ives, was due tomorrow evening. I'd stay the weekend. And be back to see her the following week.

'The surgeon has my phone number.'

'Did you have a nice time at Selina's?'

'Yes.'

We remained silent.

'I'm going to close my eyes now.'

After she woke, I said I would leave as I wanted to pack and close the apartment.

On the open front door I saw the name-plate.

'Who is Mr Thomas Sachs?'

'A bachelor,' she said.

In the Union Station, waiting for Henry to arrive, I am early and having a coffee. And think how lucky I was to have grown up with painters. Painters are much more open than writers. They seem to enjoy their work more—more extrovert. And Henry was like that. When I first knew him and his wife, Kath, were working in a café opposite Porthmeor Beach. And Henry painted when he could. He had one of the studios (large, spartan) facing the Beach. And let me use it. The tall end-windows (that looked out on sand, surf, the hovering gulls) had a wide window-sill. I had my typewriter on the sill and wrote while Henry painted behind me. I could hear him talking to himself. 'Look at that green ... That red sings ...' And when the work was going he would sing quietly: 'Life is just a bowl of cherries.' Just that line. And when a painting was finished he wanted me to see it. I said I liked it. 'But it is so still. Quiet.'

'All good paintings,' he said, 'have a feeling of calm about them.'

Henry began to paint in Germany as a prisoner-of-war. 'I got canvas from the pillow-cases. Oil from the odd tin of sardines.' He also went hungry. After the war he married. Left a struggling working-class home, in the provinces, to come to St Ives. He had a thing about those who were (like us) in St Ives but who had private incomes or parents with money. This didn't bother me. I guess you have to be English to have this love–hate with class. I remember when one of our lot (money behind him) won a prize for one of his paintings. We met in the pub by the parish church and the War Memorial garden. He bought Henry and me a beer.

When we left the pub Henry was angry.

'A half-pint of bloody beer. Christ, if I'd won that money I'd have bought everyone double whiskies.'

After that summer, and those early years, we moved apart. I heard he was teaching in an art school near London. I read about his exhibitions in the paper. Sometimes I saw him, briefly, in London. It was still a struggle.

More years passed.

Then in the spring of 1980 I came to Toronto. I was living in a modest high-rise in Yorkville. When Henry phoned. He was in Toronto. He had flown from Alberta and was on his way back to England. Could I come to this restaurant and join him for dinner.

The taxi brought me to a seedy street near Kensington Market. I went up a narrow worn-out staircase. Turned into a barn-like room. Lots of tables. No customers. A man was behind a small bar by the wall near the door. A woman, in a simple all-black dress, came towards me. I asked for Henry. She led me through a door to a room in the back.

It was all red. The wallpaper was a deep red. Red lights were on the walls. The tablecloths were red. The small lights, on the tables, had red lampshades. There was only one person in the room. Henry, sitting by a large red table and smiling.

'It's a brothel,' he said.

We had a platter of seafood. We drank and talked. About our friends, our children, and what we had been doing. He had been a guest lecturer at Banff for two months. Things, he said, were beginning to pick up. But he still had to hustle.

After the meal we went into the other room, stood at the bar, drank with the proprietor and his wife. Neither could speak much English. She was telling me that her husband played football for Portugal when a slight man, in a light-grey summer suit, joined us. He must have had his meal somewhere in the large room. But we didn't notice. He said he was an American. After a while he said he worked for the CIA. Still later, Henry and the CIA man began to dance. I danced with the proprietor's wife. Then we all put our arms over the shoulder of the person on either side. The proprietor joined us. And we moved around the empty restaurant as a chorus line. Henry singing 'Life is just a bowl of cherries.'

Out in the street we asked the CIA man where he was staying. The Windsor Arms. So we walked to the nearest main road and waited for a taxi to drive by. The grey light of early morning. It was cold and shabby. A gusty wind. Loose newspapers. And no cars. The CIA man began to take out dollar bills from his jacket pockets and threw them up into the air. The wind blew them away. Henry and I went after the loose bills ... on the road ... the sidewalk ... across the street ... and stuffed them back into the man's pockets. Then he took them out again and threw them in the air. And again we went after them ... Until a taxi finally came along.

Since then Henry has called that night magical. A word I never use.

This time he had flown from England to New York. Spent four days looking at galleries and museums. Then took the train to Toronto.

'It's marvellous,' he said in the taxi. 'I don't have to lecture or teach or flog my paintings. I can do just what I want to do. Enjoy myself. And I have enough money not to pinch and scrape. From here, I'll go to Vancouver. See Expo. Then fly back.'

He liked Fred. I showed him his room. We both got dressed up. Henry in a light blue silk jacket, a silk shirt, light blue trousers, a black beret.

'How's your mum?'

'Dying.'

'She knows you know,' he said.

Henry is tall and stocky with a grey moustache and glasses. A woman I know, who saw us walking down Yonge Street, phoned up after he had gone and asked, 'Who was that policeman you were with?'

We were having a drink before going out. His eldest son was acting in the West End in a Stoppard play. His youngest was studying languages in Munich. 'And playing cricket for the MCC.'

'I didn't know he was that good.'

'The Munich Cricket Club. After a game if he's done well he will phone. If he doesn't phone I know he didn't get many runs.'

It is only after we have told each other about our families that we get onto work.

'I've never been so busy,' Henry said. 'I can barely cope. I think it's to do with age. It is so strange to be so busy that there is never a minute to spare. Not until I sit down in the evening and fade out in front of the TV. I can hardly believe it. My early work continues to sell. I am so confused. I don't know whether to stop letting the last few things go or just treble the prices.'

The taxi arrived.

He was excited.

'Where are we going?'

The taxi stopped on a badly lit street by some garbage. There was an open door, a worn-out staircase.

Henry was smiling. 'It's the same place.'

There was the man and the woman. They said they remembered us. I don't know if they did. The front barn of a room had no customers. We asked if we could go to the back. She said, in poor English, it was closed.

We sat, by a table, against a wall. And all those white laid-out empty tables stretched in front of us.

The proprietor sat in front of a large TV screen. It was raised and could be seen all over the room. Benny Hill was chasing some girls who kept dropping their clothes.

The woman in the black dress came to take our order. In a firm but friendly voice Henry said, 'We'll have champagne.'

The woman went away.

Henry looked relaxed and happy.

She returned to say no champagne.

'No champagne,' Henry said. 'Bloody hell.'

'Last night a wedding. No champagne.'

He looked upset.

'Shall we have a Scotch?'

'Yes,' I said.

She went away.

We were silent.

'You know,' Henry said, 'I wanted to come and see you. Go to a restaurant. And just say: We'll have champagne. I remember at The Tinners ... I was strapped for money ... I was nursing a half-pint of bitter ... When in walked John Friel. And it was the way he said, in that arrogant plummy voice of his, a bottle of champagne. I thought, someday I'm going to do that.'

We started with Portuguese sardines.

I told him that last summer I went to Paris and Marseille with a woman who opened up France for me. And it was in a small fishing place near Marseille, called Cassis, where I had the best sardines.

'I was in Marseille,' he said, 'before France fell. I was in the cavalry. We went to a brothel. There were three of us. All young. We kept coming back. They began to charge us hardly anything. They were glad to see us. I wondered why.'

'Did you come back to the same girl?'

'Yes,' he said. 'I decided that they had two-way mirrors. They made their money from those who watched my ass going up in the air.'

'Did you like the girl?'

'Oh yes,' he said. 'I liked her.'

Next night I took him to an Italian restaurant, on St Clair West, where I knew the food was good and Henry said he liked Italian food. And the same thing happened. He asked for champagne. The proprietor, who was our waiter, looked sullen.

He came back with a bottle of Asti Spumante.

'I don't believe it,' Henry said. 'That's no champagne.'

We drank bottles of Asti Spumante and were having a fairly good time. The proprietor remained sullen. Finally he walked out.

'He probably has a mistress,' Henry said. 'Or else he has gone gambling.'

His wife was the cook. A small pretty woman in a low-cut dress. Black hair, very white skin, large dark eyes, perspiration above her top lip. She had to finish serving the meal.

'I stayed in London with Adrian Oakes,' Henry said. 'The night before flying over. He had a girl, staying with them, that he had just before breakfast. His wife doesn't mind. It's the upper classes. His father gave him a mistress when he was twenty. He's been used to it since. Not like us.'

When we got back we walked Fred around the park. Ahead, in the sky, I could see Orion.

Back in the house we drank and talked about Peter Lanyon, Patrick Heron, Terry Frost, Alan Lowndes. And the crazy things we did.

'I remember,' I said, 'how we all got dressed up in suits to go to Peter's funeral. And one of your sons saw us walking in the street. "You look like a bunch of gangsters," he said.'

'Who is normal?' Henry asked. 'Do you know anyone who is normal? My mother's sister was called Ida Bolt. As Ida Bolt she was quiet and passive. And no one took any notice. But she also called herself Jennie Dempsey. And as Jennie Dempsey she would wiggle her hips, pretend she was dancing to the radio, jump with excitement. A complete extrovert. When she died the only people who came were those she played the piano for in a mental hospital.'

Near the end he said, 'There's hardly anybody left in St Ives. No one to talk to. Oh, I talk to a lot of people—but we don't go back very far.'

Next morning, before seven, Henry was up. And we took Fred out for his morning walk. I have to give Fred a tennis ball so that he doesn't bark and wake up people. He gets excited as I open the door. And will leave the ball for me to throw. He doesn't wait but starts to run fast ahead. Then stops, crouches. And looks at me. When he was young, when I pitched the ball, he would catch it in his mouth. Now he misses. So I throw it over him or to one side so he can chase it. He also chases the black and grey squirrels. They always get to a tree before he can get to them. I don't think he would do anything. He just likes chasing. Then he goes off into his own world and will sniff the grass and not move for several minutes. I whistle. I call 'C'mon, Fred.' Finally he does. Or else he goes on his back and twists his body on the grass.

Walking with Henry ... he was noticing shapes and I was noticing colours ... then he saw Fred was waiting for us.

'He's smiling.'

'He always has that expression on his face,' I said.

We went to the galleries in Yorkville. Saw some early Hans Hofmann. 'I wouldn't mind having one of those,' he said. At another gallery he liked the Borduas and the Riopelles. As we came out from a gallery on Scollard we came out above the street.

'There's a painting right here,' he said.

I saw a red mail-box, a green metal container beside it, a cluster of three glass globes at the top of a lamp-post, a cherry tree in blossom.

'What do you look for?'

'Surfaces,' he said. 'That green beside the mailbox. That has a flat top. The red mail-box has a curved top. Then the cherry tree. The shape of the streetlights.'

We went to the Art Gallery of Ontario. I knew some of the paintings. Van Gogh's *Woodcutters in Winter*. A lovely little Renoir landscape. We go up a ramp and, on the wall, beside us, Patrick Heron's *Nude* of 1951; Peter Lanyon's *Botallack* of 1952; and Henry's *A Snow Day of Grey* of 1953.

Henry looked pleased. 'I didn't know it was here.'

For lunch, in The Copenhagen, we ordered duck with red cabbage.

'Gino came to see me in Cornwall,' Henry said. 'I can't remember his second name. It's my memory. He was in the Italian army. In the last war. He fought on the other side. He came to see me because he likes my work. When I told him I would be in Toronto, he said to go and see a sculpture of his. Here's the envelope with the address.'

In neat small writing: *Bell Canada H.Q. Trinity Square Building. Business Hours.*

We went to find it.

I don't know about Henry but I didn't expect too much. But there it was. Impressive. A tall piece of metal, with a gold coating, as a central column. And from it rods came out at right angles, as if from a spine. And these rods were close together. They went up and down the centre column. Not in a straight line but a gentle curve. And then back. The effect—when you looked at it or walked slowly around—was as if those rods were gently moving.

'Breathing,' Henry said.

It went up several floors.

'It really works.' Henry was delighted.

We both went to see where it had Gino's name. And what he called it. But there was no plaque, no sign, nothing to say that Gino had done it.

I asked a travel agent, on the first floor, whose door was open. She didn't know who did it. 'It's just there.' I asked a commissionaire on the ground floor. He didn't know.

When we left the building, to walk to Union Station, both of us were angry.

I remembered the man in St Ives who lived down the road. A widower, in his late seventies. It was a hot summer's day. I was coming back from mailing some letters when he suggested I go for a drive in the country with him.

'You could use a break.'

He had a Riley. He drove up the Stennack, turned left at the black-smith's. And there was Rosewall Hill with the decaying engine-houses on the slope of moorland. He drove towards Towednack. Ahead were low out-houses painted white, a piggery. And near them, this tall brick chimney, neatly made, tapering as it went up. Then, at the very top, it became wider. As he drove near it, he turned his head and said, 'I did that.'

After Henry left I tried to get on with some work, but I couldn't. I phoned the hospital. My mother was the same. As it was Sunday I decided to go for a walk. I walked north until I came to Roselawn. And saw fields on a residential street. They were Jewish cemeteries. On one side were the larger fields. Stones here had MDs and PhDs after the names. There were several families called Kurtz. On one it had: 'His name will live for ever.' But it was the two smaller cemeteries, on the other side of the street, that I was drawn to. On a wooden board, the paint fading, one had *Poland*. The other had *Minsk*.

I sat, on the side opposite, on a green park bench. Looked at these two small cemeteries. And thought, this is where she belongs.

I walked back from Roselawn. Down Forest Hill Road ... down Oriole Parkway ... to St Clair. It had taken over an hour and as it was a warm day I sat on a bench in a small park on the corner of Avenue Road.

A few trees ... green benches ... I sat and smoked ... when I noticed a sapling with a metal name-plate. I went over. *In Memory of My Beloved Papa Joseph Podobitko*. This was a good twenty-minute walk from the reservoir and the little park where I lived. What was Joseph Podobitko doing here?

I phoned Sarah.

'She has stopped talking,' Sarah said. 'She just points with a finger. And I'm supposed to know what she wants. When I get the wrong thing, she just moves her head.'

I talked to Selina.

'She's frightened of dying,' Selina said. 'You can see it in her eyes.'

Next day I packed a white shirt, a dark tie, a suit, in case I had to stay for the funeral.

In her apartment. A feeling it's all coming to an end. The money was gone. I asked Sarah if she had taken it. She said she had.

After three days I had to return to Toronto. I went to the hospital to say goodbye. She looked thinner and smaller. But there was a youthful astonishment in her face. A luminous quality. The eyes looked very blue. She didn't have her teeth in. And the dark opening of her small mouth was in a smile.

This, I thought, is the way I want to remember her at the end. And I wanted it to end.

Weeks went by.

Selina phoned. 'Why hold onto the apartment? It's paying rent for nothing.'

'She needs to know she still has a place to go back to.'

'She'll never go back there.'

Two weeks later, Sarah phoned.

'You'll have to come and help me break it up.'

'There's not much there,' I said.

'I can't do it myself.'

More weeks passed.

My mother started to get better. She started to take some food. Every time I now came to Ottawa another plant had died, something else was missing: the samovar, the pestle and mortar, the silver candlesticks, the silver tray, the silver coins. But she was getting stronger.

She was moved to a lower floor. They were going to try and build her up. I dialled her number at the hospital.

'Hello,' I said.

No answer.

'Hello.'

'Hullo,' she said, out of breath.

'How are you, Mother?'

'I'm fine.' Still out of breath. 'Are you in Toronto?'

'No, I'm in Ottawa.'

'In Ottawa ... I just fell out of bed ... to get to the phone. I'll have to call a nurse ... I'm on the floor ... We'll talk later.'

When I went to the hospital, I asked the staff nurse where her room was. She said she would take me.

'All the nurses are fighting to look after your mother.'

I wondered why.

'Because she gets all the other patients involved. She includes them in whatever she says. And she doesn't talk about herself. She doesn't turn the talk to herself.'

'A doctor came to see me,' my mother said, after I sat down at the end of her bed. 'He was the only one who said I was not dying. That I had something. That I hadn't given up.

'You know what I get from people—respect. Some people, whatever they have on their chest, they get it out. Dinka, if she had anything she tells it. I don't. I don't tell about my husband, my children, or any of my business. They tell all ...

'I wish I had done something in medicine. In research.'

And I remember a visit. A knock on her door. A thin elderly woman stood with her arm in a makeshift sling. 'I was told to come and see you. I fell. You would know what to do.' My mother examined the woman's hand, tried to move the fingers. Then announced. 'Call an ambulance.'

'Look what she has to read.' She pointed to the books of the woman in the bed beside her who was out of the room. 'Trash. You can tell she is common.

'Sarah ... doesn't have a head. You and me we have heads.'

I tried to interrupt.

'I'm not finished,' she said.

'There is a little Chinese lady. I take pity on her. She can't talk English. If I go, she goes. She talks Chinese. I talk Yiddish. She has a bowl of noodles. She gets her a fork. And me a fork. And she wants us to eat out of the same bowl ...

'A doctor who went away, on holiday, came back to see me. When he saw me he was crying. He was so pleased I was still alive.

'Where are you going? You don't have to go out.

'The Chinese lady. She is a little thing. Hardly eats. But I show her this pudding with raisins is good ... by eating it. So then she eats. She doesn't know a word of English ... just Chinese. But she can't walk well ... something is wrong with her feet.

'A Polish man came up to me and began to talk in Polish. So I answered him in Polish.'

'How did he know?'

'A nurse told him I came from Poland.

'Afterwards she'—indicating the bed beside her—'said, I see you have a boyfriend.

'She's *prost* ... common.

'We walk with our walkers. ... First the little Chinese ... then me ...then the Polish man ... the nurses look at us. I tell them ... this is a masquerade ... a cabaret ... They don't know whether to laugh or not.'

I looked at my watch.

'What is it like outside?'

'The leaves are falling. The sun is shining. I'm going back to Toronto.'

'How is the apartment?'
'Fine. I've taken my books that you have in the bedroom in the drawers.'
'Good. I don't want anyone to have them.'
I got up to go.
'You'll phone me tomorrow?'
'Yes. When do you finish lunch?'
'About twelve, twelve-thirty.'
'I'll phone you at one.'
But it was she who phoned at nine.
'I just finished breakfast.'
'What did you have?'
'Juice, an egg, toast. But I couldn't eat it all. Did you have a nice time?'
'Yes, now that you're better I don't mind being here.'
'What will you do with the food left in the fridge?'
'I'll give it to Mrs Tessier.'
'That's good.'
'Your plants ...'
'My plans are to go back to the apartment. Will you go to the Château Laurier and get a bus to the airport?'
'No, I'll call a taxi and take a taxi to the airport.'
'That's better.'
'I'll write from Toronto.'

Fred was the first to go. It was the end of October. A fine sunny morning. I was getting ready to take him out for what will be his last walk. He barks as he always does before he goes outside. From his bark you couldn't tell he has cancer that has spread. Fred looks up and wags his tail whenever I pat him. He is twelve and a half. It's a fine sunny day. The leaves on the ground are some of the colours of Fred, the browns. He has also white on his neck and some black on the sides, but mostly a light brown. I am waiting for the taxi to take us to the vet. Fred is sniffing the air. His head is up. His tail up and curling ...

The next to go was Mrs Tessier.

She died in her sleep. I read her obituary in *The Citizen*. Sometimes I would see her sitting in the all-glass connecting lounge, between the buildings, with a few other ladies who lived here. They all spoke French. She always looked jolly. Her feet not touching the ground. Her husband died a few years ago. A tall nervous man with glasses. He was also quiet. They had no children. Whenever I saw her she asked, 'How is your mother?'

I would tell her.

'Will she come back?'

'I don't know.'

And when I was to leave the apartment early next morning for Toronto, I would knock on her door the night before and give Mrs Tessier anything perishable in the fridge. I would knock on the door and a tallish thin woman with grey hair, in a fringe, opened it apprehensively. She looked sullen. She must have been, like Mrs Tessier, in her late seventies or early eighties. Then I saw Mrs Tessier appear to the right, sideways, wrapping a dressing-gown around her. She was naked underneath. And she was wrapping the dressing-gown around as if she didn't mind being seen like this. The other lady was fully dressed.

After that, whenever I knocked, the thin sullen woman was always there, always apprehensive. Once I saw her going to Mrs Tessier's door carrying cut flowers. Sometimes when I arrived, or was leaving, I heard light laughter from behind Mrs Tessier's door. I didn't know what was going on. But I hoped they were enjoying themselves.

There was going to be a meeting with the doctor and the social worker. Sarah, Selina, and my mother would be there to decide where she would go from the hospital. I had to be in Halifax on business.

When I got back to Toronto I phoned her.

'You sound better.'

'Of course,' she said, 'I'm eating.'

'How did the meeting go?'

'You should see how mad Selina was when the doctor said if I want to go home I can try it. Oh boy, was Selina mad. She wanted me to go to some nursing home, an old age home, to an institution. Anything but to live in my home again.'

'How about Sarah?'

'She said nothing.'

'How do you feel?'

'I'd like to try and see if I can look after myself.'

'I'll come and take you back. When will that be?'

'Next Wednesday.'

'I'll come on Tuesday.'

That night I spoke to Sarah on the phone. I asked about the meeting. 'To get back to her place she put on some performance.'

On Tuesday when I went to see her she was standing by the window with her walker watching a blizzard.

'I'll need my boots. Put on the light in the hall. I have no light in the cupboard. But you will be able to feel, at the bottom, the boots. Take a scarf from inside a sleeve from one of my coats.'

When I came back next day, after lunch, she was dressed ready to go in a wheelchair.

I gave her the green and brown silk scarf. Then the boots. She put one on with difficulty. Then tried the other. It wouldn't go. She tried again. Then I tried. It only went so far.

'You brought me two right feet,' she said. 'How can I go like this?'

'It's not far to walk,' I said. 'From the taxi, over a bit of snow, to the front door of your building. You have your walker. There will be the taxi driver and me to hold you.'

'Two right feet.'

She thought that was very droll.

Without the samovar, or the plants, the apartment looked empty.

'It's so nice,' she said. 'It lights my eyes up. I feel so good. It's home.'

'The plants ...'

'It doesn't matter. This one is the healthiest. And this cutting from the rubber plant I think I can save.'

She sat by the window looking at the snow-covered park. 'Oh boy, Selina was mad. She wanted me to go to a nursing home. If I go to a nursing home I don't get any money from the government. This way I'll be able to leave some money to all the children.

'The sun is strong.' She turned her head away from the window.

I phoned Selina at her office.

'She should be in a nursing home. I want my grandmother to live a few more years. And she will in a nursing home where they can look after her.'

'She wants to be in her apartment.'

'But what happens if anything goes wrong? Mummy is in Carleton Place. You are in Toronto. I'm the one who will have to look after her.'

'She also said she wants to be back because of the monthly cheques.'

'That's a cop-out. She doesn't want to lose her independence. That's what it's all about.'

I phoned Sarah and asked if she would come and stay with Mother for a while.

'I'm too tired. The place is too small. Why? Did she want me to be there?'

'No. I just wondered if you thought of it.'

I asked Mother, 'What about having Sarah come and stay with you?'

'I don't think so. I feel better by myself.'

It had rained during the night. Then it froze. On the train back to Toronto the smaller trees were bent over. Some were broken by the weight of the ice. But it all looked pretty. Mile after mile. I thought of a friend, a professor of mathematics at the University of Toronto. He has devoted his life to mathematics and to logic. I asked him, what did he make of it all.

He said. 'Nothing lasts. Everything changes.'

Was this why we keep making connections? Why do I connect Gino's sculpture to that tall brick chimney to those saplings with Joseph Podobitko to Mr Thomas Sachs on the door of the hospital room to those little Jewish cemeteries on Roselawn?

But then, whenever I go to a new place and walk around to get to know it, I inevitably end up in a cemetery.

My mother had been in her apartment a half-year when I phoned to tell her I was going to England to see my daughters. I would be away several months.

'The children have to know they have a father,' she said.

I told her I would come tomorrow. 'I'll see you around one-fifteen.'

'Any time. You will be a good guest.'

She had put on weight, and now could walk without a walker. But she still looked frail.

The place looked clean. The two surviving plants looked healthy. But without the samovar it seemed empty.

'Selina has it in the basement,' she said. 'What is a samovar doing in a basement?'

She wanted to make tea. And did, taking her time. I brought in the cups and saucers. She brought in the teapot.

'When I came home … everything was dirty—the dishes.

'Not any more the people who used to be—the apartments are empty.'

She talked about Mrs Tessier.

'People in the building told me because I wasn't in my apartment Mrs Tessier couldn't go to sleep.'

'How often do you go to the hospital?'

'Once every two weeks. When the doctor looks at me—the big smile. He is so happy.

'If I was in a nursing home I would be dead.'

She left the table and disappeared into the bedroom. Came back with several twenty-dollar bills. Put them in my hands.

'For the children.'

She sat down, slowly, by the table. 'You know the money I was saving for a trip to England.'

We were silent.

'Only another seven years and you will get the old age pension. That's wonderful,' she said. And began to take out her hearing aid. Then put it back in. 'It should make a noise if it is working.' I tried a new battery. It still wasn't working. She finally gave up and said she would get the nurse tomorrow to find out about it.

After that it was difficult to have a conversation. There were silences.

'Did you watch *Shoah* on television?'

She didn't answer. I didn't know if she heard.

'It's about European Jews being taken to concentration camps in Poland.'

'No,' she said quietly. 'I watch *Guiding Light* and *The Young and the Restless*.'

I must have looked puzzled.
'It's soap,' she said, raising her voice.
I said nothing.
'It's soap opera,' she said loudly.
And she was angry.

From a Family Album

I RETURN TO ENGLAND to see my daughters who live in different parts. Early this March I returned to Cornwall, to St Ives, to see the youngest who was starting work as a French teacher. While there, my late wife's mother, Christine, eighty-one and on her own, had a fall near where she lived in Redruth.

I took the morning train. And bought two hot pasties from the bakery in Redruth near the railway station where I could smell fresh bread ... flowers (yellow roses) from a seedy florist on the road to her cottage. And I had a tin of Canadian salmon.

I always bring her a tin when I come over.

'I'll keep it,' she said, 'for a special occasion.'

We sat in the small main room (a mixture of neatness and disorder) with little daylight. Ate, slowly, the pasties. They were still warm. She only ate half of hers.

Old Staffordshire plates were propped up on the dark wooden dresser. And in front of them photographs, in simple frames. A black and white of her late husband, Sydney, when he was young. He is dressed for the occasion. Dark straight hair combed back, a dark suit, white shirt, dark tie. He is smiling.

I remember him as a handsome man reluctant to take risks. Because of asthma, he was in the Home Guard during the war. And worked as an accountant in a company that made containers: for toothpaste, shaving cream, and shoe polish. When he went off in the morning, in his Homburg, carrying *The Daily Telegraph* and a brown leather case, he looked elegant. But he had to stop, struggling for breath, before the station slope, and use his atomizer. He also worried about losing his job. And taught himself to be a carpenter. When we married he gave us a wooden, folding ironing-board that he made without using a nail. And on the day the doctor told him he had six months to live he went straight home and built his coffin.

His younger brother, Albert, had been a Lieutenant Colonel in the British Army in India. After the war, Albert started a dating service in Brighton where he lived. When that didn't work he started a business assembling crucifixes on wooden crosses. Then sold them to Catholic institutions, hospitals, bookstores. When he became bored with that he left his wife and children in Brighton, bought a trailer to his car, drove to a field above a deserted beach in Cornwall, and wrote two novels which did not find a publisher. Sydney and Albert's favourite uncle, Stanley, was in the British Army. Sent to Canada. A Canadian winter finished him off. He is buried in a military cemetery in Quebec City.

Next to Sydney was a black and white photo of Christine when she was the manager of a small Express Dairy by the station. Outdoor-looking, lots of energy, active in sports and Girl Guides. She did everything in a hurry. And when angry, slammed doors. They both liked musicals, especially Harry Welchman. In the house she sang

Blue Heaven and You and I
And sand kissing a moonlit sky
The desert breeze whispering a lullaby
Only stars above you
To see I love you

In January 1952, Elizabeth and I were married. Then went to live in Cornwall. When we were leaving for our first holiday in London, the taxi brought us to Penzance open-air station. As we walked by the standing train, I saw an elderly man in a camel-hair coat get on. Sometime after the train started, while Elizabeth stayed in our seats with our ten-month-old Ellen, I went into the dining-car to have a coffee. The only other person there was the man in the camel-hair coat. We got to talking. He said he now lived in the country near Penzance. And asked what I did? Having just had a first novel published, I said I was a writer. He said he was Harry Welchman.

The name meant nothing to me. I remained silent. He said: 'I'm the Red Shadow.' I said that I was brought up in Canada and had not long lived in England. He said, before the war, he was well known in the West End of London. Suddenly he began to sing, the opening lines of *The Desert Song*. And this medium height, elderly man, red in the face, largish nose, filled the empty moving dining-car with a magnificent sound. Then just as quickly he stopped, slightly embarrassed.

On Saturdays, Sydney went to the public library in Eltham High Street and came back with books for the week. In the front rooms, in with his books on accountancy, there were editions of W.H. Hudson, Conrad, and Thomas Hardy.

Chris went as far as elementary school. But kept in touch with her teacher (a widow, Lily Hay) long after Lily Hay retired. Chris pronounced Michigan—<u>Mitch</u>-igan. Menu—<u>Mean</u>-u. And when, as a widow, she came with us on a day trip to Dieppe, her daughter said, 'When you want to say everything is all right, OK, say *d'accord.*' When Chris said it, in public, she said *Dachau.*

Whenever she phoned from the lobby of a hotel she put on, what her daughter called, her posh accent.

Beside the photograph of Chris there was a photograph of Chris's mother, Grandma, a Jehovah's Witness. When she was in her eighties. A tall woman, now stooped, in a new hat and coat, about to board a ship at Southampton for a Jehovah's Witness get-together in Germany. She became a Witness after her husband was killed in a road accident.

'Left with five small children, I didn't know what to do. I went to the Bible, opened it, and read: "Go out and do good."'

Then a photograph of Chris's late daughter, Elizabeth (my wife), when a schoolgirl. Someone had hand-coloured the blue summer-dress, the short blonde hair, the blue eyes. She looks like her father. And smiles like him.

But the room, the cottage, was dominated by Chris's paintings. Unframed they were everywhere. On all the walls. In the entrance hall, in the main room, in the small kitchen, on the side of the stairs, in the toilet, and in the two cramped bedrooms upstairs. They were copies of other paintings. And they were all unbelievably bad.

One, a small seascape, she had not copied. I told her it was the best thing she had done.

'I painted it in Scotland while on holiday. You can have it. Why don't you take it?'

'I don't want to take it now.'

It was a good visit.

She talked about her mother when her mother worked (before she married) as a teacher on the Royal Estate in Windsor. And how, after her mother died, she went to Windsor and was shown the handwritten punishment cards where her mother recorded who was caned, who was sent out of her class. She insisted on going up the stairs (one at a time, with her stick) and came back with copies of these punishment cards. They gave them to her as a momento.

'You can have them,' she said.

I remember Grandma coming with Chris to see us in St Ives. She always had on some little thing we had given her: a silver maple leaf, a brooch, a scarf. She never tried to convert us to being a Jehovah's Witness. But after a visit we would find a copy of *Awake* on the piano. In summer she would walk down to the front and the harbour. And sit out the afternoon on one of the green benches. Listening to the Salvation Army Band at the slipway. When she came back she came back smiling.

'Everyone talked to me.'

Then all of us (the children as well) sat around the kitchen table having tea. And Grandma, her eyes opening wide, talked about her grandfather.

'The miser. He would sit at the kitchen table with tea in a glass and cut the flies that landed on the table with a knife.'

And about a brother, Willie.

'He went abroad and married an African person. He sent us photographs of his fine and handsome children.'

On another visit (as they were leaving) our Cornish neighbour, Martha Leddra, a spinster in her late seventies, a ship's captain's daughter, a strict Methodist, on her hands and knees scrubbing the outside granite steps to her house, called out to Grandma.

'We'll go off to the South of France, my girl, and you shall spend all my money.'

The last time I saw Grandma was in Truro hospital. Very alert. She said to Chris, who talked about her going home,

'Do you think I ever will?'

As we said goodbye, Judith blew a kiss. And Grandma put both her hands to her mouth and waved them towards us.

Then Chris talked about her teacher, Lily Hay, who had died since my last visit. She looked shocked as she told me that Lily Hay's son, a doctor, had left his wife to live with a man. And because of that, Lily Hay left all her money (her husband had been a builder) to a society that arranged séances. Then she told me about her annual treat: going with her art class to London to see this year's Royal Academy exhibition. Afterwards, a good meal at Simpsons in the Strand. And in the evening a musical (this year it was *Spread a Little Happiness*) before coming back.

When I left her I left feeling cheered up as I walked through the rundown streets of Redruth to the railway station. No train to St Ives for two hours. I got on a train that was there going in the opposite direction—to Truro.

I hadn't seen Truro for several years. It hadn't changed. Not the turning road, the narrow sidewalk, down from the station. The bookshop at the bottom with books on trains in the window. The store where I would buy Manx kippers and homemade Kea plum jam. By the Cathedral, feeling hungry, I went into a restaurant that had red chequered tablecloths. It was crowded and noisy. And those inside seemed to know one another. On the walls were black and white faded photographs of people in old-fashioned clothes. On the wall, where I sat, there was a photograph taken in a field. A slim young woman with dark hair. In one hand she has a wicker basket. In the other the hand of a girl in a white dress. The girl has curly blonde hair. Beside the woman, a man with a cap on, jacket, grey trousers. About the same age as the woman. They look handsome, optimistic.

I sat and ate. All around others were also eating and talking. I wasn't curious about them. But I kept looking at these faded photographs.

I asked the waitress. She didn't know.

I asked the owner.

'No one knows who they were. Or anything about them. They were there when I bought the restaurant over forty years ago. And no one knew anything about them.'

On my next visit she couldn't put on her shoes. Her feet were swollen. I got the shoes on but I couldn't tie the straps. She didn't want lunch. But asked if we could walk to the nearest pub, The Miners Arms.

She walked with a stick, and rested often. Along a narrow passage-way—by the backs of terraced houses—the ground was uneven.

'This is where I fell.'

The pub (opposite a fish-and-chip shop called The Jolly Friar) was old and small. The saloon bar empty. We sat by a polished wooden table near the door. She ate slowly, one crisp at a time. Took a long time over the shandy. And looked around the room with an intensity, an awkward fixed smile, as if she was looking at these things for the last time.

'I always come here to collect for cancer,' she said. 'They always were very good.'

I phoned the doctor. She phoned the following afternoon.

'The doctor came. She left me all kinds of pills and tonics to take.'

I met Avril on the next visit. A widow, short, energetic. Her husband had been a miner. He had given her a parrot, Lucy, now fifteen years old. Since Chris had her fall she came twice a day. Tidied, washed dishes, clothes, did the shopping, put the garbage out, mailed letters, went to the bank, paid the bills.

The following Wednesday, at noon, Avril phoned. She sounded upset.

'The doctor was here this morning. Chris has gone into hospital. The ambulance just drove away. She said to me, "Don't be sad. I've had a good life."'

Next morning I took the early train to Redruth. Then walked through the town. And into the country, to a small hospital at Carn Brea. It was at the bottom of moorland. Five other patients were on one side of a ward, in front of their made beds, waiting for the doctor. She was last by a window. (The moor began a few yards outside). Washed, dressed, her hair combed. She looked better than she did in her cottage. In her lap a letter from my daughter Judith who lived in Norwich. And photographs of the two great grandchildren.

Before leaving Canada I had arranged to see Ellen and her family in Derbyshire. Ellen wanted Chris to come and live with them.

'Could you bring her with you?'

'I don't think she is strong enough for the train.'

'Then Kevin will come and drive her back.'

'I don't think she is strong enough for that.'

Three days later, on my way to Derbyshire, I got off at Redruth. Chris was in bed, sitting up. In a new woollen sweater that had large outlines of squares. It suited her. We talked quietly about the family. And just looked at one another. She looked younger than her years. When it was time to leave it felt awkward and incomplete. I said I would see her when I came back in four days.

Late Thursday I was back in St Ives.

Friday morning. The gulls woke me. It was still dark. I made coffee, went to the attic, looked across the bay. The orange lights of Hayle and Camborne were going off and on as if faultily connected. Gulls, dark shapes, were over the roofs of the houses and cottages and narrow streets. Then the sun, not yet on the horizon, began to lighten the sky. Across the bay a mist began to clear. I could see the white-blue water of the bay. The browns, yellows, greens, of the far shore fields. Godrevy Lighthouse. And Carn Brea.

At seven the phone. The staff nurse said she had died in her sleep.

My daughters came. And what was left of Chris's family. A younger sister ... her two children ... a nephew, a director of Rolls Royce in Derby ... Members of her local Art Class in Truro. And Avril.

Afterwards we packed into the saloon bar of The Miners Arms. Had coffee and sandwiches that Ellen had organized. (The sandwiches that she made from the tin of Canadian salmon she offered first). I had told Ellen that Chris wanted to come to this pub for her last outing. I also told her that Chris got better as she got older.

'I'll miss her,' Ellen said. 'She was, above all, straight.'

I saw Chris's friends from the local art class. They had, like her, started to paint when they came here to retire.

Most had lived abroad.

I had met them once before. When Chris took me to the annual exhibition of her art class. It was held in a large house in the country (fields in front leading to a river). The woman whose house it was (a handsome woman, a widow, her husband, a doctor, had been mayor of Truro) didn't belong to the art class. But grew up with one of the women who did. So she provided the food, the drink, the household help. And these large rooms with spacious walls.

It was a French evening. With aperitifs we had pâté de foie gras on toast. Then sat down to melon. Followed by lampreys in a dark chocolate sauce. The lampreys had no taste but a texture, that of crumbling liver. A delicious tomato salad (light mustard on top). Cheese from different regions of France. Wine from the Medoc and Saint Emilion. Everyone seemed to be enjoying themselves. We danced to the music of Sydney Bechet and Barney Bigard. And the songs of Yves Montand. While on the walls were these terrible amateur paintings.

I talked to a lively blonde woman in her sixties. Colour in her face. Large eyes. She sat most of the time. She said she needed to have a new knee.

'I'm near the top of the waiting list.'

We began to talk about dogs. I asked about her dogs.

'All gone to heaven.'

I told her about the dog I had in Toronto.

'Who is looking after it?'

'There is someone.'

'You married again?'

'Yes,' I said. 'It's my wife's dog.'

'I was forty when my husband died. Had a heart attack. I couldn't fault him on anything. It's living on your own that's not nice. I was a planter's wife in India. We had to have six gardeners because of the caste system. One gardener wouldn't do another gardener's job if he was of a higher caste.'

'Did you know Mrs Goodhand?'

'Oh yes,' she said. 'We were friends.'

'I liked her. But she found it difficult to adapt.'

'You do come down with a bang when you return to England.'

From The Miners Arms we walked to the cottage. There were too many to go inside. So we stayed outside on the gravel. In twos, threes, and fours. Not quite knowing what to do. Then Ellen came out from the cottage with one of Chris's paintings. Holding it, in front of her, her arms fully extended, she walked, directly, to a person. And, without saying a word, gave the painting formally. Then she turned. And walked back into the cottage. And soon came out holding another painting in front of her. And walked towards someone else. We watched in silence as she solemnly gave one bad painting after another. To all the relatives. To all the members of the art class. To Avril. I had the small seascape.

Twenty-nine years earlier, not long after his fifty-second birthday, Sydney died. We had not long moved to St Ives. The children were small. I stayed to look after them and my wife went up to London for the funeral. After she came back she said she had a pain in her right foot. Then she began to limp. The doctor gave her cortisone injections. And told her it was probably a reaction to the death of her father.

In the spring, she heard that an art class was being given in the St Ives library. She signed up for it. And looked happy when she came back from buying the material she needed. And excited as she went off to her first class. But she only stayed two sessions.

'As soon as the others arrive, they all know what they want to do. And they get on with it. I don't know what to do. An elderly man beside me has been going there for years. As soon as he comes in he arranges everything neatly, the way he wants. And begins to paint.

'"That's a nice sky," I said.

'"I can only do this one sky," he replied.'

A year before she died she told me:

'After I finished school I wanted to go to art school. It was the only thing I have ever wanted to do in my life. But my mother and father didn't approve. They made fun of the paintings I did in my bedroom. When I said I was going to show them to a principal in an art college—to see if I was good enough to get in—they thought I was foolish.

'I brought my portfolio to the principal of St Martins. He looked at the paintings and drawings. And said he would write and let me know within two weeks.

'I couldn't wait at home. I went to Cornwall. Stayed on the farm where I was evacuated to during the war. Went for walks on roads that I knew. And all I could think of … that what I'd be doing with my life … was being decided in London.

'When I came back I asked my parents if there was a letter?

'They said no.

'Days. Weeks. Months. Passed. I did nothing. Something had happened to me.

'My father arranged that I work in the bank. I didn't last a year. Then I went to Teachers Training College. Then we met.

'After my father's funeral I began to turn out things for my mother. In their bedroom, in a drawer, I came across an envelope addressed to me. It was opened. Inside, a letter from St Martins. It said I had been accepted.'